Cake Eater

CAKE EATER

Allyson Dahlin

HARPER TEEN
An Imprint of HarperCollinsPublishers

Library of Congress Control Number: 2021952887
ISBN 978-0-06-309677-6

Typography by Julia Feingold
22 23 24 25 26 PC/LSCH 10 9 8 7 6 5 4 3 2 1
❖
First Edition

In memory of Jim Dahlin.

ONE

May 13, 3070, 8:14 p.m.

Our empire is fading.

My mama told me this an hour before I boarded a cruiser and left the Austro Lands forever. We were in her stateroom, one of the few ancient places left in Schönbrunn Palace. The tall, echoing ceiling was full of cracks that turned up faster than the repair droids could detect them. Sometimes, I imagined I could smell candles in there, phantom scents from a thousand years ago. My mama liked that ancient aesthetic. She had barely any neon or holos, just a bit of purple glowing around the red curtains.

She stood at the huge windows with her back to me. Big gray snowflakes fell like ash, making the light strange and greenish as it slanted through the clouds like a bad photo filter. Snow in the middle of May was usually a sign that the weather was going to glitch even more. Big storms with high winds or blazing heat for three weeks.

Her holo-cat circled her feet, twitching its big white tail. I tried to avoid its giant yellow eyes, which flickered just slightly, showing the hem of my mother's dress through the projection. Holo-cats always creeped me out, but Mutti was allergic to the real ones.

Her giant black dress made a crinkling sound as she turned

to me. It looked like a heap at a plastics landfill, all shiny, crumpled ruffles. Her crown twinkled to match her eyes, the delicate twists of white LEDs and gold filigree catching a neon glow. "Our empire is fading, Maria. You and your husband will have to forge a new path into the future if we're to survive."

"What do you mean, Mutti?"

"You're still a frivolous young thing glued to your holofone. But you're only seventeen. You'll grow, and you'll learn, until you find your way as a queen in your own right. It won't do to repeat the mistakes of your parents. I hope you'll learn from mine."

I couldn't remember her admitting to a mistake before that day. Not once. Not the empress of the Austro Lands. I asked, "Which mistakes, Mama?"

"There are those who will tell you that tradition is the way to victory. . . ." I expected her to continue, but she trailed off.

"What do you mean, Mama?"

She was silent. We watched the little worker droids in the courtyard as they blasted air over the paving stones to stir the snow away. When my mother was a little girl, snowfall used to be pure white and shimmering. My tutor told me that. Then some eco disaster happened. It turned the snow into the dull, dirty stuff that swirled around the chrome columns of the palace, leaving dark streaks as it melted that had to be scrubbed away by worker droids.

"It's hard to see past yourself . . . past the crown. You'll find out soon enough what I mean. Change is not just inevitable, it is natural. We may not like to think in such terms, but I believe it's foolish to ignore reality. Now that I'm older, I can see. Our empire is fading."

That phrase again. . . . It meant nothing to me yet made my stomach a glitch of fluttering nerves.

"I don't understand." I had been prepared for a lecture about how small-minded I was. This was . . . something else.

"Are you afraid?" she asked.

I wasn't sure if she meant about the supposed fate of the empire or about the fact that within twenty-four hours, I would be sent to marry Louis-Auguste, dauphin of the Franc Kingdom, a complete stranger, a total mystery with almost zero social media presence. Of course I was scared. But when you're a princess, you say what people want to hear, not how you really feel. I had strong smile muscles, so I flexed them.

"I'm excited, Mama. I'm going to be the Franc dauphine. I'm going to make you proud."

"Good. There's no reason to be afraid. All empires pass."

She hugged me then. I can still remember exactly how warm she was, how her perfume smelled like roses and amber. She placed her hands on the back of my neck and my left shoulder blade.

I can feel it as clearly as if it were happening now, even though I'm miles and miles from Schönbrunn Palace and my mutti. The memory makes a lump rise in my throat, but I breathe in the cooled air of the cruiser and calm myself.

We flew across the border of the Franc Kingdom about an hour ago. I've looked at the tracker screen above Ambassador Mercy's head a thousand times. It shows our clunky cruiser as a blue square, flanked by the white triangles of our escort, blinking toward the grid of lights labeled *Parée*.

My heart skips a beat. Parée is the most lit city in the world. Literally. It is filled with legendary amounts of neon. Thousands of Franc kids have been hashing me in photos and videos of parties and clubs and cafés leading up to my arrival, all to greet me.

I press my face to the cool glass for my first real glimpse of Parée. In the dark, I can't see much but the realm's escort cruisers. Way more chic than our model. They're off-white, with a long, pointed nose and a curving pilot's window like a big eye. There's no passenger section because they're small and made for speed, kind of like a sport cruiser. I bet they're way more fun than our behemoth with red velvet seats, stiff as old antiques. I can barely tell we're moving.

Except for the lights of Parée, growing closer and closer until they become a big tangle below us. Traffic flashes in the air lanes beneath ours, weaving a pattern of headlights over the multi-colored glow far below.

Rising above the city like a dagger dropped into the earth, La Tour Ancienne shines brighter than anything in the city, a spire of old rusting iron twisting to the sky, pumping with neon lights. It sparkles and shimmers, defining modern marvel and old-world mystique. The Francs dressed up its ancient bones in gleaming color and gave it new life. They don't know who built it or why, but the people have made it the epitome of Franc style.

The glow-grid covering the tower advertises JetVolt cruiser batteries. A rocket blinks upward, growing smaller and smaller as it reaches the top, then the lights shimmer to turn hot pink and form a bubbling bottle of Mountain Jam Lime drink.

"Ambassador Mercy, it's La Tour Ancienne!"

I really should practice keeping the volume down, because

Versailles will be very strict. I won't be able to simply blurt things out. But for the first time since I left home this morning, I'm actually excited to be in the Franc Kingdom. Maybe I really am as lucky as everyone tells me.

Mercy doesn't even glance my way. He's sitting stiffly with a leg over his knee, wearing a perfectly starched suit, dark except for the iridescent dress shoes shining in the soft blue cruiser light. "Good. We'll arrive soon."

His eyes are glued to a news report where someone is yelling that androids are going to take over everything, like that's even real.

I open the camera on my holofone and grab a selfie with the tower behind me—quickly, before it passes from view. Not my best work. The intensity of the glow blurs out the advert and clashes with my iridescent skirt and pale pink blouse.

To show my millions of followers a terrible photo or no photo at all? The influencer's constant question. The answer is: perfection only, at all times. Especially when you're about to become the Franc dauphine.

"Are you posting a photo of La Tour Ancienne?" Mercy asks.

"No." I groan. "It looks bad."

"Well, I was about to ask you not to."

"Why not?"

"The entire kingdom doesn't need a live update of our progress."

I roll my eyes. "You sound like Mutti. Always yelling at me for being on the Apps."

"I should be so fortunate as to sound like your esteemed mother. There's more to life than posting on the Apps. You should be focused on making a good impression. We'll land in twenty minutes."

"The Apps are the whole reason everyone likes me so much, and that's my entire job, is it not? Being liked?" I get sick of Mercy and the courtiers downplaying the hard work I do. One doesn't simply gain a million followers and keep them without putting in the effort. One must be perfect. One has to be familiar, relatable, but not flawed, or at least flawed in the right way. Perfect, polished, and totally tradigital and original. That's my brand. I'm the bubbly fashionista princess and icon. I take a glitching LED gown and accessorize to make it work. I take a rained-out garden party and turn it into an impromptu film festival highlighting young and trendy artists.

Mercy presses a hand to his graying temple. "I will not even begin to unpack that statement, Marie."

"You know it's true," I mumble, and turn back to watch the Tour pass out of the corner of my window. It's still strange to hear my Franc name. Just one little syllable's difference. Marie, not Maria . . . The Francs will totally transform me, morphing everything Austro into something Franc. Even my name.

Ahead, I see something strange and murky blurring out the city lights with a different kind of glow. It isn't neon, but something orange and inconsistent. "Is that a . . . fire?"

Mercy wouldn't get out of his seat for the Ancient Tower, but apparently he'll get up for this. He frowns, furry brows pinched together. Then he goes to the tracker screen and presses a few buttons. My window goes solid black.

"*Was zum Teufel machst du?* I'm trying to look at the Franc Kingdom!"

"I need to speak to the pilot. You ought to settle, Marie. We land very soon, and you have a lot to remember. Like speaking Franc. Franc only. You're perfectly fluent, and Austro will not be acceptable in any circumstances."

I thump my head back against the blacked-out window.

Mercy pauses as the pilot's door slides open. "Please compose yourself. You look like a sulking girl. We need you to become the dauphine."

A nervous jolt streaks through me. He's right. I can't mess this up. If I do, I will be sent home disgraced, and the Austro Lands will lose the tie that makes the Franc Kingdom our ally. Mama said my marriage will end our hundred-year feud, so my job is very important. If the Francs love me, they'll start to love Austros too.

I sit up straight and tug out the creases in my skirt. I practice my smile. I can feel it nudging at my cheeks when it's just right. Tip of my tongue pressed to the back of my teeth, chin forward like I'm having a photo taken. I tell myself a few times that I *am* lucky. It's how I get through pretty much any situation—repeat it until it is real. Just like finding the perfect angle and filter for an image—framed the right way, and cast in the right light, just about anything can seem beautiful and perfect. Even when it's not.

Watching the tracker get closer to the little gold Versailles icon is making me kind of sick. I yank out my holofone and open Pixter. This App is my most popular. Currently I'm at 1,254,376 followers.

A few pastel-themed photos are matched perfectly for my Top 6. One has my brother, Josef, in a light blue sweater, and another has my pug, Mops, curled up on a pink satin bed.

Ugh. Home. Looking at Pixter was a mistake. I smack my

holofone facedown on the seat beside me. They wouldn't let me bring Mops to my new home. He's an Austro dog. And I'm Franc now. I can only have a Franc dog.

The minute my toe touches Franc soil outside this cruiser, I will be the dauphine. *The Franc dauphine doesn't cry. The Franc dauphine is going home, and she is delighted to meet her people and her lovely future husband.* I repeat those things twice.

It doesn't really work. My stomach knots up again.

I've known my whole life I'd marry young. Younger than girls who aren't the duchess of the Austro Lands. I found out a few years ago that my husband would be Franc. After I got that news, I dreamed up all these pictures of what he might be like. Probably handsome, dark-haired, and suave. Franc guys are all charming and cultured. Or at least that's how it seems on the Apps, and the Franc diplomats who arrived at Schönbrunn acted like they were born with perfect manners.

Nothing could have prepared me for the text I got last week.

With a glance at the pilot's door, I pick up my holofone again. Not that Mercy pays attention to what I'm doing on the Apps anyway.

I open Pixter and click to my old messages before my eyes can linger on Josef and Mops. I bring up the message thread from "Anon4427."

It was a bizarre thing to land in my in-box because my permissions are set up so that chats from randos are blocked. I'd be flooded if my in-box were public. All the messages would probably crash the App.

For at least the sixteenth time, I read over the thread.

It says:

Anon4427: Hi 😊

Duchess_MariaAntonia: hi?

At the time, I wrote it off as a spammer or a bot. The time-stamp shows that it took forty-eight minutes for him to respond. When he did, he wrote:

Anon4427: sorry it's Louis

Anon4427: like the Franc guy

Duchess_MariaAntonia: Oh! Hi

As if it wasn't obvious from the fact that he wrote in Franc. I remember thinking there was no way this was *Louis*. Like, *my fiancé, Louis*. I thought someone was trolling me. When I learned we would be engaged, I asked Mama if I could chat Louis, but she said we weren't allowed to talk.

Anon4427: yeah just wanted to say hi before we meet and everything.

Duchess_MariaAntonia: that's sweet. But how did u chat me? I've got it blocked & we aren't allowed to talk

Anon4427: yeah . . . i'm not supposed to do this. Don't tell anyone ok?

Duchess_MariaAntonia: ok

Anon4427: thought this would make everything less weird. Maybe. It will prob be weird anyway. I'm not really sure what people expect from a prince. So FYI or something.

Duchess_MariaAntonia: expect? In what way? 😊

Anon4427: all the ways 😊

Anon4427: ur really hot

I'm not usually a blusher, but my face caught fire when I got that one. I buffered, trying to decide if I was being trolled. Franc guys are meant to be confident. And I suppose I should have been happy my husband-to-be liked the look of me, but this message made me even more nervous. Luckily, the feeling didn't last long.

Anon4427: omg. I'm so sorry. That was my brother. He took my holofone. Sorry.

Anon4427: he says I'm a turbo-nerd and can't talk to girls.

Duchess_MariaAntonia: Which brother? Philippe?

Anon4427: yeah. How'd you know?

Duchess_MariaAntonia: I've checked out the Bourbon bros on the Apps ☺ Easy to figure out from that. I'm basically an App genius.

Anon4427: yea ☺ I could tell from your pixter.

Duchess_MariaAntonia: you looked at my Pixter? ☺

Anon4427: srry g2g

The thread ends there. I close out the App window on my only conversation with my husband-to-be, Louis the Unexpected.

I had stalked his Pixter, of course. He wasn't exactly the suave prince I'd dreamed about. I wouldn't call him handsome. But he's cute, I guess, with a round face and dark brown hair that curls up at the ends. He's really tall and he always looks serious, like having his photo taken is torture. The only posts I saw with any personality were one of him cuddling a hound puppy and one bizarre snap that looked like a bunch of computer code.

I can't figure him out, even though I can usually dig up every account someone has on any platform and get a read on them. Knowing Louis's youngest brother, Philippe, is a flirt and a brainlag? Not exactly nanotech science. He never fails to post a photo on #AbDay. Then there's the middle brother, Stan. He clearly sees himself as the smart one, with his *très chic* watches, designer ties, and opera photos. They have a sister, Elisabeth, who doesn't post as much. Nature photos, some latte art, biology stuff . . . She strikes me as the brainy type.

But Louis? Who knows. All I have is that string of messages.

The pilot's door opens with a quiet whir.

"We're starting the descent," says Mercy. "When we land, you'll be greeted by Countess de Noailles and begin the garb change."

"Of course." I've been briefed on every step in emails from Countess de Noailles herself, my publicist and guide on all things Versailles. "Will you take the dimmer off the window so I can see the palace?"

"You'll see it soon enough."

My stomach is fluttering like crazy, and it's not just from the sinking cruiser. The garb change is to strip me of all things Austro. When I exit the cruiser, I will leave everything about my old life behind except Ambassador Mercy. My mother and brother will still be a text away, but I won't be Austro anymore.

I am Franc now. Marie Antoinette. I wonder how many times I'll have to repeat that before it becomes true. If it ever will.

The sinking feeling stops, and the cruiser stills. I remember my posture. Chin raised and extended, stomach drawn in, shoulders straight. With a hiss, the cruiser door swings up and open. I have a second to be dazzled by neon light and a pattern of black and white tiles before a stern woman with a tight ponytail and a navy-blue pencil skirt marches in. She's followed by a small army of attendants dressed in royal blue and two ladies of the court in satin gowns with blue LED collars.

"*Bienvenue*, mademoiselle." She curtsies expertly, hand

poised in front of her chest. "I am Countess de Noailles. I'm pleased to be of service."

I reach my hands out, thinking, I don't know . . . that I should embrace her? "I'm so happy to meet you in person, Countess. I'm sure I have so much to learn from you."

Much more to learn than I thought, because she stiffens right up like an old-school droid. I've already done something wrong. Have I been too informal? But I'm going to work closely with this woman. That's so silly.

Not silly. I must not think of Franc court rules as silly.

Noailles's smile is as mechanical as a bot's when she says, "Ah, yes. No sense in waiting. Let's begin the garb change."

I follow her to the cruiser's bathroom, with the attendants flocking behind like ducks after crumbs. My stomach is cramping with memories of my final Austro dinner. I haven't eaten in twenty-four hours.

The cruiser bathroom holds all of us somehow. If Josef were here, he'd say there wasn't enough room to load a gigabyte. Noailles looks at me, waiting for permission to begin, so I nod.

A maid reaches for my zipper and it starts. A flurry of hands yank my dress over my head. I raise my arms to help, and they feel weirdly like both jelly and stone. The moment the dress is off, I'm freezing, goose bumps everywhere. My underwear goes next. I suppose I can say goodbye to privacy at Versailles.

I might start shaking, so I tense all my muscles, willing them still. I stretch out my arms as Noailles passes a UV wand over me. Gotta kill those Austro Land germs. But the worst is yet to come. There's a reason I haven't eaten in twenty-four hours.

Noailles raises a Franc silk robe for me to step into, then hands me a small plastic cup. Her face is blank like a statue. I won't even carry the Austro contents of my stomach out of the cruiser. I'll be like a newborn. That's how Mama described it to me. I toss back the liquid in one quick swallow.

I avoid the many eyes staring at me and instead focus on the dull glow of the soft lights above the sink. I'm pale in the mirror, truly stripped of myself and washed out in the bathroom lights. Cold sweat prickles at my scalp and my stomach clenches.

An attendant places a bowl beneath my chin. It might be real gold.

After a moment, it's flecked with spatters of my spit and bile, thick and pale with a bit of yellow streaked in. I keep retching, puking mostly water. My throat burns and I think my brain is trying to push my eyes out of their sockets.

I'm gasping when I'm done. In the mirror, I find bright red eyes and a snot-smeared nose, and to my total embarrassment, I buffer and crash. Sobs claw up my throat to replace the retching.

No one seems to know what to do except a kind-eyed court lady with tight curls and a pink satin dress. She gently dabs at my face with a handkerchief. A toothbrush and a bit of mouthwash are shoved into my hands, and when I get control of myself, I use them, arms shaking and stomach sore. I'm so annoyed that I've cried, but at least I did it here instead of in front of the whole court.

I turn to find Noailles right in my face, nostrils flared. I think . . . she's smelling my breath. It must meet her approval because fresh underwear appears, lacy and bright white. I step into it, just a little wobbly. Next, the waist trainer/bra combo is wrapped around me. Someone does up the three sets of clasps down my back. The material is stretchy, but meant to slim and smooth.

My dress is pale blue like my Austro one, a good color for me that matches my eyes. I raise my arms to slip the small ruffled sleeves over them. There's no hiding my trembling.

Once it's smoothed into place, I decide I do like the dress even if it's a little plain for my taste. Cinched at the waist, flowing elegantly to my ankles, it leaves my shoulders bare and the collar makes a sharp, deep V. My hair and makeup aren't done yet, but I'm beginning to look less like a scared girl and more like a dauphine should.

They powder my face, line my eyes, tease my hair to be full and dress it with ribbons. When I face the mirror again, I see a stranger. This can't be me. Those aren't my highlighted cheeks or long-lashed eyes. I'm not sure whether I'm thrilled because my makeup is celestial, or scared because I don't know this girl. They put a diamond necklace around my neck and then I'm finished.

There's nothing Austro left on me or in me—except memories and the Austro heart beating hard in my chest.

"Madame . . ." With an elegant tilt of her wrist, Noailles gestures to the doorway. I leave the bathroom and go straight for the exit of the cruiser. No looking back. If I look back, my knees will shake so much I'll fall over.

As I set one silver high heel onto the checkerboard stones of the Versailles courtyard, I let myself feel the slight impact. I am no longer Maria. I am now Dauphine Marie Antoinette.

A warm breeze stirs my dress and all my nerves tingle. The wind smells funny. Sort of like old garbage. It stuns me for a moment because it doesn't at all match the glamour my eyes behold. The pure beauty of this place kicks my senses into overdrive.

Unlike Schönbrunn Palace, a lot of ancient Versailles remains. Schönbrunn was thrashed a lot harder during the wars and weather of the Event. I've never seen so much brick and marble on a building in my life. This is why thousands of people come to marvel at the old stones decorated with gorgeous busts, lit in pink to show off the features of ancient people with names we've forgotten. Things this old are *très* rare, absolutely priceless. This palace is built out of treasure.

My eyes skim the roofline, where gilded fleurs-de-lis have survived to line the eaves and many windows. The parts of the palace that fell apart are patched with modern material. Gold and iron replaced by bars of neon, like the building has veins of light and bones of shiny chrome. It would overwhelm anybody, even me, even though I grew up in my own palace. But no one can know. Not any of the hundred or so faces gathered can see one gigabyte of my fear, or awe.

There are perfectly painted faces, hair teased tall, elaborate with bows, braids, and tiny lights. Gowns and suits in all colors. I've never seen people as fashionable as these, and I'm not sure my dress, or my makeup, or my Austro hair color and eyes measure up. Surely they can see my foreignness written all over my face and in my stupid, careless walk that I should have practiced more.

One foot, then the next, Marie. You can do this. I let those phrases circle my mind until I'm an appropriate five or so steps from the king of the Franc Kingdom. It feels like I use every muscle of my face to tug a warm, gracious smile into place.

The king steps forward. This is Louis the Well-Beloved, my grandfather-in-law, tall and strong for his age, with square shoulders and jaw. I admire the flattering cut of his royal-blue suit. A faintly glowing holo over the breast pocket depicts a rose. He carries a cane full of bubbling liquid lit neon blue. Dark-tinted glasses band across his face, making him look more like a fly than fashion-forward. I heard he has cataracts that he doesn't like people to see.

Before I can stare at him too long, I do my very best curtsy, taking my time to make sure I do everything right. Foot forward, arm bent, I bend to sweep slowly and gracefully downward like a wave. I hear a rustle as Noailles and the attendants behind me do the same.

I rise with a small smile. The king must speak first.

The glasses weird me out a little. The tint obscures his eyes, making it impossible to read him. But he's smiling too. I just don't know what kind of smile it is.

He puts a foot forward and ducks into a sweeping bow. "*Bienvenue*, young mademoiselle. Welcome home."

"Majesté, thank you. I'm so happy to be here, and you are responsible for that happiness."

His smile twists up at the corners. "You're very welcome, Dauphine. But I think you ought to meet my grandson if you want to know who's really responsible for your happiness."

He chuckles, head thrown back like he's made such a great joke. I'm not sure if I should laugh too. A few of his retainers join in. He must mean well, but it kind of feels like he's mocking either me or Louis-Auguste or us both.

I glance around at the faces, trying to pick out Louis. I thought he would be front and center, but he isn't. I think I'll fry a hard drive if I have to wait another second to meet him. A few shoulders shuffle around to make an opening. I spot his dark-eyed brother, Stan, before I pick out the prince himself.

"Come on, boy," says the king. "Greet your fiancée."

His Majesté reaches back into the crowd and yanks on the dauphin, who stumbles just slightly as his grandfather practically shoves him at me.

Louis-Auguste catches himself quickly, drawing his shoulders and chin up. He's as tall as he seemed on Pixter. Something about his soft face and stooping bow make it seem like he really wishes he were smaller.

I so wanted the sight of him to make me brave or at least release an insta-crush wave of nervous butterflies, but it doesn't happen. He's just . . . there. I curtsy to him while he bows.

As we both rise, our eyes meet and he blushes.

"*Bienvenue*, mademoiselle." His voice is soft, as if we're in a library instead of the courtyard of Versailles.

Why does he look so terrified of me? He messaged so we could break the ice, didn't he? All I can think to do is reach out my arms and walk the few steps to hug him. I hope this shows him that more than anything, I want us to be friends.

It's like hugging a tree, he's so stiff. He barely moves his arms to put two hands gently on my back. I think he's shaking a little.

Does he hate me because I'm Austro? He wouldn't be the only Franc with a super-bias, but we're going to be together for the rest of our lives! We're going to rule the country together—have a family together!

If we were alone, I would take his hands to steady them. If we were alone, we could ask each other some of the hundred questions that are swirling around my brain and probably his too. But we're not going to be alone until after we're married.

Louis turns back to his grandfather. Apparently our greeting is over.

The king stretches his arms out in a grand gesture. "Well, young Miss Antoinette. Let us give you a proper welcome."

The court whistles and claps. A little extra glow lights the courtyard from a hundred holofones as the courtiers start snapping pics. All my mama's etiquette reminders spring to mind, but there are so many people I can't tell who I should smile at. As a cruiser swoops low over the palace, probably filming us, two squat worker droids shaped like discs scoot ahead of the king to attach to the golden front doors and swing them open. With barely a glance at me, Louis offers his arm and we step forward to enter Versailles.

TWO

May 13, 3070, 9:30 p.m.

The party is a sensory bomb.

Flashes of laser cut through the dim light, and everything is swirls of glowing gowns, bobbing feathers with LED fronds, and iridescent shine. The air feels hot and close as courtiers dance to a beat that rattles through the marble floor and shakes through my heels. A little bot floats overhead and blasts us with bubbles that have a strange, sweet smell like soap and sugar.

I run a finger along smooth glow-in-the-dark plaster used to fill a crack in the marble pillar beside me. Oil-paint-and-canvas portraits have been re-created with soft, glowing holograms. The ceiling is giga-old, though. Against all odds, the paint up there has survived. I try not to gape at the fading, flaking fresco that shows a range of men with long coats and curling white hair, and girls with huge dresses that have no LED lights but are somehow as flashy as our own. I tear my eyes away from an image of a long-forgotten blonde girl who could have been me a thousand years ago. The king plants a kiss on my knuckles and then fits a glass of champagne into my fist.

I finish it off quickly, ignoring the sting in my throat. I'm not used to drinking, but I'm sick of straining to smile. Maybe the drink will loosen my expression into something genuine. Louis hasn't said a word. He stares into his glass while his siblings descend on us. Through shouts in my ear, I'm introduced to a family I've only glimpsed through the Apps. The youngest one, a wiry boy with fair hair, is Philippe. The one who looks like a bulkier, flashier Louis is Stanislas, or Stan. A pretty girl close to my age with glossy brown hair and a kind smile is Elisabeth.

I've just finished my drink when Philippe produces three more, shoving one at me and downing two himself. Damn, he's, like, fifteen. The Francs must have different rules about drinking. Or different rules for royals.

Maybe sensing my nerves, Elisabeth grips my arm and smiles. She reaches for a silver platter that floats by on a hoverdrone and gives me a fluffy little pastry with an adorable cherry on it.

I pop the pastry into my mouth and almost melt along with the light, buttery icing. It's so sweet and tastes like fresh cherries. I chase it with a flute of champagne, which Philippe promptly replaces with another.

"Let's dance! Come on!" he shouts.

I turn to Louis. "Do you like to dance?"

"Huh?"

He leans down, but he's so tall I still have to go on tiptoe to reach his ear. "Do you like to dance?"

He shrugs, shaking his head no.

So Louis doesn't dance. I get a sinking feeling in my gut. I love dancing and do it as often as humanly possible, but it's rude to dance without your fiancé. Stan and Philippe practically throw themselves out on the floor. Elisabeth gives me a nudge and raises an eyebrow. It kills me to smile politely and decline again. She rolls her eyes and tugs at Louis's sleeve. "*Allons.*"

Louis goes red. "You know I can't."

"You can. You won't."

Louis nods toward the dancers. "Is Stan trying to crowd-surf Philippe?"

"Not again. Stan, put him down!"

Elisabeth rushes off in the direction of Philippe's foot bobbing over the crowd of glittering hairpieces.

Louis and I are left as alone as we're going to be tonight. I look up at him. He's sweating and chewing at his bottom lip with his eyes fixed on the crowd. His blazer strains around his big, slouching shoulders. I'm not sure what I expected from our Pixter conversation, but this is awkward. Why has he got me on ghost mode? I take a big swig of champagne for bravery and press as close as I can.

He shifts. Glances in my direction, then away.

"It was sweet of you." I have to nearly shout over the music. "To message me. It made me feel better."

Finally, Louis looks at me, but his eyes are bugging out like I just told him my mama is an android. He glances over his shoulder and leans toward me to answer in a mumble I can barely hear: "Please don't talk about that."

"Well, why not? It was really nice! I know we weren't supposed to, but too late now. I'm sure it's okay." He glances around again, even though literally everyone else in the room is either dancing or drinking. I nudge his arm. "Hey, how'd you do it, anyway? My in-box is private."

Louis shakes his head. "We really can't talk about it."

I'm in a hyper state of glitched out and a little tipsy from the champagne, which bubbles up in a laugh. I glance around the whirl of dancing and drinking. There are some curious eyes on us, but they're not crowding us. "No one is listening."

He leans close to me now. I smell champagne on his breath and my heart flutters. "Someone is *always* listening."

My skin prickles and now I'm giga-focused. "What do you mean?"

He downs the rest of his champagne. "You should go dance. I don't mind. Elisabeth will look out for you. *Allez-y.* It's okay."

"Won't you come with me?"

He mumbles something that sounds like "You wouldn't want me to," and before I can stop him, he's slipping away.

What did he mean by that? And why did he buffer and crash?

I'm sure no one could hear our conversation over the music. There's nothing to do now but dance and find more champagne.

The crowd has given the Bourbon siblings their respectful amount of space, so it's easy to spot Elisabeth and weave my way through to her. The crowd parts, full of faces smiling and curious. I try not to look too closely, and let the music and champagne move me. I feel it all uncurling in my belly, and it seems like I'm dreaming in the neon half-light, dancing in the court of Versailles with my new family of strangers.

Elisabeth gently takes my arm to guide me toward them. Stan and Philippe yowl and clap me on the back, jumping around like maniacs. Stan grabs my hands and spins me around in a few circles.

Not a good idea with my champagne belly. I can't stop laughing. Everything is spinning.

"Stan, relax!" I hear Elisabeth yell.

With Elisabeth's help, I stop laughing and straighten up. The whole room tilts sharply to the right. Lasers, mirrors, people, bass. These things repeating, tipping, falling, creeping.

"Get her some water." Elisabeth shoos Philippe away.

Yes, water. Thanks, Elisabeth.

Maybe this *is* my family. Maybe it's really, *really* my family now.

Mein Gott . . . This is nothing like home. I was barely ever allowed liquor at home. We had dances sometimes, but never this loud or this . . . much. Do I even like to drink? I'm not sure. But everyone here seems to, so I feel like I just . . . have to. Is this what the rest of my life will be like? Shouting down my fears with fake happiness and champagne while I do what everyone wants?

Elisabeth guides me off the dance floor back to where the king is seated on an enormous wingback chair. Elisabeth and I both bob quick curtsies. He gives us a nod. "Enjoying yourself?"

I curtsy again. "Yes, Majesté." The motion makes my head spin.

"I think she must be very tired, Grand-Père," says Elisabeth.

Noailles sweeps up, apparently waiting to pounce the moment I was done dancing. How did she hear Elisabeth over this noise? Doesn't matter. The champagne and exhaustion have me almost happy to see her.

"Well, then. Have pleasant dreams, Dauphine," the king says. Then he frowns over the bobbing heads, craning his neck. "Louis!"

The dauphin appears from nowhere. Where has he been? He doesn't acknowledge the king, just sidles up to me.

I don't know what to say. I have no idea what he thinks of me, but he's pretty much ignored me all evening.

"*Bonne nuit.*" He kisses my cheek, light and quick, pauses by my ear. He says, "Sorry." Then he's gone at mega-speed.

"I will show you to your rooms, mademoiselle," says Noailles.

It feels like we walk forever. Every hallway is a maze of holo-gram portraits of ancient people in weird wigs and capes. I could have sworn one of the portraits moved, and not in a holo way. Like someone's shadow moved out from behind the faintly flick-ering image of a guy with a huge mustache. Or maybe I've had too much champagne.

We arrive at my room. It's very white, and the decor isn't as old as what was in the ballroom. The furniture has plain gold and brass handles and embellishments. The only pop of color is the red canopy over my bed, backlit with pink neon. We step behind a privacy screen that glows softly with a holo image of a preening peacock.

Mechanically, I move my arms as I let the attendants take me out of my dress. Noailles presents me with a nightgown and—gigs! It's so sheer. Will I have to wear this when I'm married? Louis could barely meet my eyes. I try to imagine him looking me up and down in this nightgown and flush.

I think of Louis saying sorry. Sorry for what? Glitching when I asked him about the messages? Sorry for not dancing? For the fact that I'm here?

The attendants flick back my blankets as I climb into bed. Once that's done, they all line up before me. This seems point-less. Also kind of creepy.

"Good night, mademoiselle," they all murmur and bob little curtsies, like a flock of pigeons pecking toward the ground.

"If you need assistance, mademoiselle, you may summon us here." Noailles gestures toward a small black com-box to the left of my four-poster bed. "This is Georgette. She will be your lady-in-waiting."

A round-faced girl with mousy hair pinned in a knot gives

me a bow. She looks around my age. At least I don't have to deal with another Noailles. "It's nice to meet you," I say.

This seems to catch her off guard. She blinks a few times, then bows again with a flicker of a smile.

They all bow again. I nod and sit all stiff until they file out.

When the door shuts, I flop backward onto my pillows.

The curtains above have swirling, intricate patterns. I click a light on my nightstand. One switch makes soft, gold, star-shaped lights dance over the velvet canopy.

I've never felt so glad to be alone.

A quiet voice from deep in my mind made bold by champagne and an empty stomach asks what I'm doing here.

"I'm a princess," I say out loud. "The dauphine. And I had fun."

I silently repeat the "fun" part a few times, but the quiet voice is a traitor, reminding me of my unease.

"I did have fun. Screw you," I grumble, and turn over, swallowed by my dozens of too-soft pillows.

I reach one lazy arm upward so I can snap a pic of the stars on my four-poster curtains. It looks so cozy. I should share this.

But when I open Pixter . . .

"What the hell?"

I can't log in to my account.

A few clicks show a message over my locked profile:

Follow @Duchess_MariaAntonia at her new account, @Dauphine_MarieAntoinette.

They set up a new account with no input from me. As if the giga-success of my old account wasn't all due to my hard work. As if I didn't post every photo, write every bio, compose every message myself! What if my old followers *don't* follow my new account? What then? Was all my work for nothing? What about the friends I DM with?

I bet Mercy swapped out my holofone and shut down the account during the garb change! The rough pink jewels on the case of the holofone feel just like they always have under my thumbs, but I bet this is a brand-new Franc holofone and case. Can't keep my nasty Austro one after all.

I fling it onto the bedside table, where it lands with a clatter.

It's not fair! This is *Scheiße*. It's not like I wouldn't have made a new account myself in the morning. They don't have to force me. They could let me say one last goodbye on my Austro Lands account. One small thing to show the little bridge between who I was and who I will be after my wedding.

If there's a time and a place to cry, I guess it's here in my dark, strange bedroom. Angry, burning drops streak down my cheeks while I stare at the drifting stars and try to repeat positives instead of the truth—which is that I hate it here.

THREE

✳

I've been in the dressing room for hours without looking in a mirror. I'm scared to check, because the last time I was dressed by the Francs, I didn't recognize my reflection. In a minute, they'll finish my makeup, then I guess I'll have to see.

There's a gigaton of layers to the skirts of my wedding dress. Lace and tulle and satin and ribbon. It was designed by Givernée, the top Franc designer. I'm studded with little LED lights, silk gloves up to my armpits, and my hair is stacked high, all woven through with extra wefts. The tightly piled updo, sculpted to perfect smoothness at my forehead and temples, pulls at my scalp. Georgette dabs me with a makeup brush. She's going to make me sneeze if she isn't careful.

"There is little you have to remember or say," Noailles tells me. "Walk with grace as though you are floating. Smile. Be warm toward the dauphin. Respond 'yes' to the priest and 'amen' to the prayers. That's it, but it's crucial. All eyes are on you today."

The brush is finally off my face, and I open my eyes. "I understand, Countess de Noailles."

She smiles. "Of course. You are a vision. Take a look."

"Are you ready?" Georgette asks.

"I think so."

Georgette spins me toward the mirror.

My breath catches in my throat. I don't look like a princess. I look like a queen. The lights on my dress alternate in waves between a gentle white and a glowing gold. My face is pale, with makeup sculpting my cheeks to look high and regal below soft eyes powdered around with gold. Ribbons and pearls drape in elegant strands over my stacked hair. A long, cloudlike veil billows behind me. I look like a proper adult. I look otherworldly. I look like art. I'm amazed by what they've done to me. But I'm also frightened.

I will never be the same after today.

"Do you like it, mademoiselle?" asks Georgette.

I squeeze her wrist. She seems so genuine, and it makes me feel less alone. "Yes. Yes, of course. Thank you."

This brings tears to her eyes.

Mein Gott, that's going to bring tears to *my* eyes, and then my makeup is going to run.

Noailles must sense the danger, because she herds me toward the door. Attendants hold up my train and the edges of my dress. You'd think I was a doll made of glass the way they fuss at me while I'm angled through doorways and down stairs.

Walk carefully, Marie. You can do this. You look great. You can do this.

I take empty, windowless private passages through Versailles to get to the palace chapel. We stop in a small waiting room with a holo-screen broadcasting live footage from the front of the palace. There's so many people that I can't see the paving stones of the courtyard. Is everyone in the Franc Kingdom here?

The reporter says that they're all waiting for their first glimpse of Marie Antoinette.

What will they see? A scared girl in a dress? An Austro glitch in their system? I have to make sure they see their dauphine, and I have to make sure they love her.

There are so many of them. So many of them, all with a different idea of who I am, when half the time *I'm* not even sure who I am, so what exactly am I supposed to present to them?

I can do this. I suck in big breaths. *I can do this.* I've trained years for this. No one is more ready for this than me. No princess is really as confident as she appears.

I just have to get through today. And tonight. It has to get easier after that. When I wake tomorrow, I'll be Marie Antoinette and I'll know exactly what to do and what to say.

I might vomit.

The holo-screen shows a reporter interviewing a guy with long hair and dark eyes, handsome in the way I always imagined Franc boys to be.

Then I hear what he's saying. "An expense of what? Millions? For what? For what purpose, when electric prices doubled two weeks ago? It's absurd. It's unjust."

The disgust on his handsome face is plain. The heavy tulle draped on me feels smothering and sticky with my cold sweat. I never thought about how much this wedding might cost. Besides decorations, food, the reception, the music, there's the security to contain all the people lining the avenue. I try and fail to do the math.

"What do you think should be done?" the reporter asks.

The man's brows furrow and he starts talking, but it sounds

all distorted, quick snaps of sound as the image pales out and then goes black. There's a few seconds of nonsense code language in the top left of the screen. It disappears, replaced by images of the cheering crowds again. This time it's narrated by an excited female reporter while an ad for Bombazique headphones bounces along in a banner over her head. There's no sign of the angry man who was interviewed.

Was zum Teufel?

I stare, trying to wrap my brain around what just happened, when the door opens and Mercy bustles in. He glances up at the holo-screen.

"What are you watching this for? It won't help your nerves." He switches off the screen, then reaches for my hand to plant a kiss below my knuckles. "You look like a splendid dauphine. The people will be thrilled to see you."

"I just saw something weird there." I point to the screen.

"That's why you shouldn't watch it."

"Some guy said the wedding cost millions. He seemed . . . angry."

Mercy frowns at the blank monitor. "Really? That's highly unusual."

"Then he just sort of blacked out, then it was on to something else like he was never there."

"Must have been a broadcasting error."

"Does this wedding really cost millions of bits?"

Mercy sighs and places his hands on my shoulders. "Marie, state events are always expensive. And someone will always complain about the expense. It's just the way of the world. Put it out of your mind. Are you ready?"

I take a deep breath. He's right, of course. No use going out there with some rando from the news on my brain. "I'm ready."

"You remember the ceremony instructions?"

"Yes, I've heard them a million times."

"Wonderful. Your mother sends her blessings and her love." Mercy holds out his hand. "Now, holofone, if you please."

"Are you serious? It's not like I'll have it out during the ceremony." I can't believe I'm about to be married and he's treating me like a little kid misbehaving at church.

"Then what is the point, my dear?"

I sigh and hand over my little bejeweled holofone. "You'll take a lot of pictures?"

"Of course."

My procession files in behind me while attendants adjust my hair and fill out my train. A woman with a headset waits at the door, muttering into the mic. Nearly time to go. My heart flutters like a bird.

It's fine. All I have to do is look nice. That's so easy. I repeat "easy" to myself a few times and fidget with the dress's little lights.

The music thrums, an ancient organ, a sound rarely heard anymore, mixed with a bass. I guess it's supposed to be grand, but it's more like a moaning monster. Trumpets blare, and the woman with the headset signals to us. A few little girls who are Louis's cousins or something go before us, tossing big pink flower petals.

The chapel is a huge, bright space filled with the scent of flowers. Tall columns support a ceiling painted with fluffy clouds and cherubs. More paintings are projected on the white marble walls, drifting slowly in sharp high-def. There's so much to see in here, how could any of the guests settle on one thing? How are they all staring at me?

The aisle is not so long. I'll be able to cross it quickly in careful steps on my tiptoes like I'm floating, the same as all those painted cherubs. *I can do this.*

I follow the little girls while they toss arcs of floppy pink petals to be crushed beneath the feet of the procession. The king presides on the altar behind the priest with his grandchildren arranged below.

Louis looks nice with his hair brushed back and wearing the ceremonial dress: a blue sash and badges on a dark suit. But he also looks scared. About as scared as I am. I get it. I really do. But I wish he'd stop. There's no way I'm that terrifying, and his fear is contagious.

I take my place beside him and he holds out his hand to take mine in a loose, damp grip. When I look into his large, frightened eyes, I can see the kindness in them. Things could be worse. Things *have been* worse for a lot of girls in my position.

The priest starts talking, but I don't listen. I'm focused on breathing and smiling gently. There are thousands of eyes and cameras on us. I don't stare too long at Louis because I think it makes him nervous. Instead, he watches the priest. I don't think he's listening any more than I am, because although everyone says our families were granted their positions by god, no one really believes in any god anymore. We go through these motions because so much of what humans were like before the Event is lost now, and Mutti and my tutor said traditions and our family's actions give structure and meaning to our people. They say it makes us feel connected to our ancestors to marry off princes and princesses in ancient places. I say that's a weird idea; people clearly just like to admire idols on the Apps. They look to me for style ideas, not traditions.

The room is very hot and the priest is still droning on. I feel like the weight of my hair might crush me, and Louis's hand is sweaty. But oh! The soon-to-be husband said something! Finally. We're at the part where we must swear to be faithful and loyal and godly and all that.

I will.

Yes.

I will.

I will.

I do.

Amen.

Louis's hands shake when he puts a heavy ring on my finger. I search his eyes, looking for answers. *What are you so afraid of, Louis?* I smile at him in a way I hope is comforting. Why is he shaking like a caffeine junkie?

Oh, right. We're at the kissing part. For a second, because of all his shaking, I'm afraid he'll just peck at my face like a chicken, maybe miss my mouth or something. It's quick, but he does all right. Soft, like the rest of him, just barely pressing over my lips.

I'd be lying if I said it was my first kiss . . . or my best. That award goes to Duke Francis, who kissed me all thrilling and secretly in a parlor room when we were fourteen.

Louis makes me feel a little sad. He shuffles, cheeks all rosy. That may not have been my first kiss, but is it possible it was his? Even though he's a prince? Weird.

Gigs! I've been married for thirty seconds and I'm already

calling my husband weird. That's bad. I need to be nice. Really, really nice. My holofone is going to buzz any second and Mama is going to remind me how important it is that I make the dauphin happy. Wait. No, it won't. Mercy has my holofone. And Mama can't read minds. I don't think.

I mouth the final prayers, thoughts swirling, then trumpets start again, and the rest of the orchestra follows with the huge electro-organ rattling through the chapel, thrumming the floor beneath my feet.

Everyone rises. I hear the shuffle behind me. Louis glances at me and gives me his arm, but he still won't look me in the eye. All my focus is on keeping up with his long strides, which is really hard when I'm supposed to look like I'm floating. They should have given me a Holotex hoverboard. No one would have seen it under my dress.

As we cross the threshold out of the chapel into the courtyard outside, I make my first public appearance to the Franc people. The music blares everything into a frenzy that overwhelms me into a light-headed panic.

I've greeted my Austro subjects before, but I've never heard a crowd this wild. Loud, riotous screaming and clapping, lights flashing, arms in the air clutching cameras and holofones. It all looks like a big, slow-rolling wave of arms and faces. Holo rose petals fall from the sky to disappear over the crowd. The bright red sunset behind the mass of people blinds me. I stumble on a bump in the bricks. Louis tightens our arm-lock and tugs me a bit closer.

Wave. I need to wave. I twist my wrist in small, delicate motions. Everything seems to move much too slowly, drawn out

by that booming music. We move down a path lined with soldiers facing the leaping crowd. Hundreds of people wave at me
like they're my best friend I lost in a crowd and they're showing
me, *Here! I'm over here!*

We head up a wide set of stairs leading to a dais built to display us to the masses. The higher we climb, the farther I see this
crowd stretch, no end in sight, people lined up for miles, who
won't see us except on the big screens lining the roadway.

When we pause at the top of the stairs, Louis pats my hand.
"Are you okay?"

"Yes!" I must have had his jacket sleeve in a death grip. There
is no other way of telling that I'm not even a quarter as calm as
I look. At least my smile is real, because the cheers, the screams,
are contagious.

Louis nods out to them. "They like you." He waves and his
smile is small, but his eyes are warm while he extends his hand
out to them, waving like he's reaching and grasping. Louis seems
to care for them. I make my own wave bigger, like I've got a flag
I'm raising over my head so even people far away can see. I'm
not sure how long we go on waving. Until my arm aches and my
shoulder strap slips out of place.

Our handlers urge us inside the palace, back into the same
ballroom where my welcome party took place. Everything is
dressed up more formally now. Less neon, more crystal—and
ice sculptures made to look like fish and roosters, the beasts on
the Bourbon coat of arms. The court gathers into the ballroom
with Louis and me at the center.

There's a live band, all wired and amped so it's loud, loud,
loud. I've got to keep count while dancing with Louis. He's a lot

taller than me and he doesn't exactly move gracefully. I stand on my tiptoes and get a hand on his shoulder. Not easy. Not even a little. I hope this isn't a bad omen of . . . other stuff we might not be compatible for. The thought makes my stomach drop.

I want to talk to him. Say anything. Just a few friendly words will make what's coming seem a little easier. But there are so many people watching us, and I really can't afford to trip or be anything less than flawless in this dance.

No sooner do I think this than I trip over the hem of my own gown.

It's a small mistake, a misstep, but as panic shoots between my tripping feet and my brain scrambling to choose a method of damage control, I pitch forward.

Louis's hands tighten on mine, and he turns so I spin into his broad frame to steady myself.

There's a breathless moment where we stare wide-eyed at each other.

Someone behind me snickers.

Another one gasps.

"Did she really just? She has one job. Dance."

Before I can decide what to do and process what just happened, Louis spins us to face the whisperers. A couple with sharp cheekbones and unforgiving eyes.

"My fault," he says quietly with a clumsy shake of his head.

He saved me. He really stepped up for me.

Maybe saved me. People are still staring.

I squeeze his hand. "Thank you."

His cheeks flare red. "It's nothing. Everyone knows I'm a bad dancer."

Before I can think of what to say next, the dance is over. We bow and separate.

Then we're promptly matched off with others. I dance with the king next. He's Pixter-famous for his graceful dance moves, so if I trip again, everyone will know it was me. "You were exquisite," he says. "The Francs love you already; you were so charming. I couldn't feel better about this alliance."

I blink and say a breathless thanks. How did he not notice our fumbled dance? The king's approval will heavily influence the public's. I glow with pride and gigabytes of relief, until I catch him looking down my dress. The dance can't end soon enough after that.

I partner up with three dukes. Only one of those looks down my dress. Then I dance with both Stan and Philippe, and they both make me laugh, which I hope is not against etiquette. Four more dukes and lords, and then I'm surprised when Mercy is my last dance. The sight of him is like a bubble bath after a long day, a comforting face, almost like family. He gently takes my hand, and when he does, my holofone is in my palm.

"Oh, thank you, ambassador!" I slip it into a discreet pocket in my dress lining.

"Plenty of pictures on there. You did well. Very warm welcome from the people. Positive reports on all the Apps. They admire your youth and spirit."

I giggle, still overcome with relief. "The king praised my performance! Even Louis-Auguste! He said the people liked me. I was so afraid they wouldn't."

A line appears between Mercy's fuzzy gray eyebrows. "Yes, well . . . generations of bad blood won't go away with one beautiful wedding. There will still be some who are suspicious of Austros. That's why you can't afford to slip up. Not even a trip in a dance. The Francs highly prize grace under pressure."

The relief that flooded me when Louis saved me and the king praised me disappears. "I'm sorry . . . I . . ." But there's no excuse for my mistake. I've practiced formal dancing since I could walk. It was stupid of me.

"It's no longer a worry for this evening. There are more immediate concerns."

He frowns. Neither of us wants to have conversations about my marriage bed. The skin-crawling feeling I get each time I think of my wedding night creeps over me. Dread when I think of what I have to do. A flutter in my chest when I think of Louis's kind eyes. I don't know what to do with such conflicting feelings.

"There's really nothing to fear. Of course, tension will be high, but matters should be . . . simple enough." Mercy clears his throat gently.

I nod. There's really nothing to say. He's trying to make me feel better, but he's made my nerves a lot worse.

"It should all get easier after tonight," he adds quietly.

More nodding. Just because I have to have these conversations with him doesn't mean I have to like it.

"This silence isn't the norm for you. What's the matter?"

"I'm just nervous, Mercy. Gigs, wouldn't you be?"

I stare him down, because if I have to answer his questions, he should have to answer mine.

His eyes widen. I've stumped him. "I don't know. I suppose . . . I would be."

"But you will never have to know, because you aren't a woman."

His grip on my hand loosens and our dancing becomes mechanical. After an awkward minute, he says, "I'm sure the dauphin is nervous as well."

As if Louis glitching out improves the situation. I'm not sure if I'd feel any better if he seemed eager to seal the deal, but his nerves don't make me feel . . . appealing. And I'm supposed to be appealing, though that thought also makes me feel small and worthless. The idea of being *presented* to the dauphin makes me a little angry, like I'm less than a person and more like some doll. Or a prize achievement unlocked in a holo-game. But then the way he avoids my eyes disappoints me, and I worry that there's something wrong with me.

My mind is awhirl with feelings that don't make sense all at the same time. Is this what it's like to be a princess? Will everything just suck no matter what?

"I've barely spoken to the dauphin. I'm not sure he even likes me. Everyone acts like the most important thing I can ever do in my whole life is to look beautiful and act perfect and someday have Franc babies. They act like this is all I'm good for, but there's so much I can't control."

"You'll be just fine, Dauphine. There are many people who will help and advise you. The dauphin knows his duties as well as you do. He's been shy all his life, so his reserve doesn't surprise me. But I'm sure he'll like you just fine. Any young man would."

Like everything else Mercy has said, this should make me feel better, and yet . . .

The dance ends and we take our seats for dinner.

Etiquette says I have to eat at least a little of everything that's put in front of me. I nibble at the skin of a fish that still has eyes. Glitchy. I've never liked fish, ever since I came across an article on my holofone about how fish is a risky food that makes people sick, but a lot of common people eat it anyway. Even when it has three heads and six fins. At dinner a month ago, when I was about to gag over some yellow lobster thing, Mama told me seafood is healthier and easier to come by in the Franc Kingdom, so I'd better get used to it.

Louis-Auguste sits across from me with his brothers on either side of him. Philippe and Stan keep glancing at me, then they smirk and elbow Louis, whispering things in his ear. Louis gets redder and redder and won't look at anyone.

During course seven, Stan and Philippe say something I'm glad I can't hear. Philippe laughs so hard that a tear streaks his red face. Louis buries his head in one large hand. I'm about to tell them to cut it out when Louis finally, after seven courses full of giggles and snorts, speaks up. "If you don't stop, I'm going to make you so sorry. It'll be like after that time you loosened all the buckles on my saddle."

"All right, lay off!" Stan barks at Philippe, even though he was the one who started it, and had laughed twice as loud.

Louis glances at me before rounding on Stan. "You should say sorry to her."

"What for?"

"You're being rude."

Stan snorts, but Philippe nods. "Sorry, sis! We didn't mean anything by it."

Stan rolls his eyes and gives me a greasy smile that reminds me of his grandfather. "Apologies, madame. We're having a laugh at our wanker of a brother, not you."

I give him my sweetest smile. "Seems to me you should apologize to him too, then."

Philippe does a loud "oooooh" and claps.

Do I look like the worst kind of stuck-up Austro princess? Maybe, but I don't care.

I don't like the way Stan looks deep into my eyes, totally unembarrassed, before he smiles that slimy grin again. "Looks like you have yourself a feisty one. That ought to be fun."

What a glitchy little creeper! It takes every ounce of guts I've got to stare right back without moving a muscle except for a little twitch that flutters in my eyelid.

Louis sets his fork down with a clatter. "I said quit it. I was serious."

Apparently a firm Louis is a rare occurrence, because Philippe giggles nervously this time.

Stan puts on a gruff, mumbly voice. "Oh, he's serious! Better stop, then."

Elisabeth was in conversation with an aunt, but we've got her attention now. "I don't know what you're saying over there, but I know you're being asses. I'll get Grand-Père to go off on you and then you'll be sorry, you little bagbiters."

"Oh, mind your own business," says Stan. He definitely mouths the word "bitch."

Elisabeth raises her wineglass for a drink, middle finger arranged just so. I underestimated this girl. She's totally tradigital.

I notice Stan doesn't apologize, though.

"I'm so sorry," Elisabeth says. "My brothers are all complete idiots. Lucky for you, Louis is the least idiotic."

"Wow, thanks; that's so sweet," Louis mumbles.

"You're welcome, brother dearest."

Elisabeth and Louis are cute. They remind me of Josef and me, the teasing and the love. Philippe is okay for now, but I'm not sure if I like Stan after that comment on my so-called feistiness. What a dongle. At seventeen, he's just a year younger than Louis and a year older than Elisabeth, though I'd never guess it after that immature episode. I'll need my guard up around him and those sneaky smiles and grating comments.

The rest of the dinner is kind of tense, but I catch Louis's eye a few times, and he smiles just a little each time. Maybe he likes that I stood up for him.

Dessert arrives, a beautiful little piece of cake with pastel purple and blue frosting along with a selection of traditional Franc macarons. I love dessert. It's even part of my Pixter brand. But today my stomach is in so many knots, just the sight of the fluffy meringues and rainbows of macarons makes my stomach queasy. I manage to eat half my selection of sweets, trying to savor every bite, stretching out the end of dinner and what comes next.

When the king rises, tapping a knife on his champagne glass, dread sets in. His majestic, booming voice fills the room. "To the dauphin and dauphine of the Franc Kingdom! May you do good work and give us many healthy heirs! Good luck!"

Oof. That's not embarrassing.

The entire room roars its approval and bangs on the tables. Philippe can't contain himself, rolling around in his chair, laughing like he's mega-glitched. He topples a wineglass, and a robo-server floats in to settle over the stain, glowing while it purifies the tablecloth. Louis looks like he would rather die than sit through this. I'm over it too.

The king motions for us all to rise. Noailles has appeared from down the table to lead me and half the damn court to my bedroom. Joy. This shouldn't be uncomfortable at all.

When we arrive, Georgette offers me a refreshing glass of water with a curtsy. Her eyes are kind. She looks sorry for me, and I feel less alone. I almost calm down, but then Noailles gestures to my dressing room. Untangling me from the wedding dress is a team effort. My heart pounds more than it did when they put it on me. Despite this room being completely climate controlled, I'm all goose bumps. I'm gonna pee. God, this is embarrassing. My stomach squirms like I swallowed a thrashing goldfish. I'm handed one of those stupid sheer nightgowns again.

I should pee. Right? I should pee before I get into bed. I can't just hop out and say I have to pee in the middle of everything, that would be really bad. Although I think someone told me I have to pee after we actually . . . do it. The thing I'm about to do.

"Um . . . Countess de Noailles?" I poke a finger toward the bathroom.

"Yes, yes! Hurry!" She waves her hands at me and I scamper through the little door from the dressing room to the bathroom.

I want to hide in the dark in privacy until everyone leaves. When they're all gone except Louis, then I'll get into bed. That sounds a lot easier.

A lot of people are excited about having sex for the first time, and I guess everyone's nervous, but not everyone glitches out like I'm doing. But how? How do you not? This is terrifying. I guess not everyone is the dauphin and dauphine of the Franc Kingdom, with half the residents of Versailles crammed in their bedroom.

I can wish for everyone to be gone when I come out all I want. It's not happening. This is my duty. It'll be fine. My mama would never send me here if something really horrible was going to happen. Louis is quiet and kind. He won't be mean or rough. Maybe it will even be nice or fun or . . . something.

After repeating this a few times, I take a deep breath, ignore the urge to cross my arms over my chest, which feels very exposed in this light fabric, and go back to my room. When I come out, dozens of people stare at me and my arms go to my chest anyway.

These people aren't my husband. Why should they look at me? But it's Versailles tradition. This is how they've always done things. It's just a ceremony.

Louis stands across from me on the other side of my bed. His pajamas look a lot more comfortable than mine. Black satin that reminds me of Georgette's uniform, also with the same gold Versailles logo on the pocket. I can't read the expression on his face. I don't feel like he's looking at me, though. Like, really looking at me, the way he's supposed to while I'm wearing this stupid nightgown. I'm not sure if I want him to look at me that way, but he's meant to, or else they wouldn't have put it on me. Someone behind me is eyeballing me, though. I can feel it. It makes my skin crawl.

I'm not putting up with this anymore. This is ridiculous.

I lunge for the bed, where I'm shadowed by the canopy. The room is already dim, so huddled against the ornate headboard with my knees hugged up, no one can look at me anymore.

An attendant clears their throat and someone steps forward to arrange the blankets. Louis glances around nervously like he doesn't know what to do. Clearly I've broken some rule, but I'm past caring. I'm grateful when he slides in next to me.

The king steps forward. He chuckles in a way that gives me that skin-crawl feeling again. "May you live long, happy lives and bless our kingdom with strong, healthy heirs. Good night! Our hopes rest on you."

He bows low to us. The whole room does. I'm trying to pick out which creep was staring at me so I can avoid them later. Can't figure it out, though.

Slowly, like a page loading with agonizingly low net-speed, everyone files out until only Noailles is left. She curtsies to us and then, at long last, she shuts the damn door.

The lights overhead dim, the window shutters turn and seal shut, then everything is pitch black. I don't move a muscle.

Any second Louis will roll over. He'll kiss me. Or say something. Anything. But the minutes plod by.

Louis is shy. Everyone says it. So . . . what? He's not moving. But if he's shy, I don't think he'll appreciate it if I climb on top of him. Or maybe he will.

My face burns just to think about it. I don't know why this is so hard. I just . . . don't know what he wants or even what I want.

"Sorry," I say.

"What for?" His voice is so quiet. Nothing like his chattering brothers or commanding grandfather.

"A minute ago. I did something wrong when I got in bed."

I feel the shuffle of blankets as he turns toward me. His fingers brush my arm, which buzzes with tingles all up and down.

That's a good sign, right?

"It's okay," he says. "You don't have to be scared."

"Oh, I'm not. . . ." That's such a lie and he must know it. "I just couldn't stand there anymore. I felt like everyone was staring at me. Well, everyone was. But with this nightgown . . . you know."

Cool air as he moves away from me. "You don't have to wear that. I can get you something else."

I can feel my heartbeat in my ears. Why is this so confusing? It's nice of him, but he's not supposed to want to cover me up, is he?

"Oh, no, that's fine." I grab his arm before he can get out of bed. He stiffens right up like he did when I hugged him at our first meeting, then sinks back onto the mattress.

Still holding his arm, I scoot a bit closer so I'm pressed against his side. Damn this nightgown, though. The whole length of his arm is warm against me like there's nothing between us.

I'm spurred on by all the times Mutti told me Louis and I would bond quickly if I touched him, encouraged him. My face feels like lava before I even say the words. "I think . . . the general idea is that I take it off. And . . . leave it off."

"Um . . ." Louis untangles his arm from my grip and my stomach drops. Was that bad to say? I thought it was pretty good. Cute while acknowledging the awkwardness.

I don't know what I'm supposed to do, and a lump fills my throat. Hopefully, it's too dark for him to see the tears blurring my eyes. I just have to stifle this sob, but it comes out as a hiccup, so now I've given away that I'm crying. Final nail in the coffin of the mood, I imagine.

"Oh, damn it," Louis mutters, and clicks on the bedside lamp before I can stop him.

I dab at my eyes, but there's no hiding the tears from him. So now I've offended him, he doesn't like me, and I'm crying on our wedding night. Perfect.

Très bien, Marie. The absolute opposite of what Mama said to do and what was supposed to happen.

"Okay . . . um. So . . ." Awkwardly, more awkwardly than I thought was humanly possible, he places a hand on my shoulder and rubs it. Like I'm a stupid little kid he feels sorry for. I want to shrug him off.

"I'm sorry," he says. "I just . . . don't know you. And you don't know me. So I think in the end, it will be much better if we just . . . wait a little while."

I do shrug away from him now, because his pity is the most horrible shame I've ever felt. Worse than anything Mama has ever punished me for. I've ruined *everything*. What if Louis tells his grandfather he doesn't like me and I'm sent home? I'll lose all my followers and I'll never remarry and I'll be a boring auntie who talks to strangers in obsolete chat rooms all day. The Francs will reject me. Our peace treaty will get ruined and Mama will never forgive me. I have to save this.

"Sorry. That was really dumb. I just don't know what you like," I say.

"Right. Because we don't know each other."

His voice is so gentle when he says it that tears threaten again, but I can't just give up. "You could tell me what you like, and I'll do it."

"I don't know what I like." He picks at the sheets, hair hiding his face. That must be code for: *not me*. I'm buffering. The entire marriage can be canceled up to the time it's consummated.

"There's nothing? I can do anything. I guess. It's my job to make you happy."

He shakes his head. "No. That's not your job. And this isn't your fault. It's not you."

I take another chance, reach out and stroke a wave of brown hair out of his face. "I'm scared too. But we can figure it out. It'll be okay. We just have to try."

He has soft hair and the petting thing seems to be working, so I keep it up. Because there's something there in his eyes as he looks at me. We can be friends. I can see it. This isn't a lost cause.

"I think we'll like each other more if we wait," he says. "Grand-Père never waits for anything, and my grand-mère hated him after a while."

"I won't hate you. I understand. Everyone expects us to . . . consummate."

"You'll see starting tomorrow that everything I do disappoints the court and my family. What's one more thing?"

That's sad, but he's smiling like this is a joke. It's not. Mama will glitch.

Louis takes the hand I've rested on his shoulder. "Be honest. Forget what everyone else wants. Do you want to wait?"

"I . . . I don't . . . I . . ."

When was the last time someone asked me what I wanted?

With the warm lamp glow and his warm hands clasped around mine, I don't know. I've never been so confused in my life.

Honestly, I might prefer to get it over with. But my husband is a stranger. He's a stranger with soft hair and a gentle voice, but he's still a stranger and I don't know what I think of him.

"You don't really want to struggle through this with me right now, do you?" He squeezes my hand. "When I don't know one thing about you?"

I shrug. I can't afford to discourage him. Mama's instructions were clear; it doesn't matter what I want. "I wouldn't mind. If you wanted to."

Louis sighs. "Even though you said a few minutes ago you were scared?"

I shrug again. "I think we'll always be scared the first time." A thought strikes me like a slap, and I blurt it out before I can think through it. "Unless it's not your first time."

He sets a record on the blush-redness scale. "It is. It would be. . . ." He groans and rubs at his face. "I just don't want you to think it's you or anything wrong with you. I just need some time is all."

"Then I guess . . . you're the boss."

He flops back on the pillows and looks miserable. "I'm sorry. I don't want it to be like that. I'm not the boss of you. I just . . . I'll disappoint you. In lots of ways. I'm trying to avoid starting out with a mega disaster, you know?"

I process this for a moment. His quiet voice, the distance in his eyes . . . he's so sincere, and my heart breaks for him. How did a prince end up with no confidence? I've never met anyone like him. I figured it would be nice to be my husband's friend before, but now I think I have to be. He clearly needs one. A good one.

"Hey." I nudge his shoulder. "If you're not the boss, does that mean I am?"

He laughs a little. "Sure."

"Good. Can you flip that thing on the lamp?"

The soft light goes off and the stars come on.

"Perfect."

Louis folds his arms behind his head. "Huh. Those are nice. Never seen them before."

He seems to have no interest in moving closer to me, content to look up at the little stars like we're in a field. We didn't *consummate*, but I think we bonded a little. It'll be okay. No one has to know we lay here looking at the star lights instead.

FOUR

May 17, 3070, 5:28 a.m.

I wake up before the sun. I tap my holofone, and it projects 5:28 a.m. over the tablet surface.

Where's Louis? I touch his pillow. Cold. I tiptoe from bed and peek into the common room, a shared lounge between our two bedrooms. A jumble of computer monitors pulse rest-mode lights, and the big screen on the wall shows a mountain with green predawn light. No sign of him. I guess he went back to bed in his own room. Why? It's not like I'm going to pounce on him in his sleep. What will my attendants think when he isn't here?

I dive back into the covers rather than face the day. Along with the fresh linen scent, there's also a whiff of some musky, manly shampoo. Weird. That's going to take some getting used to. Instead of thinking about how Louis bailed on me, I grab my holofone. I'm still locked out of my account. That will be the first thing I talk to Noailles about today, and I have no idea how I'm going to keep my chill.

A problem for after breakfast. For now, I can at least look at feeds. I find posts and pics of the wedding at mega-speed because there are so many hashtags. The cutest one is definitely *#bienvenuedauphine*.

A lot of these pictures are amazing, and the comments . . . my heart is swelling with warmth and pride. This is exactly what I needed. The comments are glowing. So much love. Things like, Belle, magnifique, je l'aime. My favorite is, Catch my dumb ass strapping a 60 watt bulb to my dress trying to get this look.

They're nice to Louis too, but sometimes people make fun of him. One comment on a picture of us at the altar says: Dauphin looks like he's pissing himself #ouioui. But some girls have rushed to his defense. Don't be mean! He's shy! I love him . . .

He just has a serious look. He always does.

Fave brother!! He is cutest of the 3. I would be

dauphine if he wanted 🌹 xoxxo

Does he look at these ever? Might give the guy some confidence. We'll ignore the fourth comment: r u kidding??! Philippe <3 #PhilippeIsStillSingle #DmMe

My favorite picture shows us waving on the dais. I know which moment it is because Louis is leaning toward me, saying that the people like me. I look really happy. We look perfect. Just like we should.

More wonderful comments. They will be perfect. Gorgeous couple. Lines and lines of hearts, emojis with heart eyes, Franc flags. People are so cute. . . . I close Chatterbox when I get to this comment: They will have beautiful babies.

We might look perfect, but will the people figure out we've let them down? If I lie and say we're all properly consummated, people will look at a picture like this and believe me, right? When Louis says wait . . . he just means a few days, right? A month, tops. It's normal to wait.

My Face2Face App blinks in time with little jingly noises from an incoming call. *Scheiße*. Lying to Mama should be fun.

It's cool. It's fine. I've lied to her before. Once.

I think about not answering, but it feels impossible. How does she still have this hold on me when she's hundreds of miles away? Ignoring this call would change a thunderstorm into a hurricane. I swipe to open the vid chat.

After a quick lag, her face settles into motion while she blinks slowly. Her lips are squeezed tight over her wobbly chin. She can have a really kind face. The type you look to for comfort. Or she can look like this. Your worst nightmare, all dressed up in black like a bloodthirsty raven. She never wears any other color. I guess she just really misses Dad. I do too, sometimes. But I don't think wearing black every day would help.

She leans toward the camera, squinting, then lowers a small pair of wire-rimmed glasses over her eyes. A few flickering lights blink over the lenses as they adjust to her screen.

"Much better," she mutters. "Good morning, Marie."

Mutti using my new Franc name makes me pause. Will it ever sound right? Who exactly is this Marie Antoinette they want me to become? "Good morning, Mutti."

The way she peers at me through her glasses makes me feel like she's right in the room, staring me down like she has on a million other occasions before she picks apart every little thing I did wrong that day. "Did you sleep well?"

"Great!"

"Huh!" She barks out something between a cough and a laugh. "I would imagine so."

This is the moment. If I'm lying, I have to start now. "Ah yeah . . . well. I was tired."

"Too tired to do your duties, it would seem."

I think my stomach has disappeared from my body and left a cold puddle of panic behind. But I'm very well practiced at wearing a mask, especially to please Mama. I let stillness settle over my face. I will give nothing away. "What do you mean? Of course I've done everything expected of me."

My mother's nostrils flare as she takes a deep breath. "Well, perhaps my instructions were unclear." It would have been better if she had shouted instead of using that whispery voice. She's giving me a chance. I can tell. She wants me to admit my failure. But I'm the dauphine of the Franc Kingdom now. What does it matter if I consummated my marriage last night or do it tomorrow night? I'm the dauphine and she can't push me around anymore.

"They're perfectly clear. Everything is under control."

We stare each other down as we have many times before. I will always break. I always have. I don't want to do it this time, but I know I will. Mutti said she does this because she loves me and that when I'm queen, I will have to stand up to much more. But my mama is an empress. The strongest in the world. She knows each of my weaknesses. What could possibly be more difficult to face? Maybe by the time she's done with me, I really will be fearless.

"Do you think that because you are hundreds of miles away you can lie to me?" she asks.

"I'm not lying."

Now the yelling starts. "Enough! How do you expect me to help you out of this situation if you insist on lying? I was prepared to be soft with you, but you'll always think the worst of me, won't you? That's why you're hiding from me like a misbehaving child."

Tears are coming, but I can use them to my advantage, wipe them away delicately. "I don't understand why you're upset."

"Because of your lies! Be honest. You did not consummate your marriage. Why not? If there is a problem, we need to head it off now."

How does she know? I haven't even left the room yet this morning. How could she possibly know?

I think back to the few times I've tried to defy her, tried to sneak lazy, uncourtly behavior by her, hung out with friends she didn't like. She caught me. Every time. She made me feel like I was the worst possible human for not admitting my mistakes. I don't know if I have more power so far from her in the Franc court with my new dauphine title. But I'm too exhausted to find out. So I let my shoulders sag, and I face my failure.

"I'm sorry. Mama, I'm so ashamed. That's why I didn't want to tell you."

She softens, sighs, and deflates like a cat settling down her ruffled fur. "Ashamed of what, Marie? What happened?"

"Nothing, Mama. That's the thing. Nothing happened."

She's leaning close to the camera, trying to see me better, but I tuck my face to my shoulder. I don't have the words to describe Louis or what happened. I wonder what would have been worse, answering her questions about how the sex was, or this.

"Nothing? Nothing at all?"

I shake my head, sniffing into my sleeve.

"He must have kissed you at least."

"No, Mama."

"Huh!" She sits back, as though I've given her a shove. "Well, I've never . . . not to worry. Many young couples are hesitant, but there's something you aren't telling me."

"There isn't. There's nothing to say."

"I know you're embarrassed, but I must have more details if I'm going to help you. What happened between you? Surely you didn't fall asleep the minute your heads hit the pillow."

I think of touching his hair and when he held my hand. I remember him saying he does nothing but disappoint people. I think maybe with time, I can understand him. I find that I wish to protect him from the harsh glare of my mother's attention. I have never felt that about anyone before.

"I think . . . we just need some time, Mama. We can have that, right? Just a little. We're strangers. Louis and I want to be friends. He told me so. I bet lots of people need time when they're first married."

I don't know what I expected from her, but it wasn't this rare variety of smile. Sad, but in a way like she understands.

"Lots of people aren't the dauphin and dauphine of the Franc Kingdom, dear. You have a duty. You have the most important marriage on the continent. A marriage that must be consummated to be legally binding and solidify the alliance. Two tasks accompany your title: forging a strong marriage for a strong alliance with my Austro empire, and endearing yourself to the Franc people to win their loyalty to the Bourbon throne. In these matters, time is a luxury. And I'm afraid it's one you can't afford."

All I can manage is a helpless shrug. "He seems scared."

"Then it's up to you to encourage him, dear. Shy or not, he's a young man and you're a beautiful young woman. Show interest in him. Make him comfortable. This situation does not have to be difficult. Did you touch him?"

My face burns. "Yes, I—"

"I don't mean to be indelicate, but I'm not talking about his hands."

"Mama!"

"This is very serious. You can't be a blushing girl. You are a married woman now."

There's a knock on my door.

"They're here to dress me, Mama. I have to go."

"If you want to avoid another conversation such as this, resolve the situation soon. Goodbye, Marie."

Her face freezes for a moment before the call ends.

I stare at my holofone wallpaper, a photo of the palace's most opulent feature, the Hall of Mirrors. How did she know? How could she possibly have known what went on in the privacy of my own bedroom?

Nothing feels like mine as I go through the motions of dressing. Noailles won't let me wear a yellow top I really like. Sniffs at it like I asked to go to breakfast in pajamas and says it's too casual for my first week. I settle for yellow pumps so the outfit she suggests isn't so boring and obsolete. Next time, I'm choosing my own outfit, but I'll tackle that later. Right now, I need to focus on what to say to Louis. I can't have Mercy and Noailles breathing down my neck along with Mama. It's just too much.

But Louis isn't at breakfast. It's me, Elisabeth, and a long, empty table. Giant windows make the dining room seem enormous. Like, awkwardly huge for only two people at breakfast. The wall opposite the windows has a great big holo-portrait. A bunch of guys in armor with long, curly hair gallop across a lush field in an endless loop. The room smells like citrus, fresh bread, and coffee.

"Where's the dauphin?" I ask Elisabeth.

"Oh. Um, sorry. He's out hunting."

"Hunting?"

"Yeah. He does this almost every morning. Goes out riding at sunrise, chases holo-deer around, helps to clean the stables, fills feed buckets. Likes the exercise." Elisabeth is avoiding my eyes. Then it hits me. Oh my god. She knows too.

How?

How do they all know?

A trickle of unease seeps through me. Louis seemed okay with everything last night, but maybe I have him all wrong. Maybe he complained to a valet. Maybe Philippe asked him how it went and he was honest. Like I was with my mother.

Elisabeth saws at a piece of bacon way more times than necessary. "Did you sleep all right?" She smiles at me, then drops her eyes again, realizing it was the exact wrong thing to say.

"Like a baby." I sigh and stare out the window, where the gardens beckon with bright color and tree leaves flutter under low gray clouds. Should I go riding out in the woods and hunt down my husband? Who else can I talk to about this? I want answers. How does *everyone* know what went on last night? Or what didn't. Did he tell? If he told, I take back every nice thing I've said about him. I'll never be able to trust him.

"Do you like to ride?" I ask Elisabeth.

She shrugs. "Not really. Why? Do you want a look around the grounds?"

"I could use some fresh air."

Elisabeth sets down her silverware and a server bot descends to collect her dishes. "I'll go with you, then. Just today, though. I'm not a very good rider. Go with Louis if you're okay with being up early." Elisabeth taps at her holofone. "I'll tell the stables we're on our way."

"Thanks."

She smiles again. I wonder if it's pointless pretending there's nothing for her to feel sorry for.

Elisabeth summons a few attendants. Even something like a horseback ride is a production, because I have to get changed into riding gear. During a quick stop to dress in a tiny room crowded with more plush antique chairs than I've ever seen, I'm changed into breeches and tall boots, then the attendants follow Elisabeth and me outside.

I love the gardens of Versailles. They seem wild and mysterious. Patterns of flower beds curling in circles and curves, growing anything I can think of, with blooms in every color, like a spilled paint box leaking over the gravel paths. Statues are crowded by encroaching hedges trimmed into shapes that twist like strange creatures clawing at the sky or bits of spire resembling the ruins of some ancient temple, all leafy green with decay. Last night, in glimpses stolen through tall palace windows, I saw hedges lit from within. They were less beautiful and a little more creepy, as if these plant creatures were stretching restlessly, waiting to pull up their roots and roam the gardens.

To the right of the Grand Canal that stretches through field after field, there's a massive solar panel network. The glass shimmers in patterns of green, blue, and deep red. Mounds of rosebushes with blooms in every color of the rainbow surround each panel, and a tall spiral shrub grows between each one, I guess to disguise the tech. Or maybe to make the tech a spectacle. Versailles is pretty good at that—spectacle.

When the horses are led to us, I squeal over mine because she's stunning! White as snow, with a downy gray mane like feathers. I'm a fair rider, and step up in my stirrup to swing into the saddle with ease. I always preferred my music and dance lessons to riding, but I can appreciate a Pixter-worthy horse when I see one. Which is exactly why I hand my holofone over to the stable boy and ask him to snap a few shots while I trot back and forth.

"Come with me!" I wave at Elisabeth.

She laughs. "That's all right! You're way more photogenic!"

Camera-shy like her oldest brother, it seems. "Oh, please! You look fabulous, and trust me, I will *make* the photo fabulous no matter how it turns out."

"All right . . . one!"

"Yes!" I get the stable boy to sort it. "We're going to trot straight at you, all right? Facing the palace. Just keep snapping, yeah?"

I like the twinkle in his eye. "Of course, Madame Dauphine," he says.

"You're the best!" I lead Elisabeth in front of the fountain and start trotting slowly, our horses taking stylish high-kneed Franc steps. "See! Nothing easier!"

I'll have a beautiful photo and then she'll see. I love to show people how fab they look, and then post so the world can see it too. Most people are beautiful, they just don't realize it. Everyone has features for the camera to love.

When I take my holofone back, there are several pictures of us laughing, carefree. We're proper princesses, a vision of what everyone wants to see from us.

"I hope my lady is happy with them," says the stable boy.

"You performed admirably, sir." I give him a salute and a wink.

He smiles big and bows low.

"And you, my sister, are a vision." I've already found the best photo and it's so perfect, it will barely need any sort of adjusting. I dramatically sweep the holofone toward her so she can see.

"Wow," she says. She has the smile of a delighted five-year-old. She passes the holofone back to me.

"You like it!"

She nods. "I'm not good at things like that. I get nervous posing for photos."

"But you were too busy riding to be nervous, and see how amazing you look?"

She shrugs.

"Elisabeth, you're a princess! Everyone wants to see what you're doing and how stunning you are."

She laughs. "You're sweet, but one photo doesn't make me stunning. Where did you want to ride to?"

"Where do you think Louis is?"

She points out to the woods. "He'll be out there somewhere."

We nudge the horses to a brisk trot, heading past the pools toward the forest stretching on into the distance like it lasts forever.

"I hope you know I was serious about your photo. You should post more to Pixter!"

"Ah . . ." She shrugs. "It's just not something I'm good at. But that's all right. I'm going to be a student in a year or two, as soon as I'm ready for university, so I don't have to worry as much. The Apps can really bite you when you're not looking."

"You mean like haters?" I ask, because I've had my fair share of trolls and bullies.

"Umm." A stray piece of Elisabeth's hair flutters as she lets out a thoughtful sigh. "Just that they can be really . . . misleading."

This one I don't understand at all, unless she means that people edit their nose and lips and whatever in photos. "Like what?"

"Oh, I don't know," she said. "Just think about what you post here. The lies go beyond photo edits, and Francs pay a lot of attention to all the fine details of what's posted on the Apps. That's all I meant."

We ride in silence for a while. I wonder if this is part of why the king chose me out of all the other girls to marry Louis. My skills with the Apps. Franc girls have a different style than Austro girls, but I think I can figure it out. No sense glitching over content until I start posting, anyway.

Dogs bark in the distance. Maybe we're coming up on the hunters.

"Louis and I don't really fit," Elisabeth says. "Neither of us. We're just sort of . . . not cut out for our roles. But we try. So if Louis . . ." She trails off, clearly uncomfortable. I'm squirming too. I want advice, but I'm not sure I want to talk about this with his sister. "If Louis is . . . slow to . . . pick up on some things, you shouldn't take offense. He's responsible. And kind. And he just goes about things differently than other people."

I keep in the sigh I want to let out. "I just want him to like me, but I'm not sure he does."

"Do *you* like *him*?"

"Of course!" As if I would tell her otherwise. Elisabeth is cool, but I don't think we're at that level of honesty yet.

Elisabeth laughs. "You've only known him for a few days."

"Is that not enough? My cousin knew right away that she wouldn't get along with her husband."

Elisabeth raises an eyebrow. "Yikes."

"Oh, it was a whole thing. I'll have to tell you about it sometime."

"I'm sure Louis likes you just fine." Elisabeth frowns, tapping at her holofone. "Hang on, I'm trying to find him."

She pulls up her horse and taps again, lets out an annoyed sigh, jabs at the holofone like it's personally wronged her, before shoving it in her jacket pocket and nudging her horse on. "Look, if it was Philippe or Stan, you wouldn't have to do anything other than be charming and pretty. But I'd be worried about you for other reasons. Louis . . . I don't really know. He's sort of . . . well, he's more than shy. He feels a lot, like he really cares but he's scared to show it, scared to make decisions. He's hard on himself. But you'll be good for him, I think."

I don't know how I'm going to help him or fix what she described. I make decisions too quickly, according to Mama, and I'm not shy at all.

"Sorry you had to marry the difficult brother," she says. "He is the nice one, though. Stan is sneaky, and Philippe . . . well, he's a little young yet. Guess we'll see in a year or two. So far he's excellent at getting in trouble."

I'm seventeen now, but I think back to when I was fifteen. I guess I was pretty stupid. I wonder if in two years I'll look back on myself now and think the same.

There's a rustling in the bushes that makes my horse prance. I tighten my thighs and grip the reins. A deer leaps from the brush and bounds across our path to disappear into the trees.

Something orange-yellow flashes on its hindquarters. I try to squint after it, but that glowing bit of something is the last thing I see before it's swallowed by the murky underbrush.

"What was that on its hindquarters?" I ask.

"Oh, it's just some paint so the hunters know not to shoot it."

"Why are they shooting holo-deer when there are real deer running around?"

Elisabeth raises an eyebrow at me. "Do you hunt real deer in the Austro Lands?"

"No, we don't have deer on our grounds. We use holos too."

Why is Elisabeth frowning at me like that? "Exactly. They're rare. We can't go around shooting them. We want them to have babies so there will be more of them."

I have never given a thought to the lack of deer on our grounds. I know we had pheasants and turkeys that Josef and my cousins could only hunt in autumn. Never asked why. I like riding, but I don't care to hunt.

There's a loud bark and a few hounds dash from the woods, noses to the ground, curving tails held high. Not sure what they track when holos have no scent. We didn't really take dogs hunting. Just had a few for pets. Maybe this little group is just for fun too.

Five riders follow the hounds, with Louis at the head of them. They all have white-and-green plastic weapons strapped to them. My brother used the same laser guns, and I always thought it looked funny to see them tearing around all serious on horseback, firing little toy guns. I think two of the hunters are Louis's cousins; the others are attendants. Elisabeth does a quick whistle and waves. The riders pull up on their reins and come to a prancing stop before us. They all give us a bow of their heads, which Elisabeth and I return.

Louis looks everywhere but at our faces. "Good morning," he says, so quietly I can barely hear him.

Elisabeth does not mumble at all when she says, "Didn't think to ask your wife if she wanted to go hunting? Jackass."

Louis looks embarrassed, which I've realized seems to be his resting expression. "Sorry, I didn't want to wake you."

I'm still annoyed with him. He really made me feel like it wouldn't matter if we didn't do anything last night, then he buggered off this morning even though the whole world seems to know about our . . . non-consummation.

"Well, she's here now," says Elisabeth. "And you know I'd rather not sit on a horse."

"Thanks, Elisabeth." Louis shifts in his saddle, the leather creaking as he leans into his right stirrup. He's gone from sitting tall and strong to slouching. "Um . . . Do you guys want taggers?" He taps the plastic gun.

Elisabeth doesn't look amused. "Do I have to spell this out for you?" She jerks her head at me.

Louis still doesn't meet my eyes, but he nudges his horse up to stand beside mine.

"Don't need a gun. I'm happy to just ride, thanks," I say.

"And I'm going home." Elisabeth watches me, waiting for me to confirm that I want to talk to her brother alone.

"Thanks so much for taking the time to bring me out here."

"Of course." She smiles at me, scowls at Louis, then wheels her horse around.

The wind picks up, full of a strange scent like smoke and

something sour. Louis's horse paws nervously and he draws himself up, bringing the horse to attention. "You like to ride?"

I don't love it, and I don't hate it. But if it's what my husband likes to do, I should probably learn to like it a little more. "I love riding."

Must have come out sincere, because he smiles. "Sorry I didn't wake you up, then. That's Estelle they gave you. She's a good mare. Want to see what she can do?"

For the first time since I met Louis, he looks confident and wide-awake. My stomach flutters a little. "Lead the way."

"We're riding ahead," Louis says to the rest of the party.

"Don't lose her," laughs one of his cousins.

"I'm sure she can keep up." Louis looks at me, a question on his face.

I can do this. Louis is kind of clumsy. How crazy of a rider can he be? "Okay. Let's pixelate!"

He kicks his horse forward into a fast trot. I thump my heels and rock my hips to urge the horse forward after him. Estelle does seem to know what she's doing. In fact, she does a lot of work for me; she's sure-footed over the rocky ground. She follows Louis by instinct and I loosen up, along for the ride.

We pick up to a canter and follow the path so we aren't thrashed by tree branches. The wind gusts up, skidding the low clouds across the sky. They break to let in dappled sunlight. Louis looks back a few times, but I'm right behind him. Did I say he was too clumsy for this? He seems right at home on horseback, sitting straight and tall, shaking hair out of his face like the horses twitch their manes. The trees end in an open field. We leave the palace and canal behind us, give the horses their heads, and just run, run, run. I feel like I'm galloping away from my problems, blowing away with the wind in my hair.

Louis slows his horse and wheels back toward me as I pull my reins to stop.

He trots a slow circle around us, hair mussed and cheeks red from the wind. "You're pretty good."

I give a slight bow. "Not as good as you there, horse master. You're literally riding circles around me."

He laughs and stands in his stirrups to straighten out his saddle.

We look at each other for a moment, and I don't want to ruin something fun with something awkward. I want to just enjoy the sun and the breeze tickling hair across my sweaty forehead. The musky, sweet smell of horse. The nice ache in my legs against the smooth leather of the saddle.

"Hey . . ." I can already feel the moment slipping away like air from a balloon. "So, my mother called me this morning."

"Oh." He tips his head a bit. "Is that . . . good?"

Is that good? Bless him. "I can use a lot of words for calls from Mutti. 'Good' is not one of them."

"Oh," he says again. "Sorry . . ."

"Yeah, it was pretty weird. She knew. About last night."

If he says "oh" again, I swear I'll kill him. But he frowns and rumples his hair, clearly thinking through something, so I go on.

"Yeah, and it seemed like Elisabeth knew too. Did you say something?"

"No!" His eyes are wide. "No, of course not."

I breathe out a sigh of relief. Though this knowledge shouldn't make me feel better. Because if Louis talking was the most obvious explanation, and that's not the case, then . . . "Who else knows? And how?"

"Well, my brothers. And if they know, then probably my grandfather . . ."

It's not like I'm surprised, but my heart sinks anyway. Elisabeth and Mama *felt* like the entire palace knowing, but I thought it was still a secret on some level. Does *the whole palace* actually know? Everything sways a little, and it's not because of the horse.

Louis reaches out as if he wants to touch my arm, then fumbles his hand back to his reins. "Sorry. Are you okay?"

"Not really." My mind races through possibilities of who spread the news and how. "I just don't understand how something so private was discovered."

He frowns again and turns away to stare out at the edge of the field, where it meets the endless woods. "Well . . . it's not like *I* told them."

"Then how do they know?"

"I don't want to glitch you out."

I snort. "Don't know if you noticed, but I'm already kind of buffering. If you know something, just tell me. Please."

He turns his horse, putting his back to the woods and to me, to face the open field. I can't tell, but he looks a little . . . angry? "A lot of stuff isn't what it seems to be."

"*Quoi?* What do you mean?"

Louis scratches at the top of his head. "Umm. Well, like, the solar panels are also a security grid that could shoot a cruiser out of the sky. A solid wall is actually a hidden doorway disguised with a hologram. Or, uh, a medallion in the ceiling is bugged.

With a mic in it. Or a holo-portrait is a—a camera."

My skin crawls like literal bugs are all over me. *Watched? Bugged?* That's . . . gross. Last night should have been the most private of our lives.

Of course it wasn't. Gigs. I should have expected nothing less from a court that *watched us get into bed*.

Louis clears his throat. "You, uh . . . don't have anything like that at home?"

I'm still crawling with goose bumps. Bugs at Schönbrunn Palace? Bugs in my home? Never. Never ever. Only in this glitchy place would that happen.

Except . . . there were the times I couldn't figure out how my mama busted me over something I thought was a secret. My throat feels so tight I can hardly force out words.

"I . . . don't know. I never thought about it." I tip my head back for a big gulp of fresh air. "*Scheiße . . .*"

"I know . . . it's a lot." Louis fiddles with a buckle on his saddle.

"How am I supposed to sleep in a room with bugs in it?"

"I don't know."

"How are *we* supposed to sleep in a room with bugs in it?"

"Uh . . . heavily medicated?"

He's smiling, but I can't tell if that was supposed to be a joke. My heart begs him to help me. We're on his turf. He's got to have more than jokes. "Louis . . . we have to just do this. Once we do, we'll get them off our backs."

He colors up, quirks his eyebrows. "In a . . . bugged room? With cameras? Possibly equipped with night vision?"

I rub at my face, which I only ever do if I'm really upset.

Touching your face gives you acne, says my mama's voice in the back of my mind.

I loose a string of non-princess words. Louis looks either shocked or impressed. Words tumble out before I can think them through. "Okay, but how about this: What if we weren't in the room? We spend time someplace private like . . . uh . . . like right here. We're all alone. The grass is tall. We could just . . ."

I'm insane. That's such a bad idea. But I can't bear the weight of possibly breaking the alliance and failing an entire kingdom. Two kingdoms.

"Are—are you serious?" Louis is bright red, but what does he have to be so embarrassed about? We've been told for years what the expectations were after marriage. This isn't information we got last week. I had months to prepare myself for the fact that the first time I'd sleep with a guy, he would be a total stranger. Didn't imagine it would be in a field, but hey, I guess it's better than being watched.

"I'm completely serious if it gets those bugs off us. I will knock you off that horse right now."

Louis's eyes look like they might fall out of his face. "Please don't."

He's so glitched out.

Am I an awful person to joke like that?

I never used to cry. Not unless it felt court appropriate to summon tears. But this overwhelming flood of expectations and scrutiny forces the warning signs. Tears prick at my eyes, threatening to well up like they have a hundred times since I arrived in the Franc Kingdom. And just as I've done those countless other times, I stifle them. "I'm sorry. I didn't mean literally. But what do we do? This is your home. Tell me what to do. I'm going to lose it if this keeps up."

"I'm really sorry you're scared," says Louis. "And I'm really sorry your mother yelled at you. And that people are watching us. They do that here. But there's always a new scandal or whatever, so if we just wait, they'll get bored fast and move on to whatever stupid thing Stan or my grandfather does this weekend. Then we'll have the place to ourselves again."

"Louis, I'm not comfortable ignoring Mama and my duties. That doesn't sound like it's going to work."

"If there's one thing I've learned here," says Louis, "it's that there may be eyes everywhere, but it's easy to fly under the radar. I make myself quiet and scarce, and they forget I'm there."

I don't believe him. I want to tell him that might have worked when he was a little boy, but one day he's going to be a king, and the world will watch him. But I need to be on his good side. Since apparently, at the moment, he'd rather do practically anything than have sex with me.

"So, you think that's easier than the field plan?" I smile a little so he knows I'm joking. Sort of joking.

He puffs out a laugh, picking at his saddle again. "You're crazy," he mumbles.

"Oh really? Last I checked, according to, like, ten romance vids I've watched, it's incredible to make love outdoors. Like the feeling just . . . *overtakes* you. Like hacking your system and overriding your code."

He glances at me. "You're really serious?"

I shrug, still smiling. I have no idea if I'm serious.

He smirks. "Thought you were worried about bugs."

"In a field?"

He points at a tiny white butterfly. "Bugs."

"Better those bugs than the other kind."

He looks at me for a long time, like he's going to say something. *Please say something.* Everything in the Austro Lands was simple. I only ever felt or thought one thing at a time. Now I don't know whether I want to sleep with my husband or not; I just know that I have to. I don't know if I'd prefer to get it over with in a bugged room or a buggy field. I'd like to see the people who think being a princess is easy find a way out of this one.

"It's going to be okay," Louis says at last, king of the anticlimax. "Come on."

He gives his horse a thump with his calves, and we canter back toward the palace. When I look at it sprawling in front of us like it's scooping us into two giant open arms, all I can picture in its windows are thousands and thousands of eyes.

FIVE

❋

Georgette taps a screen on the wall of my closet. It shows a long, deep blue gown that hangs somewhere in the depths of my giga-huge walk-in closet.

"*Oui, c'est bien.*" Noailles gives the image a nod and taps at her holofone.

The gown is phishing boring, but I'll wear it without comment just to put Noailles in a better mood. Georgette and another attendant begin undressing me. Another maid leaves to retrieve the dark blue dress. I lift my arms so my blouse can get removed, and my eyes settle on the floral ceiling medallion above. I wonder if it's hiding a bug. A tiny camera or microphone. Or both. The goose bumps that march along my bare shoulders have nothing to do with a chill, because heat rises in my cheeks. I'm angry all over again at this nasty lack of privacy. I can't do anything about the bugs right now, but I'm taking back something of mine.

"Countess Noailles, I wanted to talk to you about something."

"*Allez-y.*" She doesn't look up from her holofone.

"I need the permissions to access my new accounts on the Apps."

"*Oui*, Ambassador Mercy can help you after dinner."

"*Merci.* But I would like access returned to my Austro accounts too. I need some of the data and pictures."

This gets her to pause her typing and glance up at me. "*Pardon*, Dauphine, but you do not. You are Franc now, and that is how you are to portray yourself on the net."

I focus on keeping my expression neutral and use my prettiest words despite the pang of sadness I feel whenever someone mentions this. As if my Austro past is something that can be deleted as easily as an App account. "Of course I am. But many of my followers know me as the Austro duchess, and I just want to make a few connections between that and my new accounts. Keep a few photos, help them follow me over to the Franc accounts. I would be strengthening the alliance in a way, wouldn't I? If I don't do this, who knows how many Austro followers I might lose?"

Noailles drums her fingers on the surface of her holofone.

"*Pardon*, madame." Georgette lifts the dinner gown over my head, and I'm buried in a sea of dark blue satin.

When I surface, dress hanging loose and smooth off my shoulders, Noailles's lips are pinched, but she gives me a nod. "You raise a good point, madame. So long as you discuss the Austro content with me, we can permit this."

I want to punch both fists in the air, but Georgette is trying to zip up the back of my dress and I haven't won this quiet fight yet.

"This will be a great asset to the kingdom, Countess. You'll see. But there's one more thing." I settle my arms in photo-shoot mode, slightly lifted so Georgette can adjust the satin at my waistline. "On the Apps, I'm most known for fashion. It's my brand. It's my clickbait. I have to choose my own outfits."

Noailles shakes her head. "Out of the question."

"I have over two million followers, Countess Noailles. Two million three hundred thousand and counting! That's more than the queen of Anglia has."

If Noailles's mouth becomes any thinner, it will disappear. "Franc fashion is not like Austro fashion," she says.

"I understand. But I'll start trends. You'll see. If we don't make content in this way, the number of my followers may decrease."

Noailles stares at the ceiling, drumming her fingers again. I'm so close. I can feel it. "It would be unprecedented. It's simply not how we do things at Versailles."

"Unprecedented can be good. Unprecedented is exactly what starts trends. Unprecedented has *influence*." I know I've got her now. Everyone at every court in every country in the world craves influence, and this is the easiest way of getting it. "When the dauphine wears it, everyone will want it. I can support new patrons and designers and brands, each with a message. I will have a conversation with the Francs and the Austros through what I wear. All I ask is to choose—my own clothes—myself."

Noailles sighs. "I don't know. I will consider it. . . ."

I reach for my holofone where it rests on a neon-lit bust. "Here are my last few photos. I'm wearing outfits chosen for me and my riding clothes. Look how many likes. Twelve thousand? That's pathetic. My top photo from"—I lower my lashes—"well, from before, got four hundred thousand. I can do *much* better."

"Perhaps you must work harder to appeal to Franc tastes and social media habits," she says.

My temper is rising, but I have to tamp it down. Time for bargaining. For my whole life, the only place I have felt even a little free to express myself is through what I wear and how I look on the Apps. I can't lose this. I can't do a good job without this. "Let us have a trial run. A test! I'll make something trend within two months. Then you'll see that I'm good at this, Countess Noailles. I'm really good. If it all goes glitch, I'll wear whatever you want."

Her eyes narrow a little. I think . . . she almost smiles. "There are a few key businesses that might be very pleased to have your influence and representation. Very well. Don't let me down."

I squeal. I can't help it! Finally, something feels right again. Noailles gives me her disapproving pinched-up look and turns to type something into the screen on the wall.

"Well done," Georgette whispers.

Noailles glances over her shoulder at us. Georgette ducks her head down, but as she passes to get my shoes, she winks.

I can't believe I pulled this off. This probably wasn't what Mutti had in mind when she taught me diplomacy, but I maxed my stats on this one. I know better than to think she would be proud, so I'll try to be twice as proud all on my own.

SIX

❋

The Hall of Mirrors is stunning on Pixter. It's shiny people, shiny walls, shiny sun, shiny smiles, and at night, glowing neon. It's beautiful in person too. Every inch is opulence. From the old frescoes to the tall windows to the gilded frames to the marble with neon-filled cracks and crumbles, smoothed to glow beautifully in imperfection.

What Pixter didn't prepare me for is how difficult it is to stroll down the Hall of Mirrors at midday. It's everyone's first selfie and photo-shoot destination. It doesn't matter whether you're a duchess who lives in Parée or took up permanent residence in the palace, or a duke visiting from the southern provinces; the Hall of Mirrors makes for a stunning selfie, and it's where you go to view people like me on parade, headed for the gardens or the dining room.

This is less a walk through my home than a stage performance. I take a breath before entering from a small alcove. I stand up tall, relax my face to smile slightly, pull at creases in my sunshine-yellow satin minidress, and walk.

Something I've noticed about Franc fashion. The great stuff, the stuff I would want to wear on a daily basis, is for feeds and runways. On a normal day at court, the cuts of clothing, hairstyles, and shoes are bold. The *colors* of the dresses, shirts, trousers, are all totally rest mode. Muted charcoals and beiges, blacks and browns, the occasional burnt umber or forest green. Pastels are for decor, pastry, holofone cases, purses, makeup. Never for clothing.

I hate it. I want the yellow of my dress to bleed into each matte-silver or black outfit and bring it bright life to rival the dazzling palace features.

Instead, the courtiers snap their fans. The first time I smile and nod to a woman with a huge, artful updo sprayed over with lavender, she doesn't smile back. Her purple-lined eyes travel the length of my dress.

Eyes, eyes, and more eyes. Eyes judging while everyone snaps pics on holofones, eyes in minicameras. How will I deal with this? How will I perform for the rest of my life?

There's a knot of people by one of the open windows. A raised voice. *Merde*, it's Stan. Showing off with big sweeps of his arm, he gestures over the gardens below us. "*Oui, vous trouvez?* Replace the *orangerie* with something more practical: a cruiser landing pad with privacy hedges. We could keep a few trees for design purposes. Perhaps raise them up on platforms, hover some chandeliers." This is met with a chorus of oohs and approvals.

"*Bonjour, ma soeur.*" Philippe grins and looks up from his holofone.

"What's happening?" I ask while a girl next to Philippe curtsies to me.

Philippe shrugs. "Stan throwing his weight around about the gardens, I guess."

"They are just not *à la mode*," says Stan. "They're so outdated."

Everyone agrees. Or pretends to agree. He raises an eyebrow at me. I doubt he really cares about my opinion. This is clearly a test. "I suppose you're right, though I would hate to see such beauty and hard work thrown away. Perhaps it can be adapted to your ideas."

Stan flaps a hand. "As I say, keep some trees and grow a privacy shelter. Maybe a small pool for you glitched-out party people." This earns him a lot of cheers. I desperately wish I could roll my eyes. He pulls out his holofone. "Now, who do I call to get this started?"

"Wait, monsieur," a breathless voice comes from a small, frumpy woman who elbows her way around Stan's friends. Her clothing is more bizarre than anything I've seen at court. It's plain in a way I've never seen before. Some threaded fuzzy material with baggy sleeves over a bleak pair of straight-legged pressed brown trousers. There is no sign of LEDs, no iridescent fabrics, no shine, no glitter, no slashed sleeves or bodice on her strange baggy shirt. Her glasses are overlarge and look like an antique. "Monsieur, you can't mean to—"

Stan interrupts. "That's Monsieur comte de Provence to you, Adelaide Frasier of the Dusty Tomes."

Everyone snickers at this strange woman, who goes on, so unflapped it's kind of admirable. "With all respect, *mon prince*, the gardens are a historical landmark. They are very purposely designed from rare documents that give us a window to the past."

"That's precisely why they're outdated," says Stan.

"But monsieur, they are . . ." She grasps for words, twirling a hand about so a sleeve gets caught on her fingers. She shakes it loose. "There are so few places we can claim give us a replica of life before the Event. I daresay the gardens are unlike anything else in the world. A change to them can't be made so flippantly when they're . . . they are . . . sacred." She finishes with a sigh that tugs at my heartstrings.

Stan's friends snort and dissolve into giggles.

"I believe you'll find I can make whatever changes I wish," he says.

Adelaide's cheeks go red and her brows bunch together. "As you say." She curtsies, but as she hurries away, I think I hear curses I didn't know she was brave enough to utter.

"Gigs." Philippe shakes his head.

"Who was she?" I ask.

"Oh, that's just Adelaide." Philippe giggles. "She's a glitch-show. Weird, isn't she? Oh, I think she may be your tutor! Court historian, so they send us all to her to hear blah blah about the grand tradition of the palace and the Sun King and whatever else."

"Stan was a bit rude to her, wasn't he?"

"She's the rudest one here," says Philippe. "Walks around practically in a costume and tries to stop us all from having fun."

I wonder if there's any hope of getting Stan and Philippe to care about someone other than themselves. I decide to take some fresh air and step out onto the small balcony overlooking the *orangerie*, where Stan would like to replace the simple potted trees and patterned circular pathway with his own cruiser pad. I'm not sure I like the idea. Strange as Adelaide was, I do like the simplicity of the orange trees. I've never seen anything else quite like it.

As I stroll down the balcony, I see other open windows, hear chattering voices, but they fade as I reach the far end.

Then another voice stands out. It belongs to Adelaide.

"Yes, I see. *Non*, monsieur, he wants to level the whole thing, and he will if he's able. *Oui*, but—monsieur, they are *integral*. The gardens are the grandest, the most true to life, the most impressive piece of the illusion you've built here, and I can't manage this when . . ."

Her voice trails off, but the word "illusion" makes me catch my breath and strain to listen. I press my back to the warm stone of the wall.

"But every little piece we take away will make it crumble. What you are doing is already a farce that—I'm sorry. I only meant that what we have now is as perfect as we can make it, and we must not disturb . . ."

Footsteps clack and her voice echoes away.

I don't understand what she was talking about. The *orangerie* is beautiful, but why did the idea of tearing it down make her so upset?

Bugs, illusions, oranges . . . I try to find a pattern, but it's almost as incomprehensible as the shunning of color in Franc clothing.

SEVEN

May 31, 3070, 8:12 p.m.

I might have bugs watching me at all times, but with total control of my accounts and power over my wardrobe, I've got a little bit of myself back. A little more confidence.

I'm going to need every bit of it. So far, my App campaigns have had glitches.

Yesterday, I wore an outfit that would have trended in the Austro Lands. It was a dark crop top with holographic shine under a jacket made with double-layered pink and blue tulle. I paired it with a plastic pencil skirt full of gel-glo that shifts between pink and blue with the temperature. I sprayed some pastel blue over the topknot in my hair to match.

On my way into breakfast, Philippe said, "Nice one. I guess that is your brand, eh?" But his ear-to-ear grin made me think he didn't actually appreciate the ensemble.

Then I sat down across from Stan, who said he didn't know he needed to wear shades to breakfast.

"A splash of color on a dreary morning," I said, because it was super foggy out.

"You look like a kid threw up after getting let loose in a candy store," he said.

Since Stan has been a dongle since I arrived, I shrugged it off. "What do you know about fashion?"

"Lots. Look at my Pixter."

I sipped some chai and really tried my best to be polite. "Well, you're not a girl."

"So? I know the Francs will rip you. This isn't the Austro Lands."

I told him gel-glo is fashion-forward everywhere, and he just shook his head and said, "You'll see."

I wish I could say Stan was wrong. But what would have earned thousands of likes in the Austro Lands was a total system crash with my Franc followers.

Usually scrolling the Apps makes me happy, but tonight I feel lonely and kind of hopeless.

I keep going back to the picture of my outfit. I scroll hundreds of comments that say things like:

Austro fashion is so tacky.

Very childish. Not the proper look for the dauphine.

Adopting Franc fashion? The dauphine says je m'en fous.

Gel-glo is such a no.

I sigh and let the fluffy couch in the common room swallow me up. I wish I could ask someone for advice, but Noailles and Mama aren't options. Elisabeth is sweet, but she doesn't care about fashion, and I'm not giving Stan the satisfaction of asking him. The soft *click-click* of Louis hitting computer keys is frying my hard drive. It's so quiet.

Every evening, Louis sits at a mess of monitors and says he codes things. I don't really know what the obsession is. He types in what's basically another language full of symbols, which he says let him build things and unlock things.

Everything Louis likes to do are things you do by yourself.

He has to be the only guy I know who reads actual books and doesn't just watch vids or stream audio on the Apps. I doubt he has advice on what I should do, but I want him to turn around from his computer and talk to me, make me feel like he's at least a little happy I'm here.

"Louis, if an outfit photo on Pixter had bad comments, should I delete it or just, like . . . own it?"

The click-clacking pauses. I heave myself out of the couch cushions to look at him, but he doesn't even turn around.

"Oh, uh . . . I don't know. I'm not good at things like that."

I groan and flop back onto the couch with a dull *thunk*. "Why do the Francs hate colors?"

"I thought you looked nice," says Louis.

My heart gives a quick, excited beat. He noticed my outfit? You'd never have known. It's probably too good to be true. But if he did, he's at least paying a little attention to me. In a teasing voice, so he doesn't know I'm quizzing him for real, I ask, "What was I wearing?"

The click-clacks become slow and drawn out. "A . . . dress."

Knew it. I never should have gotten my hopes up, because now they're fried like an old hard drive. He has no idea. It stings more than I want to admit.

I open up the Apps again. I need a friend. I need a savvy Franc girl who can help me understand what is chic in a way that won't make me totally abandon my style and turn into a black-and-matte-silver snore machine.

I search through Versailles accounts. There have to be friends I can make right inside this palace. I've met plenty of people, but they all treat me so formally. All curtsies and polite follow-backs on the Apps. Nobody to giggle with through boring state events.

No one to take walks around the gardens with.

My Yakback account keeps suggesting I follow a courtier named Princesse de Lamballe, so I search for her vlog on ViewFi. I love her pink hair and the way she does her makeup. She's done a tutorial on how to do her look. This is really cute. She has a friendly voice. I scroll to her next video, where she sings and plays a little electro-ukulele. Her outfits look pretty Franc. She's got the mirror shades, the sleek skirts, the shiny peacoats. But her outfits are cute instead of boring in the name of cool and understated. I could work with this. I need to meet her—a friend and a guide!

"Hey, Louis."

"Yeah?" He actually twists his chair around this time. Probably making up for acting like a *Dummkopf* with the dress comment. Endless lines of gibberish cover the three screens behind him.

"Do you know Princesse Thérèse de Lamballe?"

He shrugs. "Yeah, sure."

"Do you like her?"

He fidgets with his chair, wheeling it side to side. "What do you mean?"

I laugh at him. "It's not a trick question."

"Sure. I like her. She's family, technically. My second cousin." He folds himself up cross-legged and props his chin in his hand. "A lot of people like her. She's very popular. She's sort of sad, though."

Sad? I look at the smiling girl in all the video thumbnails. Her eyes are so bright and full of life. "She doesn't look sad to me." I hold out my holofone so he can see.

"Well, she might not seem to be. But I think she must be."

"Why?"

"She was married, but not for long."

I smell scandal. I lean over the back of the couch toward him. "What happened?"

Louis nervously twirls a hoodie string around his finger. "He died."

Died? But he must have been so young. I wonder if he caught the wasting disease. That's the only thing that gets people young or old, royal or common. "Did you know him?"

"Nah, not really. They liked each other a lot and . . . ah, I don't want to glitch you out or put you off her. Princesse de Lamballe is nice. If that's what you were asking. Just avoid the husband talk, you know?"

"Tell me what happened."

"He fell in with a bad crowd. Parée can be dangerous."

"Dangerous how?" I've heard there are riots there, but whenever someone tried to tell me about it, Mutti or Mercy or my tutor went boss mode and shut them up.

"Started going places he shouldn't have gone. Hanging around people he shouldn't have. Started going to protests against the business leaders in the First Estate. The ones from the big corporations like JeanCo Foods and PharmaCloud. I don't really know why or the details."

I noticed a few days ago that if Louis is thinking of saying something, he tips his head a bit to the side. He usually doesn't say what he's thinking out loud. This time is no different.

"Could you introduce me to Princesse de Lamballe?" I ask.

"Sure." He tips his head again.

"What?" I ask.

"Nothing." He turns back to his screens.

"What was her husband like?"

Louis pauses his typing. I wait for the head tilt, but he doesn't do it. "*Viens ici.* I'll show you."

He pulls up Pixter, clicks a few things. All I see is that computer language he writes in. He frowns at the screen, scrolling slowly, clicks on something in the middle of it, and types things that make no sense to me. A Pixter account pops up for Louis Alexander.

"Another Louis, huh?"

"Yeah. Most people called him Alex."

"Is everyone in the Franc Kingdom named Louis?"

"Didn't they tell you? Louis or Louise."

"You're hilarious." I peer over his shoulder and see a handsome guy taking pictures at the beach, playing hoverball with light-up sneakers flashing as he passes the glowing ball. Lots of sneaker pictures on here. Must have been his thing. There are also quite a few of him with Princesse de Lamballe. They're hugging, kissing, smiling. Seems like they were super in love.

For a minute, I'm drawn away from the photos and look at the top of Louis's head, wondering what would happen if I just moved his arm, sat on his knee. Would he hold me like Alex was holding the princess in these photos?

"Hmm . . ." Louis frowns and scrolls past all the photos Alex was tagged in. Some are in monochrome, captioned with condolences and memories. Louis punches in some more code, and more photos show up onscreen like magic. As if they were hidden. These pictures are more low-bit glitchy. Nightclubs, guys in mirror shades puffing out multicolored vape rings, a wall of glowing, angry graffiti. A Pixter logo with the CEO on it that says *Smile for Rohan—Always Watching*. The next image is a wall of graffiti, dripping reds and jagged letters. Does the red text say something about *killing kings*? Louis closes out the screen before I can fully read it. "Yeah. Anyway. Just thought you should know. If you want to be friends with her. We try not to mention it."

Something isn't right here. Versailles is so beautiful on the outside, but so much happens below the surface, and the longer I'm here, the uglier the view behind the scenes. Bugs in the walls, eyes on me constantly. Angry people on the news during my wedding. And now a guy against kings dies mysteriously? What's up with that? Perhaps coincidence . . . but it feels wrong. If I dig too deep, if I think about it too much, will everything fall apart around me? The glamour stripped away to reveal some ugly truth? "Louis?"

"Yeah?"

"Did you just get into a dead guy's Pixter account?"

"Yup."

"And is that how you were able to get around my privacy settings to message me?"

"Yeah, sort of. I really shouldn't have done that. Or this."

He's back to scrolling through code like this is completely normal. But this is huge.

"How did you do it?"

"Well, the binary is a—"

I stop him. "I don't mean literally. I mean, you do this a lot?"

"Go into dead people's Pixters?" He laughs. "No, not really."

"But you *can* get into things like that."

CAKE EATER

"App accounts? Yeah, it's very easy once you understand how they're structured. You just have to sort of give the code the right answer and put things in the right place. It's a bit like how people pick locks. I can show you!"

That's not what I have in mind. I'm thinking of something very different that also has to do with security. "Can you . . . find things?"

"Yes . . . ," he says slowly. "What kind of things?"

Even now they might hear. "Insects."

He sits up straight, glances at the wall like it has eyes to stare back. "That sort of thing . . . you can do. But it usually leaves tracks. And that makes people very upset."

"Well, those people are making *me* very upset."

"Those people will forget all about it soon. They won't need to worry about you or me. They worry about people like Alex."

People like Alex. Bugs in our bedroom. Dead young men. How much of this is normal for Versailles? I feel like there's some wire connecting them all. But I can't see it.

I want to ask Louis more about these things. But I can't, because there are ears in the walls. Ears that he could apparently wipe out if he had the guts to. Instead, I force a smile and scroll feeds until I get drowsy and stop thinking about everything I just learned.

EIGHT

June 2, 3070, 11:49 p.m.

After a formal dinner, nighttime Versailles transforms into a world of neon and noise. Tonight, we're partying in the gardens. The statues are lit in a rainbow of color; cruisers come and go in a loud *whoosh*. There are tables and tents full of courtiers dancing, joking, and gambling while large speakers boom between the columns of the Grand Trianon guesthouse. The bass thrum drowns out the night noise of crickets and throws off any calm the warm air and sweet flower aromas might have given me.

Two glasses of champagne have made laser tag difficult. My feet are like lead as I stumble around one of the pillars, nearly tipping into a rosebush. A flash of long limbs and golden hair. I think that's Philippe ducking through a doorway. I squat and scurry from bush to bush. Someone shrieks, and I squash myself back into the prickly leaves. A couple giggles and ducks behind one of the bushes.

Philippe is tucked in the corner of the doorway. His shoulder is sticking right out. *Quel idiot* . . . I can move silently from practice at walking with grace. Step, step, sneak, and . . . tag.

"Traitor!" Philippe yells. "Traitor, traitor, traitor!"

He fires at my belt a million times and it lights up red. "Worth it! You aren't very good at hiding!"

He's about to protest when his belt lights up a second time.

"Damn it, who now?"

Louis sidles out from behind a pillar, smiling all crooked and shy at us.

"Too late," says Philippe. "She's a traitor to the family and got me already."

Louis shrugs. "Seems like she's on my side."

I hug Louis around the shoulders, which is kind of a reach because of his height, and he tips awkwardly toward me. "Tag-teamed with my favorite brother, obviously," I say with a smirk at Philippe.

Sometimes I like Philippe and Stan, and sometimes they get a nasty look in their eyes and I'm not sure if I should. Like right now. Philippe's smile is mocking, trouble, mischief.

"Oh really." He snorts. "I'm *always* the favorite brother." He gives me a wink and nudges me with his laser gun as he breezes by us.

I give him a good scowl, but he doesn't turn around to see. Louis cradles his laser gun, ignoring the fact that I'm wobbling around on my toes to hug him. I give up and let go. *Just touch me. Is it so bad?* "Hey, he's kind of a jerk, isn't he?"

Louis shrugs. "He's right. He's the favorite. I don't mind, though."

"Well, not my favorite."

"Hmm . . . how should I repay you for slaying my little brother?" He's leaning toward me and his eyes are all twinkly. This seems like flirting, which is something I wasn't sure Louis knew how to do. This is the perfect time to share a cute kiss. The idea makes my stomach fluttery, giddy with the image my mind conjures.

Graceful like a dancer, I reach to place my hands on his

shoulders. "What did you have in mind?"

Long pause. Too long of a pause. He looks confused. Of course he does; he's impossible. "Well, I said I would introduce you to Princesse de Lamballe."

I banish my disappointment quick as a keystroke. "Okay!" I bounce after him. We pass the same rosebush, which seems to be giggling now. I nudge Louis's arm. "I didn't know plants could laugh."

"We do have some rare breeds in the gardens." He jams his hands into his pockets.

"Are you upset about Philippe?"

He blinks and tips his head at me. "Huh? Oh, no. I'm really not. He's the baby brother. He needs the attention. He was kind of a lonely kid after, uh . . . well, you know how it is. At court and all."

He stares straight ahead at a table full of gamblers that I doubt he has any interest in, chews at his lip like he might say more. Maybe he means after his parents died when he was a young boy. I do know what that's like. Or at least a little. "Yeah, after my dad died, I guess it was pretty lonely. Mutti was busy a lot. I had my brother, though. And my cousins and aunts."

Louis tips his head at me. "Do you miss him?" he asks quietly.

This is just about the last thing I want to think about at a party. My dad had a heart attack when I was eight. He was in a cruiser and the med droids didn't reach him in time. I don't remember a lot about him. He had a really loud laugh. His eyes crinkled up when he smiled. He snuck me pieces of crumbly *Punschkrapfen* when I wanted a snack before bed.

"Sometimes," I tell Louis. "I miss my brother these days,

though. Kind of impossible to miss Mama. She texts me like a droid on JetFuel. It's stupid, but I miss my dog a lot."

He shakes his head. "That's not stupid. What's your dog's name?"

"Mops. He's a pug."

He laughs a little and scratches at the back of his head.

"The name is an Austro thing. Kind of a joke. *Mops* literally means 'pug'; it's a long story that includes my brother being a dongle."

He stops walking and really looks at me. Properly this time, instead of at my ear or in quick little glances. "I know it must be tough. Leaving home to come here."

I'm not exactly homesick. I have bass thrumming through my body, the scent of roses on the air, champagne every few feet, and Versailles glittering and glowing all around me. But this is all I've seen of the country I'm meant to rule. These thick walls with neon veins and miles and miles of carefully designed shrubs. Sometimes, I feel like I'm being crushed by gold, neon, and rules.

I often catch myself wishing to be somewhere else just for a minute. Just one quick minute leaning on a smooth, warm, chrome column at Schönbrunn, watching my brother and cousins kick a hoverball ball during a bright pink sunset. I figure small wishes won't betray what I'm supposed to be, which is Franc, a dauphine, a wife. In Austro, I'd maybe call the wish *Sehnsucht*. Longing to be somewhere else. I don't know what you call that feeling in Franc. So instead, I say to Louis, "It's weird, isn't it? How you can get lonely when you're surrounded by people."

I don't think he's ever looked at me so long before. I really like his eyes. They're very light and blue. "Yeah," he says. "That's usually when I'm loneliest."

Without confusing Austro and Franc, and without a nervous tangle, I manage to say exactly what I want to. "Do you think we could be lonely together?"

He smiles and moves closer to me, incredibly slowly, which makes my heart pound all nervous. I must be in crush territory or I wouldn't be so nervous, or maybe it's my mama's mega-levels of nosiness glitching me out, making me think I'll mess this up. Then he looks over my shoulder and frowns. He puts a gentle hand on my arm and holds out his holofone with the other.

I look behind me and . . . a hedge disappears? It's so glitchy that I jump back into Louis. I'm suddenly face-to-face with Louis's adviser, Maurepas, who also stumbles backward.

"*Scheiße*," I gasp while my brain tries to play catch-up. I definitely saw a hedge vanish and Maurepas was definitely behind it, spying on us.

He at least has the decency to look embarrassed, glowing as red as his fancy velvet jacket.

"Maurepas," says Louis. "Trimming holo-hedges?"

The old guy gapes like the big koi in the ponds. "I thought it strange." He clears his throat. "Strange, Monsieur Dauphin, that there would be a holo here."

"Yeah, you might want to think about planting them better. It was a bit obvious."

"I can assure you, monsieur, I had nothing to do with—"

"Maurepas, just leave me alone." Louis turns and stalks off. With one last glance at Maurepas, still flapping his gums like he's lagging, I chase after Louis.

He's red in the face and scratching at the hair at the nape of his neck.

"Can't catch a break, can we?" I say, trying to laugh it off.

"They think I can't do anything right," Louis mutters. "Well, I thought Maurepas trusted me a little more. He's taught me since I was six."

So, we have bugs *and* advisers listening in fake hedges to rate our attempts at romance. I try to replace the anger simmering up with something lighter. "I know how it is. Surprised it wasn't Miss Manners falling out of a hedge."

"Miss Manners?"

"Oh, whoops. Yeah, I might call Countess Noailles that. Just in my head, of course."

"Of course." He glances at me with the smallest smile, eyes all bright. Score one for me. Maybe we do have hope. He glances down at his holofone. "Stan says Thérèse de Lamballe is by the canal. Let's find her out in that . . . mass." He waves his hand at the party chaos by the water.

There are glow sticks and LED lights and sparklers everywhere. The pools reflect wavering bursts of color, crisp and bright in the cool evening air. Louis stops a server and snags a bright green drink that glows. When he winces after kicking it back, I can't stifle my curiosity. "Let me try!"

"Oh, I don't know if—"

I ignore him and grab my own glass. Stupid me. The stuff is bitter and burns, like I tried to drink battery acid or something. I gag and try not to spit it all over the ground. "*Mon Dieu*, what was that?"

"Absinthe, I think."

I shove the glowing death juice at him.

"I tried to warn you." Louis sets the glasses on a statue's pedestal and grabs my hand. I might be more shocked by this than the taste of that drink. We have to angle around a large press of people writhing to the music. They stop and stare as we pass, craning their arms to raise their holofones and snap pics.

"I love her dress," I hear someone whisper.

"*Mon Dieu*, really? The stockings make it so ugly."

My smile becomes frozen and strained. I duck behind Louis's large back. He doesn't seem to notice the comments. They have a special sting for me. I really tried with this outfit. I'm wearing a plain matte-silver dress. My nylons are a loud pink, but that's the only interesting thing about the ensemble. Apparently, I couldn't even pull off that one bit of signature style.

We come to the edge of the pool, where a load of drunk people splash and stumble around.

It doesn't take long to spot Princesse de Lamballe. It's as if everyone is gravitating toward her and the girl beside her. Lamballe has a musical, tinkling laugh and shakes around her pink hair, all teased and sparkling with glitter. She looks up, spots us, then bounces to her feet. "Louis, Louis!" She bounds over and nearly knocks him down, which is saying something, considering Louis's height and barrel chest. "You never come to parties! Never ever! I feel like I haven't seen you in three years."

"I saw you last month . . . ," says Louis, looking dazed.

Princesse de Lamballe beams at me but doesn't say anything.

Oh yeah, I have to greet her before she can greet me. A Versailles rule that's hard to remember at parties like this. Maybe Louis is supposed to go first? I can never keep this straight without Noailles around to remind me, but Louis takes care of it.

"My, uh . . . my wife wanted to meet you. She thinks you're cool for some reason."

I let go of Louis's hand. I know she's his cousin, but he could try to be friendly. I dip into a bow. "I really do! I'm so glad to meet you."

"Call me Thérèse!" She gathers me into a hug, practically leaping. "Oh, I'm so amped! I've been hoping to meet you. I'll even forgive Louis for embarrassing you like a dongle." She whacks his arm.

He shrugs. "I'm being nice. It's true. She liked your ViewFi channel."

"Oh, that's so sweet! Naturally, I've stalked you on all the Apps. You're so perfect. You have to meet Yolande too."

She waves me toward the rest of the group. They bow to Louis and me, glow sticks and LED lights bobbing and flashing. Thérèse introduces them to me in a rushed flurry of first names, except for the last girl. Her hair is not quite the fashion, yet somehow it's really cool. Dark, thick, and shiny, cut with blunt bangs and cropped near her chin.

"This is Yolande, Duchess de Polignac."

Yolande gives us a graceful bow. "So charmed. Was hoping I would get to meet you." She does a second little bow to my husband, who looks red in the face, though it might be the glow from the laser gun. "Louis. All right, then?"

"All right." He jams his hands into his pockets. "Jules here?"

"He's working. Doing husband things I know nothing about."

"Hmm, yeah." Louis nods and scuffs the ground with his toe, but rather than worry over how shy he's being in front of the girls, I feel a hopeful little bubble. Yolande is another wife as young as me. Finally, someone who might understand. Or give me advice.

Thérèse grabs one of my arms. "So, new girl. Our dauphine of the Franc Kingdom. It would be a true honor to show you around."

"I would love that!" Her energy is contagious, and I feel a surge of excitement for the night ahead.

Thérèse beams. "Fun, fun! Yolande, what should we show her?"

Yolande primly folds her arm around my free one. "Everything."

"Yes! Everything!" Thérèse starts bouncing again. "Around the pool! Up the promenade! Everything, everything."

Yolande raises one perfectly shaped eyebrow at Louis. "You won't mind if we borrow her?"

He gives me a quick smile. "Of course not. *Amusez-vous bien.*"

"You'll never get her back!" Thérèse tugs us forward. "Never ever! *Bonsoir*, Louis! I miss you at every party!"

I say goodbye to him over my shoulder. He seems relieved to escape.

"So, Jules is your husband?" I ask Yolande.

"Yes. Not that it matters. You'll never see him. Always working." She doesn't seem upset, though. Just smiles a little. Maybe she loves him? I want to know that people in arranged matches can be happy.

"Working at what?"

"Oh, you know. Something social marketing, something

politics, et cetera. Who knows? He's had the job a year and he's still in the honeymoon phase of it."

"Husbands always have the worst jobs," says Thérèse. "Well, except yours, I guess."

I laugh. "I guess."

"So who have you met? Any social kids?" Thérèse asks.

"Social kids?"

"Yeah, you know . . . like the ones who are always at Versailles, famous on the Apps."

"I don't think I've met anyone like that, besides you. I've mostly met Louis's family, but I scanned the Apps and picked you!"

Thérèse unleashes a squeal that reminds me of a cross between a puppy and a glitching HD screen. "That's so, so sweet! I love her already! We'll meet everyone!"

"But first, drinks." The things Yolande gives us are pink and taste way better and sweeter than that green monstrosity Louis had. I could get used to this one. We promenade like Thérèse promised, downing pink drinks.

"Ah, that's Kianique. The rising techno star."

A tall girl with neon-green strands braided into her beautiful hair giggles with a small group of kids lit by their holofones' glow.

"Her dress is amazing!" I gasp.

She's glowing blue and purple because the flared minidress is covered in LED infinity mirrors.

"Bold choice," says Yolande.

"How did she get away with it?" I say quietly, more to myself than anything. It's the kind of thing I'd love to wear, but that

Pixter incident has stopped me.

"They're a bit more gaudy in the rave scene," says Yolande.

"I love it. I actually wondered if . . . well, maybe you could help me with my style?"

"*Your* style? Your style is a legend! You should be giving tips to me!" Thérèse squeaks.

"That was when I was Austro. The Francs disagree."

Yolande takes a prim sip of her drink. "We are a bit of a culture shock."

"Yeah, and they were apparently shocked by one of my outfits."

"Ohhh yeah . . . I saw." Thérèse winces. "But honestly? People can be such viruses on the Apps. They might spread hate, but people know that you know what's up."

"Do you think I should just keep wearing what I want, then?"

"Yeah! Just go Franc-inspired instead of full Franc. I mean, check it out. . . ." Thérèse stands on tiptoes and waves her drink over at a group of girls sitting around a fountain with Philippe. "You see the jacket?"

I can hardly believe my eyes, but it's the one I wore on Pixter. The girl has layered it over a black minidress with a silver belt. It's plainer than I would have chosen, but it's the same jacket I wore that got trashed so badly! The sight makes me feel hyperdrive. It's a big step but not nearly enough to prove myself to Noailles.

"See? You've got some influence already," says Thérèse.

"You're the dauphine," says Yolande. "Haters can hate, but they'll look really stupid when you turbo-trend and leave them in the dust."

I love Thérèse and Yolande. They're like the sun and the moon, one bright, one cool. I need friends at Versailles, and I know already that these are the ones I want in my orbit. This conversation has already given me back more confidence than Louis's fumbling and apologetic support has.

We dance and drink and dance some more. Under the bright lights and thudding rhythm, we dash from statue to fountain, posing like the carved stone figures for our cameras. At some point, Philippe finds us, and he must have been in the fountain because he hugs me with a sopping-wet shirt. I shove him off, screaming and kicking pebbles at him.

We stumble back to the tents, where the older courtiers are dining, drinking, playing some guessing game on their holofones.

Thérèse and Yolande stop their chattering and bow low. I turn around and find Grand-Père King with Madame du Barry, his mistress, on his arm.

"Looking quite red in the cheeks, madame. You must be enjoying yourself." He chuckles and shakes his head.

"*Oui, merci*, Grand-Père. I apologize if you don't approve. I forgot myself since I'm in such good company."

He chuckles again. "Not to worry. To be young. Enjoy it all. As long as that little grandson of mine didn't push you to overindulge."

"Philippe? No, but he tried."

"Tell him what's what! Takes after his grandfather! Not always such a good thing!"

Everyone laughs with him. You must always laugh along with a king. Du Barry laughs the most. I've barely spoken to her because I have no idea what you should say to a king's mistress. In the Austro Lands, nobles are more private about affairs. Du Barry has this LED fan that's really cool, and I'd like one of my own. It flashes and flickers with images, like a tiger, but as she flutters it, it shows something else for a second . . . was that a naked person? Damn. Talk about a bold accessory statement. I blink, and it's gone. A tiger paces the pixels again.

"Yes, Philippe needs some strong-arming. Your husband, on the other hand . . ." He looks sad for me, and my smile, which had started to ache from wearing it for hours, falls apart. Everything is quiet for a moment while Du Barry flutters her fan again. She wears the only remaining smile.

"Well . . ." Grand-Père chucks me under my chin and I wrestle my features back into something happy-shaped. "So charming. Just a bit of encouragement should do it soon enough."

He gives me a wink. I wish I could evaporate on the spot. It might be possible to die of embarrassment.

"Dauphine, I have . . . *very* many suggestions. If you need some advice. Just between girls." Du Barry gives me a cheeky tap on the arm with the fan.

I would probably blush if I weren't already flushed from the alcohol. The king kisses Du Barry's hand. "No doubt. But they are young and maybe need some more time before you share such expertise."

"I can be most delicate when I wish." She waves her fan at him with a cheeky flap.

"Oh, really? I've known you to be a lot of things, but never delicate."

As Du Barry gives me a good look up and down, I can feel the full judgment of her stare, and suddenly my nylons are super itchy and possibly very ugly. The king can't seem to look away from her. Du Barry is here to sleep with the king and make him fall madly in love with her. I can barely get Louis to touch me, let alone look at me the way the king is looking at her. Maybe I do need her tips.

"It seems you're in need of a little guidance in style too. It will change the way your husband sees you."

Now my ears are definitely burning. I have to do a very pinched Miss Manners–type smile to stop myself from calling her a *Kotzbrocken*.

Thérèse comes in clutch with the save. "Perhaps you could settle a rumor I heard, Majesté or madame."

The king smirks and raises an eyebrow at Du Barry, who mirrors him but flutters her fan. "That would depend on the rumor, madame," he says.

Thérèse glances around and whispers, "I heard there might be *androids* here."

"Huh!" The king suppresses something like a cough or a laugh. Du Barry raises her fan just below her eyes. Another good reason to have one. You can hide behind them. "Where did you hear such a thing, young madame?"

Thérèse curtsies. "His Majesté can't expect a lady to tell!"

"Wild rumors sometimes have substance," says the king with a wink. "But if an android truly were present . . . well, best not to overwhelm him. It wasn't long ago that androids weren't ready for society."

"Mmm, badly mannered," says Du Barry.

"You'd know about that, I suppose." The king's eyes glitter with a mischief that reminds me of Philippe.

Du Barry gives him a whack with her fan. She is possibly the only person who could get away with something like that. "His Majesté suggests I have bad manners!"

"Perish the thought!" he laughs. "I meant you had some experience with androids."

I catch Yolande rolling her eyes.

"In passing," says Du Barry. "You should have a care not to spread rumors yourself."

"Of course." But the king gives Thérèse a wink and leans in. "Some esteemed members of the First Estate are here tonight. Including Monsieur Angoulême, head executive of the Franc branch of SveroTech. There's your android expert, and it seems he brought guests."

Thérèse beams. "How fascinating!"

I'm confused. Is Thérèse really interested in androids? What for? They just carry things around and deliver stuff, and maybe some can drive cruisers. There's glitchy rumors about new ones that are super advanced, but Mama told me sophisticated AI is years away. The tech isn't ready to be relied on.

Thérèse gives Yolande a small nudge.

"I'm so sorry, Majesté, but I believe the comte de Provence is summoning us to the canals," says Yolande.

"Another troublesome one. Stan can surely wait, but go."

My grandfather and Du Barry bow.

The king has lost interest in us already, turning toward an old woman supported by a hoverchair. Du Barry pauses before she joins him. "I'd avoid him if I were you. Angoulême."

"Thanks for the tip," Yolande says, with an icy glare.

"We can't avoid everyone who has business with androids. Just think about how many people we couldn't address." Based on the pointed smile Thérèse adds to the statement, I'm really missing something. More than just the androids thing.

"Girls who get too nosy about members of the First Estate get themselves into trouble. Smart girls would listen to me. Run along to Provence now." Du Barry gives us half a curtsy and half a flick of her fan.

Thérèse and Yolande steer me away.

"The nerve of her!" Thérèse mutters. "Considering her past . . . and you'd never guess she was talking to the dauphine."

I hate feeling like the outsider. The person who knows nothing. But I'll never catch up if I don't ask. "I'm . . . confused. Aren't androids just, like, vaguely human-shaped robots?"

"Yeah, maybe five years ago," says Yolande. "But they're in the military now."

"What?!" That's the opposite of what Mama told me.

"It's true," says Thérèse. "Jules has met them, hasn't he?"

Yolande nods. "He said they're just like us. The AI is so advanced now. He says they're charming and everything comes naturally to them."

"But what does Du Barry know about them?"

"Ooh, that," Yolande says. "Well, the rumor is there are some dealers who sell them to brothels."

I've heard so many new things that my head is spinning. "And Du Barry?"

Thérèse shrugs. "That's the rumor. That she traded in 'service' bots."

"That's so . . ."

"Scandalous, right? I wonder if I can find Monsieur Angoulême." Thérèse glances around.

"The king said to leave him alone," Yolande says. "Come sit by the fountain with us instead."

"Oh, now you sound like Du Barry!"

I glance between them. I don't know much about the First Estate except that they're the most important people in the Franc Kingdom, and they support the monarchy in countless financial ways. They own all the businesses and the Apps and pretty much everything. I wonder if Du Barry's warning has something to do with Thérèse's husband. Did he get himself into trouble by tangling with someone in the First Estate? Someone like Monsieur Angoulême himself?

"Just for some chitchat! There's no harm. Oh, I see him! He's wearing the red suit and—*mon Dieu*. That has to be one of them."

I squint and catch sight of a deep red suit. But my eyes drift right over him to the face of the man beside him. He's the most beautiful person I've ever seen. He's surrounded by people like he's giving an interview. Maybe he's a famous actor or a musician, but no way. I would have seen him on the Apps and recognized him. The twinkling eyes, the perfect smile, the softly curling golden-brown hair are made for fame. Surely this isn't the android Thérèse and the king were talking about.

Yolande stumbles to sit on the edge of a fountain. "Ugh. Whatever. I need to sit. Too much to drink."

"But Yolande, look at the android," Thérèse hisses, practically bouncing.

"Pretty. I don't care about them, though. Jules is already obsessed. I've heard too much about them."

There's no way. There's no way that guy is a machine. His smile, the way people are drawing toward him, are too magnetic. Giga-levels of charisma.

"*Allons.*" Thérèse grabs my wrist and drags me over to

Angoulême and his handsome companion, the crowd parting as we approach.

Angoulême's suit is really nice. An Hermonds, maybe. He bows deeply and I do my best to curtsy with grace despite my swimming thoughts and sloshing belly and blushing cheeks as the young man in military uniform standing next to him bows to me and smiles.

"Madame Dauphine. *Enchanté*," says Angoulême.

"*Enchanté*, monsieur. May I present the Princesse de Lamballe?"

"Lamballe . . . ," Angoulême says slowly as Thérèse curtsies. It seems like he might comment on her name, but the moment passes. "A pleasure," he says. "And may I present Captain Axel Fersen?"

"It is a true honor to meet you, madame." He has a rich, rumbling voice. There is nothing mechanical about it. He bends low, hand poised in offering. I place my fingers lightly on his palm. It's warm, smooth, *real*. Is this really skin hiding wires for veins? He plants a light kiss below my knuckles. His lips are warm too, his breath tickles over my wrist, and my stomach prickles like a fizzy Mountain Jam Lime drink. This is *human* charm. This can't be an android. Angoulême tilts his wobbly chin back toward me. There's something off about his movements. A little too slow. Or maybe his eyes are too sharp and searching. "Have you met an android before, madame?"

"No, monsieur, I've never had the pleasure." I hope I'm not blushing. That would be so embarrassing.

"The pleasure, if I may say, is mine," says the handsome android. So it's true. He really is a machine. Fersen's smile is slightly crooked. Must be a flaw manufactured on purpose, but

I can't keep my eyes off it.

"Ah, yes . . ." Angoulême studies me. "The Austro Lands have yet to forge a trade agreement with SveroTech. Your esteemed empress mother has reservations."

My cheeks burn and my champagne belly flounders, because I've never discussed this with Mama and can't begin to comment. "I'm sure she has her reasons."

"Yes, well . . . it seems you and Captain Fersen may make a fine team. I would be pleased to establish him as a palace guard. Consider it a gift."

I'm giga-glitching. Fersen in the palace? As my guard? And how can Angoulême "gift" him as if he were a gown or a holofone or a necklace?

"How generous to spare one for a palace guard when there aren't very many to begin with," says Thérèse.

Angoulême gives her that slow look again. "Our technology and production improve by the day. I can certainly arrange such a gift. It would be a pleasure."

"I . . . I don't know what to say." Sometimes the truth is the best option.

"Say you'll accept, of course."

I look at Fersen. I can't help it. It's his job and his life, after all. I want to know what he thinks. He smiles again. "It would be an honor, Madame Dauphine." He gives a light bow. "To serve at Versailles is a position of honor for all in the military."

"Of course. But perhaps I should discuss this with the dauphin."

"Very well," says Angoulême. "Where is he?"

"I'm not sure. He might have turned in. But I'm sure he'll

reach out with the decision."

"Then I hope to hear from him soon. Eh, Fersen?" Angoulême raises an eyebrow at him.

"Certainly." Once again, Fersen bows low. "Madame Dauphine . . . I hope to see you again soon."

I thank him again, curtsy to his bow. I'm through with the conversation, which I'm a second away from crashing. I turn back toward the fountain where Yolande is reclined, playing with her holofone. But Thérèse doesn't make to follow me. "Go on," she says. "I'll be right there."

When I join Yolande and sit, the fish statue in the fountain seems to sway. I'm exhausted.

"Where's Thérèse?" asks Yolande.

"Oh, she's right over . . ." But when I look up, Angoulême and his crowd are moving toward the tents and I don't see Thérèse with them. I don't see her anywhere. As I look for her, I see the back of Fersen's golden haired head turning my way, as if he senses me.

"I—I'm not sure. She was right there."

"She disappears all the time. Distractible little thing." Yolande yawns. "She'll turn up."

The stars spiral on and the music pounds as Yolande and I flick through pics on the Apps, posting our own and watching the comments pile on. Starry, neon-lit pictures of perfection. Everyone wants to be here with us. Tonight, Versailles is the center of the world.

NINE

June 3, 3070, 9:47 a.m.

This is a morning of firsts. First hangover ever. None of the parties before this left me with a dull headache and squirming stomach. Must have been those dumb pink drinks.

This is also the first morning Louis has been at breakfast. Not a single breakfast with him since we've been married. The absolutely awful weather kept him from hunting. Pouring-down rain and whipping wind. All the hundreds of windows of the palace look like they're crying. At least the air is cleaner here. If we were at Schönbrunn, the windows would get streaked with dirt and ash in a rainstorm.

"I would destroy you at calc," Elisabeth says. "You should take the phycalc preps with me. I'll prove it."

"I beat you at math last year," says Louis.

"Algebra by two points, you little bagbiter."

"Still beat you." Louis shrugs.

"So come to my lessons today and then we'll see."

"Can't. I've history with Vauguyond."

"History is stupid." Elisabeth smirks, clearly goading him.

"Think like that and you're doomed to repeat it."

Stan slams his hand on the table, upending the bowl of hard-boiled eggs he'd been popping into his mouth at an unreal rate.

"Shut up already. Elisabeth, you're dumb as a drone if you think they'll ever let you be a doctor when you're a Bourbon princess. So stop arguing about pointless bloatware."

Elisabeth goes pale. Her trembling hand rattles a fork. She has a comeback for everything. Why is she holding back now? Louis, who normally can't be bothered to get worked up about anything, tosses his napkin on the table. "I'll be king someday, and then she can do whatever she pleases."

"You won't do shit. Even when you're king."

"We'll see." Louis goes back to eating his toast. I wish he would be firmer. He's right. He'll be king and then Elisabeth should get to be a doctor if she wants! Why shouldn't she? Louis and Stan are both older than her. What are the odds she'd need to take over?

Stan's eyes have a wicked glimmer. "Well, Louis, seeing as you can't do shit now, I don't really see what's going to change. Can't even get it up, can you?"

All the defenses I use to school my words, my face, my movements drop at mega-speed. I should be cool, dignified, and brush him off. But he's crashed the systems, and clever princess retorts are off-line. A hot flash starts in my face, then spreads through the rest of me. "Who turned *you* down at the party last night, donglehead?"

Stan jumps from his seat so fast his chair falls back. For one second, I'm really afraid. I'm not sure of what. "One day you'll see that you can't say whatever you want here. You might be a Bourbon in name, but you're still an outsider."

He spins away and storms off, shouting for an attendant. A drone buzzes over to right the chair. I hear every little click and whir in the silence. What the frag was that supposed to mean? Why do *I* have to keep my thoughts to myself? Where are the glitching rules for princes and the stuff they're allowed to say?

There's a little snorting noise from Philippe, who's giggling into his napkin. "It's hilarious because he made a pass at Louise Bertière and she shoved him in the pool."

Philippe doubles over with barking laughter, but I feel my face warm again.

"*Mon Dieu* . . . I didn't know. That was too much. That was mean." Knew it was a finishing move, but I didn't know it was such a low blow. Even so, I'm sick of everyone making what happens, or *doesn't* happen, in my bedroom their business to comment on.

Philippe shakes his head. "No, no. Come on. He's been a *tête de noeud* all morning."

Elisabeth shrugs as if to say he deserves it, but I can tell what Stan said rattled her, and that's enough to banish my guilt.

Louis smiles at me in a lazy way. "That was giga-cool. Please marry me."

He has a twinkle in his eye. And a bit of a dimple, but just on the left side of his mouth. I twist my lips into a cheeky smile. "Maybe, but we'll need to go on at least three solid dates first. Bare minimum."

He goes bright red and looks down at his plate. "Cool. I'll clear my schedule," he mumbles. I can see his smile, even if he tries to hide it. He really can be cute when he wants to be.

Philippe shakes his head at him, and there's a nudge at my arm. Elisabeth pushes a glass of water at me. "Don't forget this. You're probably dehydrated from drinking."

I chug the delicious, freezing hangover cure. "You'd be a great doctor."

She shrugs and turns back to her yogurt. Can't tell if she's eaten any or just traced patterns in it.

"She will be," says Louis. "Ignore Stan. He's phished because . . . well, you'll probably find out soon."

Elisabeth raises an eyebrow at him. "Something other than Louise Bertière?"

"Never mind. Did you like the party?"

I hesitate, looking between Elisabeth, who's glaring at Louis, and Louis, who is clearly begging me to let him change the subject.

"I love Thérèse and Yolande. They introduced me to so many people. I'll have to check through the Apps or I'll never remember names. So many of them were named Louise."

"So call them all Louise. Told you, everyone is named Louise here," Louis says with a shy glance my way.

I giggle. "Or Louis. Gigs! You are so basic!"

He claps a hand over his heart like I've wounded him. "It's a prince name with a long, honorable tradition."

"Married people are weird," says Philippe.

Elisabeth doesn't look amused. "*Tell me* your dirt on Stan."

Louis shrugs. "Ask Grand-Père."

"No." She rolls her eyes. "Just tell me."

Louis hops up from his chair. "I have to go to history lessons. Bye." He pauses like he might say something to me. Sort of leans in my direction like he might come around to my side of the table. I squirm in my seat, not sure if I should stand, if I should go to him, if I should kiss him. Why don't we know how to act like we're properly married? Before I can decide what to do, Louis strides away in the plodding, clumsy way he has.

Elisabeth shakes her head and shoves away the yogurt. "Unbelievable. All three of you boys."

"What'd I do?" says Philippe.

"You breathe. You exist."

"Nice. Well, I could tell you what's going on with Stan."

"You don't know."

"I don't know for sure. But I can guess." Philippe raises a glass of water to his lips, eyes twinkling with laughter. "Bet you Stanny's getting married."

Elisabeth gasps. "No . . ."

Philippe shrugs. "Makes sense. It's about that time."

"I don't believe it."

"I guess we'll see." Philippe looks sly. I think he knows more than he lets on. They would keep these matters private until the match is made official, but if Louis has heard something, then I bet Philippe has too. I bet a lot of people have, since gossip is like oxygen at court. Even though I don't understand my husband at all, this morning I'm glad that I'm married to Louis and not Stan.

TEN

※

June 5, 3070, 11:23 a.m.

I'm not sure my history tutor likes me any better than Noailles does. I haven't been sure what to make of Adelaide since the day I met her and overheard her strange conversation. She is older than me, but younger than Noailles, and I had hoped we might have some kind of friendship or at least a better time than I do in my lessons with Noailles. But so far, she's bookish and teaches me with a twitchy fervor that makes it seem like every scrap of information we study about the old regime and the world before the Event is the most important thing I have to learn. Although Versailles itself is a historical icon, no one is truly that interested in the people who built this place over a millennium ago. We just get nostalgic and admire the beauty and leisure they enjoyed in this place.

But if I share those opinions or don't get the point Adelaide was trying to make, she sighs and her giant glasses seem to weigh down her small face.

Her clothes distract me constantly, because I can't figure out what inspires her fashion and what her aesthetic is. Today she wears a thick-necked black sweater and high-waisted brown pants. The look is so plain, so boring, that it stands out just by being blander than any clothes I've ever seen.

"Are your clothes retro or something?" I ask her.

Adelaide pauses with a finger hovering over her holofone. "*Quoi?*"

"Your clothes. They're . . . different."

Of course she blinks a whole lot. "Oh, I . . . erm—I'm inspired by the past, I suppose."

The only past clothing I know of are those giant dresses and goofy short-legged suits in the holo-portraits all over Versailles and Schönbrunn. "Really? I've never seen anything like it. Where did you get them?"

Her eyelids are really glitchy. She flutters her lashes a lot, but not in a flirtatious way. "They are, um, custom-made. There's a group of hobbyists who—" Adelaide shakes her head. "Never mind that, Madame Dauphine. We're here for a lesson, after all. Not clothes."

The way she glances at my holo-necked top makes me think she's judging me. I cross my arms. She has no right. I've heard Du Barry mocking her glasses and clothes, and Grand-Père King often cuts off her little speeches at events of state. She fits in far worse than I do.

"Did you watch the vids I sent you?" she asks.

No. I haven't done history lessons for the past year and a half. I've been too busy preparing to be a dauphine, and now I'm too busy *being* a dauphine. "I . . . didn't finish them. But I got the idea."

Adelaide sighs a little. "Dauphine, I know you are very preoccupied with things like"—her eyes dart over my outfit again—"fashion. But this is very important."

I don't like her judging my interests as less important than hers. Every other person pressures me to be liked, to be a brand and an icon. I roll my eyes. "It was about the Event. I know it already. Those lessons were covered when I was Austro." I shiver and pull my microfiber sweater tighter. The shiny threads scratch at the goose bumps on my shoulders. The East Wing is full of annoying little meeting rooms like this one, where the window shutters are sealed tight and everything smells like pine air freshener and the musty metallic smell of a cooling unit that never shuts off.

"I have to see how much you know," says Adelaide. "Your education was likely not sufficient."

"Just because I'm Austro?" I scoff.

"No, madame. Because you were a duchess and now you are dauphine." She does not blink when she says this, so I believe she's being serious, not trying to cover her Austro prejudice. But what she said doesn't make sense.

"I'm sure I was taught much more history than most people. Most people don't care about it at all, you know."

"I am aware, Madame Dauphine. I am painfully aware." She pauses by a purple neon lamp. Her eyes look deep and older than her face. "Perhaps you could tell me what you know of the Event."

"A long time ago, pollution and gas in the air or something made things get really warm, then really cold, then really warm again, and a lot of forests burned or flooded, and there were huge storms. Water got scarce and there was a big war over it that damaged everything so it was in a worse state than it was before. More than half the human population died, and the survivors carried on with the scraps that were left behind." I shrug, because this is basic stuff. The kind everyone knows, and I'm annoyed at having to repeat it like I'm a child again.

"And of the world before . . . how much survived?" Adelaide asks.

"We don't really know. Everyone fought over the remains of the old net data and now we aren't totally sure which kingdoms have what information and how much they've released." This feels like a trick question.

Adelaide watches me with an intensity that unnerves me. "Yes, but what remains? How much are we like our ancestors?"

I throw my hands up. "How are we supposed to know if the information is either burnt to a crisp or in someone's bio-encrypted data stores in the king of Anglia's palace? They say the Cizhou Provinces were entrusted with a bunch of it because they have the biggest knowledge base and best universities of all the kingdoms."

Adelaide shakes her head. "This doesn't answer my question. Are we anything like our ancestors? What do you think?"

This is definitely a trick question. I don't like it when tutors play games with me instead of just telling me what I have to study. "Well, based on the portraits and stuff, we're nothing like them, but me—the Bourbons, my mother—we are the most similar. The monarchy is one of the last remaining connections to the people who came before us. We're the best reminder that this isn't a new world. We lost so much before us. That's why we're so strict about traditions and etiquette and rules; we're trying to be that reminder for everyone, for the people. We're the only glimpse any of us have into the old ways of life."

I've repeated everything every tutor has always told me, what my mama has told me. I think it's a good answer, but when Adelaide slides into the red plush chair across from me, she isn't smiling. "You are right about two things. The codes are strict and you are indeed a reminder. But we are very much like our ancestors, much more so than you have ever been taught to believe. And we are not heeding any warnings the previous royal family provides."

"What are you talking about?" I've never heard anyone be so extra about a history lesson. "What warnings?"

"You walk in the footsteps of your predecessors. Do you know where those footsteps led?"

Obviously not. She's supposed to be the expert on the Event, not me. "Burned up or drowned or dead from illness from the Event. I know. What's the point you're making?"

"You think the Event was random chance?" Adelaide asks. She's staring at me over the rims of her glasses, with her hands clamped on the table edge so tightly her knuckles are straining.

"No." I'm getting pretty glitched now. Who is this woman exactly? In a way I can't place my finger on, she's scarier than Noailles. "It was caused by weather and climate disasters that humans made."

"And what about the disasters, the crumbling of society that went with these events? People with the least, left to die; people used to plenty, suddenly in want. Desperate people doing desperate acts in the name of survival. Could it happen again? Is it happening again now, as we speak?"

"No, we're much smarter. We've learned a lot since then."

Adelaide closes her eyes as if my words hurt as much as a slap to the face.

"What?" I ask. "Teachers aren't supposed to be all hypothetical! What are you trying to teach me in this lesson?"

"I'm trying to teach you why the past is important, Dauphine. Those who have power *must learn and must protect those who have none.* You're letting people steer you and all the rest of us into disaster because no one has learned anything! Not a damned thing! It's bad enough that so much history was lost or erased without this court's foolish attempt to re-create a beautified past!"

Adelaide's bangs look sweaty and she shoves her glasses up her nose after this outburst. She sits there a moment, her breathing heavy. I'm so shocked I don't even call out her impertinence. People don't talk to me this way. I don't understand what made her so glitched.

"I apologize, madame." Adelaide rises from her seat. "I—I . . . there is no excuse. I was out of line. And I'm not innocent either. I was hired to support this . . . endeavor. Perhaps I should excuse myself today."

I want to let her go. But something about what she said is adding up with other things I've heard about Versailles and the state of the Franc Kingdom. "Wait."

She doesn't meet my eyes. I realize she thinks I'm going to dismiss her as my tutor. I should dismiss her. But despite how rude and glitchy and strange she is, her honesty, her feeling, is refreshing. I can't remember the last time someone spoke to me without pretense, without treating me like I only needed to know the bare minimum. "Who is steering me, Madame Frasier? Besides people like Noailles and Mercy."

"The same sort of people who have always wielded power,

madame. The ones who always turn others into cogs in a vast consumptive machine."

This answers nothing. I stare and wait for her to continue.

Adelaide runs a hand through her messy, staticky hair. "There are those who know far more about our history than the rest of us, and that information, that historical data, is strictly controlled. And then it's used, particularly on you and the rest of the court. You are a recreation, a distraction, a scapegoat, a tool they think they can wield more successfully than in the ancient days. Your names, your alliances, your causes, your words, they are scripted by those who have put the Bourbons on the throne. But no matter who controls a monarchy, an oligarchy, whatever name chosen, whatever trappings dress it up . . . it is a cycle doomed to repeat itself. Unless the wheel is broken or is steered in an entirely different direction."

I shake my head. "You're still talking in circles. Who is steering what wheel?"

"There is much you don't know because you aren't allowed to know it. They have ears and eyes everywhere. I shouldn't have even told you this much." She grabs the door handle, as if she could run from her words.

I think of Louis telling me someone is always watching. Has he already learned all this or is Adelaide just paranoid, delusional? Cracked by too many years at court? Just as she reaches for the door handle, I ask, "Why should I believe you?"

She looks from me to the door, then down at her holofone. "I've already done the damage. . . . Why not. Has anyone shown you this?" Adelaide taps at her holofone, then sets the projector to show me a hologram. Chaos spills out over wavering pixels like light underwater. The hologram image shows fires blooming in apartment buildings. People in dark clothes waving signs that say things like THEY STARVE US and NO EGALITÉ, NO LIBERTÉ and CAN'T LIVE ON GIGS.

Police cruisers hover amid the chaos. Shadowy figures run from the blaze, many of them small, terribly young.

My heart picks up its pace. "Is this . . ."

"Parée last night," says Adelaide. "And no one told you, Dauphine. Am I right?"

"No. No one told me." But how could Mercy have forgotten to mention it in this morning's meeting? I look at the riots in front of my eyes, at the anger and fear on the people's faces. Surely this should have been the first thing he told me?

"They don't want you to know," says Adelaide, and flicks the holofone off. "You are only useful to them ignorant. It's not for you to worry your pretty head over."

"I have a right to know! I can't do a good job without this information."

"I'm glad you feel this way." Adelaide's eyes grow bright, her breath shaky with excitement. "You must seek the truth," she says. "And you must do it carefully."

"How will I do that if I don't even know who to watch out for?"

Adelaide glances at the door and drops her voice to a whisper. "Anyone in the First Estate. Anyone in the police force. The comte de Provence and perhaps the comte de Artois as well. Trust your husband. He's timid and afraid, but he's intelligent."

Not even Stan and Philippe? They're irritating, but surely they aren't trying to use me or hurt me?

There's a knock at the door.

"Speak of this to no one," says Adelaide. "We'll talk more in the next lesson."

"Why should I trust you?" I ask, because so far I've come across next to no one I can trust in this place. "You could be making all this up to scare me."

"Mention the fires." Adelaide shrugs. "See what that gets you. You'll see that I'm telling you the truth, and that is a rare commodity in Versailles."

She manages to erase the contempt on her face as soon as Noailles sweeps into the room. "Important matters to discuss. I'm afraid I must cut this short. Frasier, you are dismissed."

Adelaide bobs a curtsy without another word and slips out.

"I wasn't done with my lesson," I say.

Noailles arches an eyebrow at me. "Indeed. But more pressing matters demand your time. Madame Valois of the First Estate requested crown support of the vaccination banks," says Noailles. "This is a good cause. Free vaccinations throughout the kingdom. She'd like you to promote the banks on the Apps. Time for you to use that influence you assure me you can put to use."

"Fine. I can do that." I squirm a bit. I want to ask her about the fires like Adelaide said to, but the thought makes me nervous. Why did Mercy hide this from me? "Can we do something to help the people affected by the fires in Parée last night?"

You would have thought I'd just asked for a divorce by her expression. Noailles's eyes widen. Then she clears her throat. "Did the dauphin tell you about this?"

"No, I saw it on the Apps."

"You what?"

"On my newsfeed."

She shakes her head and drums the surface of her holofone

with rapid-fire tapping. Confused, I continue, "Anyway . . . so many people lost their homes. Children got injured. I'd like to give to them."

"A lovely thought, Madame Dauphine, but this is a large amount of money," says Noailles.

"Then think how much good it will do."

"The fires were started by protests that became riots. When a situation is . . . charged like this, then it won't do to be partial to any one side of it," says Noailles.

"How could caring about the people be viewed as a bad thing?" Mama always encouraged charity. I remember handing insta-dinners in little aluminum packets to young kids with big eyes and sticky hands. I'd give them a Hapsburg badge to pin on their shirts before they moved down the line to get food credits added to their holofones.

"Messages are never so simple. Anything the crown supports has any number of other implications, and each event, each charity, each appearance is chosen carefully. That's why you must do the promotion of the vaccine banks. The Bureau of Business Owners wants to leverage your skills. This is a good thing and exactly what you asked for when you wanted control of your social media platform."

I can't believe how callous she is. I cross my arms. "I want to help the fire victims. They need it more than the First Estate. They need help right now."

Noailles's eyelashes flutter, which always happens when she's trying not to snap. "The First Estate heavily supports the crown. We work closely with them and must accommodate their wishes."

I want to ask what the point of being in charge is if we just do whatever the *dumme* businesspeople in the First Estate tell us to. Instead I say, "Fine. I'll just ask Louis for money for the fire."

"Good. Perhaps your husband can explain my position to you."

"Louis will give to them. He's a good person." I'm not sure if that's true, but somehow I can't imagine Louis's soft face going as cold as Noailles's if I show him the scared figures running from the blaze.

"My advice, Dauphine, is to concern yourself with influencing him in *other matters* first."

There it is. *The consummation*. I knew it was coming eventually. "I can handle it."

"Can you? Evidence would suggest otherwise. We are very concerned. Perhaps you don't understand your duties."

"I understand them! I'm working on it, and I really don't think it's anyone else's business how I'm going about it."

If Noailles had claws, she would bare them, if her grip on her holofone is any indication.

"It will get better soon. My mother gives me lots of advice. You can ask Mercy and he'll tell you."

"Well, this advice does not seem to be working."

"I'm doing my best. And I've helped so much with Louis's image on the Apps! He got ten thousand more followers last month when I took some photos of him with hunting dogs, and it was so popular, *#DauphinandDogs* trended. No one knew Louis before. Just his face. Now the people like him more than ever! With my help, they'll be thrilled to support him when he takes the throne."

"Helpful as that may be, this is meaningless if there is pressure to annul your marriage. An unconsummated marriage is an unnecessary risk." She slips her holofone into her pocket. Apparently, she's done nitpicking me. Noailles waves a hand to show I should rise first because we're done here. "I will arrange the publicity shoot for the vaccine banks. Go find the dauphin. Time spent together is the way out of your situation, I think."

I scowl. "Are you saying he doesn't like me?"

"I'm saying he's bound to, the more you're around each other."

How am I supposed to do all this? Be liked on the Apps, help the people, make Louis like me? The perfect princess, dauphine, wife, App sensation. All while some things are hidden from me and others are completely out of my control. Despite years of training, I can't believe I'm prepared to do any of this or be the person who history or Adelaide or the First Estate think I'm supposed to be. I'm just Marie, and before all this, I thought I knew who that was and what I would become.

ELEVEN

June 5, 3070, 8:37 p.m.

When I'm back in the common room, I get a text from Thérèse:
Stan is def engaged. Heard his fiancée is awful. Snaps at
her maids and doesn't brush her hair.

Maybe all the Bourbons are doomed to unhappy marriages. I
open the window for air and to smell the sweet lilacs, but they're
drooping after two days of pouring rain. Instead, I smell mud
and that nasty garbage-dump smell that gets stronger when it
rains. I flip a switch by the windows and watch the white storm
shutters fold in and seal over the depressing sight. Their under-
side has a hologram, and I switch it to the golden sunset I wish
were happening.

"Can I get you anything, madame?"

Georgette stands in the doorway, hands folded. I wonder if
she is as exhausted by formality as I am at times. "You could call
me Marie. Especially here when it's just us."

Georgette does a slow nod, and I think she might try saying
it. But she smiles and says nothing instead.

"Oh, and I don't need anything. I'm just . . ." Homesick. *Das
Sehnsucht.* "Where are you from, Georgette?"

The question seems to startle or confuse her. She frowns.
Maybe calculating her answer like I often have to when reviewing the etiquette. "I'm from a place on the edges of Parée."

"Oh, so you're a Paréesian!"

Her face flushes. "Oh, no, not exactly. It's . . . not the city. It's very different from Parée."

"Really . . . How so?"

"Well . . ." She grows thoughtful again. "It's closer to nature. But still harsh, like Parée can be. Just in different ways. People live quite closely together like the city, but they have to depend on each other much more so."

I hear so little about people who live outside cities. Most places outside them aren't habitable, but of course small villages exist where people harvest whatever they can from our damaged earth. "Were you a farmer?" I ask. "Your family, I mean."

"No," she says with almost a laugh. "Well, a little. I'm sure this isn't that interesting, mada—Marie."

"It's very interesting! Not quite a farmer from not quite Parée. You're very mysterious, Georgette. I ask because I was wondering if you ever miss home."

"I was lucky to come live in Versailles. Very lucky, but . . . yes. I miss home sometimes." Georgette nods.

"Me too," I say. "I feel just like that."

She smiles. Sad for me. A girl who works so hard, from somewhere harsh. Sad for *me*. It seems wrong. But I can't make sense of anything lately. "You know, if you ever want to go visit, I'm happy to give you the leave. I'll argue with Noailles if I have to."

"Thank you. I appreciate it," says Georgette. "Speaking of Madame de Noailles . . ." She taps at the micro-tab strapped to her wrist. "I think I'm needed. Unless there's anything I can do for you."

I wish we could just keep talking. But I don't want Noailles barking at her like she always does at me. "I won't keep you. I know how Miss Manners gets."

"Miss Manners?" Georgette asks with a giggle.

"I'm sure you've noticed her turbo-obsession with 'the rules.'"

"Her job, I suppose," Georgette says with a shrug. "By your leave, then."

"Of course. See you later."

She leaves with a curtsy that I know I can't talk her out of. When you've been trained in the court dance, it feels unnatural to get out of step.

After flopping on the couch, I switch one of the HD screens on and flip channels. Hoverball, no. True crime, gross. Cooking show, no. Live feed of people at a rave, no. I settle on some film where a girl with big mirror glasses dashes around Parée after a stray cat to the beat of an electro-accordion soundtrack. Her hairstyle is a lot like Yolande's. I bet Yolande likes this movie, whatever it is. When I text her about it, she's shocked that I've never seen it. Some kind of cult classic, I guess. Something about the director's use of color and the red teapot at the café where the girl works symbolizing death.

There's a whooshing noise as the door to the common room slides open. Louis plods in, soaked like he fell in the pool.

I jump up from the couch. "Were you outside?"

"Well, I wasn't in the shower."

"You might as well have been." I dash to the bathroom for a towel. "Why were you outside in the storm?"

"There's a weather station on the roof. I wanted to see the data on the storms."

"What for?" I toss the towel up over his head.

"Uh . . . I don't know. I just worry about them, I guess. Could be a superstorm, you know?" He scrubs at his hair with the towel and goes into the bathroom. I back up to the couch to give him space.

He yanks his hoodie over his head, and it falls to the floor with a slap like a wet mop. He has big, strong shoulders, probably from working in the stables. He's built like a defenseman for hoverball, thick-chested and a little soft around the belly, like he might get pudgy someday. As I take in the places that are hard and soft, the smooth spots and the patches of hair, I look away because it feels like I'm doing something I shouldn't, even though it should be the most natural thing in the world for my husband to have his shirt off around me. He wraps the towel around his shoulders and scoots to his room. I buzz with this feeling I can't get rid of. Part of me wants to follow him; the other part holds back.

When he emerges, he's wearing a hoodie again. He must own a million of the things. Before, he was wearing the black staff hoodie with the little Versailles logo. He wears that a lot. I think he hopes people won't recognize him or something. This hoodie is also black, but it says, *if(!empty($stomach)){keep Coding( );}* *else {orderPizza( );}*. Some code joke, like his other hoodie that says, *There's no place like 127.0.0.1.*

He looks like a turbo-nerd with his damp hair sticking up and his code hoodie, but even so, it's moments like this that I'm very sure I can like him. That I already like him quite a lot. There's something charming about how he takes up a lot of space but shrinks up with shyness.

But does he like me?

"You must be cold." I take a few steps toward him.

"Yeah . . . a little."

I take his clammy hands, so much larger than mine. One hand could probably cover my whole belly. The thought makes me tingle. I'm not sure what to do next. He's staring at our hands like they're some math problem he doesn't understand. I tug him toward the couch.

"Have you seen this film?"

"Don't think so."

"It's about a girl who works at a café. Then her cat runs away, and then she finds a body, and then that drone repair guy is trying to help her solve the murder."

"Hmm." Louis blinks at the screen. He looks like he doesn't even know what room we're in. "Interesting."

"Yep. She keeps using a red teapot at the café. It symbolizes death."

He relaxes a little. "Yeah? How'd you figure that out?"

I wave it off, since I completely stole this from Yolande. "Long story. You'd have to see the beginning."

I scooch up against his side and fold my arms around his biceps. He doesn't tense up like I was afraid he would, but he doesn't try to make me any more comfortable either. "Did you hear about the fires in Parée?"

Louis frowns. "No, what fires?"

So no one has told him either. Maybe Adelaide isn't a nervous history-obsessed glitchshow. Maybe she's right about us being watched and kept in the dark about the most important things. Maybe she's paranoid, and the reasons for keeping this from us are innocent at best, or the king lacks faith in our ability to handle the situation at worst. "I don't know the whole story. My history tutor told me about them. Then when I asked Noailles about it, she glitched and tried to change the subject."

"The court historian told you this?" His eyebrows furrow.

"What's wrong?"

"Nothing. I'll talk to Maurepas about this."

I wonder how much I can tell him. How far Adelaide meant when she said I should trust him. Talking to Maurepas doesn't help much, as far as I can see. "Why didn't anyone tell you about it? It seems important."

"They keep things from me all the time. Maurepas and Grand-Père don't like me making decisions." Louis slouches farther into the couch and crosses his arms.

"But you're the dauphin. What use are you if they don't tell you what's going on in Parée and let you make decisions?"

"Good question," he grumbles.

He looks totally miserable. I didn't mean to blame him, I just can't figure out what the frag is going on. "We could do something to help. I wanted to give funds to the victims as one of my charities. But Noailles wouldn't let me. She said I can't show favor to any side of the protests."

Louis scratches at his wet hair, eyes glued to the screen, where the heroine and the drone repairman pore over clues on a computer screen. "Yeah. It's like that when these things happen."

"But it shouldn't matter, if our subjects need help."

Louis nods. "You're right."

"So, what can we do?"

"Anything you do will make Miss Manners mad at you."

"She's always mad at me anyway."

He looks at me, finally with less sulking and more interest. "Yeah. I know how it is. I can never keep anyone happy either. I could give money from my personal account. Noailles and Maurepas won't like it, but they can't stop me, and it's important. Like you said."

"That's a great idea! I could do the same."

"Settled, then." He smiles and his hair is still sticking up. He looks cute, casual, happy. He looks like the Prince Charming people want to paint him as. I could kiss him right now. This could be so easy if he would let it be. I want to. I lean forward and then my stomach knots and I change tactics, because I'm just not used to making first moves.

Every time I lean in, every time I think about his lips, things start glitching. My stomach goes giga-flutter and I wonder if he doesn't want me kissing him. "Let's post about it on Pixter. So the people who are suffering will know we're with them. Then no one can stop you donating, because we've already promised."

The color in Louis's pink cheeks deepens. "I don't know . . . I don't really—I don't know how to get photos taken. I always look constipated."

"Because you need to relax. Just trust me. You don't even have to smile, because this is something serious. Here, let me sort your hair. Just a little." I flick a button on my holofone and a few tripod legs extend from the bottom. Instant selfie mode.

I don't want his hair too neat because the tousled look is working for him, so I just flatten a few cowlicks and ruffle out the middle. He really has beautiful hair. Thick, with a natural wave. Soft and smooth between my fingers. I want to run both hands through it. Touch the nape of his neck. Heat is pooling in my belly and rising in my cheeks. Instead I reach for his hand and hold it up to shoulder height in view of the camera.

We've never looked so closely at each other. Looking him straight in the eyes makes my head feel like champagne bubbles. Everything is a bit unreal.

Blushing, Louis looks down and then at my collarbone, then away again. "I—uh, I probably look all tense still."

"Close your eyes, then," I say.

"Huh?"

"Trust me." I lean my forehead against his. He twitches, backing away. I close my eyes, silently begging him to trust me on this one small thing. Allow me this one little victory. He gently tips his forehead against mine again.

"Snap," I say quietly, almost hating to wreck the moment with the shutter trigger. There's a soft *click* from the camera.

Photography is a beautiful thing. Because the finished product shows us nothing like we are and all that people wish us to be. We look solemn, hopeful, united, strong together. We look close. Close to each other and close to the people. The photo is vulnerable and firm at the same time.

"This is perfect. Thank you." I'll worry about the caption later. Something like, *Our hearts are with the fire victims in Parée. We pledge aid for everyone affected.* With our success giving me courage and a feeling like taking a plunge into a chilly pool, I throw my arms around his neck and don't let go, willing him to move, wanting to kiss him near his ear where his soapy-smelling hair is curling up. After a heartbeat or two, he shifts his arms so they're around my waist.

"You're a good photographer," he mumbles into my shoulder.

His arms go slack, but I ignore my cue to let go.

"Noailles thinks you don't like me."

"What?" He leans away to look at me, and I release him. "She said that?"

"She implied it."

"She doesn't know. No one ever asks me what I think; they just guess. I like you."

I fiddle with the edge of my skirt. I don't have the right words. I know I like his eyes, I like how his shampoo smells, and I like how strong his arms feel when he offers one to escort me. And that seems like enough to get on with. "You don't show it. We've waited a bit, and now . . . could we just . . ."

I blush. I never ask about consummation directly. I shouldn't have to.

"What about the bugs?" he asks.

"I don't even care anymore. I want people to stop talking about us."

"And you think it would be . . . that easy for you?"

I shrug. "I don't know. Would it really be so horrible, though? Am I that horrible?"

He shakes his head. "No. I don't really . . . I can't really talk about it. I just need some more time. It's hard to explain."

"What will time change?"

"A lot of things." He mumbles this so quietly I barely hear him. I don't understand him. I don't know what he wants or what magical transformation he thinks I'm going to make. He can say he likes me all he wants; I don't believe him. I cross my arms and try to dip my chin so he can't see the tears escaping. I can't believe I'm into him but he's not into me. It wasn't supposed to go like this. The courtiers will spread that news like it's trending if they find out. "You can be honest, you know, if you don't like me."

I don't know what I expected, but not to be squashed against his chest while he strokes my hair. "Please don't cry. I like you."

He's quiet for a minute, and I don't know what else to say. "I just need some more time," he says again.

"Okay."

He settles back to watch the film but lets me lean against his chest, warm and soft. It's nice. I guess it's progress. But I'm lost. Is he really just shy? Or is it something else?

His heartbeat is in my ear. It's strange to be so close to him, but also so far. I keep my ear pressed to this one part inside him that I can hear and feel. I listen to the slow and steady rhythm like it could tell me more of his secrets while I watch the girl with bobbed hair and the drone mechanic fall in love. My own heart fills with feelings that are strange and terrible and hard to understand. A little hope, some sadness, a lot of confusion, and something new and aching that feels kind of like *Sehnsucht*, but not exactly the same.

TWELVE

June 7, 3070, 2:38 p.m.

The photo of Louis and me was well-received by the people. I've had a spike in followers and engagement, and many compliments with their thanks for our aid. As well as some comparisons to Stan and Philippe that are less than favorable toward them. Their feeds have nothing to do with charity or goodwill for the people. It's all fashion and laser tag and, in Philippe's case, shirtless workout pics. Normally, that would be fine. But my recent post has put a spotlight on the rest of the Bourbons, and not in a good way.

Stan has not been happy.

But I don't care. I feel like I made this bet with him as well as Noailles. And now with Thérèse on my side, I'll be unstoppable.

She's rooting through my closet, digging for pieces that are Franc chic that still have my personality. We want to ride the wave of my popularity and post content that will be popular among the influencers and people our age.

"How about this one?" She shows me a solid black minidress, which I would normally hate, but it's made from a material that looks kind of like leather and kind of like spandex, with geometric patterns woven through, creating illusions of harsh edges where I should have curves.

"It's cool, but I'm not sure it's quite—"

"Wait a minute." Thérèse checks the collar. A soft array of blue-white LEDs, more subtle than any I've seen, lines some of the patterns, making the illusion deepen and take on a 3D effect.

"Okay, I'll never doubt you again. That's really cool. We can probably find a statue in the gardens that would look perfect with this."

"Or the black-light gallery!"

Thérèse is a genius. "What else?" I ask.

"You tell me. Quiz time."

I reach for my favorites in the wardrobe. A turquoise dress with a hot-pink grid pattern gets a no from Thérèse. So does a black-light graffiti-print blouse with a miniskirt. An iridescent crop top, skirt, and jacket combination gets her seal of approval, and so does a neon-green cardigan with black shorts and silver heels.

My favorite outfit hangs unworn, sad and forgotten in its gel-glo glory. "Can't we give gel-glo one more go? It's my favorite."

"Hmm . . ." Thérèse flicks through Pixter. "You know . . . some popular Pixter models have been wearing it lately. I think you low-key grabbed some interest. Especially after your last photo and your support for the fire victims were trending."

A small flicker of hope warms me. I was beginning to think I would lose my bet with Noailles. But trends can appear overnight. "So . . . a risk I can afford? Like a bold, set-a-trend risk?"

Thérèse chews her lips. "I'm not sure . . . if we shoot the other outfits and do something really cool for the gel-glo, and you publish them mixed together and in sets. Yeah, I think it might be bold enough to work."

"What about paintball? That's perfect for gel-glo."

"Oh, yes!" Thérèse squeals. "And you could get the boys in on it too. That should go over great."

"I'm not so sure. People have been pretty glitched over Stan and Philippe online. Have you seen? The public thinks they're spoiled." I feel only a little guilty over this. After all, it's not my fault Stan and Philippe never take part in social action or get involved with family charities.

"True," Thérèse says slowly. "But I don't think it will hurt to show you're making an effort at being part of the family. And maybe this will take some heat off them, since people are loving you at the moment."

I grin at those words. I don't even worry if she means it will make people look more favorably on Louis's and my awkward union and the alliance between rivals. They're loving me. For the first time, I feel like I'm doing my job right. And for the first time in weeks, I can look at my clothes in excitement instead of worrying they all hide mics and trackers.

"Shall we shoot tomorrow?" Thérèse asks.

"Absolutely! I've got lessons this afternoon."

"Of course. They must teach our poor Austro dauphine the Franc ways, I'm sure. But soon you'll slay us with fashion."

"That's the plan."

"*Salut!*" She gives me *la bise* and dashes, leaving me just enough time to gather my purse for lessons.

I stop for a few selfies on my way to the classroom, because I'm finally feeling like I've got my footing, doing my job. Things are now what they should be, and I'm managing to make everyone happy, including me.

When I get to the classroom, it's dark except for the purple neon around the smart board. The air conditioning is full blast as usual and pinpoints my bare arms with goose bumps. I'm wearing a silver picnic dress. No sleeves; should have brought a sweater.

What will Adelaide have in store for me this time? I've been wondering what to ask her about the fire. It was hidden from me, just like she said, and hidden from Louis too. But so what? Who did it and what am I supposed to do about it?

My holofone says Adelaide is five minutes late. Staff are never late, from what I've seen. But who knows, maybe being the court historian is a busy job. There's a flicker in the corner of my eye, and I turn hurriedly. Was something on the smart board just now?

A voice— "She's here" or something like that . . . Was it outside? I shiver. Where is Adelaide?

I can't stand to be in this room another minute. Maybe nothing happened to the smart board at all, but I'm wasting time sitting around in here. I'm about to open the door when it hits my toes. The little squeak that escapes me is not dignified.

With my heart racing, I realize it's just Noailles. But she's not who I expected to see.

"*Pardon*, madame," she says. "Take a seat, if you please."

"Where is Adelaide?" I ask.

"I will be covering your lessons today."

"But why?"

Noailles hates questions. I can tell by the pinch of her lips. But she is duty bound to answer them. "You will have a new history tutor presently. Madame Adelaide is no longer employed at Versailles."

The goose bumps return. I try to hide the panic that flashes through me. Was it because I spoke up about the fires? "Where did she go?"

"That is not your concern, madame."

"It is! She was my tutor. We were in the middle of important lessons."

Noailles cocks an eyebrow at me. "It was not my impression that you were overly concerned with your history lessons."

Anger raises heat to my cheeks. Her passive-aggressive comments are a virus that bugs my code. It takes all my training and willpower to keep a cool head. I arrange a fake smile to match her own. "I was not, but Madame Adelaide made them fascinating."

Noailles is silent for a moment too long. "I have no doubt . . . but for now, you will have to make do with me."

"Perhaps I can keep in touch with Madame Adelaide. There were a few follow-up questions I had about my last lesson."

"That would not be advisable."

Panic flashes through me again. Noailles turns her back to me and pulls up materials for today's lesson. But instead of anything about the Event, she just brings up some stupid video about Versailles's founder, the Sun King. While her back is turned, I flip through my contacts and find the folder with my tutors, then Adelaide.

I type: What happened? Where are you? You were right about the fires.

I wait all lesson for her to answer me. I never receive a reply.

THIRTEEN

June 9, 3070, 10:14 p.m.

"Are you going to fold?" Stan stares me down across the table, face blank except for his dark eyebrows scrunched up a little. He's got a really good poker face. So good that I yank the VR goggles off my head for a better look at him, wincing when the band catches at my hair. The swirling stars, planets, and droid dealer disappear, replaced by the minimalist setting of Stan's rooms.

"Taking the goggles off won't help you," says Stan.

I try not to glance at Thérèse or Yolande, because last time Thérèse whispered to fold, Stan disqualified me. Vingt-et-un isn't my best game. I prefer the VR slots. My hand is worth eighteen, not bad. Stan is being pushy, so maybe he wants me to fold. Stan is always pushy, though.

My eyes stray to the big fish tank behind him. Some spiny thing with big eyes stares back at me. Fish still creep me out, whether they end up on my dinner plate or swim through one of the many tanks Stan has. I can always smell them in here too. The lightest swampy stink under all the lemon air freshener.

I should play it safe. Last week I went a little overdrive with the slots and had to ask Louis for money. There's a small *pop* behind me, and I glance over my shoulder. Louis is sprawled on a leather couch, aiming a Kurbo gun at the ceiling. It's a goofy-looking kid's toy that shoots sticky darts. The ceiling is too high for it to reach most of the time, but there are three little darts stuck up there. I think he's aiming for the people in the frescoes.

I don't know why Louis is even here. He's not talking to us, and he hasn't slept in my room in a week. Says he has a cold. I'm just hoping I didn't scare him off last time we were alone together.

I raise my bet by four hundred francs-bits. No reaction from Stan except a raise of his brows. Thérèse and Philippe fold, Yolande raises fifty, then we reveal our hands.

Yolande has sixteen and Stan has seventeen. "I win!"

"*Bien, bien,*" says Yolande.

"You thought you were so clever," I tease Stan.

"I am clever," he grumbles. "And still ahead. Can't win them all."

"She's been winning a lot these days," says Thérèse. "Queen of the comeback. Did you see you got gel-glo trending?"

"Of course!" I couldn't tell if Noailles was pleased or phished when I showed her my trending style. She always has the same pinched smile. But either way, my fashion is now officially in my own hands. I'm going to wear green gel-glo for that vaccines photo-shoot thing, and she can't do anything about it.

Ever since I put the outfits together and we did a Pixter photo shoot, the Francs can't resist gel-glo. Last week, I couldn't remember the Austro word for a dessert I was trying to explain to Thérèse, so I might be a Franc for real now. That gives me a bittersweet happiness, *bonheur doux-amer.*

"I still think gel-glo is tacky, and so do probably a lot of other people," says Stan.

I snort. "*N'importe quoi*. Half of fashion is errors that become trends. You need to take risks."

Stan rolls his eyes. "Just start another round."

The holo-cards shimmer in neon colors so bright and real, but my fingers pass through them like smoke when I flick them upward to sit in a fan.

"She's right," says Philippe. "Gel-glo was supposed to be a cruiser paint, but a mechanic spilled some all over his coveralls. He lit up like he was radioactive, his girlfriend put it on Pixter, now ding! It's everywhere, and our sis is turbo-trending."

"You know a lot about fashion, Philippe, considering you rarely have a shirt any time you post to Pixter," Stan says.

"I'm going to ignore that and go easy on you, Stanny, since you've only got a few weeks left as a free man," Philippe says.

We've all been trying to be nice to Stan since he's really miserable about getting married. Everything we've heard about his fiancée makes her sound awful. She's super snarky on the Apps, which I would have imagined makes her a perfect match for Stan, but he seems to think otherwise.

"Until I'm married to a pig," he mumbles.

I feel my face go red and regret doing anything nice for him. It's one thing to call her out for being rude. But a pig? Unnecessary. I can see this doesn't sit well with Thérèse either. She glares at him, but it's not her place to criticize a prince of the blood.

There's a whistling sound as one of Louis's foam darts smacks Stan in the back of the head. "That's mean," Louis says.

"So what? It's true. She's ugly."

Another dart bounces off Stan's ear.

"So are you."

Stan's face is danger-zone red and purple. "Knock it off, you little dongle."

Another one bounces off his shoulder.

"Louis, please. Just let him play." I hate it when Louis and Stan argue and spoil everyone's good time.

"You're siding with him? What if it was you, and he was saying that stuff about you?" says Louis.

"I'm not siding with him. I just—"

But Stan talks over me. "Doesn't matter, because you got a hot wife. Not that it matters much with you."

Before I can worry about resisting the urge to slap Stan, Louis sits up and fires three more darts that all bounce off Stan's head. Stan jumps up and charges at Louis, trying to wrestle the gun from him.

"*Mon Dieu*. Really?" says Yolande while Philippe cheers them on.

"*Arrêtez!*" I get to my feet too. "Knock it off!" I reach into the tangle of them, trying to get the Kurbo gun, but one of them twists his arm to the left. Thrown off-balance, I fall on my *der-rière* with a stinging *thud*.

"Stop, stop!" Despite the breach of etiquette, Thérèse dashes over and grabs one of Stan's arms. But Louis has already abandoned the Kurbo and knelt next to me.

"I'm sorry. Are you okay?"

I don't want to look at anyone. Don't want them to know how glitched I am over what Stan said. "I'm fine."

Philippe does a loud whistle.

"Have you ever considered chilling out?" says Yolande.

I ignore Louis trying to help me to my feet and stand up on

my own. "I think I should go to bed. Luckily, I'm fine, but if you guys ever fight like that again, I'm going to go boss mode."

I smooth out my gold skirt in a way I hope is super dignified.

"Sorry," Stan mumbles, but he doesn't even look at me.

Yolande and Thérèse both hug me and say good night before I march back to my rooms. I so want to just collapse into bed, but you can't do that at stupid Versailles. I'll have to summon the maids to help me change. Louis is following a few paces back, shuffling along. He's acting like Mops used to when I scolded him for something. The thought of my dog makes me want to cry, but I don't.

After I'm changed, I crawl into bed and scan the Apps, looking at photos of people who are happier than I am.

I was pretty sure Louis would stay in his own room again, which is fine by me. But of course, the one time I don't want him to, he turns up. I'm on my side with my back to him, and I don't turn over when he slides under the blankets.

"Sorry," he says.

"Thought you had a cold."

He clears his throat. "Getting better. But I can leave if you want."

I think of telling him I just want to go to sleep. Or ignoring him. But Mama will be phished if she finds out I kicked my husband out of bed. My stomach twists. It feels like it's been a knot of nerves for weeks. I take too long deciding what I should say to Louis and the blankets rustle as he gets up to leave.

"No." I hold in a sigh. "It's okay. Stay."

The blankets settle back heavily on me.

"Are you sure?"

"Yeah."

It's like I can feel the tension in him through the blankets. The same tension that's sitting in my stomach. I flip over to my back. "What did you do all that for? Stan usually picks fights. Not you."

"Bad mood, I guess. He's an ass. He shouldn't say things like that about his fiancée. Or you."

For a second, I'm annoyed, because I'm not helpless and I've proven I can hold my own against Stan. But then I think of Louis's face when he shot the darts at him. Louis is normally so calm. I'd never seen him look that angry. I nudge his leg with my toes. "Were you jealous because you thought I sided with him?"

In the dark, I see the shadow of his elbow as he rubs his eyes. "No . . . I don't know."

"Well, you don't have to be. That's really dumb."

"Is it? I don't know. I just got really mad. Don't know what came over me."

"Come on. Stan is like my competition. He's always taking a swing at me and trying to mess me up on the Apps."

Louis doesn't answer.

"You know when I say you're my favorite brother, I'm not kidding, right? Like, if I got to choose, I'd still pick you. Even over Philippe."

He snorts like he doesn't believe me. I nudge him with my foot again. "I'm serious! I got bored the other day, so I took one of those dumb quizzes for kids. 'Which Bourbon Brother Should You Marry?' And guess what? I got you."

He's silent for a minute. "What kind of quiz?" He sounds like I just told him I used advanced calculus to determine we're meant to be. Is he serious?

"You know. Like a quiz from those dumb preteen feeds?

'Who's Your Royal Soul Mate?' 'What's the Best Boy Band?' Come on, there's loads of them about the Bourbon brothers."

"Why? Like, why are there quizzes about me?"

I don't know whether to laugh or be frustrated that he's buffering over this. "I don't know. It's just something girls like to do. They think you're cute."

"No, they don't."

"Yes, they do."

"They like Philippe. I know that much."

"And you!" I give him a sharper prod with my toes. How does he have no idea? He's a prince. And princes have fans. "Some people even like Stan, for some reason."

"Ew. Not as flattered, then."

"Right?" I giggle and he laughs a little.

"That's still really awkward."

"Not really. People like you. Didn't you see the comments on our wedding photos?"

"No."

"Did you even look at them?"

"Yeah, but I just kind of glanced. I didn't read the comments."

I groan and open Pixter. "Seriously? You're hopeless. Look. Look at these comments."

"I don't want to. It glitches me out."

"But they're good!" I hold the holofone out to him, but he twists away and grumbles.

"Look at them, look at them!" I lean over his shoulder. "Look at those heart eyes!"

He covers his face like a little kid. "Nooo. Stop."

I give up and toss my holofone at the nightstand. "You're so weird."

"Yup."

I wish I knew what to do for him. Quietly, I ask, "Why are you so embarrassed?"

He flips on the star lights, then rubs his eyes while he unleashes a heavy sigh. "I'm always embarrassed. That's like . . . my permanent state of being."

"Why?"

"Don't know." He's frowning at the patterns of stars revolving over the canopy like they've got better answers than he does. I grab his hand.

"You know you can talk to me, right?"

"Yeah." He raises my hand up and kisses the back of it. Twice. I hold my breath. For a second, there's only him and the warm, dry press of his lips on the smooth skin of my hand. I've been kissed on the hand a hundred times, and it's stupid how this makes me jitter like I'm buffering. But it feels precious. From Louis, I think it means a lot.

The sensation lingers, and makes me wonder what it would be like to really kiss him. I'm too afraid to find out. Instead I tuck my face into the crook of his shoulder and try to enjoy the moment as it is. At Versailles, it seems like anything beautiful, anything lovely, becomes something sad or scary if I think about it too much.

"I'm going to make it up to you." Louis's voice rumbles in my ear.

"It's okay."

"It really wasn't." He places a big hand on my hip. "I want to do something nice for you. Will you let me?"

It's like all the blood inside me has rushed to the point where his hand rests. "I'll let you be as nice as you want to be."

Too much. He goes shy again. "You're funny," he says, smiling, but looking away. His hand shifts, and my heart lurches. I grab his arm, above his elbow. He freezes. I feel like if he takes his hand away, something will be lost that I can't get back. Hope, maybe.

He settles and his hand stays. My heart slows. Louis looks at me like he's reading my code, can see it in my eyes. The passing minutes are strange. I'm not sure if the quiet is really uncomfortable or as peaceful as I've ever been with another person. I think about kissing him. A lot. The thought keeps creeping in, every other breath. But there's some energy passing between us as if we're both running the same program. A kiss might break the code.

FOURTEEN

June 15, 3070, 1:23 p.m.

When Mercy asks me to meet him in the courtyard, I'm sure I have to go meet some straggler guest from Stan and Josephine's wedding. It wasn't as big a deal as my marriage, but the palace has been packed with dukes and duchesses from all over the kingdom and a few from the Sardinian States, where Josephine comes from.

When we enter the courtyard, I'm greeted by a yapping little blur that runs straight for me.

I can hardly believe what I'm seeing.

It's Mops!

As I drop to my knees and reach out for my little friend, I think my heart might burst. My pug scampers into my arms, trembling with excitement just like I am. I snuggle him close and bury my nose in his bristly fur while he covers me with slobbery kisses. He smells like home.

"Mops, my little Mops! I can't believe you're here! Are you sure you're not a holo?"

Mops wiggles so much I can barely hold on to him. I manage to get to my feet, still holding my squirming dog, and stretch out an arm to Mercy.

"Thank you, Ambassador Mercy! Thank you so much!"

He leans down and gives me a very formal hug, patting me on the back. "Well, it wasn't all me. Thank the dauphin."

"Louis brought Mops here?"

"Of course."

"Where is he? I need to find him."

Mercy laughs. "Well, goodness. I don't know."

It's a sunny day, so he's probably taking lessons outside. I race into the gardens, Mops speeding along after me. He barks and bounds like a rabbit. He's going to love running around in the gardens!

I check three different fountains before I find Louis tucked up beside the one with the horses. He's bent over, reading a book. Mops seems to sense a friend and beats me to him, pawing his little feet up Louis's leg.

Louis sets down his book and scoops him up. "He's cuter than his pictures!"

I nearly knock both of them into the fountain, trying to hug them at the same time. Mops cries and yaps. He can hardly contain himself, and neither can I.

"Thank you, thank you!" I kiss Louis on the cheek a few times and once in his hair. I'm kind of hoping he'll kiss me properly, but he's too busy wrestling a jittery Mops, who is, I admit, an adorable distraction.

"Hopefully this makes up for . . . everything," he says.

I sit on the grass and scoot back so I can take a picture of them. "This is so cute, look!"

He barely glances at it, embarrassed like when I showed him he had fans.

"I'm going to tag you on Pixter. It'll get so many likes. You'll see."

He hands me Mops, who leaps right into my arms.

"Are you happy?" Louis asks.

"Of course!" I cuddle my Mops and think of home. No *Sehnsucht* this time.

Mops yaps, and I follow his pointing snout to see Stan and Josephine wandering up a garden path. They both walk all rigid, Stan with his hands in his pockets. Josephine has a vape. She's a few steps behind him, like it's a coincidence that they're walking in the same direction. Mops barks again and she looks over. Maybe she likes dogs. I wave, meaning it as an invitation, but she speeds up a few steps to catch up with Stan.

I'm not sure why she's so hard to talk to. I tried my hardest to be kind to her, remembering how nervous I was when I got married. So at the wedding dinner last night, I asked her what music she liked, and she shrugged. Then she picked her teeth. With her finger! I thought Noailles was going to pass out.

"They're both so miserable, you would have thought they were made for each other," I say.

"He could try to be decent if he won't be welcoming," Louis says.

"Is he really just that much of a dongle?"

"Yes." Louis shrugs. "Well, I don't think he was ready to get married at all. There was some girl he was trying to hook up with. Louise Bertière, maybe. And he had a boyfriend like a year ago, but then he stopped coming around and Stan was super glitchy about it."

"Really?"

"Yeah. Not that getting married stops him from having someone else. Doesn't stop the king."

Louis is so different from his grandfather. Even though I'm

struggling to get closer to him, I have the feeling that I won't have to worry about competing with mistresses and favorites. Stan and Philippe will probably continue their grandfather's tradition.

"Maybe we should try to help her. Do something fun," I say. "They're definitely bombing on the Apps."

"Any ideas?"

"Not really. But I'll think about it."

Mops is so excited, he's shaking. I'm afraid he might pee on my leg or something, but I'm so happy to see him that I probably wouldn't care much if he did. I scoop him up and hug him close. He grunts and whines, happier than I've ever seen him.

"I know. We'll never be apart again now."

"I know it must be hard," Louis says. "Being far from home. I hoped Mops would help a little."

"Oh! I thought he was a birthday present!" If Mops wasn't a birthday gift, that means I could ask for the other thing . . . the one that's been on my mind since Thérèse mentioned it.

"No," says Louis. "Coincidence. We'll have a party for you, and other presents."

"Well, I really don't need presents." I give him a slow smile. "There's only one thing I need."

Louis glances around like he's looking for an escape. "Mops was no problem. We can't just not give you gifts."

"I didn't mean Mops, though there is no cuter present. Thérèse and Yolande are going to a masked rave in Parée on Friday. We could go too, totally disguised. No one has to know it's us."

Louis scratches his jaw. "That's going to be really difficult."

"That's what makes it fun! It'll be a giga-rush! Oh, oh! And Stan and Josephine could come. She'll love it. It'll be perfect. Stan and Philippe go out to Parée all the time, don't they?"

"Yeah, but it's not as bad for them to get caught at something like a rave as it is for us. No one would like it. They'd say we have enough parties here without going to Parée for them."

"Come on. We could see what Parée is really like. Just forget all this and have fun for one night."

"I don't know . . . I already pulled a lot of strings to get Mops."

"We won't get caught. Yolande's husband will help. He'll pick us up."

"It'd make you really happy, huh? For your birthday?"

"I'd be totally pinging! I was dying to go when Thérèse told me about it."

He smiles. It's a very cute smile. "How could I say no, then?" he says quietly.

"You're the best! I'll get it all arranged. It'll be great, I promise. Oh man, I can't believe I'm going to a Parée laser *soirée*! I've seen so many on the Apps." I bounce Mops up and down while he barks and wiggles.

Louis just smiles again. His smile needs to be all over Pixter.

FIFTEEN

June 16, 3070, 8:27 p.m.

I'm seated between Josephine and Philippe at dinner, with Stan and Louis across from us. She doesn't like roast lamb, so I try to bond with her.

"Me neither," I tell her. "Lambs are so cute. There are so many other things to eat."

"Cuteness is meaningless. Lamb is not sustainable. I would prefer to never eat meat." She sighs. "I'd just as soon have tofu instead."

I've seen it on the Apps, but I've never had it. "Is it good?"

"Duh," she says.

"What's tofu?" Philippe asks.

Josephine sighs, rather unnecessarily. We all know he isn't the brightest, but there's no reason to be rude. "You know, soybeans? It's, like, the most common meat substitute."

"Well, I've never heard of it," says Philippe.

"Of course you haven't," Josephine mutters.

"I haven't either," says Louis.

This surprises me. It's a bit glitchy. Like, such a common thing to overlook. "You're kidding," I say to him. "You know, it's square, kinda cream-colored, soft. Gets grilled and covered with sauce a lot. Or crumbled up."

Louis frowns. "I had no idea. That sounds odd."

I glance at Josephine. She rolls her eyes. Clearly she just thinks the Bourbon boys are uncultured, but I know Louis better than that. I give him a puzzled quirk of my brows, and he shrugs.

"We eat meat here," says Stan. "There are more and more farms every year. Thinking about meat like it's a commodity gets us nowhere."

"If people thought of it that way ages ago, maybe we wouldn't be in this mess," says Josephine.

"What, like if people ate some soft bean cubes, the Event wouldn't have happened?" Stan snorts in disgust.

"My god," Josephine says. "You don't know what tofu is either."

"No, and I don't care what it is."

I look from Stan to Louis, because something about this just doesn't add up. How does a simple concept like tofu not exist at Versailles? "You've never seen it on the Apps?"

"Nope." Louis shrugs. Then again, he's not one for scrolling the Apps. Maybe I'm making something out of nothing. But the smallest things have glitched me out and felt weird. Ever since Adelaide vanished.

"Is this some Sicili thing?" Philippe asks.

"No, you brainlag, it's from Shinkoku, I think."

But before we can get to the bottom of the tofu mystery, there's a big clattering noise as everyone rises to their feet because the king has entered. This is a formal dinner of state, so we couldn't eat a thing until his arrival. Late, but the king can be late to whatever he wants.

"Good evening, *mes amis*." He gives the great expanse of table a toothy grin. "Sit, sit. I assure you I'm already ahead of you on glasses of wine."

Server bots scoot in above us, gleaming and glowing brighter than the cracked old fresco. They descend and deposit the aperitif, a flute of champagne, and two canapés. I'm still thinking about tofu, trying to remember if I've had it before. Maybe Francs shun it because they're foodies and have really particular ideas about meals.

Before we eat the canapés, the king rises again, which means we must all do the same. I glance at Louis and he shrugs at me. No idea what Grand-Père is about to announce.

"Before we begin eating, I must introduce new members to court. And they are novel, I must say. Just novel!" The king gestures toward the grand entrance to the dining room. There's a slight tremble to his hand, and I can't tell if it's from nerves or excitement. "Monsieur Angoulême and SveroTech have kindly gifted us with two android guards! They will be personal guards to our family, and we welcome this great advance in technology to Versailles." He raises his champagne in toast.

I copy him mechanically, but I'm glitching. I never responded to Angoulême. Never brought up my meeting with Axel with Louis. Is it really possible that . . .

I look at the entrance, school my face into a neutral, subdued photo-shoot expression. Because of course it's him. Axel Fersen and another android, nearly as handsome. But I prefer the curl to Axel's hair. The glimmer to his eyes. He's a robot, so why is my face burning? Why am I panicking? Why do I feel like I can tell from one look at his face that I prefer him to his colleague? It shouldn't be like this.

Fersen gives a respectful bow to the king. But then—it really, really shouldn't be like this—he looks *right at me*. And he smiles slightly. I think my cheeks are molten lava. How much concealer do I have on?

I glance down at my canapés.

"Are you all right?" Elisabeth asks from her seat across from me.

"Yes, why?" I say far too quickly.

"You looked kind of spooked. Do you not like androids?"

Elisabeth is really perceptive, apparently, though not quite correct.

"I—er, I can hardly have an opinion. I've had so little experience with them." I can hear how stiff the answer is. Elisabeth, a gem and a star, has the good grace to drop the subject.

Stan does not. "Handsome enough, aren't they? You can tell they were originally used for pleasure."

"Oh, stop," Elisabeth says. "These are soldiers."

"Do you think they'd let me have a look at their code?" Louis's eyes are bright with curiosity.

Josephine nearly spits out the champagne she was drinking and snorts into a napkin.

"What?" Louis asks. "Is that rude to ask or something?"

"Do you think they're handsome too?" Elisabeth teases.

Louis squints down the table. "They're very interesting, but yes, I suppose they're handsome fellows."

I dare to follow Louis's gaze. The blond android beside Axel is busy greeting a duke and duchess. Axel is also engaged, but then seems to sense the stares of the royal family. He could look at Elisabeth or Stan or Louis. Instead, once again, he looks directly at me. Then he raises his glass in a small toast and turns away.

I promise myself not to look his way again for the rest of dinner.

SIXTEEN

June 17, 3070, 11:52 p.m.

This is more exciting than anything I've ever done in my whole entire life. It's rave night, and Georgette is sneaking me out through the servants' staircase. The *servants' staircase*! Miss Manners would fry a chip if she found out.

Georgette threw a Versailles staff jacket around my shoulders. With the hood up, no one notices me while we pass. I follow close behind her, head ducked, hiding my face and, most of all, my smile. I can't seem to erase it!

We duck through a humid hallway. Clatter from the kitchens echoes somewhere to the right. Georgette opens a little door. Outside, a chef smokes under the dim light of one blue neon arch over the door. He gives us a nod and a "*bonsoir*" that Georgette returns before rushing me behind a hedge. She ducks between trees and shrubs, skirting along the edge of the *orangerie*. A giggling pair stumble across the path in front of us. I tuck my chin closer to my chest, but they don't even give us a glance. Now I understand why Louis lurks around in the staff hoodie. It really does make us invisible to the courtiers.

Georgette stops near the edge of the Grand Trianon. A figure standing near the round pool turns toward us. I see a flash of pink hair.

"It's Thérèse," I say.

"I think you'll be fine from here." Georgette gives me a nod toward Thérèse.

I take her by the elbow. "You really should come with us. It will be so much fun."

Georgette smiles and shakes her head. "I really couldn't."

"But why not?"

"Have fun tonight." I know she won't go for reasons I don't quite understand. She looks so much older than me somehow, even though she isn't.

"*Bonsoir* and thanks again." I throw my arms around Georgette's shoulders in a quick hug. She seems startled and barely returns it with a loose and awkward wrap of her arms. Maybe she doesn't like hugs and I shouldn't have done it. But when I let go, her smile matches mine.

She helps me shimmy out of my staff jacket, then we wave goodbye and I dash over to Thérèse, who gushes over my dress.

I'm wearing a flared multilayer black dress studded with an array of blue, green, and purple LEDs. We compare masks, which glow with emoji faces. Mine is purple, just two round Os for eyes and a tongue sticking out of the curving mouth.

Yolande had Jules bring their cruiser around and land by the back of the Grand Trianon. No would think it was me and Louis or Stan and Josephine in that black cruiser. We'll seem like random courtiers out for a night cruise.

This is my first time meeting Jules. He's very serious, with a square jaw and really neat hair, but he's funny beneath the seriousness.

Louis laughs at him when he tells a story about an old guy

from Kursk they met on a cruise who tried to build a campfire on deck.

"Seventy-five degrees out and wearing the most outrageous fur hat," says Yolande.

"Turns to us and says, 'No fire. No fishing at sea. Thirty meters from rails when in air. I pay them to scold me like child!'" Jules says this in a flawless Kurskan accent and Louis chuckles again.

I'm glad he's having fun, because I was afraid I'd dragged him out to have a bad time. Josephine really *is* having a bad time, apparently, and barely speaks. She's covered her dark eyes and plain, makeup-free features with her mask, flipping it on and off. It's red with two Xs for eyes.

The cruise story seems to have perked her up, though, because she stops tinkering with the mask to say, "Did you see any air pirates?"

"Air pirates? *Merde, non.* That would have been awful." Jules waves away the idea.

"Sounds boring." Josephine goes back to flipping her mask.

"They're viruses," says Jules. "Toss people overboard so you end up as a splat in a field somewhere. That's what happens if you come across them. None of that romantic stuff in films."

Josephine sighs and props her chin on her hand.

"If you want to get the shits from radioactive fish, go be a pirate. Be my guest," says Stan.

"Maybe I will. Better than being here," she grumbles.

Louis looks at her all sad, then at me. Maybe we shouldn't have invited the unhappy couple. I take his hand and give it a squeeze.

I can't help but do a very Thérèse-style squeak when I see La Tour Ancienne. It flashes neon yellow, then green, then it shows all these bubbles and a message across the middle for Diet Volt. We're skimming lower and lower, passing through fog, steam.

"Remember! Fake names if anyone asks!" says Thérèse. "I shall be Charlotte." She plunks her mask on, and it glows pink with hearts for her eyes.

"I'm Louise!" I yell.

Louis thinks that's hilarious, but of course no one else gets it.

The cruiser takes a dip to the right as we descend. I reach inside the neckline of my dress for the switch on my LEDs. Thérèse squeals and applauds when they light up.

"Masks on, yeah?" Yolande slides hers on, lit up with swirling turquoise eyes. "And call me Mirabelle."

"What's your name?" I ask Louis.

"Albert." He lights up his mask, which has a mouth all lined like it's got stitches.

I yank him to his feet because I can't wait another second to leave the cruiser.

Jules lowers his mask and says, "Remember, there will be some courtiers from the Second Estate here who could recognize you, so lie low, *non*?"

Yolande and Thérèse ignore him. Shrieking with laughter, they bounce out of the cruiser.

Stan and Josephine follow them. They constantly do this thing where they kind of glare at each other in quick glances. Mama was glitching after their wedding, because she thought they would have a baby before me and Louis, or that Grand-Père King would like Josephine better, but both of those things would take a miracle. Louis hops out and extends a hand to help me out of the cruiser, all princely.

We're greeted by a swarm of LED masks. Some people wear glowing face paint. The masked and twisted faces are eerie but exciting. A group of people fix curious stares on us, trying to tell who we are behind the masks. Jules hustles us inside.

The laser *soirée* is in an old church that's been redone as a club. A bunch of creepy statues of saints hold LED lamps and black lights. Tiny little lights climb the walls to the towering ceiling, fading from pink to purple to blue. It might look a little sketch, but it's easily one of the top ten most aesthetic places I've ever been.

Yolande tosses a glow ring over my head. I grab Louis's wrist and drag him after us. The dance floor is so crowded that I barely have to dance, because I can't move.

The place is a mass of bodies bending, twisting, spinning. It's smoky in here, with a burning-grass stench. Someone in a glowing skeleton outfit dances snakelike and I can't look away. It's like I'm in a dream or a music vid. Stan shows up with drinks that are gone in record time. Josephine barely dances, just kind of rocks back and forth.

Thérèse arcs a glow hoop in circles and that clears us some room to hop around. And of course, that's the moment Louis yells in my ear that he's going to the courtyard for air. The moment he could actually dance a little. I know he snuck us out for me. I know dancing is out of his comfort zone, but I wanted him to have fun with me. I wanted him to see what I like. Maybe find out there's more to life than his computer and riding a horse around and mucking out stables. I've tried to show an interest in Louis's hobbies. The least he could do is get more involved in mine.

"Dance with me!" I pull his arm.

He blinks, looks around. Looking for an escape. "Uhh . . . in a few minutes?"

I won't force him. If dancing with me is so painful, I'll let him escape. "Whatever." I turn away from him. Enough drinks and dancing can dull the disappointment. Can stop me from wondering for the thousandth time what's between Louis and me that stops him from getting closer to me.

"Teach me, teach me!" I point to Thérèse's glow hoop, and she puts it over my arms. I think I've had too many drinks to spin it right, because I keep dropping it. It goes flying and nearly hits a guy, but he grins with his big painted-on smile and dances over to give it back.

We dance and dance, and then there's this huge rumbling bass and everyone cheers, then crushes in closer. I can barely move. There's knees and elbows everywhere. Someone steps on my foot. Another girl spills a drink down my arm. It's getting hard to breathe behind my mask, but I can't take it off. Where are Yolande and Thérèse?

A tall guy with thick arms backs right into me and I almost fall over. There are so many people around, and I feel small and made of glass. I look for openings and duck toward them. Keep jumping and darting for exits until finally, I squeeze off the dance floor.

I gasp for breath while a couple dashes by, shrieking and laughing. Everything's under control. Nothing to be worried about. It's just my first rave outside court. The only time I've been outside any court without parents. But I'll be eighteen in a few days. I can handle it.

"Are you all right?"

I turn around and nearly glitch.

Axel Fersen is here.

We are all busted.

He looks so amazing that I forget for a moment that I'm wearing a mask. Maybe I'm not revealed yet. But no, I must be. He must have followed us. He's not dressed for a rave. Nothing glowing, except his perfectly pressed shirt is all weird neon green, shining under the lights.

Do androids like raves? What do they do for fun? Can they even *have* fun? I can't stop my thoughts from spinning. I don't know what to say. I can't tell whether he recognizes me. Even though his expression, his kind dark eyes, are friendly, it's difficult to tell what he's thinking. His face is too perfect. I think that's why.

I'm married. I probably shouldn't analyze his face for imperfections. But here we are. Perfect teeth, perfect nose, perfect dark eyes, perfect light brown hair. Just a slightly lopsided mouth. Whoever designed him is a genius for that one quirk. "Do you need help?" He smiles in a calm, cool way. Nothing nervous about it. Nothing self-conscious. He has the grace I've been taught to have as a princess, except I need to fake about 60 percent of it. His seems real.

"No, no! It's just crashing out there, right?" My laugh sounds glitched. Thank gigs I'm wearing a mask.

He takes a few smooth steps closer. "You don't like to dance?"

"Oh, no, I love it! But I thought I'd get crushed. Needed some space."

He looks out at the dancers, smiling a little. The lights catch bits of shine in his hair. He's way too much. Does he recognize me, though? I still can't tell or guess what he's doing here.

"You know . . . ," he says. "I don't know how to dance. Maybe you could show me."

That answers the androids raving question. "Nothing to learn! It's easy. You just . . . move."

I haven't once been embarrassed of dancing in front of anyone, so why do I suddenly feel like I've forgotten how to raise my arms and sway? "See? Easy . . ." I could take his hands and dance with him. No one would know. I'm wearing a mask. For one short minute. One minute, then never again.

There are a thousand reasons I shouldn't. Because he works for the palace. Because he's an android. Because he's a beautiful android. Because I'm married.

But has Louis tried to find me since going out for air? No, he hasn't. No sign of him. The loneliness that emerges whenever I wish for Louis to touch me or hold me aches.

I grab Axel's hand and slide closer to him. His hand is warm and smooth. How is it possible that he's not made from flesh and blood?

He rocks and moves all fluid, like the no-dancing thing was a lie. I step back so I can twirl around once, and then he spins me back toward him. My shoulder blade brushes his chest and I'm way too aware of it. Unspun and arms untangled, I drop his hand and hop back. He sways and steps like an expert.

"Don't dance, huh?"

He stills. The soft smile hasn't left his face once. "I'm a fast learner."

"Really fast."

"Yes. Really fast." He holds out his hand and I hesitate. He's trying to dance again when I really, really shouldn't.

"I should get some air." Repeating Louis's excuse. That's a

sure sign he really was trying to run from me. Axel gazes at me in a way that makes my heart feel like it's going to pound right out of my dress. Looking at me like the last thing he wants to do is run.

"You must be really warm under that mask," he says.

"Nope! I'm fine."

"And, I imagine, very beautiful."

And blushing like a twelve-year-old under here. "Masked rave. I must maintain the mystery."

He leans down toward me, eyes twinkling. He has to speak right into my ear for me to hear his low voice, which tickles the little hairs at the nape of my neck. "It's all right, Madame Dauphine. I'm not here by coincidence."

Son of a glitch, I'm such an idiot. Of course he knows me. Maybe the stiffness that seizes me is visible, because he speaks again. Still right in my ear.

"My job is to keep you and your husband safe. Including your secrets. They're safe with me."

I'm grateful for the mask, because I catch my jaw hanging slack in an undignified way. "Really?"

"You have my word." He gives a bow.

Someone has stopped to stare at his weird behavior. They're wearing a huge pair of neon goggles, pointed right at Fersen. He snatches my hand and plants a kiss there, covering formality with flirtation.

Oh gigs. This is danger. This is bad. I need to find Louis. I need to channel all this attention toward him. Need to convince him to dance or go for a walk or something. "I—I should find Louis." I want to say *my husband*, but my mouth can't form the words.

"Of course." Axel nods.

I'm not sure if he'll follow. Not sure what he'll do.

"I won't be far," he says. "But I see no need to alert the others. Just know that coming here was a dangerous decision. But you are safe so long as I'm here. You won't see me, but I will be following till all of you are safe—till *you* are safe—back at the palace."

"Thank you." He probably can't hear me because my mouth is so dry.

My eyes want to stare at Axel some more, but my feet send me out the door to the courtyard as fast as I can possibly go.

It's packed here too. Can't find that husband who I need to be glued to immediately, so I put my back to a wall and hoist myself on top of it so I can see better.

Where is Louis and his geeky green mask? There's a group of kids below me, all vaping, puffing out smoke in purple and blue rings, showing off. The smoke smells awful. Really strong and musky.

"I heard there's Bourbons at this party," says a girl.

I grip the edge of the wall, frozen still, like that will somehow make me disappear. How do they know? Who did they spot? I need to find Louis. We need to leave. I don't feel right staying any longer, forcing Axel to protect us all.

"Bourbons at this dead disco? You're full of shit," says one of the boys as he coughs out some vape clouds.

"No, Madeline saw them! It was Stan, and I think she saw his new wife too!"

"The one that's not as hot as the Austro one?"

"Yeah!"

Of course it was Stan who doxxed us. The boy puffs out a

few rings. "The Bourbons are a bunch of weird fucking kids who never leave their house. They're not here."

I've never heard anyone talk about royals that way. I feel stuck in place, muscles all tensed up like I can disguise myself as a statue on the wall.

The girl crosses her arms and juts out a hip. "Stan goes out. He posts it on the Apps. And Madeline's not the only one who saw him. Someone said he showed up with a bunch of people. What if it's the dauphin and dauphine?"

"They'd never set foot in here. People like them consider people like you garbage," says vape boy.

"That's not true! They love us! They probably want friends. They're so cute. I wish I could meet them."

"They can buy rich friends. Wake up. Royals are pigs, and they consider us the shit they roll in."

"Oh my gigs, that is like straight-up radical anti-monarchist stuff! Stop! That's for wackos with podcasts. Do you want the safety officers to block your Pixter?" The girl glances around wide-eyed, like arrest might be imminent. For all I know, it might be. I glance too, but see nothing but ravers and glow sticks.

"It's for people who aren't dumbasses."

I've heard enough. I want to hug the girl who wants to be my friend. My stomach is in knots and my limbs feel watery. If the guy with the vape knew who I was . . . what would he do? I'm sure he wouldn't hurt me, but would he say those things to my face? Would I know what to say back if he did?

I drop off the wall and dig for my holofone to text Louis: where r u.

Thérèse and Yolande find me first. I scream when they startle me, hugging me from both sides.

"Really sorry, but we should leave," Thérèse says. "Stan and Josephine had an argument."

"And got recognized," Yolande adds.

"Seriously? Damn it," I groan. That explains how those kids knew we were here.

Should I tell them about Fersen? Probably not. They'd glitch. Did he mean it when he said he'd keep our outing a secret?

We all leave the club without hassle, piling into Jules's cruiser, parked in the alley. I look around. No sign of Fersen. I think I'll keep his presence to myself. No need to tell anyone. No need for them to ask how I found him, why he only spoke to me.

"Did you have fun?" Louis asks.

I have a hard time looking him in the eye. "I did. I . . . would have liked to dance with you."

"Oh . . . ," he says quietly. "Well, I'm a very bad dancer. I thought you'd have more fun with the girls."

I feel sick and guilty. I went to pieces over a glitching android when I'm married to the glitching dauphin of the Franc Kingdom, who's willing to break rules for me. And apparently some of our people think that we're so far above them, we consider them dirt. Nothing about this evening turned out how I hoped. And it started so well.

The whole way back, the words of the vaping kids keep sneaking into my thoughts. I want to talk to Louis about it, but I'm not sure how to explain what I heard. I'm sure their words would be just as much of a shock to him.

Fersen's face keeps coming to mind too. One of the cruiser lights outside must belong to him.

He has dimples. Dimples! Why did they make a bot with dimples?

"Are you okay?" Louis touches my arm gently. Can guilt drown a person? He did this whole thing for me. He's perfect. Not that robot.

"I'm just tired." I grab his arm, lean on his shoulder.

"Yeah, me too."

He yawns and falls asleep a minute later. Cute, cute, cute. Repeat a million times. Forget about android smiles. Only creepy people with gadget fetishes are into bots.

SEVENTEEN

✳

I put on extra concealer to hide my baggy eyes and create the illusion of perkiness. After my night out, I need to make sure nothing seems amiss to Noailles in my lesson today.

Noailles requested we meet in the library for this lesson, so I wait there for her arrival. It's quiet in here, and the windows full of sunshine help me feel more awake and alert. There are a few tall shelves containing ancient, dusty volumes that probably interest no one but Louis. For some reason, there's a chain and a bio-encrypted lock around an antique bookcase. I wonder why. The books may be expensive relics, but Versailles is full of relics. Not many that I'm aware of are kept under lock and key.

Our main resources are the big holofone desks with interfaces shining on each surface. The first one I sit down at is glitching, apparently. It shows the spinning wheel of death and it won't unfreeze.

Just as I'm about to hop tables, the screen flickers and brings up what the last user must have gotten frozen on.

Some vid, paused on an image of Louis's great-grandfather the Sun King. I play it just to see what it is. The title appears in the corner of the screen: *Historical Models and You*. What the frag does that mean?

"The Sun King understood better than anyone the power of

taking on a name and a legacy. In an age when much of human history is lost, destroyed, or hoarded by rivals, this knowledge is currency, and most important, it is power," explains the narrator.

The Sun King leads a man in a gray suit with a holo-tie through the portrait gallery near the Hall of Mirrors. Today the room is full of monuments to the Sun King himself. It holds the shining neon sun he placed behind the throne. A mural made of fiber optics depicts him in a gold suit. But in the video there are other things in the gallery: Bits of fresco framed in neon. Old, ripped canvas placed beside projections of what these paintings once looked like.

The Sun King and the man in the suit pause before an enormous holo displaying a man with a ridiculous mane of hair. It's full of curls and trails down his back. He displays one toned leg extended out of his voluminous robes. He wears stockings to show off his legs like I might do to model shoes.

"This is my namesake. This is Louis XIV. They called *him* the Sun King, and he was glorious. We know he led this land to many great victories and built this palace, and the bones were still standing when we reclaimed it. Artwork of him still exists when millions, billions of other names have been lost to time, wiped away by the Event. This is glory. This is power. We retrace his footsteps; we rebuild what this man created. We know so little of him but the lands he conquered, the awe he inspired, and the dance he created at Versailles. He understood the importance of a good show, a strong illusion. To direct the courtiers in an elaborate pageant of etiquette, to dazzle the people so they think of the Bourbon family as gods, untouchable, unattainable, but still belonging to the Franc people. That is the legacy we create, the one the First Estate has helped us to build. This is how we direct this kingdom to the future. What little history we have, it is so important to use it . . . so important to wield it."

"And to learn from it?" the man in the suit asks.

"*Oui*, and make our kingdom into something better, I think." The Sun King glances at the portrait of the ancient man, who to me seems like a figure in a movie, someone made up, imaginary. "I'd like to think he would agree."

"What are you watching?"

I gasp out loud, a little shout as Noailles's hand slaps down onto the table. I'd been watching so closely I didn't hear her enter.

The Sun King's image disappeared with Noailles's touch.

"I don't know," I say, hand on my chest as if it could press my heart to calm. "I didn't know that—there was another Sun King? The man with the long, curling hair? There was an ancient Sun King?"

Noailles swipes furiously through screens on the holofone desk. "Who showed you this?"

"No one. It was frozen that way when I came in."

"*Merde*," Noailles hisses under her breath. "When I find out who . . ."

I have never heard Noailles curse before and never imagined I would. I don't even understand what I just saw. "Countess, what did he mean by the 'legacy'? I thought we didn't even know the names of the people on the walls and in the paintings."

"It's none of your concern," Noailles says as she types into her holofone.

I'm so sick of her saying this whenever I ask a question about how Versailles is run. How am I supposed to learn if I don't even understand this place? "What is a historical model?"

Her lips become thin as she presses them together. "It is

simply a tradition we have here."

"But it sounded more important than that."

Noailles shoves her personal holofone at me. "What's more important is this."

It's a news site. A headline flashes between *RENEGADE ROYAL COUPLE* and *BOURBONS GO INCOGNITO AT PARÉESIAN RAVE.*

There is no denying that's me and Louis and Thérèse and Yolande and Jules crowded into the courtyard. My face is pointed in the camera's direction, looking at something, I don't even remember what.

"What have you to say about this?" Noailles looks more glitched than I've ever seen her. Pale, cheekbones prominent with the clench of her jaw.

"I—I am sorry, Countess. I just—I know it was foolish, but I desperately wanted to see Parée, and tomorrow is my birthday, so I—I convinced the dauphin. It wasn't his fault. I wanted it to be a chance for us to bond."

Noailles's nostrils flare. "A bonding opportunity? A bit of birthday fun? No one else views it this way. They see flagrant disrespect. A foreign princess who thinks she's above the rules. The dauphin has never strayed like this before, so everyone knows it was your doing."

I frown. I'm just a girl who wanted to go out where the other Franc girls party. Surely it wasn't that bad a thing to do. "I haven't seen any comments like that on my App profiles. Maybe the younger subjects are pleased."

Noailles closes her eyes, which I have learned is a replacement for the disrespectful act of rolling them. "Those Apps are a child's game. This is what matters. You told me you understood image and the power it holds. Clearly, you do not. I will have to involve myself in your media presentation again."

She can't. I've worked so hard to earn that right and prove myself. "But Countess, you've seen the progress I've made!"

"Progress you undid in a night."

"I don't believe that!"

Noailles scrolls with an aggressive flick of her wrist.

The comments here are far less forgiving than anything I've seen on my Pixter profile.

She is above us all until she wants to party.

The streets of Parée are a spectacle to the royals.

They don't understand the dangers like the rest of us.

Foolish. Wish they'd gotten caught in a riot.

They'll show up for this but just toss a few bits to fire victims? They could have visited the people in the hospital.

My heart races. Because now I understand how this looks to them. And Noailles is right. I never thought of this, and I should have considered what could have happened if we were caught. "I can fix this," I say. And I'm sure I can. It was one mistake held up to many more good deeds I can do. They'll forget about it in a week.

"We'll discuss this after today's lesson."

Noailles brings up the lesson on the holofone desk, but I can't pay attention. I'm already running through plans. Things I can do, things I can say, apologies I could make, to Louis first, then the king, then our subjects. I know I can make this right. News stories, rumors on the Apps—they come and go as quick as the weather. But I can't help wondering who took the photo. It could have been anyone. But I hope it wasn't Axel Fersen.

EIGHTEEN

❋

"Left . . . right . . . elbow out just a little. *Belle. Magnifique.*"

I try to let my smile beam natural and bright to match my outfit, because it's my birthday. To appeal to the Francs, I'm decked out in matte silver, but I've got my own special touches. There's a hologram sheen and a check pattern on the sleek mini-dress. My jacket is lined in pastel purple. I've got round mirror glasses on, a touch of purple shade to my lipstick, and, to top it off, a silver wig. The first picture has only been posted for a few minutes, but so far, the rave reviews are rolling in along with the messages of *Bon anniversaire, Dauphine!* If I do this right, serve enough looks in my photos and donate the value of my gifts to charity, the rave incident will be overshadowed by my birthday.

I've done a few different poses on the wide stairs. The cool natural light from the moon along with the soft blue and white light from the huge chandelier make my dress twinkle and shine for the camera.

When the photos are over with, I race upstairs for my grand entrance, greeted by a round of cheers when I burst into the glittering ballroom in the East Wing. My closest friends are front and center with me, but the room is jammed with courtiers and influencers who vied for an invite to the social event of the season.

Despite the number of people, the room doesn't feel crowded. I chose it for the tall windows and big mirrors, reflecting light. A gold shower of bubbles streams from a hovering droid into what seems like an infinite and airy space. Even the king rises to greet me with the biggest smile. He's already forgotten our rebellious trip, only pretended to scold us in the first place.

Philippe bounces over to put a silly LED crown on my head. It has a glowing holo of a cake on it. Speaking of cake, there's loads of it here. Cake and cake and cake! In so many colors. You could feed an army with this cake.

Angoulême is back and he's brought the android regiment with him, along with their tech specialist.

Axel is among them, reuniting with his old . . . friends? I haven't been able to speak to him since the rave. I want to. Which is exactly why I shouldn't.

I give him only the slightest glance and attach myself to Elisabeth. We giggle and drink champagne and pick at the most fluorescent pieces of cake. We both keep glancing at the small group of androids. There are six of them. Each one has a flawless appearance and is dressed in a perfectly pressed uniform. Just like us, they laugh, they smile, they try to catch the attention of others with their beautiful eyes . . . like Axel is doing to me now. He's looked over here twice.

"They seem so real, don't they?" I ask Elisabeth, who's blatantly staring in their direction. I wonder which one she likes best.

"Huh?" She blinks. "What do?"

"The bots," I whisper.

"Oh, right. Well, they *are* real."

"I mean . . . human."

Elisabeth stares in their direction again. Axel's talking to a girl in a pink dress. Who programmed bots to flirt, anyway? "They're perfected AI. Loyal to their purpose, but so human they feel and have opinions, and grow and learn. Or at least, that's what they say."

There's a young woman in uniform standing beside Angoulême. She looks our way and winks. Elisabeth almost spills her drink down the front of her dress. Oh. Maybe Elisabeth wasn't looking at the androids at all.

"Well, let's find out. We should talk to them!" I give Elisabeth a nudge.

"Um . . . Sure." She's gone very red in the face. Yikes. She's going to need some help. Unless I get her in trouble? Elisabeth isn't betrothed yet, and anyway, if the king can have a mistress, why not Elisabeth?

"Come on, come on!" I tug her arm and bounce in time with the strobe.

"Dauphine, *joyeux anniversaire.*" Angoulême bows elegantly. "May I present Sergeant Amélie Mercier and our tech specialist, Jeanne Bisset, and, of course, the rest of the android unit."

I have no idea what the etiquette is for addressing androids, so I curtsy to them the same way I would to show respect to human guests. "Thank you so much for attending my birthday party."

The bots bow, so perfectly in sync, it's unnatural.

"It's a true honor to present them, Dauphine," says Sergeant Mercier.

Jeanne the tech specialist pipes up. "I suspect you've been

happy with Fersen? I don't like to play favorites, but . . ."

Axel turns to me, smiling so that his dimples are showing.

I have to use every social grace in me to will my heart calm and stop from blushing. "Certainly."

"The social events help them learn to be better mannered, more at ease," says Angoulême. "The more humanlike they become, the more useful they are."

Something about this gives me a shiver. "May I ask why?"

Angoulême's face is noticeably still, like the first time I met him. Maybe he's hung around bots so much that he's started acting like them. "We don't want the androids to be easily identified. For their safety. Not to mention, the more familiar they are, the more . . . accepting the public will become."

"I'm glad to hear that you're satisfied. I'd dare to say they're charming. Some even have a sense of humor!" says Sergeant Mercier.

"Eh, if they're funny, it's cheating. I programmed all their jokes," Jeanne says.

"If we can cheat our way into jokes, explain why I'm way funnier than Nilsson," says Fersen.

"You might be funnier, but I'm more charming." Nilsson bows and kisses my hand. "It's an honor, Madame Dauphine."

"Over there are Bergen, Fager, and Linden. They've all got Sved names, but they've been doing crown and country proud, I promise. The Kingdom of Sved developed and sold the tech my programmers have perfected, but they insisted on the Sved names in our contract. You know how they are about their tech," says Sergeant Mercier.

Fersen clears his throat. "Bit rude to talk about someone's

developer, don't you think, Sergeant? It would be like if I mentioned the conditions of your conception."

I burst out laughing and Jeanne nearly chokes on her drink. "Fersen! Trying a little hard with the jokes thing, aren't you?"

"But it was funny, wasn't it?"

"No need to get a big head," says Jeanne. "That's your developer's humor."

"And I suppose you can take credit for whatever your brain produces, but I can't?" Axel gives Jeanne a tap on the head.

"Fair enough. I could tweak your code to get you less jokey, though."

"You'd like to talk with my brother Louis," says Elisabeth. "He's into coding."

Jeanne grins. "Maybe. I'd rather talk with you, though."

Elisabeth blushes, just a little. "You have excellent taste, then."

Maybe she doesn't need my help at all.

Angoulême frowns. "Forgive Ensign Bisset and her casual manners. She's in the program on scholarship and lacks professional experience."

Jeanne's lips thin and she looks down at her polished boots, a curtain of blond hair blocking her face.

"Oh, that's quite all right," I say. "Now I've seen that the androids are as funny as claimed."

"I'm glad you approve of them," says Angoulême, who apparently is less comfortable with humor and fun than the androids are. "Fersen assures me he is more than satisfied with his position here."

I wish I could cancel blushes. Abort, disavow, delete. "Your generosity in sending him to us is appreciated, Monsieur Angoulême."

"I'm happy to send them. Your promotion of the vaccine banks brought about a record-setting turnout, so showing your support for my tech does help me a great deal. Perhaps some promotion with our esteemed and handsome Captain Fersen would benefit us both."

I can't look anyone in the eye. I can't tell what Angoulême is insinuating. Maybe nothing and I'm reading into it, my mind going down paths it has no business on. Or maybe Fersen really did bust me. Maybe he's a reminder that I'm to be kept in line. All I can manage is a muttered, "Perhaps."

Elisabeth is definitely giving me a glitched look and Axel is staring.

"Apologies, but I have many other guests to greet." I curtsy and try to avoid Axel's lingering gaze.

"We hope to see you at Versailles again soon, then," says Elisabeth, covering for my shoddy manners.

As I turn away, I see Jeanne give Elisabeth a slow smile. "That would be a real pleasure."

Elisabeth's blush is more vibrant than mine, but I owe her one and rush our exit.

The crowd of other guests swallows me up, full of people who hug me and kiss my cheeks. Dukes and duchesses smile and nod while the band plays. I picked a super-sick group from Parée called La Pluie Toxique. They wear these turbo-trending helmets that flash emojis and little messages.

Mon Dieu, is Fersen still looking over here? It must be because I'm the dauphine, and I'm the prime target to protect. That's all.

"Talking to Fersen again?" Yolande sweeps up beside me. "Who has the obsession? You or him?"

"Definitely not me!" I peek over my shoulder. He's talking to that girl in the pink dress again.

Thérèse appears and hugs my arm. "I finally met the androids! They're really charming, aren't they? I don't know why some people hate them."

"Hate them?"

"Oh yeah. There's a group that's really glitched out by them and thinks one day they'll take us over or something. Probably because the First Estate buys them. Plus, they hate the bot lovers."

My stomach squirms up. "I bet all that is just a rumor anyway."

"Bot lovers? Nah, they're real. Just very hush." Thérèse raises a finger to her lips. "Only the First Estate can afford them, and they're very quiet about it."

"Then I don't see how it was appropriate for Angoulême to suggest a photo shoot with Axe—I mean, Captain Fersen." I had hoped to sound casual, so much for that.

"Ooh, really?" Thérèse squeals.

Yolande raises an eyebrow. "Goodness . . . better behave."

Thérèse gasps. "Yolande! She's not a bot lover!"

Good thing I'm holding champagne so no one will question why my cheeks are bright red. "Of course I'm not!"

Yolande shrugs. "Well, if she were, why should she be ashamed? They act like us and they're designed twice as beautifully. I'm not sure what's so taboo."

"They're machines," Thérèse says. "So it's creepy. They're

programmed. There's like chips and wires in there somewhere."

"One big wire, if you know what I mean." Yolande makes her eyebrows jump and I almost choke on my drink, while Thérèse shrieks and slaps at her.

"I can't believe some of the things you say!"

"I'm not saying I would," says Yolande. "But I don't think we should humiliate people who do. And Marie, darling, it's okay if you think a bot is hot."

I know they're just joking around, but I'm getting really annoyed. It doesn't matter what I think of the "bots"! "Don't be ridiculous! His stupid perfect face is made of plastic. That's why it's perfect."

Yolande gives me a sassy smile as she sips her drink. "Not plastic. Bio-grown skin compound. But okay."

My semi-drunk brain keeps prodding at me to turn around and see what Axel is doing right now, but I need to change the subject. I need to get away from him. He doesn't matter. "Where's Louis?"

"Oh, I think he went to bed," says Thérèse.

On my birthday? Nice. I feel like hurling my champagne glass. "Then I should go to bed too."

"Why go to bed?" Yolande asks. "I'm sure others could keep you company." She takes another sip of her drink with a pointed look in Axel's direction.

Why won't she stop teasing me about this? I roll my eyes. "Seriously, I should go."

"Just talk to him," said Yolande. "Who cares? It's innocent flirtation. You deserve to have some fun."

My heart aches in a way I wish it wouldn't. *Sehnsucht* with a mix of crush. It's a glitchy combination.

"I don't know, Marie . . . you wouldn't want to get more bad press after the work we just did and the rave . . . ," says Thérèse.

"Don't be boring. She knows how to keep it clean for the feeds. She can't have a little fun on her birthday?" Yolande says.

"I'm just worried about her," says Thérèse.

I'm full to bursting with feelings, squashed by a heap of exhaustion, and sick of everyone making decisions for me.

"I think I'll have a chat with Captain Fersen, then off to bed. Don't worry about me, girls." False smile in place, I wave ta-ta.

"Well, you have a good night there, Princesse." Yolande winks.

"Happy birthday! We love you!" Thérèse scoops me up in a hug. "Marie, just be careful, okay?" She says this quietly. Only I hear her.

I give a little shrug. "What could the harm be?"

Besides, it's just a chat. And after my husband abandoned me on my birthday, I don't want to go to bed feeling so defeated. She frowns like she might say something. I don't know why Thérèse is so interested in androids. First she seemed excited, now fearful. The moment passes. She smiles. "Have fun!"

If I were an LED, I would burn out. Every nerve feels like it's flashing on fire. I smile to each person who greets me as I pass, but I look only at Axel because if I look away, I think I'll bail. I think this probably is a stupid decision, but at the moment, I don't care. I want to ask Axel about the rave. And Louis shouldn't have left. People should understand why in a room full of people, I might be lonely.

Axel's smile is warm. Inviting. He bows to me. "Good

evening, madame. You grace me again."

I curtsy. "Captain Fersen, I . . . well, I had hoped to talk to you."

"Of course, madame. I'm at your disposal."

"Perhaps . . ." I nod toward the balcony. I don't want to be overheard. I want the rave forgotten.

"Say no more." Axel offers me an arm.

I follow him to the balcony, and when the crowd becomes thick, Axel says, "*Pardon*. The dauphine needs some fresh air."

They part without question and soon we're under the stars. The noise is muted, though there are plenty of shouts and laughter and lights in the gardens, which are rarely quiet at night.

"What did you wish to speak to me about, madame?"

It's ridiculous, but his brows and eyes even manage to express concern handsomely. "I . . . well . . ." I can't accuse him when he looks at me with such concern. "The night we were at the rave. Our secret was exposed."

His features rearrange in surprise. Over and over I have to remind myself that Axel is a machine, because nothing else gives him away. It's nearly impossible to believe. "Not that we spoke or—" Danced. I can't bring myself to say danced. Because it's not as if we . . . my mind wanders. Wonders what Axel's hands would feel like on my face, my rib cage. "Just the fact that we went! It was on the Apps and Noailles was very cross."

"Ah, yes," says Axel, and his expression goes neutral again. Pleasant and warm. "I am sorry, madame. I hope she wasn't too harsh."

"She's always harsh." I lean on the balcony edge with a huff. A large bit of stone crumbled here and was replaced with purple neon. Warm to the touch, it gives my skin an eerie glow, similar to the moon. "I just . . . I wondered how the trip was leaked to the press."

"Oh, I see. You feared it was me." Fersen says this quietly. So mild, as if I wasn't accusing him.

"No, not exactly." Lucky the neon hides my flush. "It could have been anyone. I don't know what happened."

"Unfortunately, the comte de Provence and Madame Josephine were discovered, and then word spread quickly. Anyone at the party could have taken the photos."

"Of course." I shake my head. Because I knew this was the case. It was a crowded place and I'm the dauphine. Half the kingdom knows my image well enough to pick me out from the crowd. Surely someone could have recognized me, even in my mask. It was a bad decision and I was stupid to think I could pull it off.

"I'm sorry, madame," Axel says again.

"Can you understand why I wanted to go? Why I want to forget myself at times?"

I don't know why I ask. But everyone has been so upset ever since that day, and I guess I just want someone to sympathize.

He leans on the rail beside me and tilts his head. The gesture is so human that I feel, suddenly, that he's capable of understanding me.

"I can," he says quietly. "You are given so many rules, your appearance is so detailed and stylized, that sometimes to find yourself you have to escape and get lost in a crowd."

I simply wanted to have fun with my friends. But he's right. There are times I have no idea who Marie Antoinette really is. "Sometimes I'm afraid I'm nothing more than what others have taught me to be. And at those times, I'm not sure I like who I am."

I've never said this out loud to anyone. I don't know why I'm telling Axel.

"That's something I can understand very well," he says softly.

I stare at him. There is some pain in his eyes, I think. Something I recognize. Of course he understands. He is programmed. He's entirely someone else's invention. I have no right to complain in comparison. "I'm sorry, I didn't think, I—"

Axel shakes his head. "It's good to talk like this. I mean it when I say I'm at your disposal and that your secrets are mine." He leans close, a smile quirks his lips and lights his eyes, and a bit of teasing creeps into his voice. "Your wish is my command."

Perhaps I could kiss him. Just to practice. Just to help me understand how to approach Louis. *Would you kiss me?* I want to ask. But if he says yes, would it truly be his choice, when he's programmed to do so? Instead I say, "Will you dance?"

"It would be my pleasure."

He takes my hand and puts his other on my waist. I can't tell which of us decided to move close as we turn in small circles, stepping back and forth. He watches me intently, as if memorizing my face and every hair on my head. No one has looked at me so closely before.

If I could just kiss him, I'd feel less broken. Less flawed when Louis pulls away from me. It could just be on the cheek. It doesn't have to be the soft smile of his lips. As soon as I decide to do it, I freeze, nearly miss a step in the dance.

I have kissed and been kissed before, but now it's as if I don't know how.

Because like Louis, I'm not sure if it's welcome. I don't know what he wants. I don't know how to ask.

Axel's expression is gentle, but unreadable.

Like a warm blanket, he can wrap me in safety and comfort, but he will never lean down and kiss me on his own . . . because he can't. He can't! Of course he can't, without permission.

In a rush of breath, before I can change my mind, I say, "You can kiss me if you wish."

The dance doesn't miss a beat until I stumble. His grip on me stays firm. My chest touches his, we're so close. "Do you wish me to?"

I can't meet his eyes. I wouldn't have offered if the answer wasn't yes. Maybe sensing my hesitation, he leans down and kisses my cheek. I'm so glitched, I can barely feel it, barely process. He stays curled around me, looking into my eyes. If I want to kiss him back, it's my moment. That's what his posture says. It's less confusing than dealing with Louis, but confusing all the same, and when I think of Louis, I feel pummeled with guilt, heart hammering. I should be with *him*.

"I should go."

"I've offended you," says Axel.

"No, no, of course not." I let go of his hand, back away, curtsy. "Good night, Axel."

I rudely ignore several guests as I push through the party in a rush to return to my rooms.

NINETEEN

✳

June 20, 3070, 12:38 a.m.

After I change into my pajamas, Georgette and I eat some cake that I brought to share with her. I was hoping Louis would be in here waiting for me, but silly me. Of course he isn't. Maybe he just felt awkward, knowing Georgette would turn up.

My cheek still tingles where Axel's lips brushed it. I'm filled with a weird frustration I've never felt before. Like I want to run and yell and sweat. Like I might burst right out of my body.

When I enter the common room it's dark, but not pitch. The blinds are open and Louis sits in the window. A flash of lightning brightens everything all blue-white. I go cold with nerves and guilt and fear all jumbled into one. Here is the boy who I should kiss.

"Hi," he says in that quiet way he has.

He doesn't make any move to get up, so I go to him. I'm so nervous, you'd think he was a stranger.

"Sorry I left," he says. "There were a lot of people."

"It's okay." I put my hand on his shoulder. I think I can feel my heartbeat fluttering somewhere in my neck. "I didn't know it was storming. I didn't hear thunder."

"Yeah, the walls are thick. You can hear it a little bit. If you barely breathe."

The lightning is purple, a minute later, almost blue. I bet Louis could explain why. The same fear that held me at arm's length from Axel at the party and has turned me away from Louis over and over is still there. But I push against it and slide my hand around his shoulders, bend my knees to perch lightly on his leg. Some of my nerves uncoil a bit when he steadies me with his arms. He's staring at me, but his eyelids look heavy. He seems tired and sad. I need to kiss him. I just feel like my entire birthday will be ruined if I don't. I'll feel like I betrayed him with my moment with Axel if I don't.

"Louis?"

"Yeah?"

I don't know what words will work. This would be, I don't know, the fourth time I've kissed anybody? But I can't just say that to him. It's embarrassing to have limited experience. No wonder we never know what to do around each other.

I put my hand on his face. His cheek is warm with a little bit of roughness, stubble I can't see. It's different from Axel's flawless skin, neutral in temperature. I see the loneliness in Louis. I see sadness and hope when his eyes meet mine.

Before I can think twice or he can come up with some excuse, I press my mouth to his. No disasters happen. I'm firm, but I don't knock against his teeth or anything. We just sort of sit like that for a few seconds. It's nerve-racking. He doesn't really move, and when he does, it's his arms. He tightens them around me, instead of wiggling away. I break off the kiss, if I can call it that, and take a breath like I just came up from underwater, all quick and sharp, because I need to try again. Brain seems off-line, but my arms and my mouth and my heart are saying *Do it again*.

He moves this time, like he's catching my mouth with his, moves so we fit better. It's still a bit awkward, but it gets . . . nice. Warm and soft and something else I can't name. One of his hands is on my leg and it's weird, but I sort of feel that more than I feel my mouth.

Lightning close by. It startles me and we stop. But okay, that was step one. I'm ready for step two, and it seems like he is too. I think I'm more scared than I was when the cruiser first landed at Versailles. I take his hand, slide off his lap. It seems to take ages to step back, pulling his hand until I've stretched his arm out, and then with just the littlest stumble, I stop dead. Louis hasn't budged.

I don't know how he can be nice to me in every single way and so horrible about this. I drop his hand. "Louis, please. It's my birthday. Please." I sound pathetic. Everything about this is pathetic.

His chin drops. "I just can't. I'm sorry."

Anger burns through me and the pain makes me want to tell him that plenty of others would be happy to kiss me, like Axel. But I stop myself because I know that won't help, and I feel like there's something here I'm missing.

He won't look at me, so I kneel on the floor and peer up. He can't hide anymore. I won't let him. "Why? Everyone says I'm pretty. Why is it so hard?"

"You *are* pretty. That's not the problem."

"Then what?"

"I can't explain it."

He shifts like he'd rather I stopped leaning on him, looking at him. I almost shrink away, ashamed to think that he's disgusted by me. I think of Elisabeth and the way she looked at Jeanne.

"Louis . . . ," I say, more gently than I think I've talked to anyone. "Do you like boys?"

He shakes his head. "No . . . no."

"It's okay if you do. Stan does. I'd keep your secret if you prefer it that way."

"That's not it."

"Then . . . are you scared? Because I'm scared too."

"I'm scared, yes. But that's not all of it. I just don't . . . There's something wrong with me."

"Talk to me. What's wrong with you?"

"It's not as easy for me as for other people. I don't . . . feel the same things."

"What do you mean?"

"I don't like boys. But I never really liked girls either. Not in the same way someone like Philippe does. I like the look of some girls, I just . . . don't feel what I should feel."

This hurts to hear. I don't know what I imagined the problem was, but it wasn't this. "So . . . you didn't like kissing me?"

"No, I liked it."

"Are you sure?"

"I did. I'd do it again."

This also takes me by surprise. My heart flutters.

He puts his hand on my face. I feel his breath and it makes me jittery. How does he not feel what I feel? "I don't understand," I say.

"I don't really either. I just know . . . the sex part. I've never wanted to have sex. I still don't want to."

"But you said you want to kiss me. I'm confused."

"Kissing isn't the same thing, and, well . . . before really recently, like the past few weeks—I never wanted to kiss anyone either. If that can change, maybe other things can change too. I'm not sure. I just know it's like . . . now that I know you more, I started to feel some other feelings. Kissing-type feelings. But it's not a power switch like it seems to be for other people. Not off or on. It's not a simple 'yeah, I want or don't want that person.' It's like a fire. Spreading. But slowly."

"So, this has happened before?" I ask.

"What do you mean?"

This is like trying to understand how someone breathes something other than air. "I mean you must have had a crush before?"

He stares over my shoulder, thinks this through. "I . . . don't know. Maybe?"

"How could you not know?"

He shrugs, helpless. "I don't know. There was this girl, Annette. She helped her père at work in the stables. We were friends. I liked her a lot. When I was fourteen, we were loading hay into the loft and she asked if we could kiss. I kind of panicked. I wasn't sure if I wanted to or if I just thought it was the thing I was supposed to do. Anyway, it hurt her feelings and I didn't know how to explain why I couldn't do it, and she never talked to me again. I spent a while wishing I had just done it.

"But you're different. I knew I wanted to kiss you. I knew since the rave, when I saw you dancing around and so happy. So, see, I like you more than anyone else."

He says this last part in a rush like if he messes it up, I'm also going to leave him in a hayloft. "I think I understand, but I'm just trying to figure this out. Why can you kiss, but not try to go further?"

"It doesn't feel right." Louis shakes his head. "I just . . . it feels wrong."

"Am . . . I wrong?"

"No." He seizes my hand. "No. Please believe that. It's something I have to work out for myself."

"Maybe with . . . practice?"

He nods. "Yes, I think that might help."

It's not the answer I wanted, and it doesn't exactly set a romantic mood for kissing. It's hard to imagine what he's describing, but I guess not everyone works the same way. I'm relieved he trusted me enough to explain this to me, but I'm still stuck in the same situation. "What if you never want to? What if you never get past kissing?"

He shrugs and looks at his knees. "I guess we'll figure something out, or I'll just have to . . ." He shrugs again.

If he never wants to have sex, I don't know what we'll "figure out." How could I be with him that way if he doesn't want to do it? That would be horrible.

He follows me to my room, and in bed, he curls around me like a puppy. I hold him to my shoulder and pet his hair.

"Sorry I'm so messed up," he breathes against my neck.

"I don't think you're messed up. You're just you. And I think people expect a lot from you. From us."

He mumbles, voice thick with sleep, "Happy birthday. Thanks for marrying me and stuff." Then he gives me a really light kiss on my neck and my heart dances around again. I feel sorry for him, and sorry for us, but happy for his trust, yet still really frustrated in a way that's not exactly directed toward him. I kiss his lips gently. Then he kisses back. Kissing him makes me feel closer to him, makes me feel warm like a little flame inside, even now. I think I prefer it to Axel's kiss, but I guess, like Louis, I don't understand what I feel.

I kiss him until I think less. It's gentle; it brings us closer. It lulls me toward sleep.

TWENTY

June 26, 3070, 4:30 p.m.

I'm curious, to say the least, to see Stan's photo-shoot setup, his birthday gift to me. His style is nothing like mine. But like Yolande said, it's very Franc. Between this and my birthday photos, the Francs should forget all about my rave mistake.

I can't even guess the theme or setup, though. I just got a pin in the gardens and a text from him that said Bring Mops.

"I'm only doing this for you. Not Stan," Louis grumbles as we make our way out to the gardens.

"It could be fun if you relax a bit." I say it in a teasing way, but I hope he will. There are so few good pictures of us together, and I replay our kisses in my mind over and over. Would he kiss me in a picture? Will he kiss me again tonight, alone in our rooms?

I try to focus on the shoot, what it could be and my goals for it, while Mops leads the way through the gardens. We round a fountain and head for one of the hedge enclosures. I hear voices from within, and when I step through the archway into the little enclave, a smile so big and genuine takes hold that I'm photo-shoot ready in a nanosecond.

Stan, Philippe, Elisabeth, and Josephine are all here, and so are a big rack of clothes, a mound of flowers, a tea party, and a little cottage made of sticks and thatch and more flowers. But best of all, there are sheep! Three woolly creatures, necks tied with ribbon, fleece pale as the marble in the palace entranceway. There's also two little lambs, pink-nosed and bleating.

There is not a bit of neon in sight. This is natural, whimsical, simple, and in its fairy-tale way, with no embellishments, it's bold.

"We have sheep? Where did we get those?" Louis asks.

Stan preens. "I have my ways. What do you think?"

"It's beautiful!" For the first time in weeks, I'm compelled to hug my brother-in-law. I hold my arms out and he smirks in his Stan way.

"Thank me when we see the results."

"What's the theme?"

"Family togetherness and tea parties and rustic, simple, day-to-day life. Not exactly how people imagine us. I had a chat with my PR adviser and he liked the idea of us showing some humble, wholesome content. Save the glamour for state events."

"Isn't this kind of fake?" Elisabeth asks. "I mean, has Philippe even seen a sheep before?"

Philippe crouches in front of a lamb, making something like a "baa" noise that isn't quite right.

"*Ma soeur*, this entire place is fake. What exactly would we shoot that's authentic?" Stan takes a dramatic puff of his vape, taking no care to aim his exhale away from his wife. Josephine waves away the plume irritably.

"This seems ridiculous," she says.

"Well, it's not your birthday gift, is it? What does Marie think?"

"I'm excited! I love the sheep, love the flowers. Let's do this."

I make a beeline for the clothing rack.

The options are quite plain, no neon, lots of solid colors, but I don't mind for once because the outfits are covered with dramatic ruffles, big bows, poufed shoulders. The looks are totally retro, some soft, others creating angular silhouettes and interesting symmetry.

I'm halfway through choosing some styles when I realize Louis probably needs help. He's flipping through jackets too quickly to really see them.

"Hey." I bounce over and sift through options. "Blue and green are your colors."

"How do you know?" He smiles but practically hides behind a jacket. Maybe I'll never cure his bashfulness.

"Your eyes, and vibe, and general cuteness." I shrug. If he's already embarrassed, might as well flirt a little.

He smiles, but it doesn't reach his eyes. "I'll wear whatever you want."

"What's wrong?" I ask him.

"Oh, it's just . . ." He fiddles with a jacket as if he'll try it on, but it's an ugly yellow shade that even Louis must know enough to avoid. "I wish I had thought of this as a present. Instead of Stan. Even though I'm glad he did, since—you know—it made you happy and everything. Never mind, I'm being stupid."

These are the moments I know that Louis cares. I just wish he'd learn to show it at other times, instead of only when he's afraid he's not good enough. I want him to just grab me around the waist, smile for the camera, do something spontaneous and fun.

But maybe I'm asking for too much, because Louis might never be spontaneous or graceful or anything but this sad boy lost in his thoughts. I don't know if this is something I can change or fix. This might just be who I've married.

I squeeze his shoulder. Again, I can't help but notice the toughness there and feel a warm fluttering at the strength beneath the soft exterior. "Hey, I love what you did for me. Mops, the rave . . . we couldn't ever replace that. This is cool, but you still win."

He smiles, more fully this time. "Sorry, I said I wouldn't be jealous of Stan again. And I'm not. I just feel stupid."

I wonder if he's thinking about our conversation a few nights ago. "Don't feel stupid. Put on this jacket and have fun." I brandish a deep blue blazer at him. "I'll show you what to do. You'll see that it's so easy."

It takes a bit of practice. Louis poses unnaturally with his teacup until I pop a bottle of champagne in his direction and he almost topples off his chair. The photographer clicks furiously.

After an outfit change from our champagne-soaked clothes, I suggest posing with the sheep, because Louis seems more comfortable with animals than he is beside his camera-loving brothers. Though he and Elisabeth posed to examine roses, and I think they'll get some cute photos out of it.

Louis places a lamb in my arms and I let my delight shine through, forgetting that the photographer is there for a moment.

Louis reaches around me to scratch at the lamb's ears. She stirs and bleats a little, maybe sensing my beating heart as I realize Louis could put both arms around me. Hold me like we're the proud parents of a little lamb. The proud parents we're expected to be someday.

I think I'm blushing, but it will just add to my sunshiny glow. I wish he would. I wish I didn't have to ask.

And then Louis moves. I almost startle and bump into him, or worse, drop the lamb. A brush of lips on my cheek.

Now I can feel the warmth in my cheeks, warmth in my belly. I wasn't ready and probably looked surprised.

"Adorable," says the photographer. "Again!"

"Uh! Oh . . ." Louis looks at me, round-eyed.

I smile back. Almost like I'm shy. The butterflies in my belly remind me of dancing with Axel and at once, I feel guilty but also different. Louis makes me feel different.

He kisses me again and lingers this time.

It's so rare, so sweet and unlike when I kissed him last night. I let my eyes flutter closed and enjoy it.

Like a true Franc prince, he kisses my other cheek. Then back to the first one. I'm overwhelmed, like I drank the whole bottle of popped champagne, giggles bubbling up. "Louis!"

"What?" His smile is quick and nervous.

"I think we got some really good pictures."

He smiles in that way I want to capture and show off on Pixter.

"You're a real prince," I say.

He takes the lamb from my arms, sets her on the ground at my feet, gentle and slow, then takes my hand. He bends forward to kiss it, bowing low.

The sun slants golden light over the flowers and faux cottage. This really is a fairy tale.

TWENTY-ONE

June 28, 3070, 7:08 p.m.

The thunder on my birthday was a warning for a coming super-storm. The palace started preparing yesterday. When I went for walks, I saw staff, both human and drone, moving things inside that could get swept away by the wind.

The Franc Kingdom gets worse storms than the Austro Lands. But I've never seen one howl and wail with as much force as this one.

We're in Philippe's apartments, because he called a storm party. He's set up multiple screens for VR games. I can tell that Louis is upset by the storm, because he loves VR games, but he's not playing. He pulls up security cameras on his computer showing the front gates, the garden, the Grand Trianon. Everything is all gray and blowing rain. Branches and debris rip by or tumble over the ground. I can barely see the canals beyond the *orangerie*.

"What are you looking at, Louis?" Philippe groans. "It's just rain."

"It's *just* something that can kill people." Louis shoves his laptop away and starts pacing.

"Touchy," Philippe snorts.

"You have no idea, Philippe." Louis shakes his head.

A smashing noise from somewhere upstairs shatters louder than the dull roar of wind. My heart beats double time as Josephine lets out a startled yelp.

"*Merde*." Stan gets up and glances at the ceiling like he'll magically be able to see through it. "Was that a window?"

"Probably," says Louis. "We should go to the basement."

"We're fine," says Stan.

"I see rotation in the cloud patterns. There could be a tornado," says Louis.

A tornado? I've never heard of one in real life. I thought they were just in vids.

"Thanks for the update, Captain Weatherman," says Stan.

"I'm serious. Why aren't any of you serious?"

"I'm serious," says Elisabeth. "I think you're right."

"Wait, wait, wait!" Philippe jumps off the couch. "Basement equals pool! Pool party!"

"In a storm that has lightning? No!" says Louis.

"Dude," says Philippe. "The pool won't get electrified. It can't because chlorine. It stops it."

There's a loud clap of thunder.

"Are you glitching?" says Louis.

"You know what?" says Elisabeth. "Go for it. Go jump in the pool, Philippe."

"Would everyone just chill out?" says Josephine.

"Yeah, I'm chilling out in the pool." Philippe drags a towel from the bathroom.

"Philippe, I can't believe I'm explaining this to you. But that chlorine thing is . . . not how science works," says Louis.

"Lightning's gonna blind me with science!" Philippe leaps up to give the doorframe a childish smack as he zips out the door.

"The lightning might get those synapses of his firing," says Elisabeth.

Louis groans into his hands. "*Mon Dieu . . .*"

"Should we . . . stop him?" I ask.

"I'll go." Louis squeezes my shoulder. "I'll be right back. Don't go anywhere."

Everyone is silent. I can't tell how much danger we're in, but Stan has muted the VR screens, which makes everything tense. I can hear the wind, this distant roar like the bass beneath the track of thunderclaps.

"Do you really think we need to go to the basement?" I ask.

Elisabeth shrugs. "Not sure. The staff will tell us if we do. It happened once a few years ago."

"It's a bunch of panicking over nothing," says Stan. "Versailles is like a fortress."

Stan is right. I try to imagine going to the basement while everything upstairs is swept away, and I can't. It's like a strange dream. To think of all the windows, statues, paintings, and my bed, and—

"Mops!" I yell.

"What?" says Elisabeth.

"I left Mops in my room, and he's probably scared! If we go to the basement, I can't go without him."

"That's crazy," says Josephine.

"He'll be fine," says Elisabeth. "I promise."

But I can't stand the thought of abandoning my scared little pug to the storm. "I'm going to go get him. I'll be so fast. I'll run the whole way."

"Marie, no," says Elisabeth.

"Louis won't like it," says Stan.

He won't, but I can't leave my dog. "This place is a fortress, remember? So I'll be fine."

"Yeah, and so will your dog."

But I'm already out the door. As soon as I enter the hallway, I'm faced with the storm out the window. The clouds are strange. Almost a greenish color. As I stare, a big branch all bright with leaves whacks into the pane. I jump back against the wall, nearly toppling a bust. If that branch had broken the window, I would have been obsolete.

I need a route without windows. If I run a hand along the wall, I might find a holo-door. One of the staff passages. Courtiers use them to sneak too. The Espagnic ambassador disappeared behind one once when I caught him eavesdropping on Louis and me.

But there's never a holo-door when you need one. I rush down the hallway, fingers brushing along the wall, until, finally, I hit air.

I've never passed through one of these before. The sensation is shivery and tingly. I emerge in a long, straight hallway, dimly lit with a strand of hanging bulbs. Dust and a musty smell tickle my nose.

I start running. There's nothing here to trip me up. No decorations or anything. Just wallpaper and the lights. I come to a staircase and dash up. When I get to the next hall, everything goes dark. Like pitch-black-blindness dark. It happens so fast, it takes my brain a second to catch up with reality.

My breath is pulled straight from my lungs and for a minute, I feel like I'm drowning. Everything is so, so dark. I've never been in darkness like this. Even though I know the hall is empty, I feel like this darkness hides things. Terrible things.

My hands are shaking almost too much to control them, but I pull my holofone from my pocket and use the glow to light my way.

I open my messages to tell Louis I did something dumb and I might need help, but *merde*! My holofone won't work. There's no service or something.

This has never happened. I feel like someone just cut off one of my hands. What if I need help? How am I going to find help? The dark is pressing in on me. I feel like it could crush me, and my breath is coming in short, painful gasps. My heart hurts. What's happening to me?

I force my breath to slow by drawing it in through my nose.

Get it together.

The last thing I want is to be trapped in here.

I just have to walk. *Just walk, Marie. Keep walking until you're out.*

With these thoughts on a loop in my head, I try to focus on putting one foot in front of the other until I find the nearest exit. When I push open the door, it's dark out here too. The whole palace must have lost power. I start running. I can't tell where exactly I am because in the dark, everything looks kind of the same. Holo-portraits that I use for landmarks have gone black and still. I learned a lot of the hallways by knowing to turn right at the Sun King portrait and that type of thing.

But oh! I know these stairs. I'm by the Hall of Mirrors. Yes, there it is. The storm seems huge and never-ending here, reflected in all the many windows in the long line of mirrors. It's strange to see it now. Dark. It's normally the brightest place in the palace between the large windows and huge gilded mirrors framed with tubes of neon light. They're all dark now. Everything is plain, like I've traveled back in time a thousand years. The frescoes on the ceiling ahead are shadowed and I feel like each face, each angel or king, is glaring down at me, telling me I shouldn't be here.

I make a run for it, pelting down the deserted hallway as fast as I can.

A loud smash startles me so much that I trip and fall to the ground. My knee collides with the floor with a sharp twinge. I flip around to look behind me and find a million shards of glass and a big branch across the hall. One of the gigantic mirrors that I had imagined as so indestructible is cracked and splintered into a hundred spiraling images of storm clouds. Rain spatters in from the hole in the window.

"Madame Dauphine!" shouts a voice behind me.

I can't seem to stop staring at the cracked mirror. What if I had been standing there? I would have been smashed like that glass. A gentle hand on my shoulder makes my heart lurch. Axel Fersen leans over me. I haven't spoken to him since my birthday. I stare at him, stupidly gaping, thoughts off-line.

"Quickly, please, madame." He holds a hand out to me.

I let him pull me to my feet. Then he huddles over me, hands on my shoulders, a barrier between me and more danger from the windows. "The Hall of Mirrors is off-limits in a storm like this, madame. It's dangerous. Now you can see why."

"I got lost," I say. "When the electricity went out."

"Why are you wandering around alone?"

"I needed to get my dog."

He laughs, a short, breathy sound. I don't really think anything about this situation is funny. "How did you find me?"

"I can always find you," he says, and steers me away from the mess.

"Where are we going?"

"To your apartments, where you must stay until the storm passes. You'll be safe in your common room."

We're out of the hall, but he still huddles close to me. Shoulder to shoulder. I could ask him to step away, tell him he's being impertinent. If I made it through the black hall alone, I'm pretty sure I can manage this walk. But I don't want to tell him to step away.

He stops when we're outside the doors to my apartment. "Your maids are sheltered in their quarters. I'll keep watch outside the door in case you need anything."

"What about the dauphin?" I ask.

"I believe he's on his way."

"Good. Good." Why am I still standing here? Axel is staring at me like he might be wondering the same thing. His face is blank and impossible to read, a bit like it was on my birthday. Does he think I'll ask for a kiss again? I don't know if I ever can or will. "Well, thank you."

He bows. "Please, madame. Your common room is safest. The window has storm shutters. The worst should pass soon."

Right. Forget kisses. Forget what he's thinking. I need to find Mops, anyway. When I enter my room, I have a second of panic again, calling for my dog with not so much as a whimper in return. On my fifth try, I hear a little yap from under my bed. I drop to my belly and stick my head under the heavy blankets. I can't see a thing.

"Mops?"

There's a scratching noise as he scoots toward me, then a slobbery tongue pokes me right in the eye. "Ew. Come on, Mops."

I drag him out and hug my trembling little friend. All I have to light the common room is my glowing holofone. Me and Mops huddle in the corner of the couch, sheltered in its pale glow.

The window shutters are sealed tight; the thick metal protects the glass and blocks any view of what's happening outdoors, but I can still hear the wind. I'm afraid, but not of the storm, exactly. I don't know what I'm afraid of.

The door to Louis's room opens and he bustles in all wide-eyed. "They moved you?"

"Uh, well . . . I remembered that Mops was up here."

"You came up here alone?"

"No, Captain Fersen helped me." I mumble it, embarrassed to talk about him to Louis.

"Good, good." Louis plops down beside me. "Those androids are fascinating, aren't they? The net is down. Nothing working except emergency power to the security system and the droids' systems."

"The androids can find us? Because of their programming?" Mops whines and I hug him closer.

"Well, yeah. Part of the point of them, I guess. They can do things an ordinary human can't."

"Don't you think it's kind of creepy?" I don't think it's creepy. Honestly, I'm just looking for reasons to dislike Fersen. I might still be a glitched-out wreck on the floor of the Hall of Mirrors without Fersen's tracking. Louis's eyes crinkle up.

"I guess it's a little strange," he laughs. "I'm more glad than anything. He kept you safe, after all."

"Hey, I can find things too." I wave my holofone around. "With the magical power of my GPS App."

"An App that's currently useless," he says.

"Not for long, I'm sure." I drop my holofone on the couch between us. It might as well be a brick. "Never had the net go out before."

"It's because they're powering on the generators and had to shut things off, I think. You know, a long time ago, before the Event, like way long ago, there was no net, no holofones, no electricity. People just had that map on your holofone as a piece of paper. And they used things like the sun and stars to navigate."

"Believe it or not, I didn't sleep through all my history lessons. I've seen a map before."

Louis shrugs. "Some people haven't. A lot of people. Not sure Philippe has."

"You think I'm like Philippe?"

Louis clears his throat. "No, sorry. That's not what I meant. I just . . . I like talking about this stuff, I guess."

He gets up from the couch and goes to his bookcase. He's brushing this off, but something in me still smarts. Sometimes I'm pretty sure Louis thinks I'm dumb.

He yanks some old, old book from the shelf. All leather-covered.

Right as Louis sits down, the power comes back. "That's

convenient, I guess." He opens the book with gentle hands. "You know your constellations?"

"I think I'm a Gemini, but I always felt like more of a Scorpio."

Louis laughs kind of nervously. "Uh, well. Not exactly . . . like that."

He's way too serious. It's not like I actually believe in astrology. I just take quizzes and play with a horoscope App when I'm bored. Speaking of, my fingers are itching to check the Apps. But Louis shoves this big star chart at me. "Yeah, people could tell where they were and what direction they should head based on the position of the stars."

I lean over him and look over the charts. They're pretty, I guess. Really intricate lines tracing out creatures I've never seen before. "You know what Scorpio is based on?" he asks.

"Nope." This whole conversation is making me feel stupid, and I just want to use my holofone.

"A scorpion. It was this little bug thing that went extinct during the Event. They were pretty cool. They had a poison stinger."

"Yeah? Me too."

"Really? Can't believe I've never noticed."

"You've never seen it."

He pokes at his holofone and it projects a simulation of this totally creepy thing with claws and a curving tail. "Hiding one of those, huh?"

"Ew! It's gross."

"They were giga-cool. Super fierce. Like you." He flops over, lying across my legs, bringing the book with him.

"Excuse you." I lean my arms over his chest, free to read the App feeds at last.

I open Pixter first. The last thing I posted was a storm photo and my well-wishes for everyone to stay safe. Why did my notifications explode? I always have so many. More than I'd ever get to read through if I had seventy years to check, but this is like double my usual amount. Super weird. Something must be bugging from the storm.

The comments keep ticking in. What's this latest one say?

Like u care what happens to us Austrobitch.

What? Seriously? That's really classy. People get glitched out during storms, though.

The next few are normal. Stay safe. Storm party at Versailles 🌀 That kind of thing.

But then:

Dauphine—hundreds live in a floodplain. Nowhere to go. Ppl probably dying as I type. They could be sheltered at Versailles. Why aren't they there? If you cared, you would petition the king.

There are a hundred comments below it. My hands shake as I click to expand:

Yeah uh. She doesn't care.

Message clear from the monarchy: let em drown.

#MadameClueless #MadamePixterWhore

I've never seen messages like this. Did something really bad happen during this storm? It must have. People are so angry. What do I do? I thought I had made a responsible post. I linked to the National Disaster Services and everything. Are people really drowning?

I close out Pixter and try Chatterbox instead. The storm tag shows exactly what people are talking about. Flooding, wind damage. People are sharing an article with the title *STORMS*

WILL NOT STOP UNTIL FACTORIES STOP.

It's loaded with comments:

We have learned nothing from climate disasters.
NOTHING.

It's not us wrecking the atmosphere. It's the factories
and industry of the First Estate. Our blood is on their
hands. They're bathing in it.

Another article says: *DON'T PANIC. WIND SPEEDS
VASTLY EXAGGERATED. SOCIAL MEDIA STORM RAGES
ON.*

These comments are harder to follow. A lot of arguing:

Everyone gets so worked up. Love and peace! Don't
cause a panic. It's dangerous.

You know what's really dangerous? Storm surge 4
with cyclone potential.

Stop spreading the anti-monarchist fearmongering.

Storm is not nearly as bad as it was predicted to be.

Looks pretty bad out my window, mate.

Windows!! Very authoritative and scientific source.

Regardless of the real surge strength we have: Seine
flooding, power outages, cruiser crashes, shortage of
provisions #WhereIstheKing?

Getting it on with Du Barry in a gold-covered room
safe from all this shit. #WhereIstheKing?

I feel light-headed. There's a strange tingling in my belly and
my mouth is dry. "Louis?"

"What's up?"

"Something . . . bad is going on."

He heaves himself up, leans into me to see my little screen. I can't tear my eyes from the holofone. "Can I take it?"

I let him pluck it from my numb fingers.

I feel like I'm dreaming. This can't be real. Louis seems to read for an age. Finally, he places the holofone back on my lap and crosses the room to his computer in a few quick strides. He opens up like six Apps and scrolls through them quickly. Then he opens a few screens of code. His nose is practically touching the monitor.

Slowly I rise, feeling as though I'm underwater. I grab the back of Louis's chair for support. He's opened up a document, where he copies and pastes big chunks of code.

"Louis, what's going on?"

He holds up a finger. "Sorry, I need a minute." He grabs a stylus and scribbles something on the holo on the wall over his desk. It's more code and some jargon I don't understand. He falls back into his chair and keeps inserting things into the code. Pulling bits from other places and dropping it into a new file.

Finally, he sighs and flings the stylus at his computer screens. "Forgot I know how to code, huh, assholes?"

"Louis, what's going on?"

He drops his head into his hands and doesn't answer me for a long minute. "Security firewalls must have crashed when the power went out."

"What?"

"They're lying to us," he says. "Nothing's changed."

"Who's lying to us?"

Louis drops his hands to the desk with a *thud* that knocks over a mug. "Who knows . . ." He shakes his head. "Who even knows."

"You're glitching me out."

"Well, *I'm* glitching out. But now I have the code. I can unlock this whenever I need to, if we're careful."

"Please talk to me. Unlock what?"

He swivels his chair slowly. "I don't want to scare you."

"I'm already scared, obviously. You don't have to baby me."

He rubs his eyes and sighs. "I'm . . . look, I'll always protect you, okay? Whether you want it or not. Just know that." He looks so pained. I've been scared out of my mind a few times since coming to the Franc Kingdom. This one takes the cake. "That stuff you saw on the Apps? It's . . . always there. They just don't let us see it."

This is like a nightmare, where someone is saying something to you that's really important, but the words coming out of their mouth make no sense, a string of random phrases that don't mean anything even though you really need to understand. "What are you talking about?"

"They block things, Marie. They filter out what they do and don't want us to see when we use the net."

"You mean like the fires that time?"

Thunder rumbles, rattling the walls like it's in the room with us. Mops barks at the ceiling. Louis runs his hands through his hair. "Check your holofone."

I think of those comments and hashtags, frightening and hateful. "I don't want to."

Louis turns to his computer and opens Pixter. "See? Gone. They reset everything."

I do take out my holofone now and go back to that storm picture. He's right. Most of the hate I saw is gone. Back to the usual stuff. A few things of concern about floods. But it's gentle information. Information meant to coddle me. Just enough so I would never suspect the truth. That what's happening out there is ugly. It's a disaster.

I sit on the floor at Louis's feet. Mops takes this as an invitation to walk all over me. "Why?"

"Because it's easier to control us when we're ignorant."

Slowly pieces fall into place. Each strange thing that's happened since my arrival here. The bugs, the historical models, the hidden information, Adelaide's banishment when she gave me a little bit of truth. It's like we live on the set of a film. How do we stand up to something this big and invisible? "What do we do?"

He shrugs again and stares blankly at his computer screen. "They'd like us to forget we ever saw this."

"I can't. No chance. I can't forget something like this."

"You might have to," he mumbles.

"Well, I won't!"

Louis jumps out of his chair, eyes flicking over the ceiling and walls. "*Merde . . .*"

"What?"

He leans back over his computer. "I need another minute."

"What's going on?"

"I'm serious. Please."

The damn code is back. Lines and lines of it. Louis clicks and types furiously. So fast, I wouldn't be able to keep up even if I could read code. I pick Mops up and start pacing. Pacing, pacing while the thunder gets softer.

Finally, Louis pauses what he's doing. He seems to hesitate, pressing his fist to his mouth. Then he hits enter. He refreshes a few things, nods to himself, and at last, he turns away from the computer. "That was stupid. We sat there and talked about that with the bugs online."

"You just took the bugs off-line?"

He nods, but avoids my eyes.

"I'm not sure whether I want to kiss you or punch you. Why didn't you do this sooner?"

"Because I'm trying to explain to you that this is dangerous."

"What's dangerous?"

"Knowing!" He paces and scrubs at his hair again. I've never seen Louis like this. "Them knowing that we know."

"Well, so what? Maybe they should! Who's even doing this? And what could possibly be more dangerous than us having no idea what our subjects really think about us or what's happening to them?"

He shakes his head. "You don't understand."

"Obviously! And I know I'm just some idiot who can't read a map, but I'm pretty sure no one can read minds! So unless you want to explain to me what's going on, I'm going to continue not understanding!" My rant causes Mops to start barking, and I snuggle him calm.

Louis ambles over to the couch and buries his face in his hands. I roll my eyes and turn away. I try. I try really hard. I care about people and what they have to say, and I try to help. Then everyone just treats me like I'm brainless and tells me nothing. My husband does it, my subjects do it, and I shouldn't be surprised that some mysterious other power, the king or the First Estate or whoever, is doing it to me too.

I round on Louis, ready to tell him all this, but I see his shoulders shaking. Is he . . . crying? I feel like my heart has jumped into my throat to strangle down the angry words I was about to unleash.

"I'm sorry. I didn't mean to yell." I take a step toward him, but he holds a finger up and I stop in my tracks. Did I hurt him so badly? Why do I just start yelling things the minute I get upset? When he turns away to rub at his eyes with his shirt, I realize he's embarrassed. Not upset with me.

When he looks up, red-eyed, I sit beside him and put a hand on his chest. He covers my hand with his own. "I couldn't talk about this with the bugs on," he says quietly. "I've never talked about this with anyone. Except Elisabeth, a little. It's the reason I wouldn't do anything about the bugs before now. We'll be okay for a few minutes, because they'll just assume it's the storm. Or they'll just . . . I don't know. I don't know what to do, Marie."

I put my free hand on his cheek. "Talk to me. We'll figure this out."

"I'm not sure we can," he says.

"Louis, what's this about?"

He takes a deep, shuddering breath. "It starts with my father."

TWENTY-TWO

✳

Louis stares at the shuttered windows and scratches at his jaw. "Or maybe my brother. My older brother. Xavier. Did they tell you about him?"

Xavier was the eldest Bourbon brother, who died of the wasting disease when he was young. No one knows what causes it, whether it's the food we eat or stuff in the air or our water. But when it strikes, especially when it strikes someone as young as Xavier, it takes hold quickly. Big tumors and sores drain the life from people. They become skin and bones, they lose their hair, their skin dries into big flaky patches. It's only now that I've really thought about how terrible that might have been for Louis, like I forgot that he had this whole other life before I showed up. Stupid of me. I just nod and rest a hand on his knee. He's still running a thumb against his jaw, eyes wide and lost.

"Yeah . . . Xavier . . . ," he says. "Everybody loved him. He was all the things I'm not. Clever like Stan, confident like Philippe, charming like Grand-Père. So, at that time, my père was dauphin and Xavier was heir apparent after him, but now we're stuck with me. It's kind of a joke."

He shakes his head, lips pursed like he swallowed something bitter.

"Louis . . ." I hate it when he talks like this. Like he's such a bad dauphin.

He shrugs. "Well, what were the odds? That both of them would die and I'd be the one left? It was never supposed to be me. That's why I didn't get any of the training until I was ten, and by then I was just kind of . . ."

He gestures helplessly in the general area of his face, as if he's some unremarkable piece of furniture. My brain finishes the sentence for him. *Perfect*, it says. I've never thought of him this way before. It's a surprise to feel this, that "perfect" is the word my brain stuck into that sentence. I should say the word out loud, because I think he needs to hear it. But the feeling of it is so new, the connection he formed by telling me is so fragile . . . I can't break it. Instead I ask, "You were left alone, weren't you? They ignored you to train Xavier, and then Stan and Philippe were born and they're kind of . . ."

"Annoying?"

"I was going to say chatterboxes, but yeah. That too."

He smiles. Just a little.

Then he frowns, stares down at his hands. "He got so thin. I don't know if you've ever seen someone with the wasting disease, but it's like they just melt into a skeleton. To see him like that, my brother . . ."

I rub his broad back, and he keeps talking.

"My père was never the same after Xavier died. I remember him as kind of a sad guy before and after Xavier. Wore black a lot. Had morbid taste in music and stuff." He laughs a little like he's remembered something, but then he rubs his eyes and goes on. "It's because he had a wife before my maman. I don't know much about her, except she had red hair and died of the wasting disease too, a year after they were married. He loved her a lot, so losing two people . . . It just broke him, I guess. After Xavier died, he hunted way more. Like, you think *I* hunt a lot . . ." He smiles, but it's forced, as if it hurts him.

"He would be gone for hours. All day. Elisabeth and Philippe kept asking after him. I'd pick Philippe up and swing him around or take them both for walks. We were all worried about how our père kept disappearing, even Philippe, even though he was only seven. Stan was angry all the time. My maman and père would have arguments late at night. I never understood what they were fighting about. Until one day Papa asked me to go hunting with him. I was really happy. It had been forever since he took me with him, you know? Stupid . . ."

The way he says this is like he has a list of everything he's ever done that he thinks of as a mistake, and he won't forget a single thing on it. Once, I found little square notes stuck to his desk that said things like, *Rude to Thérèse*, *Crashed Elisabeth's holofone*, *Balanced the account wrong*. Something about them seemed so terrible that I crumpled them up and tossed them in the toilet. Then I felt guilty, like I'd read a diary. He never brought it up, and the sticky notes never appeared again. I'm sure they're not gone from his brain, though.

"We rode forever," he continues. "That's how it felt. Farther into the forest than I had ever been. We ditched the attendants and rode the horses hard. I was afraid I was going to fall or get lost because we were off trail. I had branches in my face and my legs ached. Then he stopped. Everything looked normal except there were signs stuck to the trees. Signs like I'd never seen before. They glitched me out because this is my home, and those signs said 'Danger' and 'Défense de Passer.' All bright yellow and red.

"Père was restless on his horse, walking it up and down. He asked, 'Do you think the woods go on and on, Louis?'

"Weird question, but I answered the best I could, told him they go from Orsay to Saint-Cloud. Then he reached up into the branches, pulled out an acorn, and tossed it into the trees by the signs. It just kind of disappeared. I thought I lost track of it, but he did it again and again. The acorn would vanish before it hit the ground. I was glitched, but I thought it was, I don't know, a magic trick? He did it one more time, and the air around the acorn flickered a little bit like light on glass. Then I started to figure it out. Papa asked what I saw. I said, 'It looks like a holo, sir.' What else could it be? But why the hell was there a holo in the woods? It felt so wrong.

"'What do you think lies beyond that holo?' he asked. I just shrugged, because how would I know? I was ten. 'Would you like to see?' he asked.

"No. No, I didn't want to see," Louis says to me. "I'm not brave enough for that."

"You were ten," I remind him.

"Ten and almost pissing myself," he sighs. "My père reached out a hand toward the holo and it flickered for a minute, then the air kind of pixelated and made a reflection of his hand. It moved and changed as he flexed his fingers. 'Smart tech,' he said.

"I didn't want the answer. I really wasn't ready for it. But I asked anyway. 'Why is it here?'

"'So we don't see what's on the other side, of course. Now, shall we look?'

"But I couldn't. My horse was fidgeting around, I was shaking so much. My père looked ashamed of me. Stupid, shaking me. And he said, 'I'm showing you this so you don't grow up to be a coward like the rest of them.'

"My père had never talked to me like that before. He was . . . I don't know, he was firm, but he wasn't like Grand-Père. He didn't make me feel like . . ."

Louis trails off and runs his hands through his hair.

"You were so young. Of course you were scared. Anyone would be."

"Would they? Would Stan or Philippe have done the same?"

"Who cares what those dongles would have done?"

He drops his hands from his head and when he looks at me, there's so much warmth. No one has looked at me like that before. But he also looks so sad.

"Anyway . . . Then he asked me, 'Do you know about the Wastelands?' Of course I knew about them. I had learned about them in lessons, so when he asked me where they were, I told him: Northern Anglia, the Sardinian States, the Apennines, all over the Americas, and at the edges of our kingdom. Then he just looked at me . . . dead in the eye, and he said, 'How about right on our doorstep, son? How about right on the other side of that holo? There are dust and death and heat and people living in tents somewhere out there, hunting deer with two heads and sick meat. Right next to our own lands.' And I just . . . I was horrified. I cried."

Of course he did. I could do the same in this moment. I don't understand. Wastes? Right outside Versailles? How is this possible? Why would they hide it? All my guesses scare me. They scare me so much. This doesn't seem real. Nothing about this night should be real. Louis takes my hand and squeezes it, nods once. His skin is clammy, too real to be a dream.

"Papa said, 'I'm showing you this because I don't want you to forget. Because I don't want you to be a useless pawn like your grandfather. If we can't face the truth and govern accordingly, then there's no point to us. The king has been trained well not to see. But that's not how I'll raise you. Do you understand me?'

"I didn't understand him at all, but I said 'Yes, sir' anyway. He never made me go through the holo, but he told me one day I'd have to. It couldn't be ignored. I never did see what was on the other side. My père did, though. More than once. It's where he went when he disappeared hunting for hours. Then one day Maman came to me . . . crying . . . and she told me Papa had fallen from his horse and broken his neck."

I hold tight to his hand. "I thought he caught the wasting disease," I whisper.

His throat bobs as he swallows and shakes his head. "No. And he didn't fall from his horse either. I'm not quite stupid enough to believe that. There was never a body. Try explaining that to Elisabeth when she asks, 'Where's Papa?'"

His voice goes hoarse, but he keeps talking. "Maman started to go the same damn way as Papa. She got all pale and thin. She'd be gone half the day. Stan was so mad. He's still mad. Can you blame him, really? Once, he broke a statue on purpose and Grand-Père glitched, yelling at him to behave like a prince or he'd send him to our cousins at the Espagnic court. I said to Stan, 'Next time you want to hit something, hit me.' So he did. Gave me a black eye, then cried over it."

He laughs a little.

"That's so Stan," I say.

"Very much Stan, *oui*. Anyway, Maman came to my room one night, completely exhausted. Way too thin. I've never seen anyone look that tired before or since. She set me on her lap even though I was too big for it, and she told me I was a good boy, and so honest. Then she begged me to tell her if Papa had shown me anything strange in the woods. I didn't want to tell her. I had tried to forget about it. I whispered the truth about the huge hologram in the trees that Papa said blocks out the Wastes.

"I don't know if it was right. To tell her . . . it was a like a shadow fell over her face. I'll never forget what she said. 'Louis, you're a good boy and a good brother. You'll be a good man. But I'm afraid of what will happen when you're king.'

"I didn't know what she meant. I just don't understand . . . still don't understand . . . how the things people say are my best qualities are also my worst."

I reach out and brush a tear off his face. "You're perfect," I whisper. It comes so easily this time.

"Far from it." He gently kisses my hand. "I've made so many mistakes. Like telling Maman about the woods. She was dead a week later."

This is too much. My heart aches. "That isn't your fault."

"It's someone's." His brow furrows and he stares at the rustling trees on the holo-wall's screen saver. "Grand-Père said she was ill and took too many pills. Whatever the hell that's supposed to mean. I don't know who's responsible . . . but someone is. Maybe the First Estate, who probably got Papa. Or maybe I should have just kept my mouth shut. Like I'm supposed to . . ."

"You were a child, Louis. A scared little boy."

"And I should have been anything it took to save Maman. But I wasn't anything. Just scared little me. I haven't changed.

"Grand-Père scooped me up after the funeral. Like he was comforting me. But he said in my ear, 'I know what your father showed you. The crown is a dangerous game, but if you don't play, bad things happen. Understand?'

"That scared me, but once I got into coding, I started messing with hacking. Just small things at first. Games, my brothers' Apps to prank them. Then I found some filters on my net access, hacked around them, and from there . . . I found the blocked stuff. Stuff I wasn't supposed to find . . . stuff about my père. Conspiracy theories. Except the further I dug and researched, the less crazy it sounded. People linked the death of Louis the Dauphin to the Bureau of Business Owners in the First Estate. He wasn't supposed to see what was out there. He asked a lot of questions. He fought Grand-Père's decisions. And Grand-Père's decisions are really the First Estate's decisions.

"Grand-Père went on a walk with me one day and stopped me by that stupid statue of Apollo that I hate now . . . and he said, 'I heard you have a taste for tooling around with computer programs.' I'm not exactly a great liar. I just shrugged, since I knew damn well I wasn't supposed to be on those sites.

"Grand-Père said, 'As a king, you don't make all the rules. I know you remember when I told you that you must play the game. To win the game, you follow the rules. Do you understand me?'

"I said 'Yes, sir.' I was thinking how it was the same feeling as when my père dragged me out in the woods, but the opposite message.

"He looked so fierce when he said it. So brave, so much like the king. But all I could think of was when Papa called him a coward that day he showed me the holo-boundary.

"I've never figured it out, Marie. Who the real cowards are or what the right thing is. I've just listened to Grand-Père because I'm a coward too. That's why I wouldn't touch the bugs. I'm so afraid of losing my siblings or Grand-Père or you. But it kills me. It just eats at me, you know? How do I make Grand-Père happy and honor my père's memory? How do I be a good king? How is any one person supposed to handle any of this?"

I squeeze his big hand. If I could give him whatever strength I have left that hasn't been scared out of me, I would. If I could take half his pain, all his loss, I would. But I can't.

"I don't know," I say. "But that game your grandfather told you about? It has two players now."

TWENTY-THREE

June 28, 3070, 9:52 p.m.

The thunder has grown distant, a low grumble like Mops makes when he stares down a squirrel. Louis sprawls across the couch, dull-eyed and exhausted.

I can't imagine what he's been through. I'm tired just from listening, and my heart . . . hurts. I've never felt anything quite the same, but that's what it's like. It hurts.

I should be more scared. If you break the rules in Versailles, you're dead, apparently. And I've broken plenty of rules. But I can't find it in me to be scared for myself. All my feeling right now is for Louis. Nothing has ever ached like this before. Like if I just hurt enough, I could take it away from him so he doesn't have to look this wrecked.

"So, you were afraid about the bugs . . . because you think the First Estate killed your dad. For finding things out and trying to fight them?"

"I'll probably never know what really happened. But . . . yes."

I squeeze his knee because it's what's closest to me. "If I had known all this, I wouldn't have been so harsh to you about the bugs."

"It's okay," he says quietly.

"Not after everything you went through. I wish I had known."

He shrugs and gives the smallest smile. "You had to be a level-four friend to unlock my tragic backstory."

"What does that mean?"

"You've never played RPGs?"

"You really think the answer to that is yes?" I swat his leg and my heart aches again when he smiles all sad. "What now? How are we supposed to act like none of this is happening?"

I would do anything to help him. Louis is family now. I can feel that now more than I ever have. I love him as much as I love the rest of my family. I have no idea if I love him like people normally love their husbands, but it's love and it's worth a lot more than nothing.

I'm surprised when he reaches his arms out to me. Slowly, I lower myself, and I feel mega-gig shy. He's holding me right on top of him and we haven't exactly been in this position before. "What . . . what should we do?" I whisper, and I'm not sure if I'm referring to the filters and the secrets or this horizontal state.

"All that stuff I wrote down? It's so I can build us a way around the filters. We might not be able to use it often or they'll notice. But it's a start. We have to be careful, you know?"

"Of course." I touch his face. "Louis, you're a lot better than everyone tells you."

"Not really," he says. "If I were better, I'd know what kind of king I want to be. I just don't know what's right."

"Who . . . is really in charge? It's not your grandfather, is it?"

"No. I don't think it is."

"You'll figure it out. I'll help you."

He strokes a hand over my hair and rests it there on the back of my head. "You're . . . the best person I have."

The best? I've been far from the best. I've whined at him and gone to parties without bothering to learn how to help him be a better king. I never even bothered to wonder how his parents died. "I've been useless. I want to do better."

"You're really far from useless," he says. Then he kisses me. And he doesn't stop. He kisses me long enough for me to wonder if tonight of all nights, our marriage will become complete in the minds of the court. He kisses me long enough for me to stop thinking of much at all.

When he does stop, I feel like I just woke up from a long nap, but also buzzing like I just drank three Mountain Jam Lime drinks. "What level of friends do that?" I ask him.

"At least a five or six."

He's going to fall asleep. I can tell. I kind of want to tell him I love him, but I'm afraid he'll get all buffer and crash. So I don't.

TWENTY-FOUR

July 1, 3070, 8:24 a.m.

Three days later, when the storm passes and the rain finally stops, Louis asks me to meet him in the gardens. His text says, By the Proteus and Aristaeus statue.

The what? I write back.

The dude tying another dude to a rock.

Okay, Louis, sure. I search the statue name and see that it's by the Château du Soleil all the way on the other side of the gardens. He must want to avoid the bots and the staff scurrying around, picking up branches and leaves and smashed flowerpots.

It's a half-hour walk that takes me farther and farther into the wilder parts of the garden, where I feel I could lose myself. The morning fog softens the hedges but hides things like an eerie photo filter. The gardens feel changed. It's like the storm was a reminder that no matter how much we build, how much of the past we preserve at Versailles, nature can still have her way.

After making my way around a downed tree that crushed a rosebush, spitting red petals like a spray of blood over the grass, I spot Louis in a dark hoodie, leaning on a statue with his face buried in a book.

I rap my knuckles on the base of the marble statue, where a super-ripped guy is wrestling another ripped guy to the ground.

They're kneeling on a panther or something? I don't get half the statues here.

"Dude tying another dude to a rock," I say. "Hot."

He turns around and gives me that sleepy smile he does. "If you say so."

I pluck the book from his hands, thinking it's the only way to get a proper hug, but he scoops me around the waist and tugs me close for a kiss. I'm so shocked I have a couple-seconds-delayed response, but it's a really nice kiss. I want to tease him, ask him if he's been practicing, but I find all I can manage is a breathless "Well, hello to you too."

"I missed you," he says, all quiet and rumbly.

"I saw you this morning."

"I know."

The fog has made his hair damp. I push a tumble of it behind his ear, hand him his book back. "What are you reading?"

"David Hume," he says like it should be super obvious.

"Okay."

"You know, the philosopher. He's, like, the chillest."

"Sure."

"He said, 'It's not contrary to reason to prefer the destruction of the whole world to the scratching of my finger.'"

Louis taps the tip of my nose with his finger. I wave him off. "What's that supposed to mean?"

"Well, people still argue about exactly what he means. He's basically saying that emotion wins out over reason when people make decisions. He's the 'reason is a slave to the passions' guy."

I tug on his hoodie string. "Passions? Are you trying to make me blush or something?"

He shrugs, his eyes all twinkly. "Read it and tell me what you think," he says, and passes the book back to me.

I'm not going to read it, but I take it to make him happy. "What are we doing out here?"

"We're avoiding the eyes and ears. As much as we can." He glances around. Doesn't look like anyone is nearby, but you'd be surprised. Once, a finance minister fell right out of a hedge trying to eavesdrop on me and Mercy.

"Hmm . . . *Allons-y*." He puts his hand on the small of my back and guides me off the path into the trees. "I've been thinking a lot."

"About the blocks on the net?"

"Yeah, everything. I just think . . . well, I can't forget about this. Can you?"

I'd like to. I really would. It seems clear that Versailles is a distraction. A distraction for the people, a distraction for us. They've given us everything we could want. But to ignore the truth when we're supposed to lead feels wrong. I shake my head. "I don't think so."

"Good," he says. "I mean, it's not good, and I'm sorry you had to come here and get thrown into this."

"The Austro Lands are probably not much different . . ." I think of my mama. How many lies has she told to protect me? To train me well for my role? My role as a puppet.

"Probably not. But we'll rule someday, and maybe now we can be a little more prepared. Maybe we can get some answers."

"I agree. But how?"

"I have an idea. But I really need your help. You're an expert at the Apps," says Louis. "You're good at finding things out about people. You're good at talking to people on there. Good at presenting yourself. I need you to use all of that."

"Music to my ears," I say. "What exactly are you thinking?"

"I have a way around the filters. It can't be used for too long at a time. It can't be used when you're in the palace and everyone is watching. Just out here. Just for an hour or two, once or twice a week."

I can hear my heartbeat along with some little bird singing out in the trees, muffled by the fog. "What do you want me to do?"

"I need you to learn more about what's hidden from us. What's really going on out there. I need you to see what the people really think of us so we can try to think of ways to solve the real problems."

Fear prickles through me but also . . . a little excitement. "Yeah, I can do that. Of course." I think of how many followers I have on the Apps and the thousands of glowing comments. I used to think I was a guru. But if there are a thousand terrible comments I've never even seen, am I really such an expert? "But what if I can't fix anything and I make it all worse?"

"If you can't, nobody can," he says, and kisses my forehead. "You'll be anonymous. I'm going to give you the name of a forum that I used to find stuff about my father. You'll just be a screen name there. And your IP and proxy will always change."

"Is this dangerous?" I ask.

"Yes," he says quietly. "But I trust you. Work for no more than two hours at a time. Always somewhere like this." He gestures around at the woods.

"Are you sure this isn't something you'd be better at? You're the computer guy."

"I'm the guy who gives you a way in," he says. "You know how to talk to people. You know how to make people like you.

You can do things that I can't. I need you, Marie."

Those are like magic words. I think I would do anything for him in this moment. I just want to make him happy. I just want to do something, anything that will make me feel less helpless. "I'll do it. I'll do anything."

"You know that band Dukes and Bakers?" he asks.

They're this totally morose Anglian arena rock band that are kind of classic now, I guess, but they were popular, like, twenty years ago, when glitchgoths were a thing. "Uh, yeah, I guess."

"Everyone knows David Cass, the singer, right? Dude gets thousands and thousands of people singing or jumping or doing whatever he asks. People love them and misfits feel like they belong to them and kids can even bond with their dad over them."

"Is that what you did?" I still have no idea where he's going with this, but sometimes I like him most when he's talking about totally obscure stuff.

"Uh, yeah." He smiles all bashful for a minute. "My point is, most people think of David Cass when they think of Dukes and Bakers. They feel like Cass is talking to them when they listen. Do you think David Cass wrote the songs?"

I shrug. "I don't know. Probably? Most leads do."

"George Teller did. Do you know who George Teller is?"

"Darling, I hate to tell you, I only know, like, two songs by that band. No, I don't know who George Teller is."

"Two songs?" He looks physically pained. "Okay, we're fixing that. But not today. The point is that Teller was a bassist. The guy who hangs around toward the back and people forget he's there. But he was really the one who came up with all the music. He just didn't have the stage presence Cass did. No charisma. And he knew it. They worked really well together. He knew Cass could get people to love the band. Knew he could speak to them and make the magic happen. So I need you to be my Cass."

I get it, but it's such a Louis thing to say that I feel a rush of fondness twitch my lips into a smile. "That's really sweet. I wish we were in a band. Instead of . . . this."

"I know," he says. "But this is what we are. And we can make a lot of difference for people. But only if we know the truth."

"I feel better about it pretending I'm in a band, I think."

He smiles. "Whatever works. Can I see your holofone?"

I pass it over and Louis spends a few minutes with it. When he's done, he shows me some window he wants me to open and type some code commands into. Then he gives me a password, and we sit there looking at the code and the password until I could recite it in my sleep.

TWENTY-FIVE

July 8, 3070, 7:34 a.m.

I'm finally able to dodge people early in the morning. I tell Noailles I need a morning walk to clear my head for the day. I travel the maze of hedgerows in the gardens until I start to feel a little lost. I know the gardens pretty well by now, but sometimes they start to look the same. The paths are so straight and the hedges so tall.

I find a pagoda to sit under. Some little thing I'm not sure I've even seen before. I lean against one of the pillars and get to work.

Twice I mess up the way into Louis's server or whatever this thing is. Now I think I'm in. There's a little part of me that hopes people were just upset during the superstorm and that what I saw was a fluke because people were buffering over the storm. But I think the larger part of me knows exactly what I'll find.

Louis asked me to read the forums on a site called WhoWatches. He told me to make a screen name and interact once I feel out the message boards. I pull some breakfast from my purse, an apple and a little paper-wrapped bit of cake that found their way into my bag before anyone could see me very rudely sneaking food from the breakfast table.

While crunching my apple, I check the site out and it looks sketch. The background is all black, with bold yellow text on the banner. Reading the About page tells me that the title refers to some graphic novel about antiheroes fighting a shadow government. The site is for conspiracy theorists and total nerds. Of course Louis would send me here.

I click over to the forums to make my screen name. I freeze, jaw locked around the apple in my mouth while my thumbs hover over my keyboard. Any of my usual screen names are way too obvious. I glance around for inspiration. WillowTree, Sparrow7, FlowerGirl? Nah, those are so obsolete. The only other thing that catches my eye is my little piece of cake, all pink frosted.

I type *CakeEater* into the sign-up bar. It's kind of cute. It'll do.

WhoWatches says they're a gathering of fact finders, truth seekers, whistleblowers, scientists, misfits, and malcontents. Sounds like a party. There are thousands of users active on the forum chats, which have a few broad topics broken down into subforums.

I see: Social Engineering and You, Police and Patsies, Sins of the First Estate, The Event That Halved the Human Population, Climate Will Kill Us, Fake Facts and Historical Lies, Who Killed Louis the Dauphin?, Who Watches the Bourbons?, How to Break Free, and Who Watches WhoWatches?

I set my holofone on the ground in front of me. I don't even know where to begin. "Maybe they're all just glitching crazy," I say right out loud.

It's time to be brave. It's time to find the facts, and I won't know unless I look. I start with Who Watches the Bourbons?

What I find is overwhelming. Pages and pages of threads. The people who run this site really are watching us. Everyone is watching all the time, just like Mercy and Noailles and my mama have always told me. I think the users, the "Watchers," know more about the court and the people here than I do. A lot of topics start with RECEIPTS and then name a courtier and how much money they think that courtier wasted or how they were rude to someone or supported a law the Watcher didn't like. And me. I'm in here over and over. Dresses I'm not supposed to wear. Parties I'm not supposed to attend. Madame Deficit: The Dauphine's Gambling Addiction has, like, fifty pages of conversation. I click it and keep clicking like you poke at a sore tooth over and over. Gambling addiction? They don't know anything about me!

I want to look away, but I can't stop myself from clicking the topic labeled That Pastoral Photo Shoot.

I was proud of it. I had fun. When I think of Louis and me that day, my heart warms. If it's on WhoWatches, I'm sure it's about to be ruined.

The commentary:

❋ How can they be this out of touch? They flaunt nature and green space for those who will never see it.

❋ They play at farming like it's a game instead of a dangerous, thankless business. Let's see them defend sheep against a band of Waste Raiders.

❋ This is so gross. Is their extreme privilege meant to be cute? How much did this cost when half the kingdom is starving?

❋ Let's be honest, though. We know the First Estate probably engineered all this. I'm surprised there's no sponsorship attached to this. She said Stan set this up, so I'm sure they leveraged him in some way. Rewarded him or had dirt on him. I'm just not sure what message they were trying to convey here.

❀ Royals: They're Just Like You. Transparent bullshit meant to distract from crown spending.

❀ Spread that shit. Put it all over Chatterbox and Yakback.

❀ Right? #MadameDeficit—make them aware.

❀ Make them uninformed more like. All the masses ever know or pay attention to is hashtags. That's social engineering.

❀ @XxxMaxXxRobesxxX weigh in, dude.

XxxMaxXxRobesxxX says: Perhaps social engineering is the only way to stir the people. What we do would not be nearly as deceptive as what's used against us every day.

Who the hell is this MaxRobes and why does everyone act like he's king of the chats? I click his profile and see next to nothing about him except: Law Student, he/him, Change Maker, WillofthePeople96 on Pixter.

His comments and opinions are everywhere. On every topic, someone adds @XxxMaxXxRobesxxX and wants to hear his take.

The Bourbons are puppets of the First Estate, he writes. That much is clear. Look at how they use the dauphine as their little spokesperson for whatever wasteful consumer good the marketing teams are pushing. And those vaccines? Free today, fifty bits for the flu shot next winter. They're a mask and a prop. And we need to expose the people behind the mask.

The comments are full of his supporters.

Yeah, no kidding. The only reason people accept the monarchy is because everyone has such a big nostalgia boner.

I have hope for young Louis-Auguste, **someone responds.** I heard he's quite educated and I even heard a rumor he's a hacker. Seems like a cool guy. And remember his father died trying to expose the same stuff we are.

XxxMaxXxRobesxxX has one simple response to that: It's impossible to rule innocently.

Watching4Progress: So he should abdicate and join us.

XxxMaxXxRobesxxX: Abdicate to who? Stanislas? It may be harsh, but the Bourbons are a tree with rot, and there's no saving any limbs no matter how healthy they might look.

I can't read any more because my eyes are filled with tears and they're blurring everything. If they see Louis and me as nothing more than tools, then they would see us dead just for being used. It's so unfair. I'm nothing but what everyone has made me. They want to punish us for being exactly who we were told to be since birth. I have no answers. What am I supposed to write on these forums?

I feel like one girl against the entire net. And I know the net well enough to be sure of who would win that fight.

TWENTY-SIX

The second time I sneak away to log on to the forums, I'm still glitched out to the max. After wandering around the gardens for over an hour (procrastinating, really), I get a little lost. While wandering aimlessly like a vacuum droid, I find a field that's almost overgrown and a rock formation covered in moss. After a closer look, I find a little cave. When I poke my head in, the dark is cool and the little grotto drips small puddles on the slick, rocky ground. I take a step inside and smell mud. I've never been anywhere quite like this. But I kind of like it. It feels safe.

I take a seat on a damp rock. My leggings are going to get muddy, but I bet Georgette will cover for me. I let the dark comfort me, try to feel as sneaky as the First Estate planting every bug and spy in the palace.

After putting in my passwords and codes, I return to WhoWatches. My head's been spinning since my first visit. There's just so . . . much. I was only able to talk through a little with Louis when we went for a walk. He got pale as I described what I found. I need to learn more, no matter how scary.

There are a few names that pop up again and again on WhoWatches. With the help of some Pixter stalking, I find their real names: Maximilien Robespierre, Camille Desmoulins, Lucile Duplessis, Georges Danton, Jean-Paul Marat, Antoine St-Just.

They go to university in Parée. They're all smart. All organized. All persuasive.

Scrolling past fears, theories, outrages, a thousand problems, I feel paralyzed. I have to do something, but could I even hope to right this many wrongs in a lifetime? I scroll back to the top, to the more recent chat threads, where something catches my eye. Fire in the Wastes Means Food Shortage.

Louis would probably like to know more about the Wastelands. Maybe follow in his father's footsteps. Except we'll avoid the dying part.

I read about a wildfire that burned through miles of land, including a big irrigation plot that grew wheat and corn. As I scroll through message after message, reading about rising grocery prices and the horrible descriptions of people from the Wastes fleeing the fire into Parée but finding nowhere to go, only one thought crosses my mind: *No one told me.* And I'm sure that was very intentional.

I type: What should be done?

My post is drowned by commenters in mid-argument about whether the fire was caused by arsonists from the First Estate, Wastelanders, or simply the unstable weather.

I try again: What happened to the Wastelanders? Where are they now?

ThatDamnDanton63: Arrested most likely. Only useful thing the police do. Wastelanders only want anything to do with Parée when they get themselves in hot water that they set boiling themselves.

JP.Marat: It's cruel to blame them for their own misfortunes. Besides, there's no evidence they started the fire.

CAKE EATER

ThatDamnDanton63: There were floods in Parée not long ago. How does a fire start naturally after that?

JP.Marat: I'm going to guess you've never set foot outside the city, but try to keep up. The Wastes aren't a desert. They have grasses and shrubs, but they're sick, unhealthy. Dry. Fires spread fast out there even if it's rained recently. What's more, Paréesians aren't any better or more deserving of safety, shelter, and freedom than Wastelanders are.

ThatDamnDanton63: You're such a softie, man. But every time there's a fire in the Wastes, it sparked from a turf war. If the Wastelanders are the same as us, they should get taxed the same as us. ESPECIALLY when they turn up in Parée unannounced.

JP.Marat: They turned up in Parée terribly burned, cradling blackened loved ones. I know you have more of a heart than this.

ThatDamnDanton63: Mon ami, a burned kid is always sad. I'm just saying they have no right to turn up here asking for help when the rest of us are taxed up the arse and out of house and home. They're the ones who choose to live where no human or tech can help them.

JP.Marat: They aren't taxed for aid they don't receive. As for property tax, it's doing us a favor if they figure out how to productively live on that land. It would be unjust to tax them, and disasters call for compassion.

XxxMaxXxRobesxxX: As we strengthen our organization and look toward revolution, we need to stop seeing the Wastelanders as part of the problem. In short: They are not. They could prove very useful to our fight.

ThatDamnDanton63: I knew you'd turn up. I wonder if I can ever go a full hour before the esteemed Max graces us with his brilliant takes.

From here there's a lot of arguing between Danton and Robespierre, mixed with discussions about taxes and whether or not Danton is being prejudiced against Wastelanders or if their tax-free lifestyle is unfair. I try to cram this all into my memory, because I'm sure Louis will be interested. But my eye keeps going back to Robespierre's post. *Revolution.* This was a word I was taught to fear by my tutor in government lessons.

CakeEater: What about the current dauphin and dauphine? Can't they help the common people of the Third Estate? Can't they create change?

I'm afraid of the answer. My finger hovers over the button, then I post.

I let out a whoosh of breath, search for another topic, expecting and maybe hoping to be ignored. But Lucile Duplessis decides I deserve an answer.

LucyTruths: It's a possibility. But a risky one. Keep in mind the crown's power is funded by both the First Estate and the taxes of the Third Estate. The dauphin and dauphine could side with us. But that would mean their influence over the Third Estate on behalf of the First Estate is gone. The First Estate would have no use for them. The crown would be dangerous at that point. Louis the Dauphin tried to turn away from the First Estate. He didn't last long.

My heart races as I write: What if they were smart and careful? What if they helped the people while making the First Estate think their decisions were good ones?

LucyTruths: That would be quite the accomplishment. It would take courage and cleverness we haven't been given a reason to believe the dauphin and dauphine possess. Can I ask what makes you think they're capable of something like that?

That's a great question, Lucy. A great glitching question. What makes the dauphine think she's clever or courageous?

I almost don't answer. I almost log out and run back to the palace to tell Louis I can't do this. But I'm courageous because I'm out here. I'm clever because I'm trying, and I'm not giving up yet. But I can't write that.

So I type: They just seem different.

Then I log out.

TWENTY-SEVEN

July 17, 3070, 10:12 a.m.

I tell Noailles and Elisabeth that I've forgotten my hat and insist on rushing back to my rooms to grab it. Can't have too much sun on my skin. Really, I need my holofone so I can get back to the forums and see what's happened to the Wastelanders.

When I open the door, Georgette leaps to her feet and swoops into a curtsy. I rarely see Georgette relax, so that puts a ping in my system. "*Pardon*," she murmurs. "What do you need, madame—*pardon*, Marie?"

"Georgette, are you all right?" But when I look closer, she clearly isn't. Her eyes are damp and red from crying. "Sit down. Please. What's wrong?"

I have to take her by the arm and practically push her back into the chair before she takes a seat and a big shuddering breath. "I shouldn't trouble you," she says.

"It's no trouble. You're clearly really upset. What happened?"

She sniffs and twists a bit of stained red fabric around her knuckles. "I—I've had a message. From the Hôpital Saint-Louis in Parée. My brother was admitted and he didn't . . . he's gone."

"I'm so sorry." I hug her around the shoulders. My mind is already racing with what I might do to help her, but I catch myself. If I start babbling, I'll overwhelm her. "Do you . . . do you need to get to Parée?"

"I don't think so," she whispers.

Unasked questions hang heavy in the air. I don't want to ask how her brother died or why she won't go to Parée in case the answer is too terrible to talk about. And because I fear there was something Louis and I could have done to stop it.

Georgette keeps twisting the red cloth. It's streaked with something black, like machine grease, and other things I can't identify because they have never been allowed anywhere near my clothes. "This was his," she says when she catches me staring at it. "My family sent it. They wanted me to have it."

"You don't want to go see them?" I ask quietly, gently, so she knows she doesn't have to answer.

"I can't, really." She shrugs. "I don't think they want to see me."

I don't know what to say to this. Who wouldn't want someone nurturing like Georgette around while they're grieving? What family would leave her here alone? "Are you sure?"

She shakes her head. "I shouldn't. It isn't worth the risk."

I don't know what to say to make her open up. I got through to Louis, but I've had a lot more time with him, and he doesn't work for me. I'm not sure what to say, so I ask, "What was his name?"

"Gaspard."

"What happened to him, Georgette?"

"Fire. He got badly burned."

First, I'm horrified by such a terrible death. But then pieces fall together. Georgette is from not quite Parée and not quite a farm.

Fire.

"Georgette"—I ignore any damn bugs listening to us because

Georgette is crying and her brother is dead—"are you from the Wastelands?"

Her hands still, with the bandanna stretched between them. "Why would you think that?"

"Because there was a fire that affected Wastelanders a few days ago. I'm sorry, I shouldn't assume—"

"No, you're right. I am. I was. That's what happened. I just didn't think you would know about it. . . . How do you know?"

"It's not important right now. What's important is how I can help you. I could find a way to help you see your family."

Georgette pushes away a strand of hair that sticks to her tear-streaked cheek. "It's not so much that I can't. Or that they—well, they cared enough to send this. I don't know." She balls up the bandanna in her fist. "I'm at court because of luck. Because I ran away to Parée and a courtier sponsored me and got me a job. I saw a chance for a better life, and I took it. I love my family, but they're . . . complicated. And life out there is hard. It's so hard. But once you leave the Wastes, you don't go back. You can't understand unless you're one of us. Your convoy, the group you travel with, is your life. You don't just leave and come back. You're one of them or you aren't. And I'm not one of them any-more."

She swipes at her tears with her bandanna.

I can't imagine my family pushing me out forever, but I cer-tainly know what it's like to leave home and not come back. "If you don't want to go, I would never make you. But . . . take as much time as you need. Please don't think of working today or tomorrow."

"It might help me to work."

I squeeze her shoulder. She's really dead set on not accepting my help. Maybe this is another Wastelander thing I wouldn't understand. "Whatever you want to do."

"I can't believe they sent me his bandanna. He's had it for years. Thought it was lucky." She shakes her head. "Well, they won't be able to pay his hospital bill. So maybe when I pay that off, they'll see I don't hate them."

"Hospital bill? Georgette, I'll pay it. Please, it's the least I can do."

"I couldn't possibly accept. It's very expensive."

"Then how could your family be expected to pay it?"

"I'll contact the hospital, and have it done in installments."

I haven't been reading the forums for nothing. I know what shadows are lurking here. "What would happen if you couldn't pay it?"

Georgette's eyes go round. "Not an option. My family would be arrested, or they'd garnish my wages."

Taking Georgette's wages because her brother died? Arresting the family because they have nothing and live in the Wastes? Is this really my kingdom? Is it this heartless?

"Do you think a lot of Wastelander families have hospital bills after the fire?" I ask.

"I'm sure they must. Those who were even let into the hospital. They aren't always admitted, because they don't live in the city."

"I'm paying. For all of them."

"Madame, you can't."

"Louis will help me if my allowance isn't enough."

"That's not what I mean. I mean there are rules. Remember

last time you wanted to pay for a charity? This is . . . very different. No one looks kindly on Wastelanders. No one. Not the court. Not the First Estate, not the people."

"The Wastelanders *are* my people. And they deserve respect like anyone else."

Georgette flushes. "That's kind, Marie, but maybe because you're Austro, you don't understand. Wastelanders live how they do because to them, it's freedom. Everyone else thinks they're insane. It's a rough life and it makes them rough. People are afraid of them. Maybe for good reason."

"But they're still Franc people, no matter where and how they live. I'm calling the hospital and paying the bills."

I get to my feet and rush over to the closet to yank open one of my many accessory drawers and start digging.

"Marie, what are you doing?"

I shake loose a red ribbon, then tie it in a careful bow around my neck. It's not a bandanna, but it's more my style. "I'm going to use some influence." I turn back toward Georgette. "I'd like to post to Pixter in support of the Wastelanders. I want to encourage other Francs, especially the Paréesians, to rethink their prejudices and to show their support by wearing red. In honor of Gaspard. I don't have to use his name or mention anything about your family, but I'd like to do this, if it's all right with you."

She hesitates, but her eyes on the ribbon are bright. They're pained, but there's a fire in there. She wants to do this.

"We can change things, Georgette. In little ways that become big ways. I'm tired of wearing clothes just to get people to spend money. I want to do something good."

Georgette chews her lip. "People won't like it. You're going to get criticized. By the court and by Paréesians."

"That's why I have to do it. Because it's just a ribbon and it's just asking for kindness and understanding for people who are suffering."

Georgette ties Gaspard's bandanna around her neck, then tucks it into her collar. The red peeks out like the edge of a secret.

"Would you take my picture?" I hand her my holofone and stand against the wall for a plain background. With my chin slightly lifted so the ribbon is in full view, I pose without a smile.

After a few snaps, Georgette hands the holofone back. "Are you sure about this?"

"Not really," I say. "But I think it's right and I have to start somewhere."

I type my caption:

Today I learned a lot about the lives of Wastelanders living outside the city limits. Recently, a tragic fire claimed the lives of many people outside Parée and I learned that some of them were denied shelter, help, and medical services while others are burdened with medical bills they can't pay. I'd like to do what I can to help during this crisis, and I encourage you to see people who live outside the city borders as Francs like the rest of us. Please wear red if you agree that we are all Francs and you'd help a neighbor in need.

First, I'll call the hospital. Then I guess I'll make this live and prepare for the inevitable Noailles glitchshow.

TWENTY-EIGHT

July 19, 3070, 8:37 p.m.

I'm amazed I'm still allowed to the opera in Parée after the red ribbon post. Noailles threatened to take away my wardrobe privileges, but the king, of all people, supported me. "Let her make choices and deal with the consequences. She'll have to learn soon enough," he said. And then coughed a lot into a handkerchief. He seems tired lately.

Noailles was furious, but Louis turned up for breakfast in a bright red hoodie and she stomped away. I'm glad he wore it, because he buffered over my red campaign at first. I know it's his father haunting him, but in the end, he liked the idea because his papa would have. He told me his father would have liked me a lot. I think of that whenever I touch the ribbon around my neck.

I really wanted Louis to go to the opera. I bet he could have; he just wanted to go to sleep early. Stan and Philippe have come with me instead, and Fersen for security. I note Stan and Philippe don't have a shred of red on them. I still wear the ribbon proudly with a long red skirt.

When we land at the Parée Opera House, everyone is waving and snapping pics.

"Madame Dauphine!" A group of girls are begging for a selfie, and they all wear red ribbons.

Of course I grant their wish, leaning in close for a picture. "Your ribbons are lovely. Thank you for your support."

"My uncle is a firefighter and he went straight out to help after your message," says a curly-haired girl.

"There's so much red, madame!" says the girl beside her.

I realize she's right. It's in hats, jackets, hair streaks, bracelets, headbands. It's incredible.

"Madame Deficit!"

A chill comes over me. I've only read that word online. The sound of it out loud is feral, dangerous. "A ribbon will fix this, eh?"

Something flies over my head and shatters on the wall of the opera house, followed by a chorus of screams and a curse. My happiness at the sight of all the red vanishes, replaced by a fear that's immediate and clawing like a living thing beneath my ribs.

Philippe grabs my arm as Fersen sweeps up behind us and hustles us toward the door. The other security officers clear a path and keep the crowds at bay. I don't even want to go into the opera house; it feels like a giant trap with nowhere to run.

"*Vive la dauphine!*"

Just before Philippe turns me to the door, I see a fist in the air with a red scrap of fabric tied around the wrist.

"It's under control. Please head straight for the stairs," says Fersen.

I take a seat in our private box, covered in goose bumps like it's winter. "They attacked us," I say quietly.

The walls surrounding me are beautiful, detailed in gold floral, but they feel too close. The faces filing into their seats look like enemies, and I see too few exits. The opera house is full of statues holding neon candlesticks, but the purple glow makes the faces around us washed out and spooky, like alien creatures.

"Please relax, Madame Dauphine," Fersen says gently. "I won't let anything hurt you."

"Neither will I, for that matter." Stan crosses his arms in a haughty way, his big wristwatch glowing to match the neon. "I could deck whoever did that."

"You wouldn't," Philippe snorts.

"I would."

"They'd wreck you."

"We'll see about that."

Fersen sits right next to me. His eyes scan the crowd, flicking around in strange, methodical sweeps. Sometimes he stares at something that I can't seem to see. People below are staring back, taking pictures, not even bothering to hide it. I have to force a smile. I can't let them see me rattled and weak over a glass bottle or whatever it was. But as I look around at the faces, I wonder how many of them actually hate me.

I can't seem to catch my breath. Like I might drown or burst, similar to when I got stuck in the hallway in the blackout. My hand goes to my chest, as if that could hold the air in my lungs.

"All right, sis?" Philippe asks.

Even though I know it's ridiculous, I feel too afraid to answer. Like I don't have the breath to.

"Uh, we should probably do something," says Stan. He's frowning at me like I've grown another head.

Fersen leans close. "I'd like to scan your vitals. May I take your pulse?"

I bob my head. Why can't I stop gasping? With gentle fingers he takes my wrist, looks deeply at my eyes, seeing something I can't.

"Look at me, please, madame. Breathe with me."

He counts and I breathe in time. His hand feels strangely warm. "Can you feel your feet firm on the ground? Nothing will hurt you. It's safe now."

My breaths even out, though my heart is still thudding and my head hurts, but that drowning feeling has passed.

"Maybe we should get her some water," says Philippe.

"Or whiskey," says Stan.

Philippe snickers but says he'll send someone after water.

I don't dare to look at the faces below. "I'm sorry," I say, even though there was absolutely nothing I could have done. My body felt completely out of my control.

"Don't be sorry," Fersen says quietly. "Your panic was quite natural. But I assure you, you're safe. May I?"

He reaches for my wrist.

I feel a bit breathless again, but for other reasons.

"Stable." Fersen nods.

Stan glances between us and raises his eyebrows. The lights go dim to hide any flush in my cheeks, and a voice instructs us to put our 3D goggles on. The crowd falls away as we're transported to a junkyard on a moon base. I drift with the music, my fear melts, my anxious thoughts scatter while I follow the story of a robot, an astronaut, a moon rover, and an alien.

Sometimes we can see the stage clearly, with the performers dancing about the boards; sometimes the goggles create the illusion that they're right next to us. At one point, it seems like the robot is right in my ear, singing to me. The alien performs the most difficult soprano part in the world. Her notes are so high, so clear, they sound like they could shatter if you dared to breathe during them. The notes leap and tumble during a classical arrangement that transforms when it plunges down into a low beat and the room fills with laser light. For three hours I forget much else exists.

When the lights come up and my goggles come off, I'm not sure I want to face the world again. It greets me with a sea of faces, chattering and dazed. For a moment, my breath catches and I wonder if I'll get strangled by panic again. But it passes.

"Weird show," says Philippe. "Like, what was that thing between the robot and the astronaut? Written by bot lovers."

I almost shush him. That's so rude in front of Fersen.

"Dude, it's the most popular show right now. Everyone loves it. It's going to tour internationally. Especially with that soprano. You just have no taste," says Stan.

"Oh yeah, what's her name, Beaulieu? Alien girl? She was pretty hot, I guess."

I ignore whatever Stan fires back with. "What did you think?" I ask Fersen.

"I thought it was wonderful," he says. His eyes scan the crowd below. "How do you feel, madame?"

"Oh, just let down by . . . reality." I give him a little laugh, like this is something everyone must be feeling. Maybe it is.

"I'm glad you enjoyed it," he says gently. "If there was a way to guarantee your smile, I would do whatever it was."

What can I say to this? I blush and look away.

From the box next to ours, I see a woman with her holofone raised. Probably taking a picture. Nothing I'm not used to. But then I look again. Her cropped hairstyle is similar to Yolande's, and Yolande modeled hers after . . . could it really be Madame Rohan? The founder of Pixter? I think it is.

Should I pose for her? Should I ask to meet her? I give her a small wave. She simply nods, smiles, then follows her entourage out of the box.

TWENTY-NINE

July 25, 3070, 10:06 a.m.

I go to the gardens more and more often these days. Mercy asked me if I'm picking up the habits of my husband, always out walking or riding. I guess I am. I feel free out here. Free of eyes, able to breathe fresh air instead of palace stuffiness, chemical stink, and air-conditioned dust. I almost prefer that distant smoke and garbage funk that you can never quite escape out here. The light this morning is soft and the fog off the canals is strange, kind of smoky. I should probably go use the forums, but I just don't feel like it. Not after the broken glass, the shouts.

I see a man moving through the fog, coming closer. He has a straight posture and an even walk, maybe a duke. Oh. It's Fersen.

My memory jumps to the warm, smooth, and very human feel of his hand around mine, checking my pulse. I rub my wrist with my own hand, whisk away the memory. No need to glitch.

"Madame Dauphine, good morning." Fersen bows.

"Good morning, Captain Fersen. Thank you again. For your help the night of the opera."

He gives a small smile. His face is damp with fog and seems bright, as if he has a healthy human glow (and a really good skin-care routine). "Of course. How are you feeling?" he asks.

I look out toward the trees, sigh. The automatic response on the tip of my tongue is the polite one to be used at court, dismissive: *I'm fine.* The truth comes out instead. "Better, but . . . I'm not sure I'll ever forget something like that. I keep . . . it's like I hear shattering glass in my mind." I laugh nervously.

"I understand," Fersen says.

Does he? I'm sure bots don't have something as humanly weak as fear, anxiety, memories that creep in when they're unwanted and unhelpful.

"I want you to feel safer. I want you to have help when you need it. So I have something I hope you'll accept."

He reaches into his pocket and takes out a small box. It's velvety like it holds jewelry, but that doesn't make sense. I glance over my shoulder before I take it, like I'm doing something wrong.

There's a bracelet inside. It's delicate and gold. The charm is a fleur-de-lis, the symbol of the Bourbons. What does this have to do with anything? Why is Fersen giving me jewelry? I should be polite, gracious. Instead, I croak out a confused "Um?"

"I do hope it's to your taste, but there's more to it than meets the eye," says Fersen. "The fleur-de-lis is a button. Press it if you find yourself in danger. It will signal me and Lieutenant Nilsson if you ever need help. Even if you just need a friend."

I risk a look at his eyes. He smiles with real warmth. My own face goes warm and I look away. "I don't know what to say." I probably shouldn't accept. But it's a security measure. The memory of Fersen helping me to breathe, calming my panic, takes over. I have more enemies than friends at Versailles. I don't want to turn one away. "Thank you, Captain Fersen. This is really generous."

"You'll use it?" He smiles again.

I nod.

"I'm honored and glad that I can serve you better. May I?" He reaches for the bracelet and plucks it from the box. He handles my wrist gently as he clasps it.

"Just press if you need me. Would you try it, *s'il vous plaît*?"

I press down on the charm, which clicks quietly, then glows green from the small divide between the two sides of gold. Something pinches my skin.

"Ouch." I wince. The bracelet links must have caught a bit of my wrist. I push the bracelet down and find a small pinpoint of blood.

"Apologies." Fersen pulls a silk handkerchief from his pocket and presses it over the tiny wound. "Are you all right?"

"Of course. Just a scratch. I've had worse from Mops."

Fersen laughs a little. The handkerchief comes away with just a few blood spots, and he puts it in his pocket. He presses the charm with a slim finger and the glow fades. "It's in working order, anyway. I hope the pinch didn't put you off it," he says.

I cross my arms at my waist, cover the bracelet with my left hand. "Thank you. For everything."

He bows low, eyes locked on my face. "I'm always at your service," says Fersen. "It is good to know that I can rush to your aid if need be. But I hope you'll make use of it even if something small troubles you and you need a friend."

I play with the bracelet. What does it really mean? Is the bracelet more a gesture of security or is it truly a gift? A gift from someone who cares, someone who is interested in getting closer to me?

I do a small curtsy. I've never been so tongue-tied. "I do thank you, Captain Fersen."

"You may call me Axel if you wish."

The wind tousles his hair. My stomach knots. "Axel, then."

There is a breathless moment when the wind speaks for us. His smile says volumes. I think it answers my lingering question. The bracelet isn't simply part of his job. It was meant to express friendship. Maybe even affection.

"I should be getting back," I murmur.

"Of course. Have a good day."

"Bye," I say with an awkward wave of my bracelet-clad hand. I walk back to the palace feeling giga-charged, trying not to look like I'm running. The bracelet is small but feels heavy and as noticeable as a fiber-optic chain. I'm going to have to put on a flounce-sleeve blouse that will hide the jewelry. I'm embarrassed to have Fersen's gift around my wrist, but I also don't want to take it off.

THIRTY

July 30, 3070, 1:23 a.m.

I have a weird dream. I'm filming a livestream for ViewFi with Thérèse, helping her with a makeup tutorial, I think. But she's wearing an ugly, floppy hat, and I've got white pancake makeup on with dark circles dusted all around my eyes like a skeleton.

"Tell them your biggest fear and your most embarrassing memory," says Thérèse.

I glance at the little webcam, its tiny lens small as a beetle, glinting dark like an eye. "Ha ha, very funny."

Thérèse boops my nose. "No, *you* are very funny. It's truth or dare! You have to!"

"I don't want to," I hiss at her, turning away to avoid the camera.

"Oh, it's no big deal! It's not like we don't already know everything. So don't lie! That would be a really bad look." Thérèse taps the screen. "Your fans are waiting."

Comments are scrolling along the side of the screen like crazy.

Royal liar.

Madame Deficit.

Robot banger.

Rich bitch.

I slap the screen like it can somehow clear away all these nasty comments. "Stop it! I didn't lie about anything!"

"Are you saying you're a rich bitch, then?" Thérèse asks, all sweet, like she didn't say something completely horrible that would never come out of her mouth.

On the screen I see makeup smeared down my cheeks in ugly white and black streaks. And red. Where did the red come from? I jump from my chair. "Why are you being like this? I'm the dauphine and you're my friend!"

"Oh, honey, you're not really the dauphine," says Thérèse. "It's just for pretend because it's fun!"

"Pretend? This isn't pretend. It's my life!"

"It was your life until it stopped being fun for us." Thérèse shrugs.

"No. No, it's not a game! If I'm not the dauphine, then why do I have a palace, and a title, and a guard?"

"Because they gave you them." Thérèse does a cheeky little hair toss. "Duh!"

"Who gave me them?"

Thérèse taps the webcam. "Uh, hello, they did."

I glare into the webcam, but all I see is one dark, shiny, empty eye. "Where are you?" I shout. "Stop ruining my life!"

As if from nowhere, Fersen appears behind the computer and flips the whole table. Thérèse shrieks and backs away. His eyes are intense and his jaw is set firm. "To some there will always be a dauphine," he says.

The light behind him is all golden. He looks beautiful.

He scoops me up in his arms and we jump out a window, but we land on the ground all soft like we floated instead of dropped. We're in the gardens, surrounded by dark trees.

Fersen holds me close. I put a hand on his chest to find his heartbeat, but I can't feel it. When he kisses me, nothing seems robotic.

"They programmed you for that really good," I say.

He frowns. "Androids aren't programmed for love. You totally overrode my programming, babe."

I know I must be dreaming, because that's so stupid it's kind of funny. Somebody taps me on the shoulder. I turn around and find Louis. He looks all mopey. "What are you dreaming about him for?"

I look back over my shoulder, but Fersen is gone. "I—I don't know! It's just a stupid dream, Louis. How do you even know what I'm dreaming?"

"They bugged your dreams, remember?"

"Well, that's totally weird! What are you doing here?"

"Why shouldn't I be here?" Now Louis grabs me around the waist. "I'm way more real than that stupid robot."

"My dreams aren't any of your business!"

"Nothing is just your business anymore. Didn't you read that in the handbook they gave us?" Louis's voice kind of sounds like Fersen's, and his eyes are brown like Fersen's, instead of blue.

"Yeah, but I skipped to the end," I say.

"Okay, so you saw the part where you end up with me because you couldn't be with a dumb robot because the First Estate would, like, banish you to the West Mericas. Robots aren't even programmed for love, anyway."

"He overrode the programming," I whisper.

Louis snorts. "Rewriting programming? I'm way better at that stuff."

He pulls me closer. The sky is purple and clouds stream above us, dragging us in and out of shadow. The man I'm kissing has Axel's lips and eyes, Louis's hair and face.

Then I'm awake, sweating up a storm and covered in way too many blankets, which I kick off in a tangle.

Louis is snoring like he's glitching. I glance over at him and see he's half out of the blankets too. At some point in the night he pulled his shirt off. I stare at his bare back. Some little bit of my brain is bitter about him being a jerk in my dream. Even though that's the dumbest thing ever. It was just a glitching dream. My brain must be buffering, giving me a ridiculous impulse to flop on top of him, even though it's way too hot in here and that would wake him up.

Instead, I drop back on my pillow and cross my arms, wondering what's up with the AC. Trying not to wish to cuddle close to Louis and feel parts of him that he hides from me.

THIRTY-ONE

August 3, 3070, 11:33 a.m.

The king is dying.

I've never seen a dying person before, but the wasting disease makes it obvious. The signs are all over his lined face, saggy like the life went out of it. His skin is almost yellowish. I think of runny egg yolks and feel sick. His breath is rattly, wheezy, wet.

Du Barry hasn't left his side. Never seen her so miserable. Her makeup isn't on point like usual. She's done nothing to her eyebrows and her upper lipstick is crooked. She glares at me the whole time like his illness is my fault.

The king did get a little more lively when he saw me. I'm going to be really sad when he dies. Not just because Louis and I are not ready to take over, but because I'll miss him. He's spent more time amusing Du Barry and going to parties than preparing Louis for his role, but I like him. He's been kind to me.

He takes my hand in his knobby one. His fingers are stiff and cold with dry, papery skin. It kind of creeps me out, but I squeeze his hand anyway.

"Are you frightened, dear?" he asks.

He wouldn't ask me that if he wasn't going to die. Tears creep into the corners of my eyes. "A little. Are you?"

He chuckles, and it's a crackling, painful sound. "A little," he says. Then he clasps his other hand over mine. "You have all the makings of an excellent queen, as long as you make sure you give us a little heir. Maybe even a spare." He winks, so I try not to take this as too heavy a criticism. "You are an icon for the country. A symbol of tradition and a connection to the past. Remember that your duties, at the end of the day, are quite simple. Do as you're told and your life will be happy. It will be blessed. Like mine was."

It's like he knows about the conflict that Louis and I are facing right now. Like he read my mind. Way more likely that he heard us over some bugs somewhere or found a text we sent and guessed the truth. Or maybe he just knows his grandson.

"Your husband has no direction. Guide him. Help him take counsel from the people he ought to take it from, and help him be firm when he speaks and decides. You do those things, and you'll honor my memory and the people of the Franc Kingdom."

"Of course. I want nothing more than to support my husband and please the Franc people."

It would be so easy to listen to Grand-Père King. There's a part of me, a way bigger part than I want to admit, that's dying to do what he says. To be like I was before, who I thought I would be when I arrived at Versailles, a pretty, happy thing who people are excited to see at state events. A girl who has no idea what's really going on. But now that I know the truth, I can't go back. Now that I know this is an elaborate performance, I can't forget that. I want to ask him how he did it. How the king played the part created for him every moment of his life. But that would be cruel, and no matter what happens to me here, no one will make me cruel. I won't let them.

"Would you like me to see you again tomorrow?" I ask the king.

"I think he's seen so many people he's in a state of exhaustion," says Du Barry.

"Nonsense, her pretty little face brightens the day," says the king. "Yes, dear, if you can manage it. For now, please send Elisabeth."

I leave to send her after promising to return tomorrow.

THIRTY-TWO

✻

I don't want to check the forums, but I have to. I don't want to believe the king will die, but I do. Which means I have more work to do than I ever have before.

I return to the strange and secret grotto, but this time I walk around the hill. There must be a pond because I hear the chirp of frogs and bugs. On the other side of the hill, I find more than a pond. Something strange and beautiful. A piece of Versailles that never got propped up with a neon makeover. It's a crumbling old tower shaped sort of like a lighthouse. Tall grass tickles my hands as I go for a closer look. There's an old stone foundation beside the tower. Like there was a house or a barn. Something about this place is comforting, gently familiar. Maybe it reminds me of some part of Schönbrunn that I can't put my finger on.

I slip into a hole in the side of the tower, into cool shade and old dust, safe from the blazing sun. With a brush of my sleeve, I clear away a patch of dirt and debris and take out my holofone, then enter my password while a pigeon coos above me.

So many topics on WhoWatches make my stomach a knot. Things I'll have to deal with as queen. Things I'm not ready to deal with yet. A thread catches my eye. Androids Are Our Enemies.

I scratch at my bracelet. I keep hiding it under larger ones. So far no one has noticed it. And I haven't told anyone about it. Not even Louis. Especially not Louis. I don't have the words. But I'm curious what WhoWatches has against androids.

First, what I see is typical. Discussions about a possible robot army being built in secret at the palace. Ridiculous, of course. A lot of users have already shot that one down.

Then I find a subtopic: Androids Among Us.

Robespierre explains, The original point of an android was to use it to do things humans could not. You can imagine what atrocities the military may use them for. But recently, the research and focus has become troubling. They're trying to make them more humanlike. Seems contradictory? It isn't. They're the perfect spies.

I scroll down and see bits of code, photos of computer components.

Beneath these Robespierre wrote: You remember our friends Elias and Aveline? They're the JeanCo employees who organized a worker revolt on the production floor. They thought they'd made a friend and ally in a fellow worker. A young and efficient man who wanted to help Elias and Aveline with some hacking. He was no friend. That same worker attacked Elias and would have killed him if Aveline hadn't arrived at the right moment. If she hadn't been carrying an illegal volt-baton for protection. The baton overheated their coworker's hardware. That coworker was an android posing as a human.

She was shocked when the first strike didn't affect him. Elias held him, Aveline jammed the baton in the android's mouth and fried him. They're lucky they survived. It's notoriously difficult to disable an android. Elias and Aveline picked apart the bot, uploaded data from his hard drive, and made some shocking discoveries. He'd collected data on several colleagues. These were workers suspected of organizing the revolt. He'd left bugs on their clothes, in their bags, a tracker in a cruiser. They had never suspected. And that's what makes androids so dangerous.

The picture below the story is gruesome. A body splayed face-down on a dirty black-and-white-tiled floor. A head separated from a body. But there's no blood, just wires. A hazy smoke over the picture.

Robespierre's third post says: Some of their findings are posted above. It's unclear what the First Estate's ultimate goal with the androids is, but we have to find out before it's too late. We know two are in the palace. Are they serving the Bourbons or tracking the Bourbons? Their presence is highly suspect. Watchers, you are encouraged to post any information or experience you have with androids. Be safe and be careful. We outnumber the robots for now.

The conversation continues below. I fiddle with my bracelet. Is Fersen tracking me? Probably. But for my protection. He was completely transparent about what the bracelet is for. It summons him.

I'll just wear the bracelet less. I don't need to wear it every-where. Just in crowds. Just when I'm out of the palace. And I don't need to tell Louis about it yet. We both have bigger problems.

THIRTY-THREE

August 10, 3070, 5:17 a.m.

Louis and I are woken early by Countess Noailles, Louis's valet Cléry, and Maurepas. There's a buzzing sound from the com by my bed, which never happens this early. It's so early that Louis hasn't even gotten up to hunt yet. My heart pounds and Louis sits straight up, alert like someone just busted into the room.

"Permission to enter, Majesté," says the voice on the com.

"Granted," says Louis.

When the three of them enter and drop to their knees in front of us, Maurepas says, "The king is dead. Long live the king."

Noailles and Cléry repeat, "Long live the king."

"*Que Dieu nous aide,*" Louis mutters. God help us.

And that's it. I will not see the king again. Each time I returned to visit he was sleeping. Our last conversation was the final conversation. Louis and I become the king and queen of the Franc Kingdom while we are in our pajamas, sitting in bed with messy hair, taken by surprise. We are completely terrified.

THIRTY-FOUR

August 12, 3070, 2:00 p.m.

The coronation is a blur. It's a lot like my wedding. Except twice as terrifying. Louis holds my hand the whole time, looking brave and serious, but his sweaty palm gives away his fear. Barely three hours after his grandfather died, he had to meet with a First Estate representative. He came back totally spaced, quiet and staring at nothing. "They're even worse than I thought," he said. I know he found out about the state of the crown finances and glitched out a little. He told them he wanted this ceremony to be simpler than usual and cost less.

As far as I can tell, the planners didn't listen. There are cruisers flying over, spouting blue and gold glittering stuff, and giant holos of creatures flying overhead, like the Franc rooster and a fish thing.

There are so many people yelling, cheering. After the ceremony in the chapel, they fly us slowly from the packed gates of Versailles all the way to Parée, and there's a mob of people the whole way. They're so happy, I can't imagine where all the things we saw on the net came from. I squeeze Louis's hand. "It's going to be okay. Look at them. We can do this."

"We need to make them happy," he says. "It's more important than anything."

Eventually we leave the cruiser and Louis addresses the crowd from a neon-laden dais. I don't have to do anything, just smile, but I can't keep my mind on this simple task. I have this weird feeling that if I look at any one face for too long, I'll see something I don't want to. I keep looking back at Fersen, who stands guard right below our platform, with Nilsson and other soldiers at his side.

My brain keeps losing service all through Louis's speech. It's so scripted anyway. He got to write his own, but of course it went through about eight other people, like Maurepas and a representative from the First Estate. I know where requests to wear a certain clothing brand on the Apps or show a certain drink came from. The First Estate has been everywhere this entire time. Hiding in plain sight in every rule, every camera, every dark corner.

It's strange to see Louis address such a huge crowd with his soft voice amplified a hundred times. He's wearing a nice suit with all the regalia on, a deep blue cloak, and, craziest of all, a crown. He looks so young, but strong and sure. This isn't the Louis I know. I wonder if it's the Louis the people want to see.

They sure scream and wave their arms around and totally glitch when he's done. I'm trying to memorize it all: how Louis looks, the sound of people cheering and singing the national anthem, the sight of thousands of waving hands—many of them with red around their wrists, the signs with messages of love, and holos swirling around. The moment when Fersen turns around to smile at me.

Louis comes back to my side and puts an arm around my waist. He's smiling and waving, and so am I. We do that until my arms feel like I just did some deadlifting.

When we get back to the cruiser, the windows darken and we're through with facing the crowds. We're finally alone and Louis sags. He takes the crown off carefully, like he just took it from a fire and it might burn his fingers. The thing is ancient. A relic from before the Event. Solid gold, heavy with rows of jewels. He'll only wear it at huge state occasions like this.

"I feel like the whole universe is falling down and it's going to land on top of me and crush me."

I put my hand on his knee, right next to where the crown rests. "You were great," I say quietly. "Seriously. Almost like you were born for this."

He says something I can't quite hear. There's no way I could have heard it right. It sounded like he said, "No one was born for this." But if I think about that sentence for more than a second, it sounds pretty anti-monarchist, and there's no way it would come from a king's mouth.

"What?" I ask him, and put a hand on his arm.

But then Maurepas comes in with a marketing manager, and they start talking about what messages and quotes should be sent out to the press. We aren't left alone again for the rest of the cruiser journey.

THIRTY-FIVE

August 12, 3070, 10:18 p.m.

This long day isn't over. It's Versailles. It's Coronation Day. Of course there's a party. Maybe the first party I'm not super plugged into. When I look around, I see a lot of faces covered in makeup and glitter and glowing jewelry, and I wonder who's a friend and who's an enemy. I wonder if I'll ever get to enjoy a party again, thinking like this.

As if to prove I'm not being paranoid, a woman with a huge pink wig walks by with a friend, and I hear her say in nothing resembling a whisper, "No sign of an heir. She's useless. *Elle est un enfant.*"

She flutters a fan in front of her mouth that shows an image of churning storm clouds and forked lightning. She looks me right in the eye. She wanted me to hear her. Thérèse is right by my side and heard it too. She whips around, glaring daggers at the courtier, who pretends she doesn't notice.

Is this what being queen will be like? Exhaustion, all work, and nothing but scathing comments about one of the most private parts of myself? The constant feeling that I'm too young for my job?

I watch Philippe deejaying, hopping on the balls of his feet, pushing at sliders. He spent all kinds of money on this sound system. Stan complained to Louis about it, but Louis didn't really want to do anything. Stan was annoyed and was all like, "Well, you're in charge, so be in charge, man." Then Stan dealt with Philippe himself. For all the good it did. The sound stuff is still here and Philippe is mixing tracks on his holofone. I have to say he's pretty good at it.

Philippe looks so young. Bouncing around, waving his arms, tossing glow sticks at the people around his little table. Being in charge of your family is really different from being in charge of your kingdom, I think. Louis is their brother, not their father. How is he supposed to manage them? But if he can't manage his siblings, how will we manage a kingdom?

I've been thinking about how young we all are, but I never put it together like this. The boys and Elisabeth don't have their parents, and now they don't have their grandfather either. Who do they have?

I miss Mutti. She could do both. Manage her family and her kingdom. Maybe I can leave the party soon. Go call her.

"Good evening, Majesté."

I turn and find a woman who seems familiar. Her outfit is truly on point and made for Pixter. Her silver-blue wig complements the blue-white glow coming from within the collar of her sleek black dress, highlighting a diamond-studded necklace.

I think I've seen her on the Apps, but it's hard to say when her face is covered by a thick band of dark sunglasses.

"Good evening." I curtsy and Thérèse follows suit. It takes me a second to realize that the woman broke etiquette. I'm supposed to speak first.

An uncomfortable second passes. I think I'm supposed to know who she is. Thérèse must. She's staring. But she isn't smiling.

"Madame Rohan," says the woman with the glowing dress, and dips into a curtsy.

Rohan. No wonder she's familiar. She's the CEO of Pixter, a member of the board of directors for the Apps. I should have remembered her face. I saw her that night at the opera.

"Of course! Madame Rohan, it's an honor. I'm a huge fan of Pixter."

"I'm very aware, Majesté." Her smile seems thin despite the shaping of her deep red lipstick. "And very pleased. If I may . . . could we grab a selfie?"

I don't think about disagreeing. When someone asks for a selfie, I almost always accept. It's the height of rudeness to turn them down. Madame Rohan removes her sunglasses, revealing sharp, dark eyes flashing amid deep eye shadow. With a flick of her neat hair, she leans forward to murmur in my ear. I smell a perfume I'm not sure I like. Floral, but something about it smells like metal.

"Oh, and if Her Majesté could please remove the red ribbon around her neck. Pixter can't be seen as an affiliate of this, hmm . . . passion project."

No one is more aware of the power of a symbol worn between the heart and the head than I am, but if there's one person who might understand better, it's Madame Rohan. I've been queen a few hours and she's already trying to push me around. "But madame, that's exactly what it is. *My* project. Not even that. A simple statement. A show of allegiance to my people."

Madame Rohan lowers her voice. "I think we both know the matter is far from simple. But if Her Majesté insists."

She raises her holofone and we snap a few pics until we agree on our lighting and angles. My smile is as fake as a face-swap filter.

"*Merci*," Rohan says, and flips her glasses from her collar back to the bridge of her nose. She clicks away at her holofone, probably posting to Pixter already. "Since you are such an excellent ambassador of fashion and causes, I would love to talk about branding possibilities with you. A partnership."

It's never been more important to wear my mask and choose words carefully. I keep my smile fixed in place like I'm still posing for Pixter. "That would be *magnifique*." I touch Thérèse on the elbow. "And Princesse de Lamballe may be a great asset too. She's an excellent influencer."

Between the huge, dark glasses and the stillness of her features, it's impossible to read Madame Rohan. I can't tell if she even gives Thérèse one glance. "A queen has a lot of influence. She must be careful how she uses it. Careful who she serves . . . who she befriends." The last word is drawn out, and she raises one very thin eyebrow from under the mask of her sunglasses. "Long live the queen." Madame Rohan places her hands behind her back, gives a bow of her chin, then sweeps away.

I stare from Rohan's retreating back to Thérèse. The look in Thérèse's eyes is one I've never seen before. It's steel. It's furious.

"That was . . . strange." I feel like a dongle the moment it's out of my mouth. But I don't know what else to say. "And very rude, I think? I don't understand."

"She thinks she's untouchable." Thérèse says this in barely more than a whisper.

"What do you mean? What did *she* mean?" I squeeze Thérèse's arm and spin her toward me. The solemn look, the deadness in Thérèse's eyes disappears, replaced by the girl I know. All warmth and a bubbly grin. Like there are two of her. It's a feeling I know well.

Thérèse has a mask.

"Oh, I don't know. I'm nobody to them, you know? The First Estate. *Très* rude, but they can afford to be."

There's something she's not telling me. It's so obvious. "Thérèse, are you all right? That kind of glitched me out. It's okay if you were buffering too."

She shrugs. Either I totally misread everything or Thérèse's mask is even better than mine. "I'm fine. It's just been a long day. Actually, I have to use the restroom. Talk later, okay?" She squeezes my shoulder and bounces off.

I pull out my holofone. For once, I'm happy to see a text from my mama. And she's written the perfect thing. It wouldn't sound like much to other people, but she doesn't send stuff like this too often. It just says: How are you?

I write back: Tired, but I'm ok.

There's a long pause. Thought bubbles pulse across the screen. The next message is much less comforting. The crown is heavy.

Then: Call me when you can.

THIRTY-SIX

※

August 12, 3070, 11:43 p.m.

"I had certainly hoped that Louis the Well-Beloved's reign would last longer. So that you and Louis-Auguste would have more time to prepare."

I lean my holofone on my knees, pressed close to my screen as if I could really get closer to Mama. Bags sagging under her eyes make her look older and more tired than I've ever seen her. Still, the sight of her makes my heart ache with *Sehnsucht*.

"The people seem unhappy, Mama. Before I even began my reign. I don't know what to do." I want to tell her the truth. So badly. If anyone would know what to do, it would be her. But the sheltering canopy of my bed is a trick. Anything I have to say about my fears of the First Estate will travel from my lips to the wired ears all over the room.

"There has been a lot of unrest in Parée. More than I've seen since I was very young. But your coronation was greeted with enthusiasm. You have a young, fresh, and exceptionally lovely face. That brings people hope."

Tears prick at my eyes. I think this is one of the biggest compliments she's ever paid me. I wish I had heard it a few months ago when I could have just soaked it in. Now I know what I look like doesn't matter half as much as I've always been told. What I do will count most now.

"What can I do? I need to do more than look nice."

"And I've taught you far more than manners and charm. Now is the time to use diplomacy."

"I try, Mutti. But I'm often not allowed. Everyone had a fit when I encouraged wearing a certain color and—"

"You are queen now, and you must assert yourself. That maneuver to champion the people of the Wastes was impulsive, but you saw how it won you some allies and made you some enemies. This is the job. This is being queen. You favored one group and now you must please another."

"It's more than that." I sigh. I don't know how to tell her a half-truth and make her understand. "There are some people I have to work with, but I think it's wrong. What if what I should be doing is choosing a side and staying there?"

She's quiet for a minute. Thoughtful. Did she read the pauses between my words? Does she know about the First Estate?

"This is the real challenge of your role. You must be all things to many people. You must find balance. If an action or a decision is blocked, you must negotiate. Strike a deal. Promise reciprocation if you meet resistance. You fund fire victims this month and promote JeanCo Foods next month. Or that ridiculous photo App you use."

She doesn't understand. Not at all. She doesn't know the danger. That, or I will never be the kind of ruler Mama is. Maybe I'm just too soft.

"What if I don't want to promote JeanCo?" I mutter, the closest I can come to the truth.

Two ringed hands appear onscreen as Mama shrugs. "*C'est la vie, ma chère*, as they say in your kingdom. Contrary to popular belief, a queen often has to do things she doesn't like."

I shake my head. I'm exhausted. I'm lost. I don't think I've explained well.

"Think of a plan, Marie. Think of a problem, or a solution that was blocked to you in the past, and come up with a deal. Use me. I will help you in this. There are many businesses that would welcome Austro support and patronage. I've shied away from SveroTech . . . but for you, I can reconsider. I can negotiate. Let me know if this would be useful."

My mind fills with images of the photos I saw on WhoWatches. A murderous android facedown on the floor leaking wires. I swallow a painful lump in my throat. "I'll think about it. Let you know."

"Please do."

I fill the rest of the conversation with empty chatter. Empty promises to work on producing an heir, though that seems to have slipped down the priority list. I feel terribly alone until Louis turns up half-asleep to fall into bed.

He knows something's up because he gathers me in his arms. "Are you okay?"

"I guess."

For a minute I hide my face in his shirt, let him feel like a shield. "I talked to Mutti. She's willing to help with some things."

"Oh?" He sounds far too hopeful. I make the mistake of looking up at his sleepy face and tousled hair. I can't fry his hard drive. Not when we're this tired. So I just shrug and nod.

"That's good. I have this plan and a research team that needs funding. They're gonna do some irrigation in the Wastes and some solar farming." He yawns. "I'll explain it tomorrow."

I'm really glad he's thought of something, that he's not as crumpled as he seemed in the cruiser with the crown on his knee.

I kiss him. It's like his hands on my back and ribs have found a dial that upped my heartbeat a few notches. He doesn't pull away when I slip my hands under his shirt, over his soft belly and firm chest.

Maybe I can do one thing I'm supposed to. Maybe I can finally make the marriage official and people can stop laser-focusing on me for at least one thing.

Louis sighs or maybe takes a breath. His hand goes to my thigh. I feel calluses on his palm. Maybe from holding a horse's reins. They're warm and rough on my smooth skin. My heart changes tempo again. Maybe it's time. Maybe things change. Maybe there's hope. Maybes and maybes.

I move my hands down to the waistband of his pants. I think my blood is warm JetFuel and the engine is somewhere in my stomach, humming and prickling. My hand drifts a little lower and his hips jerk away like I'm a live wire.

I don't go cold right away, but the engine sputters. Stupid.

Stupid to think I can change anything.

I roll over and curl into a ball, trying to settle the roaring in me.

"Um," says Louis, and he puts a hand on my back. A sweaty hand on my shoulder blade.

But I don't really care. I don't care about excuses. And I'm definitely done with anything cuddly for tonight.

After a few minutes of his hand there, a few minutes where I can practically feel him thinking, struggling for words, I pretend to be asleep. I'm sure he knows I'm not.

THIRTY-SEVEN

August 17, 3070, 9:47 a.m.

I get a text from Yolande after breakfast. It says: Don't want to glitch you, but there's been some shit about you in the news. Thought you should know 😕

My holofone makes a plunking noise when a text from Thérèse comes in: What a bunch of malware. Don't listen to any of it. It happens to the best of us.

What the hell are they talking about?

Are you ok? Thérèse asks.

Then there's one from . . . oh gigs, my mama. Call me immediately.

Merde. What's happening?

I haven't even seen yet, I tell Thérèse, then book it out to the gardens.

I run for the quietest bit of woods I can find. I don't bother looking for a statue or a pagoda or any kind of landmark. I just run into the trees and keep going until I feel like I've disappeared.

My fingers fly over Louis's password. Then I'm in. Might as well go straight for the news Apps. I don't have to look for long. I don't know what I expected the gripe to be, but it wasn't this.

A sample of the headlines this morning:

QUEEN GOT COZY WITH ANDROID GUARD AT THE OPERA

IMPOTENCY ISSUES:
THE QUEEN'S ROBOTIC SOLUTION
QUEEN SHOWS FAVOR TO ANDROID LOVER

The same photos are plastered all over every article. One is a photo of Fersen and me at the opera. Fersen is leaning in close to scan my vitals, taking my pulse while holding my wrist. Except in the photo it kind of looks like he's holding my hand.

He does have my hand again in the second picture. Presenting me with my bracelet, clasping it around my wrist in the garden, when I was too tired and upset to think of who could be watching. My hand strays to my wrist automatically, even though I'm not wearing the bracelet. Ever since I learned about the robot spy, I've been wearing it less and less. But someone noticed it at the coronation. There's a zoomed-in pic of my collection of bracelets jangling as I wave to the crowd. You can clearly see Fersen's among them.

And then . . . most damning . . . there it is, and I was so stupid for allowing it, for getting swept up—there's a photo from my birthday. Fersen leaning in to kiss my cheek. My eyes are wide, my lips parted. I look as stupid as I am for allowing such a thing where anyone could see.

With numb fingers, I click over to Chatterbox to see how much damage has been done. The rumors are not exactly a stretch of the imagination. I dream about robots, after all. Maybe someone really is watching my dreams.

The commentary goes something like this:

Can you blame her for banging the hot droid? We know she's not getting any from her husband.

Do you think the king is gay?

I heard they're both robot fetishists.

Disgusting. We'll never get an heir this way. I'm not
sure I want one now. Shameful couple, turning to
robot prostitutes.
Do you think the king bought the bot for her himself
or is he just that much of a cuck?
No shame from these young rulers. None. To flaunt a
service bot in public? Classless.
I support my tax dollars paying for sexbots long as we
all get one lol
This is totally weird. I heard the queen was frigid.
I heard she hooks up with Lamballe and Polignac.
Robots too?
A Versailles staff member swears the bot is with both
the queen and king. Royal position in bed and at
court. Bots are taking over. We knew it was going to
happen.

Just when I've seen enough, something else makes me feel
somehow, impossibly, worse. It's a photo of Elisabeth at a club
with her arms around Jeanne. Apparently they really did hit it
off at my birthday. When she wasn't around much the past few
weeks, I assumed she was studying.

The photo tells a different story. She stares, horrified, into
the camera, the flash washing out both their faces. I don't
think this photo is a setup like the photos that made Axel and
me look like an item. I think some paparazzo just did a little
digging.

The first comment says: Corruption runs deep. Elisabeth's
girlfriend is a techie for the androids. Bourbons sure do love
that bot unit.

I don't want to see any more.

Some more texts came in while I was looking at the media black hole.

Mama: Call me. We need to sort this mess.

Yolande: Hey the Shinkoku are into it anyway? They made a comic about you. Like I'm serious. They love you.

She links to a cartoon of me with giant eyes and hair. I'm staring all dewy-eyed at a tall Fersen with flowing locks. Rose petals surround us.

Someone has roughly edited over the Shinkoku words with Franc. *Captain Fersen*, my character says. *I love my husband. How could I possibly . . .*

There are many kinds of love, says cartoon Fersen.

When our black-and-white-inked lips lock, there are lightning strikes in the background.

Ouch. A spark? says this blushing, pathetic little version of me.

Forgive me. A small glitch. The real Fersen has long lashes, but nothing like this drawing of him as he leans forward to kiss my character again. I don't know why I don't look away. Instead I flip several more pages, which include more and more rose petals and fewer and fewer clothes until I close it and toss the holofone away. My head feels light.

How do I get out of this? How do Louis and I recover from this? It's so stupid, so ironic that I'm attached to a sex scandal when I've never had sex with anyone, let alone my husband. When I have to hide my embarrassment over it whenever the girls giggle or gossip about what people do with their partners while I have zero experience to relate to.

How do I face Mutti? How do I face the court? How do I face Axel or Louis?

I lean my forehead on my knees and think, think, think.

I'm the social media whiz. For every person calling me a robot banger, I have someone defending me and calling it the slander it is. There has to be a way out of this.

After an hour of thinking, I'm not sure if I have answers. I need Louis's help, but I'm mad at him. I know I shouldn't be and it won't help. But I am. This is partly his fault. It just is. And he needs to help make it right.

I text that I need to see him ASAP for an emergency, and I don't care how long I have to wait because I'm not moving. I drop a pin to my location in the woods. I can't stomach walking out of here and facing a single person at court.

THIRTY-EIGHT

August 17, 3070, 1:34 p.m.

Louis says he'll be here in twenty minutes but shows up almost an hour later, puffing and sweating, hair standing on end and tie loosened.

"What's happening?" he asks as he trips on a stick and nearly eats dirt.

"Good thing I'm not dying out here."

"Sorry," he mumbles. He won't look at me. He has been quiet instead of texting me what he's been doing and memes like usual. I know it's because of coronation night.

"We've got a problem." I toss my holofone at him and it smacks his chest. He fumbles it around, nearly drops it.

I watch his face as he sniffs and wipes sweat from his eyes, then puts a hand on his hip. He frowns as he waits for Chatterbox to load. Then his eyebrows spring up. Slowly he drags a finger over the screen, scrolling, scrolling, pacing. He scrunches up his hair so it stands up even more.

I cross my arms tight as if that will hold me together, until he stops his pacing and passes the holofone back to me. He sighs and puts his hands on his hips while he kicks at an acorn.

"Well?" I ask.

He tips his head, still kicking at acorns. I can't tell what he's thinking.

"Aren't you going to say anything?"

He shrugs. "What's there to say?"

"I don't know, Louis! Anything! Aren't you upset?"

"Of course I'm upset," he says.

"I'll find out who posted these."

He just nods and paces a circle so he's turned away from me.

"It's really embarrassing. It sucks. But . . . there are ways back from this."

He just nods again, still with his back to me. "Um . . ." He kicks at those stupid acorns again. "I'm supposed to be somewhere in twenty minutes."

He won't look at me. When I most need him to, he just won't do it. "You're not upset with whoever did this, are you? You're upset with me."

"Well . . ." He gestures at the holofone, open to the picture of Axel kissing my cheek. "Look, I know I haven't given you everything you want. So I guess I can't totally blame you for going to Fersen. But yeah, I'm upset."

"I haven't gone to Fersen for anything but friendship and the security he was sent here to provide. I didn't kiss him back. We chatted and danced, and he knew I felt lonely, so he kissed my cheek formally. Just that one worst moment caught on camera."

I've been grateful one hundred times for Louis because, unlike anyone else at this stupid court, he doesn't seem to have a single bit of meanness in him. But when he narrows his eyes at me, I see it there, and it doesn't look right on him. "Come on. Don't lie."

I'm so stunned, he might as well have slapped me. "I would never lie to you."

He jabs a finger at the holofone. "Then stop lying to yourself. Look at that photo, how you looked when he kissed you. And of course you did. He's perfect. He looks perfect, he acts perfect. I'm far from perfect. That's what you want, because you're shallow. You want a perfect android. It's right there on your face."

"It isn't! You're seeing what you want to see! I only had that moment because you left me alone on my birthday!"

"Exactly." He turns to walk away, and I gather up a handful of those stupid acorns he was kicking around. I fling one at his back. He just keeps walking. I fling another one.

"You're an asshole," I yell.

"Yup," he says.

"Stop walking! How dare you say I'm shallow! You just assumed that about me ever since I got here, just because I like fashion and don't know any of your sad old bands and dumbass computer games. You're just like everyone else! You think you know me, but you don't. You don't even try." I hurl another acorn and it bounces off the back of his head.

He spins around. "How could you say I don't try? I try to make you happy. I tried on coronation night. It's just not perfect. Not exactly what you want."

"That is so unfair, Louis. And you know what? It's really damn sad. You have no idea how much I like you, do you? Don't blame me and say I don't when really, you don't like yourself." I wasn't sure if that was at the heart of Louis's behavior, but he stops walking. He turns like he might say something, but he can't look me in the eye. I must be right.

"I've shown you I cared for you so many times. *I'm* the one who's had to doubt. No idea what you think of me. You don't tell me, you just kiss me and put your hands all over me, then you jump away from me like I punched you in the gut or crossed some great big line."

"I tried to explain. I told you it's not your fault," Louis says, but I'm tired of excuses.

"I have no idea where the line even is, because you don't tell me and you keep changing it. Like it would kill you to just talk to me. I'm trying to be patient. But you just . . . you confuse me and I'm . . . hurt. When you push me away, it hurts because I don't know what I've done and I'm worried about our future."

There's nothing left to say. I've done everything I can to love my husband as well as he'll let me and it's still not good enough. So what if I look at Axel and wish for some kind of affection? Anyone would, in my situation. I drop to the ground and fold my arms around my knees. Louis can walk away. It doesn't matter anymore.

I hear the crunch of old leaves as he kneels in front of me. I'm not sure I'd rather he stayed or left.

"Okay . . . ," he says quietly. "Okay. I'll talk. I'll try, I just . . . this is pretty new to me. I never even thought much about sex. So, like coronation night . . . I panicked. What if I mess it up?"

I shrug. "Then you mess up. You think I don't worry about that too?"

"No, I wouldn't . . . have imagined you did."

"Well, surprise. That was your first mistake."

He looks at his hands as he knots and unknots his fingers. "Why would you? You're, like . . . perfect. That's why I said those things about you and Fersen. You're right, it's not you. It's me, afraid I can't be a good match for you when you're perfect. Everything you say and how you move and how you look and just . . . everything. And then when you touch me, my brain just kind of, like . . . buffers. But in a good way? I know it's not an excuse. I've just never felt like this, so I keep shutting down."

He scrubs at his hair with both hands. I think I know exactly what he means by buffering in a good way. "You know, you could have said that a while ago. That would have been super helpful."

"Yeah . . . ," he says. "Well, I haven't been close to that many people before. I think I'm closer to you now than I've been to anyone. I've probably messed this up daily. And I'm sorry."

I think of when he told me about his family. He's lost a lot of the people he was close to. Maybe some of his shyness is because he's afraid he'll lose me too. I clap a hand over his. He looks up and his smile softens me in an instant. I don't think he's losing me on any level. "You're forgiven," I say. "And I'm not going to make you do anything you don't want to. In bed, I mean."

"Oh, I know." He nods.

"But I want us to keep trying. Just talk to me, okay? Tell me what you're thinking. Tell me if we need to stop or, like . . . change something."

"Yeah, yeah. And you too, you know. Sometimes I'm afraid of hurting you. You're so small and delicate. I'm kind of . . . not." He laughs nervously. I think I'm doing a really embarrassing full-body blush, so I don't answer. "There's one other thing," he says. "Why is Fersen giving you presents?"

I'd almost forgotten about that. I let out a whoosh of breath. "It's not presents, like multiple presents. Just the bracelet. It was after that crazy night at the opera. It has a button to summon Fersen or Nilsson if I'm in danger or something."

He frowns. "Oh . . . it's just weird. With the kiss. Not exactly what I would I have expected from an android sent to guard you."

Guilt twists again. "He's . . . very humanlike. He seems to want a friend."

Louis cocks an eyebrow.

"What, do you suspect him of something else?"

"I don't know," says Louis. "Has he said anything unusual to you? The bracelet is just . . . odd. He could have given you a device like that in any other form. It's just . . . I don't want you to get hurt. It may seem like he understands you and he's bonding or flirting or whatever, but he's programmed to be that way. What if he understands too well?"

"You think he's playing me?" I ask.

Louis shrugs and I look away. My first instinct is to be angry. Louis is jealous. Of course that leads to suspicion, and I know that I'm not completely innocent. I've encouraged the connection I have with Axel. But still . . . the bracelet was totally used against me. I can see why Louis would have his doubts.

My hand goes to my wrist, but I'm not wearing it right now. Thank gigs. "I saw this thing on WhoWatches . . . some androids are spies. They plant bugs on people. I've worn it less since then."

"Yeah . . . I'm just worried it's not as innocent as it appears." Louis raises his hands, trying to keep things cool. "But I could be wrong."

Anger shoots through me all over again. But not at Louis this time. "Except I wore that bracelet everywhere at first. Including when I was out here working on the net. Who knows what they could have heard? And he acted like he was my friend. Fersen."

Louis chews his lip, unsure what to say. "What do you want to do? About the bracelet."

"You can find bugs, right?"

"Yeah, I have precision tools. I can open it up and check."

I think of Fersen smiling, promising to keep me safe, giving me an understanding ear like a friend. While planting something on me. One of the First Estate's ears. Tears threaten, but this is part of being a queen. I don't need to cry. I'll handle it. Like my mutti would. I'm sure she's had fake friends before.

"How come you didn't just tell me about it?" Louis asks quietly. "After you saw that stuff on WhoWatches?"

"I was embarrassed. You saw that photo. I knew I was . . . well, that I had a crush. I'm sorry." There's still a part of me that hopes we're wrong about the bracelet and that I can trust Axel.

"He *is* a handsome robot," says Louis.

"Yeah, well. I like you better," I say.

"Really?" His smile is contagious and he has a twig in his hair.

I might have been confused before, but I feel surer by the minute. "I do. Maybe I should have shown it more."

"I'm going to make this right. With you, and with everything else too." Louis gets to his feet and brushes dirt from his pants, then holds out his hand to me. He practically lifts me right off the ground into his arms. "We'll figure this out."

"I might have a plan already. The start of one."

"They set me up with such a smart wife."

"They knew you needed all the help you can get," I tease, and poke at his chest.

His eyes twinkle. Louis, Louis, Louis . . . for a minute he's all I see, all I can think about. I can save him, if he'll let me. I can save us both.

THIRTY-NINE

August 20, 3070, 9:03 p.m.

"Don't break it. I still need to use it."

"I've got this." Louis has the bracelet under his work lamp. With some kind of metal file–looking thing and a small pair of pliers, he slowly separates the two pieces of the fleur-de-lis charm. It trails delicate little wires like tiny electrical blood vessels. Louis points at one piece with the pliers. "It's definitely got a transmitter for emergencies and . . ." He grabs a square plastic magnifying glass, leans so close his nose nearly touches the lens. "Look," he says quietly, and points. Then he taps his ear. The bracelet has a mic.

Which means I have to choose my words carefully. "Nothing seems broken. I'm sure it's fine. Thanks for checking."

"Should I . . . put it back together?" he asks, already losing his casual tone. Louis isn't a great pretender, so I ruffle his hair for being clever instead.

"Yes, of course. I have occasion to use it."

I think I'd like to confront Fersen directly. This is personal. It became extra personal when those rumors appeared.

This is the second time I've gotten help from Fersen and then had a scandal break on the net. I'm starting to think it's not a coincidence. My brain is running on megawatts as a plan takes shape. I'm getting used to having to stifle every thought and weigh every word carefully. I mean, *mon Dieu*, there are enough bugs around here without glitching androids tying them around my wrist. But I'll set a little trap of my own. I'm going to ask Thérèse for help. She's a true friend.

"*Ma chère*," says Louis. "You're pulling my hair out."

"Sorry," I say, and smooth the mess I made of his waves. "I just had a great idea."

FORTY

August 28, 3070, 7:35 p.m.

Thérèse asked me to be in one of her ViewFi videos. I kind of don't want to show my face on the Apps after the Fersen disaster, but disappearing won't do anything for my image. So I might as well jump back into the fray with Thérèse. She's trying to make macarons.

Those little buggers are way harder to make than you would think, but Thérèse seems to know what she's doing. We make a total mess, laughing, covered in flour. The camera is shut off while we wait for Thérèse's first batch to bake.

"Oh, princess of ViewFi, I need your counsel," I say to her.

She gasps. "How could a queen need counsel from me?"

I trace a finger through some of the runny pink batter that spilled on the counter. "Because you saw everything that came out about me—the Fersen rumors."

"That will pass," says Thérèse. "Stuff like that always does."

"I'm not sure if this will. I'm afraid that if I ignore it, it will change how people see me. For a long time."

"I hope you know anything I said about androids—I was just joking! I know you're only friends with Captain Fersen."

"I'm not talking about you, Thérèse. I'm talking about everyone who believes the rumors."

"Of course." She waves a hand. "I'm just saying . . . I can keep your secrets. I won't tell. Or judge you for anything. Fersen is a very handsome robot, after all."

I lean on the counter, all speckled with our mess. The cooks looked at us like we were crazy when we said we wanted to come down here and use the kitchens, but they cleaned everything up shiny for us before bustling off, throwing frowns over their shoulders. "He *is* a very handsome robot. But he also pretended to be my friend and protector when he's a liar."

Her brows pinch together. "What do you mean?"

"I'll explain when we're not in the kitchens, but he hurt my feelings and I have something to prove. And this whole photo thing is total *merde*. I just want to do *something*. I'm sick of feeling helpless."

"I get it," says Thérèse. "But you have to be careful."

"Well, I have a plan, and I wondered if you'd help. Just a simple setup."

Thérèse raises an eyebrow. "Sounds like something wired right into my programming."

"Good. I knew you'd be down! All we're going to do is talk about sneaking out to a Parée party near the Louis-le-Grand campus."

Thérèse taps her chin. "So we're not actually going to this party?"

"No, just talking about it."

"I don't really get it. What does this prove to Fersen?"

"I promise I'll explain later. But that's all we have to do. Are you in?"

She frowns. "How'd you find out about a campus party?"

A nervous twinge floods me. The forums. I shouldn't have even mentioned it, since I can't say that. "A friend told me about it."

"Oh, really? Who?" She sounds genuinely curious, but I shrug it off.

"Doesn't matter, since I'm not really going to go."

She smiles. "*C'est bien*. Nothing else? Just that?"

I nod. "*Oui*. Just some faking. *Très facile*."

"Never knew you were so sneaky." She smiles, but gives me a searching look. It's almost like that mask I've seen her put on. "I'm in."

"There is one other thing. I think Louis and I need some good images right now, and I was wondering if you would help."

"Cute things?" Thérèse bounces up and down and claps. "Do you want me to help you spread cute things?"

"You got it."

She giggles. "I'd love it. I love couples photos. Oh, I'm so excited."

I think of her husband and how many photos they had together. I've never talked to her about what happened to him. She's never mentioned him. But it seems important. Now that I know what I know.

"Thérèse . . . ," I say quietly. "Do you miss your husband?"

She doesn't stop smiling, but she starts bustling around with the mixing bowl, stirring up a fresh batch of yellow batter. "Oh yeah. Quite a lot, sometimes."

"I'm sorry . . . I never heard . . . what happened."

"Really? People sure like to gossip about it." She stirs so quickly she almost drops the mixing bowl. "It was an accident. A cruiser accident."

I don't want to talk about things that will hurt her, but I want her to know I understand.

"It's strange," I say quietly. "It sounds a little like what Louis told me about his dad. . . ."

She stops stirring but doesn't look at me. "Sometimes accidents happen. Alex wasn't careful. He wasn't careful about who he spoke to. Or his opinions. There are people in Parée who don't like the First Estate, and they meet and make plans. When you live at court, you can't go anywhere like that. Much better to stay home. To stay online and use the Apps."

Thérèse does look at me now. I see the girl who watched Madame Rohan leave the party. Steely, careful, and tired. She knows. Thérèse knows about the bugs in the walls. She knows about the filters on the net. She knows all too well that if you cross the First Estate, you might wind up dead.

My breath feels short, but I exhale through my nose.

"I'm here to help you," Thérèse says slowly. "With anything online . . ."

Does she know about what I've been doing on the forums? Does she know about CakeEater and my other screen names? How would she have found out?

Before I can ask any more, it's like Thérèse flips a switch. Her smile is suddenly back full force. "It's your turn! I'm putting the camera back on! You have to try."

It's like the conversation never happened. On camera, Thérèse is the bouncy, bubbly ViewFi star everyone knows Princesse de Lamballe to be. I always thought she would be a great actress. I never knew how good she really was. I try, but I'm not as flawless for the camera as she is. My macarons come out looking like little blue rocks and drippy pancakes.

"Total mess! What will we serve at the tea party now?" Thérèse asks the camera.

I shrug. "I guess we'll have to let them eat cake."

FORTY-ONE

※

August 29, 3070, 9:46 p.m.

The neon in the dining room mocks the warm glow of candle-light. The flickering yellow and orange is supposed to be cozy but makes faces murky. Even the holo-portrait of the parading army looks dimmer. The riders gallop under a red sunset. From the head of the table I can see about a hundred guests at this dinner we were pressured to host for the First Estate. The room is full of shadowy figures speaking in politely low voices amid the clinking soup spoons. Our family sits closest to us, Stan and Josephine, Elisabeth, then Philippe. Across from them are Angoulême and Rohan, then some cousins, aunts, and uncles, followed by nobles. Then at the farthest end, where I can scarcely see them, the people who serve us, like Mercy and Maurepas. The arrangement seems backward. I'd rather have Mercy trying to get my ear than Angoulême.

"Majesté, I seem to recall a lovely gold bracelet you wore quite often. But I haven't seen it lately," he says.

My spoon clatters on the rim of my bowl. I can't afford to glitch right now. My Fersen plan is mere days away, and I can't bring attention to my suspicions about the bracelet now. "One can't wear the same piece too often or it falls out of fashion." I don't bother to sound light or charming or anything I used to be for these people.

"Your dress is certainly an interesting choice," says Madame Rohan.

I smooth a fringe of ruching on my lap. It's a cream-and-red dress that was sent to me by a seamstress who lives near the border of the Wastelands. She sent it in thanks. It's accented with my red ribbons of Wastelander support, and I wore it to defy Madame Rohan. I'm glad she noticed, but I'm also incredibly nervous and hesitate over a response.

"The queen is an expert on the latest fashions," Louis says. "And I'm sure you've noticed she can start trends. She has an eye for spotting new designers. I wouldn't question her."

I brush my hand over his knee beneath the table.

"Do we really have to sit through over an hour of this?" he says with a whisper he disguises as a kiss beneath my ear.

I smile, and he squeezes my hand.

"We will ask whatever questions we like," Angoulême says. I expect a hush to follow. People don't talk to the queen this way. But everyone around avoids my eyes and continues eating.

"And I will answer honestly, Monsieur Angoulême. Honesty is so rare at court." Louis is staring at me and I can feel the anxiety rolling off him, but I keep my gaze on Angoulême. "Don't you think?"

Angoulême raises a bushy eyebrow. "You think of yourself as honest, Majesté?"

"Perhaps you can answer me honestly, then," Madame Rohan cuts in. "Why won't you sponsor Pixter and promote their approved brands? You clearly have a love for my App. If the designs and products chosen aren't to your liking, I'm sure something could be arranged."

"I prefer to discover new designers and give them a spotlight.

Surely Pixter doesn't need my support to be a huge success. I draw so many users to your platform already."

Rohan's smile becomes icy. "Well, perhaps Madame Josephine or Madame Elisabeth would be willing to promote Pixter."

Elisabeth goes pale. "*Pardon*, madame, but I make a terrible model. I'm very stiff in photos."

"I've never modeled either," says Josephine.

Stan slings an arm over her chair. "I think you should try." I know by his grin that he's teasing Josephine, who whacks his chest with a napkin.

Rohan smiles indulgently. "We're experts. You'll be very satisfied with the photos. Few things inspire more confidence than the perfect dress."

"Go on, Jo," says Stan. "She'll do it, madame."

"We'll discuss it," says Josephine.

"I model too." Philippe grins. "Just saying."

"Excellent." Rohan smiles. "Such a shame the queen won't participate. We can do so much to influence your image, after all."

She raises a wineglass to her lips, her eyes still on me. A threat? I remember the first time I saw Rohan in person. The night at the opera house. The night the photo was taken of Fersen and me, then twisted against me.

It was her. I know it was her. She did it after I wouldn't remove the ribbon for our selfie.

"While you have an impressive number of fans, Her Majesté is not without enemies. Pixter has always supported the crown. We do our best to correct your image. Remove libelous photos and lies. But I'm afraid that without support, we may not have the resources to continue as we were."

"Good thing I'm helping out, then, eh?" Philippe says with a wink.

I don't know how much pressure his cooperation takes off me. If Rohan did create the Fersen scandal, what else might she do? Who will she send after me?

Dinner seems to drag on far longer than an hour. Whenever I meet Rohan's eyes, I refuse to look away first. Winning a staring contest is useless, but it's the principle of the thing. I'm not giving in to the First Estate's bullying. We keep up this silent battle throughout the dessert course. I barely taste my meringue cake.

FORTY-TWO

August 29, 3070, 10:49 p.m.

"That was awful," Louis grumbles when we get back to our rooms after dinner. "See you in a minute."

He disappears into his room and I wander into my own bedroom, where Georgette meets me. I just want a minute to sit and look at my holofone or something. Instead of following her into the changing area, I flop onto an armchair. "Georgette, no offense, but can I get changed by myself this evening? Dinner made me feel covered with eyeballs, and I need a minute."

She smiles sadly. "I understand, Majesté." She raises a finger to her lips to show that breaking etiquette will be our secret and slips toward the staff passage at the back of the dressing room.

Finally alone, I wrench off my shoes, grab my holofone, and open Pixter. For years this used to relax me, turn my brain off for a bit, but now I get a sick flutter in my stomach when it loads, even though I'm in the palace and the firewalls and filters are up. Curating my accounts has lost its fun, the excitement of creation and color matching and filtering. Each time I open Pixter, I wonder what Madame Rohan could do to me with this App. Maybe I could shut my account down for a while? Almost tempting. But if a rumor or a scandal spreads while I'm dark, I won't be able to fight back. As I scroll, churning over what-ifs and worries, I find something that brightens me up a little.

Yolande, who was sitting farther down the table with Jules and probably trying to do me a solid, snapped a pic when Louis leaned in and kissed me and another right after, where we smile almost secretly, privately, like there aren't a hundred people in the room. A young duchess, Claire Chosay, reposted the pic and wrote: How are all those bagbiters saying they aren't totally in love?? Lmao do they even know what love is?

It's been shared and liked thousands of times. Maybe it doesn't mean much for my image. It's just two pictures. But it means a lot to my tired heart. We look like I wished us to when we were first married and I scrolled Pixter looking at other happy couples. Also, Louis looks much more relaxed and handsome when he's caught unawares. The stiff posture and awkward faces he makes when posed are gone, replaced by his gentle smile and strong stature.

When Louis comes back in pajamas, he collapses facedown on my bed.

"Not everything is terrible." I show him our pictures. "Look."

He sits up and squints at the screen. A slow smile spreads over his face. He stands up and gathers me in his arms. I stretch on tiptoe to reach around his neck.

"Totally in love? I guess they finally got something right," Louis says.

I try not to smile too much and ruin a good kiss. Has Louis ever said he loves me before? I'm not sure. Can't think. Too much kissing happening. There's also entirely too much dress between the two of us, even though I've got a grip on the back of his shirt, squeezing myself in tight.

Apparently, he's afraid of being interrupted, because he mumbles against my lips, "Um, where's Georgette?"

"Dismissed her for the night. I needed some alone time."

"Oh, right." He loosens the arm around my waist.

"Except for you, obviously."

I move to kiss him again but catch a toe on the hem of my dress and wobble. Louis holds me steady. "Who's going to help you out of your dress?"

Based on his red cheeks, he clearly wasn't trying to be as flirtatious as he sounded. He tries to recover, smiles all crooked, but huffs out a nervous laugh.

I look at him shyly from under my lashes, though I'm not feeling shy at all. "I believe it's a kingly duty." I turn slowly so he can get my zipper, reaching to pull my hair over my shoulder. He places a gentle hand over mine to still me, then brushes my hair away from my neck himself. I feel his breath on my nape, raising goose bumps even though my heart is pumping me full of warmth. He pulls the zipper slowly, and cool air tickles where the dress parts down to the small of my back.

I suck in a breath when he kisses the back of my neck, then my shoulder blade, more warmth pricking in those spots. I wriggle a bit so the dress puddles at my feet with a rustle. I turn toward him and step out of it, just wearing my satin slip now. Thunder rumbles quietly somewhere beyond the thick walls. I remember the first storm, when I was afraid we might never consummate our marriage. I can barely believe this moment is happening.

Louis puts his hands on my waist. "Could we . . . go to my room?"

I don't care where we go. All I know is I feel like every one of my nerves is glitching and the layers of dress are finally out of the way. "I thought I wasn't allowed in."

Louis shifts his arms and lifts me right off the ground. I giggle a little in surprise, use my arms and legs to get a grip on him, but he holds me steady.

"You're my wife," he says. "Nothing of mine is shut off from you."

He carries me through the common room and nudges open the door to the dark of his room, where I've never been. I can't see much, but when he lays me on his bed, everything smells like him, piney soap with a bit of hay and dusty stable smell. I feel like my bones have been replaced with something warm and fluid. He slips his shirt off and I wrap myself around him again.

FORTY-THREE

August 30, 3070, 6:07 a.m.

One word circles my head.

Louis

Louis

Louis

I think I'm in love with my husband.

"Maria," he says softly as morning light edges around the heavy curtains in his room.

I must not have heard him right. Too sleep-addled from the deep slumber I fell into after our fumbling but thorough union. "Hmm?"

"Maria," he says again. "That was your name, and we took it from you. Do you miss it?"

Maria seems like a different person from who I am now. It's not that sex changed me; I feel the same and, blissfully, not very sore. It's that Versailles has changed me. Being queen has changed me. And yet Maria is still me. Still a part of who I am. "Sometimes," I tell him, and run a sleepy hand through his hair.

"Would you like it if I called you that? Maria . . ." To hear him speak my name with depth and softness stirs something in me. A feeling both nostalgic and new. A more comfortable *Sehnsucht*.

"Only sometimes. When we're alone." He smiles. His eyes twinkle, warm like the embers of a fire on its way out. I kiss him.

"Maria," he says again.

I've rarely felt so content. Louis lays his head on my bare stomach.

I think again about how difficult it was for us to take this step. "Did you . . ." *Like it* sounds childish. I consider. "Did I satisfy you?"

He turns his head to look up at me and frowns. "Well, of course."

I ignore my misgivings and say what I fear. "Then you . . . liked it?"

"Yes," he says simply, and snuggles back into me. "But only because it was with you."

My heart flutters.

"And you?" he asks.

"I liked it very much." I wonder if he'll want to go again. Yolande once drunkenly complained about how "energetic" Jules is in the morning.

But Louis is still Louis, and in a few moments, he's snoring softly.

FORTY-FOUR

August 31, 3070, 9:46 p.m.

Tonight's party is low-key, in a small parlor with red wallpaper and soft neon. I slip behind a potted plant with Thérèse and play with my hair, so the bracelet is right near my face. It's time to put my plan to the test. Before the party, I caught Thérèse up in the gardens, bracelet-free and away from other prying eyes. Now, with the bracelet picking up all my words, she leans close as I tell her, "It's at a house right near the Louis-le-Grand campus. If you could pick me up at nine thirty, I don't think anyone will see us behind the Petit Trianon."

"*Magnifique.*" Thérèse claps. "Tomorrow, then. I'll have my driver take the dark red cruiser."

"Perfect! This is going to be megawatt lit."

I giggle nervously, hoping this works. We slip out from behind the plant and almost walk over Madame Rohan's toes. The first time I saw her, I was starstruck. Now my mind fills with quotes from WhoWatches and other places on the net.

Pixter collects metadata to target ads that feed the consumer loneliness loop.

Careful what you post. Pixter has a facial ID database.

They can access the mic on your holofone too.

Pixter is identifying people who are opposed to the

First Estate. It turns over the info to the cops and you're never seen again. Please give us details if you know anyone listed in the missing persons forum.

"*Excusez-moi,* Majesté," says Madame Rohan.

"Good evening." I curtsy to break my racing thoughts and Thérèse does the same, her face hard like the last time we met Rohan.

"Such a lovely bracelet." Her eyes linger on Fersen's "gift." Is she mocking me about the scandal?

"It's nothing." I fold my hands behind my back.

"I do hope you've rethought your decision to work with us. I believe my assistant will be in touch soon with a pitch," says Rohan with an arch smile. "We'd love to do a sponsorship. We have some wonderful designers at our disposal."

"I'm sure something can be arranged." I keep my expression neutral. This offer that would have once been a dream come true rings hollow now that I know Pixter can be dangerous and beyond even my control. I won't forget that the platform I used to define myself was used to hurt me.

"Well, then. If I have your leave." Rohan gives a slight bow and turns away.

"Are you really going to work with her?" Thérèse asks.

I lift my wrist and jingle the bracelet, reminding her I can't answer honestly. "I don't know. I guess it depends what they want me to wear."

"Of course," says Thérèse, and glances away. "I think I need some air. I'll be back later."

"Do you want me to come? Are you okay?"

"Oh, I'll be fine." The bright Thérèse smile returns, and

within moments, she disappears into the crowd.

Not for the first time, I feel sure that Rohan and Pixter had something to do with the death of Thérèse's husband. But I don't know what to say to Thérèse about it.

FORTY-FIVE

September 1, 3070, 9:28 p.m.

No one has stayed in the Petit Trianon since Du Barry left. The little but lavishly decorated guesthouse was her favorite party place. It's quiet tonight. Fireflies hover among the white blooms while crickets chirp. I could enjoy this evening if I weren't glitching with nerves.

Will he show up early or late? I did a fake call with Thérèse, holofone and bracelet next to my ear, told her I was on the way over. What if he doesn't turn up at all?

I wonder if this is how girls feel when they worry they're getting stood up by a date. I wouldn't know. I've never been on a date. Not a real one. My mind jumps to dancing with Fersen at the rave. Anger coils in my belly again.

"My queen."

The anger rises like heat waves, along with a jittery sense of relief. Fersen showed up. I'm so giga-raged that he actually turned up. That he's standing by a rosebush in the moonlight like he knows he looks dashing, like the hero of the story.

"What are you doing out here?" he asks.

"You know what I'm doing out here."

His face puckers up in a frown and he takes a slow step closer. I ball my fists at my sides. "Taking a walk? Enjoying the moon? It is lovely tonight."

He really is a good liar. No wonder androids are used as spies. And not as friends. "Don't lie."

He stares closely at my face, and I let him meet my eyes. Maybe he's scanning me or something. "Why would I lie?" he asks.

"I know who's listening."

His face is neutral. He chooses not to answer. Maybe his code couldn't provide him with a logical reply.

"Well, if you haven't figured it out, maybe your data collectors have." I work at the clasp of the fleur-de-lis bracelet. My fingers tremble so I give up, squeeze my thumb to my palm, and slip it over my hand. It puddles cool against my skin. "I'm here to return this."

"I would rather you didn't," he says. "It's for your safety, Majesté."

"Captain Fersen—and whoever else is listening"—I thrust it toward him—"take it or I'll toss it in the canal. I might be a human, I might be a young woman, but I'm not stupid. This bracelet is bugged. It's not a coincidence you're out here. You heard me tell Thérèse I was sneaking out to the Louis-le-Grand campus. I never intended to go anywhere. I'm just proving a point. Guess I backdoored your programming."

He extends his hand slowly, and I drop the bracelet into it. "Your safety isn't a joking matter, Majesté. I'm not sure I understand."

"You invaded my privacy. You used me and pretended to be my friend. Who got the information that bracelet collected?"

"I did," he says.

"No kidding. Who else?"

He does two blinks that are a little too slow. Maybe his programming is adjusting to this new territory. "I have developers. Programmers. I can't control what they do."

"Then you do understand why I'm angry. Or maybe you don't, because I'm not even talking to you, I'm talking to your programmers. Does Angoulême hear me? Does he understand that I won't stand to be spied on?"

"The information collected is to keep you safe. Let's say you had gone to Parée. If you had, you would have been in danger."

I remember the time I really did sneak out to Parée before I was queen. How it was thrilling and fun and I had no idea of the risks that were out there. I take a step closer, lift my chin in a challenge. "You've been watching me the whole time."

Fersen frowns. "My job is to protect you, Majesté."

"What about when you followed me to the *soirée*? Why dance with me? A dance has nothing to do with protection."

"Because it was fun."

Something about this is chilling. I take a deep breath and try to keep my voice level. "So, it was fun to pretend to be my friend when you were really spying on me. I must make wonderful entertainment for you, Monsieur Angoulême."

"I was protecting you. Majesté, please, this is confusing. I'm not Monsieur Angou—"

I shake my head. "We aren't friends anymore. I can't trust you. That was your plan all along, wasn't it? Gaining my trust?"

"Trust is helpful for protecting you."

"Brilliant job, programmers! *Très magnifique*! Your bots could do their job without spying on me! Or you could have done your job and not made it personal. . . ."

Maybe a human would have sighed here or something. He's so strangely still. "I can't help what my developers use me for. I am controlled. Just like you."

I clench my fists so hard my manicured nails bite at my palms. "No. Not just like me. I can fight control."

Axel turns away from me, eyes squeezed shut. One hand rumples his perfectly coiffed hair. The action is so achingly human, guilt stabs at me. "I don't want to be a coward," he says quietly.

I didn't call him a coward, so I don't know what to say to this.

"We are more alike than you imagine, Majesté," he says. "Like you, I was sent here to play a part. Like you, I lose track of who I am and who I am supposed to be."

These sound like more empty words. "I fight every day to define myself and do what I think is right."

He shakes his head. "Imagine being a shadow of who you once were; imagine having small glimpses, patterns of behavior from someone else . . . someone." He shakes his head again, winces almost like something hurts him. "This is . . . I will show you my fight." He meets my eyes, strong jaw set firm. "This is highly classified information. I am at war. There is the Axel Fersen who longs to tell you this and the Axel Fersen who would never question whether to reveal it, and I must say it fast before I— I am not like the others." He blinks a few times. Clearly glitching in some way, but all his movements are still human. "I am not like the androids," he says with far too much calm. "I am something new. I am a re-creation of . . . Axel Fersen."

He trails off, stares at nothing. I'm afraid to say a word, afraid to breathe in case this disrupts whatever is going on with his programming. When seconds that feel like hours tick by in silence, I whisper, "Who is Axel Fersen?"

"I am Axel Fersen," he says. "I was Axel Fersen. I was as I am now, a soldier. I like . . . dancing. I like . . . pleasant company like yours. I like blue eyes." He stares into mine.

"You are Axel Fersen." I nod carefully, as if I understand, though I don't.

"I am his memories. I have synthetic blood in my veins that is based on his . . . true blood. The blood he spilled when we were at war with the Austro Lands. I am his behavior, recorded from years of profiling when I was a top-ranking air captain, years of missions recorded, personal logs . . . and . . ." He shakes his head again. "Classified. This is classified. I am good at keeping secrets."

The pieces form the whole of Axel Fersen. He is SveroTech's next advance. He is charming, he is hard to distinguish from human, because he very nearly is. He is a tragedy, a life lost to pointless war and brought back as a tool. His story makes my heart ache. But he is still dangerous. He is still my enemy.

"I know you're good at keeping secrets," I tell him. "You've kept so many from me." This particular lie is one he couldn't help.

"We are . . . we are so alike. I know it. You are the most similar to me out of . . . anyone. Anything."

"Then walk away from the people who want to control you," I say. I don't think he will. I'm not sure if he can. But I desperately wish he would.

"How? What do you wish me to do?"

"Be my guard truly. Don't answer to them. Don't send them

data. Louis knows programming. He can do this, and I will say I need you to guard my personal information."

"I'm sorry, Majesté, that isn't protocol." His eyes grow distant. The human I saw—the human he used to be—is retreating.

"*Je m'en fous*," I hiss. "You told me secrets because you're so desperately lonely, but you won't do this? If you want friendship, this is the price. Friends don't keep secrets and trade them like bits and credits."

"Friends trust one another," he says. "My only intention is to maintain your safety."

Anger flares in me again. "Stop saying that. If you are truly Axel Fersen, that brave soldier, you would listen to me and understand what is right." I'm not sure if I'm really angry at him, or at Angoulême, SveroTech, the entire First Estate. It's so strange to direct my anger at someone who just . . . doesn't really react.

Fersen stares at me and accepts it. "I don't know what you want me to do."

It's not exactly satisfying, and I feel sorry for him. But nothing changes this simple fact: no matter how sorry I feel for him, no matter how handsome he is, no matter how badly either of us may want to be friends, Fersen can't be trusted. Like so much else at Versailles, our friendship was just an illusion.

"I'm done with whatever games Angoulême is playing," I say. "No more gifts. No more dancing. No more jokes and fun."

I turn to walk away.

"I'm sorry," says Fersen.

I pause, but I don't turn around. "I told you my conditions. You could let me protect myself without recording my every move."

"Please, my queen," says Fersen. "You have seen very little of what's outside the palace walls. You don't understand what you're being protected from."

I can't say too much. His two humanlike ears are no different from the bug on my wrist. "I understand more than you think I do. And that was your real mistake. The more you try to control me, the more I'll push back. That goes for whoever is listening right now too."

I keep walking. Fersen doesn't try to stop me.

FORTY-SIX

✳

September 14, 3070, 4:27 p.m.

It can be hard to defend myself on WhoWatches and places like Pixter. Using a small arsenal of screen names and fake personas, I say things like, *Maybe the queen actually meant this* or *What if she feels like that?* Sometimes I get hate. Sometimes I don't. Some people loved my support of the Wastelanders and saw it as a sign that I'm working to be a champion for the people. Others thought it was a shallow and uninformed move by a foreigner who doesn't understand Franc culture. For every person who says I give them hope for the new reign, there are at least two who point to old sponsorships like the vaccine banks as proof that I can't be trusted.

She's got leverage on the Apps. She's probably using social engineering, someone said yesterday. I'm sure she posts exactly what the First Estate wants her to say.

I could have screamed. I don't know what to do next. I turned down the offer of sponsorship from Madame Rohan and Pixter. Instead, I found a local designer, Rose Bertin, and sponsored her. I commissioned an incredible gold gown layered with hidden LED beneath sheer layers of ruching. Rose's small shop became vogue. Maybe the strongest statement would be to delete Pixter . . . but without it, I feel like I'm taking away my best weapon.

Defending myself is exhausting, but I have one steady friend. One friend who steps up to my defense when I post. Their handle is "Ils-de-Françoise." I have no idea what this person is really like, but I imagine her as a girl my age. Some Paréesian, a student maybe, who lives in a little apartment on the top floor of an old building in an arty arrondissement, where she sits in her windowsill with her holofone at night, sending me DMs and defending me on the forums.

When we first chatted, I told her that I had met the queen at an event in Parée and was moved to defend her because I felt like she and Louis try their best. Françoise said she agrees with me. We don't reveal anything personal about our lives, but sometimes she's so easy to talk to that I feel like I'm chatting with Thérèse or Yolande. In fact, I've wondered if she really *is* Thérèse. If that's what she meant the day she said she could help me. If Ils-de-Françoise really is Thérèse, I'm not sure I could accept help that exposes her to the same risks I'm taking.

I prefer her help with the second part of my recovery from the Fersen scandal: some positive photos of Louis and me looking happy and android-free. These days it doesn't take much effort to show off this side of ourselves. It's been my one saving grace.

It feels like I waited seven years to sleep with Louis. It's changed everything and nothing. People online still hate me. The First Estate still watches us. Louis is still dragged into meeting after meeting and comes out of them all pale and serious-looking. But he smiles when he sees me.

It's the way he smiles at me that's made me forget about everything else. A country full of people could hate me, but he doesn't and that's all that matters. Stupid. It's stupid. Of course our kingdom matters. But if I look at Louis, I don't see anything else, don't think of anything else. It fades to background noise.

The way he smiles now when I find him in the gardens. Thérèse is here to help with a photo shoot, but I can't look away from Louis. I feel dazzling when he smiles, like I'm wearing something more chic than my breeches and bespoke jacket. I notice that only Louis's horse is here.

"Uh, am I going to walk?"

Thérèse giggles, covering a smile with her camera. Louis looks from his horse to me like he's really confused. "Is the horse invisible?"

"No, but apparently the saddle is."

Louis holds the horse by the reins, but there isn't any other tack.

"Come on, I'll give you a boost."

I'm a pretty bold rider, but that seems like a long way up with no support. "I've never ridden bareback before."

"Really?" Louis pats the horse's rump. "You'll be fine. Don't worry about it."

Thérèse giggles again.

"If I fall off the other side of this horse, that camera better disappear."

"Yeah right!" Thérèse scurries over and starts snapping while Louis grabs my heel and boosts me up so I'm draped over the horse to swing my leg over.

"Thérèse, why are you taking pictures? This is not a flattering angle!"

The horse makes a whickering sound like he's laughing, and I scoot up into position.

"Okay, now what?" I ask, but instead of answering, Louis

bounces up on the horse behind me. The horse stirs a little bit, confused or annoyed. *You and me both, horse.* "Are you serious?"

Louis adjusts his position behind me. Like, right behind me. Arm around my waist, legs around me.

"Super serious." I can feel his voice rumble against my back.

"I can ride a horse by myself, you know. This is so cliché."

"People love clichés!" Thérèse says from the ground, still clicking away.

Louis trots the horse around in circles. The horse's withers and back are tough and strong and not forgiving as I bounce. Louis seems sure of his seat, though, and keeps an arm tight around me. This position leaves very little Louis to the imagination. I'm practically in his lap. Despite our new intimacy, I'm not used to such a public display of our affection. I'm going to look sunburned in these photos.

He pushes the horse into a canter, and I could kill him.

"Hey, hey!" I grab two fistfuls of horse mane to steady myself.

Louis curls over me and puts his chin on my shoulder. "I've got you."

We do three wide circles around Thérèse, who yells, "Don't look so terrified!"

I try to loosen up. The canter is a bit easier to sit than the trot. More rocking, less bouncing. Louis slows up the horse. This involves his legs tightening around me. I can't help but wonder if he's teasing me on purpose.

"You good?" Louis asks Thérèse.

She keeps doing these sly smiles. She knows what I'm feeling. "I think I've got enough material."

"Good!" Louis wheels the horse around so we're facing the

woods. "I'm kidnapping the queen. See you later."

"Wait! What?" I try to twist around to see Thérèse, but Louis is in the way.

"Have fun," she calls from somewhere behind us.

He pushes the horse into a trot, but I ask him if we can skip that and he slows back down. "Where are we going, anyway?"

"I wondered if . . . you wanted to see the edge."

"Huh? Is that a euphemism?"

He snorts with laughter. Snorts right into the crook of my neck. "No," he says, and kisses me, which is really a mixed message. "The edge of the woods."

"Oh. Okay." That doesn't seem super romantic. It's actually a little terrifying.

"I have a few hours. I told Maurepas I need a break. And that we need time to focus on, like, family matters."

He kisses my neck again. "Oh, okay," I say, except this time my voice sounds kind of squeaky. "You know, you should look at the forums with me sometime, because there's a lot of serious stuff on there and I probably don't understand all of it. Like, there's these people, Robespierre, Desmoulins, Danton. They're smart and they're angry. And it kind of seems like, uh . . ." Louis has decided my neck is a more serious matter. So is running his hand up and down my leg. "Uh, this is . . . this is kind of like we've swapped brains or something."

"I'm just trying not to lie to Maurepas," he says. Then his voice goes low. "I believe you are the one who once told me it's romantic to make love outdoors, *Maria*."

My breath catches in my throat. "Completely willing to reprogram this line of thought. I was just trying to tell you some of these guys are dangerous."

"I know." He straightens up in the saddle and my neck tingles in his absence.

Maybe I shouldn't have said anything. "I'm scared some-times."

Louis leans his chin on the top of my head. "It's okay."

We ride for a while in silence. I think I've totally ruined this, whatever it is. Sometimes it seems like Louis and I are never on the same wavelength at the same time. "I listened to some of your stupid Dukes and Bakers."

"Oh yeah? And?"

"It was pretty cool."

"*Bien sûr.* What did you listen to?"

"I watched some live videos. Something about falling trees, and one about the sadness of Sundays, and another one about this dead pirate or something that went on for, like, twenty minutes."

Louis laughs. "I think I know which show you mean. It was in London?"

"Yeah, I think so."

"You liked it?"

"I did." I squeeze his knee. "You listen to sad music, though."

"I guess." He laughs again. "Tell me what I should listen to. Whatever you say, I'll try it out."

"You know Discothèque Rebels?"

"No."

This time I slap his knee. "Oh, come on! They're so popular. You're kidding. Okay, it's Discothèque Rebels, then."

"Got it."

I lean back against him and he tightens his arm around me.

Louis falls into a thoughtful silence until he asks, "Now that you've listened to them, can you see yourself as Cass?"

"Maybe. Seems like I'm going to need a lot of leather pants to be Cass."

His breath is in my ear when he says, "I'm sure that could be arranged."

Did he download a flirtation program into his brain? Maybe Louis has secretly been a bot this whole time. I can't argue with the results.

As if he read my mind, Louis asks, "How'd it go with Fersen last night?"

Louis was asleep when I got back. He's been exhausted with meetings, sagging with stress. "Perfectly, if you consider 'perfectly' catching him in the spying act."

"I'm sorry," Louis says quietly. "How did he react?"

"He sort of non-reacted. But he seemed a little sad."

"I used to wonder what feelings might be like for an AI. Or thoughts," says Louis. "Maybe it's better not to know."

"Who knows who I'm really talking to when he's like a walking surveillance bug? But now we know they can be tricked. I told him I backdoored his programming."

Louis bursts out laughing. It rumbles through his chest into my back, startles the horse. My stomach flutters. "Was that right? Backdoor?" I ask.

"Yes, that's amazing." Louis kisses my ear. "You're amazing."

Fersen seems irrelevant. I feel warm and loose, like I just had a bath and some hot tea. Louis stops the horse. "Look," he whispers.

We've come across the clearest little blue pond. I've never seen this. We must be deeper in the woods than I've ever been.

This pond is surrounded by deer, all drinking from the shallows. Not holo-deer like Louis hunts. Real ones. Some have large, beautiful antlers. All of them have a little glowing mark on their hindquarters. About ten peaceful, gentle-looking creatures move slowly through the water, making only the softest splashes.

"I've never seen so many in one place before," I whisper.

"They like this spot," says Louis. "Just think . . . before the Event, there used to be deer everywhere. All over the kingdom. They were really common. Now there are people who will never see one in their whole lives."

"I guess we're lucky."

"I guess so."

The sky ahead of us is a wall, an image. Versailles is a small world, like the set of a TV show, and outside that world, there are people who can't afford groceries and who have never seen a deer. I have no idea how we're supposed to change that. But for a few minutes while I watch the deer with my hand on Louis's leg and his hand over mine, I enjoy this place and I let myself feel safe.

When we move on and come across signs warning us not to cross the property line, I feel Louis's heart beating fast against my shoulder blade.

"Have you been back since . . ."

"Since my père brought me? No."

It looks so real. You wouldn't know. Until Louis, just like his dad did, grabs an acorn and pitches it toward the trees, where it gets swallowed up by empty air. This should frighten me more. But I guess because I've survived the day the filters on the net went down, I'm not scared. "Can I touch it?" I ask.

Louis goes tense and both his arms wrap around me. The horse tosses his head with the pull of the reins. "Uh, I'd rather you didn't. I don't know . . . what would happen."

"Right."

"So much is going wrong. All over the world and in our own country. There are so many problems, and I only knew about half of them when I became king. There are likely even more issues hidden from me. I don't know what we should do or what I should try to accomplish in my life. But I think . . ." He raises an arm to point at the hologram. If I squint, I think I can see it flicker. Just faintly. "I think the goal is to make that thing disappear. Even if it's scary. Even if it changes Versailles forever."

Something inside me feels empty. It dreads something I can't name or understand.

He turns the horse for us to leave. We don't rush. The horse plods in slow, long steps, but neither of us looks back as we travel through the woods back to the garden paths.

With the palace in view again, the wall starts to feel unreal. Courtiers in the gardens wave to us as we pass. They seem happy to see us like this.

Louis stops the horse and drops to the ground, then grabs me by my waist to help me down. "Sorry if that was a little much," he says quietly.

I'm not sure if he means the wall or the sharing-the-horse thing. "It was good. It was all good. I'm glad we went."

"Okay." Louis takes my hand and very formally bows to kiss the back of it. "My queen," he says with a smile that's mostly in the twinkle in his eyes. A kiss on the hand has never made me feel half-melted before. He smirks in a way that promises more later. The smirk is new, only appeared recently. Not only do I love him, but I think I have an enormous crush on him too.

My shy, gentle husband, who turned to weather-watching hobbies and hacking fascinations when he was left lonely. I never would have imagined him as a match for me. Maybe that's what gives me hope as I watch him lead the horse away. I don't know how the two of us can right a thousand wrongs or take down something as huge as that wall, but we found our way to each other despite being different and trapped in the midst of this insane neon glitchshow of a palace full of spies and backstabbers. So maybe we can do anything.

FORTY-SEVEN

I take a trip to the indoor pool for some quiet, because I think everyone but Philippe forgets that it exists. It's always peaceful down there, all steamed over from the warmth of the water. The tiles are a coral pink, the lighting purple from a spiral-shaped chandelier in the ceiling, glimmering over the bright blue of the pool. I burst in, singing a song, waving my towel around, and it takes me a minute to realize I'm not alone.

Elisabeth is sitting on the edge of the pool, dangling her feet in. She's wearing a T-shirt all damp and stuck to her from the steam. She slouches over her holofone. Doesn't look like she's in a talking mood. She hasn't been since the photo exposing her relationship with Jeanne came out.

"*Bonjour,*" she says, the word all drawn out, fake-cheerful. "What's up?"

"Nothing much. Just need some decompression time. Looks like you had the same idea." I slip in, careful not to splash her. The water is warm like a bath, soothing even through the thin fabric of my pink perma-dry bathing suit. Chlorine scent bites my nose and the back of my throat.

She's still tapping at her holofone. "Just wanted some quiet."

"Sorry," I mumble. This is awkward. Maybe I should leave her alone.

"It's fine." She shrugs, but she hasn't taken her eyes from the screen.

"Haven't seen you much. You must be studying hard."

"You could say that." She looks completely miserable. Hair all flat and damp, framing dark circles under her eyes, which look a little red. Not sure if she's been crying or if it's the chlorine.

"Are you . . . okay?"

"Sure." She shrugs again. "No."

"I know this must be hard for you. Louis and I will always protect you. And he won't force you to marry someone you don't want to."

"He absolutely would if he had to for political reasons. It's necessary sometimes."

I swim up beside her and touch her hand. "He wouldn't. I promise. You aren't alone, Elisabeth. We're your family. We'll support you."

"There's not much you need to support anymore." She drops her holofone beside her.

"What do you mean?"

"I mean there's no relationship to support."

"Oh . . . oh, Elisabeth. I'm sorry."

She kicks at the water. "Can't really blame Jeanne. That job will get her a scholarship. She can't risk it. And who would want to be involved with me when stuff like this happens? We're surrounded by all these bullshit luxuries, but the one thing I don't get is a real chance to be happy with anyone."

My heart aches for her. She's not wrong. In our world, finding friends you can trust is so difficult, let alone finding love. "Someone who loved you should stay with you in spite of everything,

Elisabeth. They would stick out the storms with you."

Elisabeth shakes her head. "No, that's not fair. No one should have to sacrifice their name, risk their job, or deal with hate just because of me. Face it, Marie. This is just fubar." Elisabeth gets to her feet and waves her hand around the room. "All of this? It's fake and it's going to crash down on all of us."

I don't know how much Elisabeth knows or if she's merely feeling the pain of her breakup. "What do you mean?"

There are tears in her eyes now and she shakes her head. "Maybe it's best if we don't fight it. Maybe they can take everything, and when they leave this family with nothing, we can finally figure out what being happy is."

Before I can say anything else, she scoops up her holofone and marches out.

Happy. Maybe that's all any of us want. Versailles trades in happiness, sells an illusion. Beauty, freedom, excitement, fame. We make it seem fast and easy, something to be swallowed down while wincing and smiling, like a hasty toast with bad champagne. The price is a lie, a world half-dead.

FORTY-EIGHT

September 28, 3070, 10:12 a.m.

Louis has been on his laptop for hours, writing up some kind of notes on a law reform. We sit in a study where Louis is watched by holo-portraits of his great-grandfather the Sun King, and old frescoes of the kings who came before him. Every once in a while, he glances at me and smiles like the sight of me is keeping him going. I wonder if I would have loved anyone else like I love him. Whoever they married me to. It isn't so hard to love someone, is it? But there's only one Louis. And all it takes is me hanging out with Stan and Josephine for five minutes to know I'm lucky.

Stan won't stop talking about the Sun King, who is one of his favorite subjects. Josephine's eyes are far away, like she isn't even here.

"So his intention was not actually to show off, but to distract everyone," says Stan. "Grand-Père never understood that, and that's why he never mastered it. And that's also why everyone in this family thinks they understand the Sun King, but barely anyone really does except for me. Are you even listening?"

"No," says Louis.

"Um, yeah." Josephine blinks a lot and glances around like she's just remembered where she is and who she's with.

"No, you weren't."

"Stan, you've talked about this so many times," she says.

"Because it's important."

"The Sun King died, like, a hundred years ago. How important could it be?"

Stan's voice rises. "Are you serious?"

"You know, the Sun King wasn't even that great," Louis mumbles without looking away from his screen. "He did a lot of bad things."

Stan snorts and fiddles with his big, shiny watch. "Oh really. And what king do you prefer?"

"Henry of Monmouth, I guess."

"An Anglian king? You're a real joke."

"Stan, if you like the Sun King so much, why don't you marry him?" I say.

He rolls his eyes. "You guys are boring."

Josephine glances at me with the smallest smile, holding in laughter. Without looking up from his screen, Louis gives me a high five.

"I need to get changed. I have a photo shoot in an hour." I rise from my chair and Louis takes my hand to kiss it.

"Try not to stun them too much. You already look amazing."

"Gross," Josephine mutters.

I ignore her, do an exaggerated twirl of my skirt, then head to my quarters.

I'm halfway there, already reviewing notes for the shoot in my head—designer from Normandy, eight tops, two dresses—when Noailles swoops out of one of the holo-walls like a ghost. I almost scream, clutching at my blouse while I catch my breath. She shoves a holofone in my face. "What is the meaning of that cake comment? What were you thinking?"

"This is impertinent," I say, still breathless and heart racing.

Noailles takes a deep breath in through her nose, nostrils flared. "I only have Her Majesté's best interests at heart. Since it seems that Her Majesté cannot keep her own best interests in mind before speaking."

"That's extremely rude." It's easy to act haughty when I have Noailles in front of me for a model. "Especially since I have no idea what you're talking about."

She closes her eyes and takes another breath. Apparently, it's that much of a struggle for her to maintain her composure around me. Noailles slaps her holofone into my hand. It's open on a video of me and a reporter. I remember him. One of many I talked to during a press junket Louis and I did three days ago. He was really young. I remember him because he had a friendly smile and a strange holo-button on his lapel, glowing with the Franc colors, red, white, and blue, but arranged in a circular pattern I'd never seen before. The reporter asked me about adding more representation to the Third Estate. When I start the video, I hear that same question again.

"Majesté, the Third Estate represents the vast majority of the Franc population, which means more representatives would more fairly express the will of the people and their concerns. What do you think of increasing representation?"

In the video I answer, "The king and I take the concerns of the Third Estate very seriously. I'm sure we would both like to hear from them, and this matter will have the king's full attention."

"Of the highest concern are the prices of basic groceries and supplies. Prices spiked after the last superstorm and have yet to come down. The cost of a gallon of water nearly doubled. The price of a loaf of bread also doubled. What does the crown plan to do?"

I remember my answer. I told him that the king was actively working on expanding means of food production and that in the meantime, I was always happy to extend more charity. I do remember that before I said the thing about charity, I hesitated a little. It was because I knew my answer was weak the moment it was out of my mouth, and I needed a moment to think of a follow-up. In the video, my second of self-doubt comes out as a bit of a shrug, a careless shake of the head. It was me clearing my mind. The words that come out of my mouth have nothing to do with charity. "We'll have to let them eat cake."

I nearly drop the holofone. "What?" I skip back a few seconds and watch it again. Then again. "This is . . . this is ridiculous."

"Certainly. Majesté, how could you let something like this happen? Others don't consider that question to be a joke," says Noailles.

"I never said that! Well, I did."

Noailles shakes her head.

"Listen to me! That's not what I said to that reporter. That's idiotic! How could I have ever said that? It's something I said in a video I made with Princesse de Lamballe! A video about actual desserts! Someone changed this footage. I told that reporter I would give to charities. People don't believe this is real, do they?"

A small crease appears between Noailles's brows. "Are you certain you didn't say this, Majesté?"

"Of course I'm certain! You believed it. You actually believed I made a joke about hungry people."

"It's rather convincing, Majesté," she mutters, and takes the holofone back.

"Please! It barely matches my mouth. And how could you believe I'd say something like that?"

She's typing furiously on the holofone. "We'll try to get this under control. I don't know how it was spread; these things are usually removed within minutes. . . . You must be very careful from now on. It's just as I've told you since the day you arrived here: everyone is watching, and you can't afford a single mistake. Only now that goes double because you're the queen."

"This isn't my fault." This also isn't the first time I've felt betrayed by the people. It's just never felt so complete or cruel. "What should I do? We must have access to the real footage."

"We'll need to put out some response. I will let you know as soon as we have a plan for how to handle this. Now, if I have your leave, I have a lot of work to do."

"Of course." We curtsy to each other and she walks off quickly, the sound of her high-heeled footsteps echoing off the vaulted ceilings.

I sink into a chair, face in my hands. There's an obvious connection between cake and CakeEater. Did they choose this line because they know who CakeEater is? They're mocking me. Or threatening me.

They don't know me. They created an image of me, like their own mock android of Queen Marie Antoinette. And now everyone thinks she's real.

FORTY-NINE

October 5, 3070, 7:27 a.m.

I shouldn't be surprised that when I log in to WhoWatches with the morning light and fog creeping through the woods near the canals, it's Françoise who has come to my rescue again. I've been dreading logging in to see the discussions about my lie of a cake comment. I have no idea how to defend myself against it. Except to post the original footage that Noailles dug up to point out that it was all obviously faked. I didn't say anything about cake. But much of the damage has already been done. People see what they want to see.

Before I even look at the thread on the video, I open the DM from Françoise. It's a good thing I do. It just says:

> Don't respond to anything. Robespierre knows who CakeEater is.

My blood goes cold. I knew it.

What do I do? My first thought is denial. I write:

> Lol what are you talking about?

Françoise must be online, waiting for my response, because she writes back straightaway.

> Don't even respond to me. Don't post as CakeEater or anyone else. It could be dangerous. He's saving your identity and everything you say as ammo. Take care.

The fog feels like walls closing in. Apart from my family, I'm alone. And losing control of everything. It's all falling apart, like what Elisabeth said at the pool.

Because it might be my last chance to look at WhoWatches, I click the thread on the video, the undoctored one, just to get a sense of the damage that's been done. I see a lot of drama between Robespierre and his friends Camille Desmoulins and Lucile Duplessis.

Desmoulition77: I'm a journalist, you arsehole. My job is to expose the truth.

LucyTruths: Calm down. We need to work together. Got an explanation, Maxime?

XxxMaxXxRobesxxX: It's close enough to the truth. They do things like this all the time. It's time to fight fire with fire. Can't argue with the results. Look what's trending on Yakback. #EatTheRich

Desmoulition77: Ok except that interview was a big deal to my career and I didn't consent to how it was used. Social engineering is like a beast. Feed it and it will grow and eat you.

LucyTruths: That's a dangerous line to walk. You should have asked Camille for permission to use his footage like that.

Desmoulition77: Exactly. Thnks Luce < 3

XxxMaxXxRobesxxX: I've only done it once. To put eyes on corruption.

LucyTruths: How is this video still up? Faked footage doesn't usually stay on the Apps long. Especially concerning the First Estate and royal family. We usually have to count on people spreading copies.

XxxMaxXxRobesxxX: I'm not sure. Perhaps the queen

annoyed someone in the First Estate.

Rohan. Robespierre might not know, but I do. Rohan might as well have sold me to them. She turned my strongest platform against me.

LucyTruths: So we're siding with them? Idk about this. . . .

XxxMaxXxRobesxxX: As I said, it's one time. We have so few vulnerabilities to exploit when it comes to dismantling the Bourbons and the First Estate. It's a weakness and it was exploited.

Desmoulition77: It's a LIE, you shady bagbiter of a lawyer. You might have ruined my journalistic integrity forever.

XxxMaxXxRobesxxX: So be a little coward, say it wasn't your idea, and piss off, you self-righteous prick.

LucyTruths: 💀 Grow up boys and let's figure this out.

Then others jumped in on the argument.

✳ Robes you faked that footage? That's fucked up, dude.

✳ That's amazing. People are finally seeing the truth.

✳ It's not the truth, it's a lie! It's like siding with Rohan and Pixter!

✳ It's a white lie. She might as well have said it. The queen serves empty words.

They go on and on like this. Then Robespierre and Desmoulins argue some more until Lucile writes, Get a room, boys, and they agree to take it off-line.

I power off my holofone, which is something I almost never do. I clench my jaw, and my knees feel like water. The danger is very real. I thought I knew how serious this was before, but now I truly understand. This was a direct attack on me. From both sides. The people opposed to me and Madame Rohan.

This is real fear. With each new horror, I think I can't be more terrified, but the fear grows deeper roots in my heart until I feel like my mind could crack. I'm out of ammo, out of hiding places, out of allies. Nothing I say is safe. Everything can be twisted. Every word, every action can turn me into an enemy, a monster.

I'm exhausted before I've even left the privacy of the woods. The sun slanting golden through the branches, the smell of lilacs, the quiet twittering of birds feel like my only friends. The only safe, true thing in a world that's fake and ugly.

FIFTY

October 7, 3070, 6:29 p.m.

I feel like this cake thing has killed me.

"We can show it's a fake, but nothing takes back the fact that most people believe I *could* say something like that." I'm curled up in the corner of the couch in the common room, cradling a sleeping Mops. "I wouldn't say something like that. When I was little, I gave out food at soup kitchens."

Louis is pacing. He doesn't look angry, exactly, but there's some kind of resolve in the way he paces around with his arms folded. "And you think you know who's responsible."

"Yes . . . ," I say carefully. The common room remains bugged like it's always been, so we must speak carefully. "Maybe I should have come prepared with better answers. Maybe I should be doing more so they don't attack me."

Louis shakes his head; his brow is drawn down. He's never looked older or more like a king. "No. They have no idea what you're worth."

His words fill me with guilt. "Louis . . . I'm not . . . what exactly am I worthy of? I haven't accomplished much."

"I won't stand for it," Louis mutters, and plops down at the computer. "Give me five minutes."

Louis at a computer asking for silence is usually a little

worrying. But since I have no ideas at all, whatever. Louis can try something that will inevitably not work. He clicks furiously for a few minutes and then says, "The bugs are off. You said it was Robespierre?"

"Yes. He changed the footage and spread it around."

"And he's the tough guy of WhoWatches?"

"Yeah, one of them."

Louis turns back to the computer and starts flipping through Robespierre's accounts on the Apps. He gives Pixter a quick glance but focuses more on his forum posts and blog. "He's smart," he says after a few minutes.

I roll my eyes. "Yeah, he's definitely some turbo-nerd creep trying really hard to ruin our lives. And succeeding."

Louis laughs a little, still absorbed in the guy's writing. I groan and flop backward, causing Mops to scamper off. "Quit admiring him. He's the worst."

"Sorry," says Louis. "He's pretty interesting. It will be a shame to get back at him."

This is worth me clambering back up into a sitting position. "Get back at him how?"

Louis turns his chair around and shrugs. "Well . . . I could get into one of his accounts easily. Like, really easily."

"Are you serious?"

"Yeah," he says, all innocence and modesty, like he's talking about whipping up a spreadsheet.

"Okay . . . my knee-jerk is to say *cassons-nous*, let's do this. But you told me to stay off the forums. Wasn't that so they target someone else besides me?"

Louis tilts his head, frowning, thinking. "What about making a dramatic exit? Could you post one more thing, then stay off the forums for now?"

I shrug. "I have a friend on the forums who tipped me off to Robespierre and the footage. She knows who I am. I do hate to leave without a fight."

"So I hack into his Pixter or something," says Louis.

"Are you sure?" I can admit that the thought of doing this is kind of delicious.

"He stole your credibility. Let's steal some of his." Louis turns back to his computer.

I get up to stand behind his shoulder. "Filters are off, but are the bugs still off?"

Louis slaps his forehead. "Uggggh, damn, they're totally back online," he groans.

I slap at his shoulder. "Stop, I almost believed you!"

"Of course they're still off. You think this is amateur hour?"

I fold my arms around his shoulders and kiss the top of his head. "No, His Majesté is a brilliant expert, of course."

My heart is pounding as he takes screenshots of Robespierre's admission from WhoWatches and makes a post on his Pixter account, then toggles it to post to Chatterbox and Yakback too. "What do we write?"

"Got it." I lean my chin on his head with an arm over each of his shoulders and type out: I hate social engineering so much that I use it myself. #AboveTheRules #EatTheHypocrites. Then I add a link to the real video, where I don't say a word about eating cake.

Louis whistles. "Yikes."

"Post it?" I ask.

"Uhh, yeah! Post it!"

"Okay, I'm posting."

"Do it!"

"I'm doing it!"

Like kids doing something they know their parents will kill them for, knowing they'll be grounded for months, we make the post. There's no time to think about whether it was a good idea. It's posted. It's done.

"There's one more thing. A post from my own account. Rohan isn't getting away with her part in this."

I upload a blank black square into Pixter, toggle to cross-post to all my other accounts across the Apps. My caption reads:

> I deny saying "let them eat cake." I would never make light of such a serious issue as hunger. Pixter and other Apps should take this issue seriously too. It's irresponsible to allow inflammatory and defamatory messages to spread. To fight misinformation, I'm logging off for forty-eight hours. I encourage followers to join me. I will be spending this time hard at work addressing matters concerning us all. Pixter is not free to use my image however they wish. #QueenGoesDark #PixterBlackout3070.

I show Louis. He lets out a big sigh. "They won't like it."

"Good," I say.

"I'm just worried."

"We can do this. We knew it wouldn't be easy." I press the button. The message is posted.

He smiles a little and squeezes my hand. "Forty-eight hours, huh?"

"Yeah, that's a record for me. But I'll monitor what's going on. I'm just not posting."

"I'll set you up a proxy. So they know you stayed logged out for real." Louis turns back to his computer. "*C'est pas vrai*! People are logging out already."

"How do you know?"

"See the metrics?"

"I'm glad you're such a geek."

"I'm glad you're so, what's the word . . . iconic?"

"That will do." We watch together as Pixter goes dark.

FIFTY-ONE

October 8, 3070, 2:12 p.m.

The text from Thérèse comes in while I take Mops for his morning walk.

Are you alone?

I glance over my shoulder and see worker bots misting the plants, a few staff raking the gravel paths. The duc and duchesse d'Agineau taking a walk, but headed away from me.

I text back: Alone as I ever am lol taking mops for a walk

Thérèse replies: Perfect. Can you meet me by Proteus and Aristaeus?

Mops and I make our way over at a jog. I toss sticks ahead of me for Mops to chase. His dark curly tail wiggles with excitement. I see the infamous two-dudes-wrestling statue and Thérèse's pink hair up ahead as Mops trips himself with a stick three times his little size. I stumble toward Thérèse, laughing and trying to hang on to a squirming Mops. Thérèse doesn't laugh. Her face is blank. Hard. Like a bot. Like the face I was trained to wear when I need to give away no thought or feeling. But with less smiling.

"*Salut*. What's wrong?" I ask.

She reaches for Mops and I hand him over. Maybe she needs doggy kisses. Mops trembles with excitement and licks at her face. Thérèse hugs him close and hushes him with some soothing scratches at the ruff of his neck. Mops stills, better behaved for snuggles from a friend than he is for me.

"*Allons-y*," says Thérèse, with a nod to the trees behind her.

I follow her while nerves chew at my stomach. The only reason I've ever pushed a path into the woods was to say something dangerous that couldn't be overheard. Sharp brambles grab at my ankles. I'm not dressed for this as well as Thérèse is. I've never seen this outfit or anything like it on her. Green-edged sneakers, plain black leggings with temp-reg panels, a jacket with a big hood that shifts between dark green and black as though reflecting the forest light. Something is wrong.

She passes a calmed Mops back to me, and I hold him close. "What's happening?"

"I'm leaving," says Thérèse.

She's so dead when she says it. Her eyes and her voice are empty.

"What do you mean?"

"I need to go away for a while. I won't be at Versailles. There won't be a way to contact me."

Thoughts and questions fly through my mind like a data stream. First it hurts, because she says it so flat. Like this doesn't matter to her at all. But almost as quick as that feeling rises, I wonder if this is my fault. If it's dangerous to be friends with me. I want to ask why, but I start with, "Where?"

Thérèse shrugs. "South, maybe. To where my family is from."

She's still so cold. I deserve more of an answer than this. So now I ask it. "Why?"

Thérèse takes a deep breath. I only notice it because I see her chest swell. "There are . . . but you know this, you aren't stupid. You know there are a lot of people upset with the crown. Angry at the court and the First Estate. Those same people have put a target on me. I need to lie low for now."

My worst fears seem to rush to my head, leaving my blood cold. "Was it because of me? What could you have possibly done to make them angry? It was the Pixter thing, wasn't it? Was it Rohan?"

Thérèse reaches for me and squeezes my shoulders. "No. It doesn't matter what I did, but it's not because of you."

"Then let me help you. Stay at the palace. No one will hurt you here. I won't let them."

Thérèse hangs her head. "That's why I needed to talk to you. The palace isn't safe. People *can* hurt you here. I want you to leave. I want you to go home. Go back to the Austro Lands."

I back away and her hands drop. "What are you talking about? People come after me online, but they can't hurt me here. We have a guard. We have soldiers."

"Look, I don't know exactly when. I just know the danger is coming, and the only way to avoid it is to leave." Thérèse takes a step toward me.

"I'm the queen, Thérèse. What about Louis? I can't just leave him and my people."

Thérèse shakes her head. "If only they knew . . . You are much braver and much smarter than anyone gives you credit for. Somehow you were exactly like I expected you to be and also nothing like what I expected."

"Thérèse, you're scaring me." Mops is squirming again, squealing like he can smell my fear. "If we're in trouble, we'll tell Louis and Mercy and Maurepas, and we'll figure out how to solve it."

"It's too late," Thérèse whispers. "This is bigger than us. It's been growing and growing, and now it's unstoppable. The people of Parée are going to rise, and the First Estate won't protect you. Ideas are strong. People are strong. You have to leave, Marie. Please. Just trust me. Say that your mother is ill and you need to visit her. Say anything."

"They'll never let me go right now, there's so much—"

"To hell with what they want!" Her eyes are wide. Haunted. "Who do you trust? Them or me? The people surrounding you here don't give a damn about you! You're a tool to them, not a person! And you're no longer useful, so they're going to throw you away and use something else!"

"Thérèse." I search her eyes, her face. I search for the missing space between the girl I thought I knew and the girl I caught glimpses of, fully emerged now. The girl who lost her husband and would never speak of it. "Who are you?"

She steps toward me and I almost back away, but for her I stand still. She hugs me, Mops snorting and crushed between us. "I'm your friend," she says. "Don't forget that, Marie. Please listen to me. Listen to me and we'll see each other again someday."

Tears catch in my eyelashes. "Don't go. Let me help you."

"It's too late," says Thérèse. "I have to go. Don't follow me. You won't catch me anyway. Not in those fab shoes."

Her eyes flick to my white-and-pink shoes, a cross between heels and sneakers. It's in that look that I realize what I'm losing. That my best friend is running away and she won't let me help her.

"Thérèse, you can't."

"I'm sorry. I'm sorrier than you'll ever know. Please take me seriously. Stake your life on it." She backs away, taking quick strides toward the heart of the woods. "Goodbye."

"Thérèse, no!"

She starts jogging and I stumble to keep up. Mops starts barking and straining at my grasp, slowing me down even more.

"Go back, Marie," Thérèse shouts over her shoulder. She flicks the large hood over her head to cover her pink hair. She's much harder to see. Like she's melting into the leaves. "Go back and go home!"

I pick up the pace, trip over a branch. I'm losing her. She's like a shadow. Her dark clothes in the strange colors blend into the forest. Mops barks louder and I almost lose my hold on him. If he got away, he'd chase after her and get lost. So would I.

I stop walking. My arms tighten around Mops, still barking in the direction of Thérèse. She's out of sight. I won't follow, but I won't quit. I turn back and stumble out of the woods. As soon as I'm back on the garden path, I set Mops down and whip out my holofone.

I open my messages and type furiously as I stumble back to the palace. I nearly trip over Mops twice, tears pricking at my eyes. I send message after message. I beg her to come back. I promise to help her. I threaten to send someone after her. Thérèse doesn't respond. Until a text appears saying, The account Thérèse_de_ Lamballe doesn't exist.

FIFTY-TWO

❁

October 9, 3070, 9:13 p.m.

My forty-eight hours off-line were up almost three hours ago, and I've been digging through the quiet aftermath. A lot of people went dark. More than I expected.

Louis is burned out, curled up in a ball, using my stomach as a pillow. I've been petting his hair with one hand and scrolling my holofone with the other. He's been trying to uncover any possible sign of Thérèse but has come up empty. Empty as my heart feels, certain that no matter what she said, she's gone because of me.

"She's a ghost," Louis says, repeating what he said at least four times while hunched over his laptop. "She's scrubbed, burned. She's either a god-tier hacker or she's friends with one. Either way, there's more to Thérèse than we ever guessed."

"I knew . . ." I scratch at his hair. "Well, not really. I just knew there was something different about her. I should have asked sooner. A better friend would have helped more."

"It wouldn't have made a difference, *ma chère*," he says quietly. "She was smart. Really smart. Whatever she was hiding, she hid it for a reason. And she hid it well. I'm sorry I can't find her."

"You tried your best," I say, sounding as hollow as I feel.

"What do we do when we have all the power, but none of it?" Louis rubs his eyes. "We can convince a few thousand people to do a temporary Pixter boycott, but what else? And what can the First Estate really do to us when we fight them? I don't have answers. I wish my père was here."

"Our empire is fading. . . ." I think of my mama standing by the red curtains, snow falling behind her.

Louis looks startled. "What?"

"My mama said that."

"When?"

"Right before I came here to marry you."

Louis frowns. "That's a strange thing to say."

I gather him to my shoulder and stroke his hair some more. What she said haunts me too. Did she know about any of this? This can't be what she was talking about. She never would have sent me here.

"Thérèse will be all right," Louis whispers.

I can't keep my eyes open anymore. So I drift into darkness and imagine all the places my friend might be. I try to picture Thérèse somewhere beautiful and far from here. Somewhere warm that smells like oranges. Somewhere like the Schönbrunn gardens on a summer evening.

FIFTY-THREE

October 10, 3070 2:12 p.m.

Thérèse's disappearance has made me restless, angry. I want to do something, I want to act on something, but I'm not sure what my next step should be. She was always an accomplice to my plans. Without her, I feel lost. I will always wonder if she's gone because of me. If she's hurt or worse. Because of me.

When I can't take pacing any longer and the awful small talk about nonissues with courtiers in the Hall of Mirrors becomes insufferable, I retreat to the library. It's often deserted, and today is no different.

I sit at a holofone desk, flicking through useless facts and information so filtered and doctored that I'm not sure why I'm doing it. I won't find answers here. There will be no map showing me how to be queen of a kingdom turning against me. No secret dossier detailing where Thérèse has gone.

I stretch and knock a pen from the table. I try to catch it, but it rolls away. I go to follow it, but it must have rolled under something. Like the bookcase.

The bookcase has bothered me a little ever since I first laid eyes on it. I used to think the books behind the glass doors were under lock and key because they were rare, delicate, and expensive. Now I know better. Nothing in Versailles is simple.

The lock is bio-encrypted. It should recognize my skin if the queen truly is the mistress of this palace.

I grip the lock. There's a rude barking buzz noise. The screen flashes *RESTREINT*. No access. I can't say I'm surprised.

I wait for the inevitable staff member to appear. He marches around the corner, shoulders squared and haughty, ready to reprimand whoever tried to open the bookcase. When he sees me, he gives a small gasp and bows. "Majesté! Please forgive me. I wasn't made aware you were visiting the library."

"It's not a problem," I say. "But I must have access to these books."

His forehead is shiny with sweat. He blinks beady eyes from the shelf to me to the empty space behind him. "Oh, I see. Majesté, I'm terribly sorry, but those volumes are so delicate that they are not to be handled."

I raise an eyebrow. "I will be most careful, I can assure you."

"Forgive me, Majesté. No one accesses these books. The king himself hasn't touched them."

Given Louis's fondness for books, I wonder if he's tried. I'm not ready to back down. I can pull the rank card. I'll wear my imperious mask and say in no uncertain terms that the queen's word is law here and I will see those books. But with each passing day, I've grown to hate that mask more and more.

I use the mask that comes naturally and put on a charming smile. "Monsieur, I do hate to put you out, but it's very important for me to have a few moments looking at these books. It's a project for the king, you must understand. If I could have but ten minutes alone, the queen herself would be in your debt."

Greed sparkles in his small eyes and a smile slimes across his face. He dabs at his forehead with a handkerchief. "I suppose ten minutes would harm no one if this is just between us, Majesté."

"Of course. I would appreciate discretion too."

"Allow me a moment to shoo the other staff member out of the data center." He is all too eager to curry favor with the queen and bustles away.

I wait, afraid he's about to call someone to scold me. But he returns, heels clacking with the same crisp walk, and clutches the lock. This time it unleashes a quiet tolling sound and the bookcase doors open.

"Ten minutes, Majesté," he reminds me with a bow, then departs.

Ten minutes.

I don't even know where to begin.

I can make out the cracked, peeling spine of a book written in an old Franc dialect that seems to say something about the *History of Louis XIV, King of the Sun*. I pull this one out, then notice something else. A frayed red ribbon sticking out near it. The ribbon is tied around a small bundle of papers. I pull them out carefully, the paper brittle and delicate in my hands. Cramped writing is squashed in the margins, with dates and question marks and names that must be references.

But I don't look deeply. Instead I turn to the next page and find a sprawling, intricate family tree. The spidery writing is almost indecipherable, and I'm about to move on when I see a name that stops me in my tracks.

My name.

Marie Antoinette is written at the very bottom of the ancient paper, a flimsy line connecting it to *King Louis XVI* and four small lines branching out from both. Children.

Reality seems to slip. Sound dulls. My hands on the delicate paper are numb.

I flip the page, still feeling detached and light-headed. But there is no more text. No continuation that shows what happened to this past Marie Antoinette, or her apparent children. There's just a handwritten block of familiar, cramped writing.

Previous notes from the Zweig book: Antoinette was frivolous, lighthearted, but kind-spirited. She was at first adored by the people, but sentiment changed as France took part in a war against England. Crown finances became strained as King Louis XVI constantly wavered between aiding his people and caving to his dukes and the Church.

But what happened?

As is so often the case, Louis and Antoinette's fate is lost. When all we have are precious few books and research claimed after the Data Wars, understanding human history is like putting together a puzzle with only a third of the pieces.

It is also possible the First Estate has this information and restricts it. They famously celebrate the Sun King's triumphs, emulate his artistry, pageantry, and glory, while ignoring the atrocities committed in his name.

Sadly, hackers might have more luck tracking down this information than historians. Maybe one day I will be brave enough to seek that kind of help, because Queen Marie Antoinette haunts me. What became of her? Without a past, do we really have a future?

Adelaide Frasier, 3070

Notes on Louis XV contain some mention of XVI and Antoinette—search for links social/economic conditions similar to our own, but agriculture vastly different & important factor.

De Gaulle book for ideas on unity and cultural shifts, notes on Sartre?

There are some scribbled names and page numbers, but that's all that remains of this parcel and the work that Adelaide left here, never to retrieve. My heart hammers as I search spines for mentions of the Marie Antoinette who is me and not me. I find a notebook belonging to Adelaide, but as I rip through the pages, I find nothing but notes on men named de Gaulle and Sartre.

I slump to the floor and rest my forehead on my knees. I've always known the royal families are built on a myth and a model. I never knew how close this model was to reality. I never knew that I had the name of a woman like me.

I have truly never gotten a chance to rule in my own way. Every step has been guided by an extensive PR team led by Rohan, a bug in Angoulême's ear, a shadow of the path forged by a woman who lived here in another world. And there is no way out because the path disappears into the hazy, unknowable distance.

FIFTY-FOUR

October 14, 3070, 10:47 a.m.

The sunny parlor is full of people with sleepless eyes fixed on a screen showing riots in Parée, cut between reports about the city's food shortage. The strain from the wildfires has caught up with the stores and markets, now empty of anything fresh and nearly out of anything preserved. JeanCo Foods is the only supplier left and they've tripled their prices. When people started looting, they were arrested.

"Blogger and influencer Jean-Paul Marat has gone into hiding. It's widely believed that an android spy leaked his whereabouts to authorities. He escaped before his apartment was raided early this morning," says a newscaster outside a dingy apartment building above a pharmacy. "Whether his exposure and disappearance are truly due to incognito androids remains unclear, but Marat is a figurehead for the Paréesian protesters. He is a champion of the people, and they see an attack on him as an attack on them."

"It was bots!" says a woman with a plastic mask over her face. "It was bots that found Marat. They can find a face in minutes. That's why I've got this." She gestures to her blank face, a smooth curve of gray plastic covering all but her eyes.

Whatever lit the fuse—Marat, the food prices, the need for

more Third Estate representation in the Estates General govern-
ing body—Thérèse was right. The people can rise, and now they
have. The streets are full of fire, hand-drawn signs, broken windows, cruisers smoldering and belching black smoke. And now
they're at the gates of the palace.

"Come out or let us in!" they chant.

I try to remember why they're acting like this. But because
I've met so few of them, have no idea what it's like to be them,
they mostly feel like an enemy waiting to drag me from my home
any second.

The riot footage shows people getting gassed and stumbling
away. Then police start stunning people with volt-batons. They
drop like flies, as if they're dead. Louis gets to his feet. "*Arrêtez*,"
he says, as if his voice could halt what's happening in the video.
"They can't do this. We can't attack our own people."

"Sire, they will destroy the city if they carry on," says
Maurepas.

"They believe we're against them. If we do nothing, we're saying we support this." Louis waves a hand at a woman coughing
into a handkerchief, choked by gas. "It proves that they're right
to call for our removal. Destroy them, and they'll destroy us."

"It's firmness, Majesté," says Maurepas. "They can't be
allowed to run rampant and set fires."

Louis shakes his head. "It's cruel."

On the screen showing the front gates, something flies up and
over, spewing smoke everywhere. The guards aim their rifles.
My blood runs cold and I raise a hand toward the screens, knowing it's useless but needing to do something. Anything.

"Stop them," Louis shouts. He presses at the glowing silver

bud in his left ear. "This is your king! Hold fire."

"Don't be an idiot!" says Stan. "Look at them!"

"What if they throw a grenade?" Philippe says, nervously pulling at his shirt cuffs.

"They won't," says Louis.

"And how can you be so sure? How are you going to send them out of here before they break in?" Stan asks.

"I don't know. . . ." Louis stares at his shoes. I can see his authority slipping. It's always been a mask on him. An illusion, like a holo. He has to keep the illusion up or we're lost.

"You could talk to them," I say to him quietly. "We could go together."

"What do I say?" he asks, low enough so Stan can't hear.

"They're your people. Tell them you want to help. Talk to some at the gate."

He nods once and turns to Maurepas. "I'll address them, then."

"Absolutely not. All due respect, Majesté. We cannot let you. This is a bloodthirsty bunch."

"You can't stop me, Maurepas. I'm the king." He places a cold hand over mine. "You don't have to do this."

"I'm sharing your dangers. I'm the queen."

He squeezes my hand. In his eyes, I see what I hoped I would. His respect for me wins out over his wish to protect me. He nods once.

"Those people aren't safe," Stan growls. "They could kill you. Especially when you're too soft to use the guards."

"'Those people' are our people," Elisabeth says while she leans on a chair, arms folded tight. "But what will you do? How are you going to stop them?"

"I'll give them what they want."

"You can't just do that! The First Estate will be furious," Stan shouts. "It's weak."

"He's doing what he thinks is right," I say.

"Right and smart?" Stan taps his head. "Rarely the same thing."

"He'll be fine," Philippe squeaks. "They've got this."

"Don't be a child, Philippe." Stan thrusts a finger at the screen. "He dies? Marie dies? I die? Elisabeth dies? You're up. This is real. This is what we're up against."

"No one's going to die!" Philippe looks like a child, all big, scared eyes. I often forget that he actually is a child and the rest of us aren't much more.

"Someone could!"

"Oh, stop," Josephine shrieks. The first words she's said this entire time. "So he dies and then you're king, Stan. Isn't that what you've always wanted?"

"Shut up, you horrible woman," Stan thunders. He looks at Louis, then at me, nervous like I might slap him or something. "I don't want that. I'm your brother."

"I know," Louis says. After all, who would want to be king after seeing this? He takes my hand. "Let's go."

"You'll need anti-shock armor, a bulletproof helmet," says Maurepas.

"For the queen. I don't need any. I'm asking for their trust. I'm giving them mine."

Stan curses behind us. I squeeze Louis's hand. "I don't need armor either. All your dangers," I remind him.

For a minute, I think he's going to argue. "Stay close," he says.

When we leave the room, we're flanked by Fersen and Nilsson. I can feel Fersen staring at me. I'm sure it seems illogical that I'm going. I don't worry about whether he'll try to stop us, and march straight ahead.

The roar of the crowd gets louder as we descend the staircase of the grand entrance. I see them through the window, through smoke and haze. Waving signs, waving fists, waving banners with crossed-out crowns sprayed on. When two droids attach to the doors and push them open, a strange hush falls. Maybe they can't believe we're here. I can hardly believe we're here.

I feel my lack of armor. I feel the breeze through my plain blouse and at the cuffs of my pants. I'm more plain and bare than I've ever appeared before them. Like I'm dressed for mourning. Someone shouts, "*Vive le roi! Vive la reine!*"

Louis murmurs beside me, "What should we do?"

I look at the press of people against the gates. A hundred staring faces. They look desperate. I feel desperate too. But now isn't the time. "Talk to them."

"*Oui,*" he says, and we go closer. The noise picks up again: shouts, mumbles.

My breath feels gaspy, like that night at the opera. There's no time for that either. I take long, slow breaths through my nose.

Louis and I approach a young woman pressed against the gate. The crowd seems to have crushed her there, with her arms wrapped around the bars at a strange angle.

As I get closer, I see that she's skinnier than anyone I've ever come across. Her hoodie and jeans hang loose, her face is gaunt, her eyes are large, dark-rimmed. Black hair hangs lifelessly in two curtains framing her thin face.

We stop right in front of her. She's shaking. Her hands jerk up and she grabs the bars of the gate, presses her face closer.

My heart is breaking. Who let this happen? Who drained the life out of her? I know it was the First Estate. It pains me to think of the ways we might have let them. She's no older than me. And she couldn't be more different from me.

What kind of world gave me everything and her nothing? I don't need to wonder why they're ready to rip apart these gates of gold and neon. The answer is clear in her face, starved for nutrition while the palace glimmers and glows just out of her reach.

Louis places a hand over hers. "*Mon amie*," he says quietly. "What can I do for you?"

Her throat bobs as she swallows. "We need food," she says. "Real food. Not nutri-tabs."

Louis nods.

"Let us meet with the Estates General!" shouts a man behind the hungry girl. He jostles forward, crushing her against the gates.

"I hear you," says Louis. "Be careful of her."

But the shout has reached other ears and there are more cries about the Estates General. Others shouting for food.

Louis's eyes are wide. We're on a knife's edge between total chaos and dispersing the crowd. We're a thumb on a detonation button, a finger on a trigger. One wrong move and we'll lose them. Louis squeezes my arm. "Can you have someone bring food? Any food. All of it in the kitchens. Have the guards give it out."

I don't want to leave him, but I nod. What else can we do?

"The queen will get you food," Louis says to the girl. A tear runs from her eye.

I touch her arm. "I will. I'll be right back."

The crowd is getting restless, milling around. Shouting, chanting, "We want the Estates General."

I turn to leave, my mind already racing with who I can ask to collect food fast. Noailles? Maurepas? The head chef? A roaring sound breaks my thoughts. Not the crowd, but a cruiser. A big one. Dark blue. Military.

"No," Louis says. "*Non*. Send them away!" he says into his earpiece. "We don't need them."

But as the cruiser descends toward the ground, the door opens a few feet over the ground and a line of men jump out. They wear trim blue uniforms. Little armor, no helmets. They all have elegant faces. They're all the same height. These are androids.

"THEY SENT FOR ANDROIDS!" someone screams.

A chant breaks out. "Bots should burn!"

Louis marches toward the androids, waving his arm at the cruiser, ordering them to go back. The crowd surges forward with so much force the gates creak. A piece of neon to my left cracks and shatters. The girl we spoke to cries out as she's pressed against the bars.

"Stop!" I yell. Grabbing at her arms, helpless. "Someone help her! *Arrêtez!*"

Hands grip my shoulders, pulling me away, and I scream.

"Come, Majesté. We must leave."

It's Fersen.

"Get off me!" I scream. "I'm not leaving! Let go! I'm the queen! I command you to let go."

"Safety protocols in place." His voice sounds strange. Clipped, mechanical, unnaturally calm, no trace of his personality. "Commands overridden."

I kick out, but there's no fighting him. He's strong. Inhumanly strong. He drags me backward and I keep fighting. It might be useless, but at least they can see. I don't want this. I'm not a friend to anyone who would drag me away from the poor girl clinging to the gate.

She reaches toward me. I'm not sure if she wants me to save her or if she wants to help me. Maybe both.

I kick and scream all the way into the palace. Three androids approach the gates. They have volt-batons, blazing and crackling with snaps of white light. Someone shrieks. Part of the crowd surges backward. The scene becomes chaos. My poor dark-haired girl disappears. I choke on a sob. Did she fall? Did she run?

"Be calm," Fersen says over and over. It's like a message at a cruiser port, lifeless, emotionless. Like the night at the opera, but the empathy is stripped away. "You're safe. Be calm."

He drags me through the front doors.

"Louis!" I yell. "Where's Louis?"

He follows me a moment later. It took Nilsson and another android to get Louis through the doors, each of them clamped onto one of his swinging arms.

"You have to stop!" he yells. "You can't do this. You do this and they really will kill us. And we'll have earned it! They'll scrap you for parts and it will be your fault! Do you understand?!"

They don't respond. Fersen, Nilsson, and a red-haired android take their place in front of the doors. From somewhere outside there's a gunshot. A fresh wave of screams. My heart seems to leap into my throat.

The androids are as still and impassive as statues. Louis

shoves between them, but of course the doors are locked. He gives the frame a violent kick, then screams in Fersen's face.

Just yells like an animal. Fersen doesn't flinch, but I do.

"Louis . . ." My dam breaks and tears flow. I've never seen him like this. "Louis, there's nothing we can do. Not right now."

He slumps, shaking, sweating, hair on end. "We've lost them," he says. "There's no coming back from this. We attacked them. We're traitors."

"We didn't." I'm shaking so much, I don't think I can stay standing much longer. "The androids did."

"It doesn't matter. It's our failure to protect them that matters."

He's right. We're lost. We've lost. I shake even more, this time with sobs.

"The crowd is dispersing," says Fersen. "There's no need for distress."

"Shut the hell up," Louis grumbles at him.

I look at Fersen. "How could you do this? You were almost one of us."

Slowly, he tilts his head toward me. "The measures saved lives. The crowd was out of control."

"We had it under control. And now it's ruined. Destroyed," Louis says. Then he takes my hand.

We lean on each other as we trudge back up the stairs.

FIFTY-FIVE

❊

October 14, 3070, 10:30 p.m.

As I vid-chat with Mutti, I feel less like a queen than I ever have. I feel young. I want her to hug me. It would be easier if she were making me feel like I've failed in every aspect of being Franc queen. Instead she looks sadder than she did after my dad died. I could crumble from being so weak in my heart. I know that I've failed every hungry person who swarmed the gates and was punished for it.

"I don't know what to do, Mutti. We can't even make a statement to the people. They would wipe the message in an instant. All the androids that attacked are still at the palace. It's like they've taken us captive."

"I believe it is time to prepare for the possibility of your return to the Austro Lands," she says.

It's like the words were spoken to someone who isn't me. Even when Thérèse warned me to leave, it never felt like a real possibility. It can't be. "How could I give up now? I can't leave Louis."

"You love him this much? In this late hour when it could destroy you?"

The thought of abandoning Louis when he's lost his parents and his grandfather and been deserted in all corners is too horrible to imagine. "Of course."

"And if the king went with you?"

"He won't give up. It's too soon. He wants to give the Third Estate the representation they asked for."

She looks beyond me, probably remembering things I'm too young to understand. Her eyes shine with a few collected teardrops. "You poor children. You never really had a chance."

"Mama . . . you said our empire is fading. Do you remember?"

She shakes her head. "This turned much faster than anyone anticipated. Including me."

I can't believe it's come to this. We are truly lost. Fugitive monarchs.

"I failed," I say quietly.

"Now is not the time for regret," says Mutti. "Now is for the present. When you meet with the First Estate, when you discuss plans with the king, remember everything I've taught you about negotiation. You will have to make some sacrifices. Some concessions. Choose wisely. I won't argue with you about leaving the kingdom. At least for now. We'll continue to monitor the situation. Stay safe, Marie."

FIFTY-SIX

I tug rumples from my sleek black dress and adjust Louis's tie, even though he flinches. "I'm going to sweat," he says.

"You can't go in sloppy," I tell him. "You can do this."

We turn to the door that hides a waiting First Estate. They're in a quiet area of the palace, full of small meeting rooms on the ground floor and guest rooms on the second floor, an odd choice when they could have gone for a stateroom or library. Louis glances at me. I nod and he opens the door.

It's dark inside. The shutters are all sealed up and the light mode is set to green and purple. Maybe the intention is to creep me out. The attempt is working.

When we enter, seven faces, murky in the strange glow, stare us down, imposing, in charge. These are the seven people who represent the First Estate's Bureau of Business Owners. These seven people more or less own the kingdom. I recognize them all. One rises from his seat at the conference table to greet us, an older man in a deep red suit and some awful wig that doesn't fit him right, hair sticking out to the sides like wings. This is Monsieur Jean of JeanCo Foods, which controls all things food and agriculture.

To his right is Choiseul. He has a strange greenish tint to

his pale skin, like he's ill, but maybe it's his thick eyeliner and murky gray eye shadow. Choiseul controls the kingdom's power grid and the cruiser-manufacturing plants. The man on his right wears an Hermonds suit, tailored to fit his hulking frame. This is Necker, a former finance minister, now the owner of our three major banking chains. On the other end of the table are Madame Rohan and Angoulême, along with a thin-faced woman with pure white hair bundled around a softly glowing band. She's Madame Valois, owner of the Franc Kingdom's pharmaceutical labs. Last is a woman with a big mass of curling neon-yellow hair and dark banded sunglasses similar to what Grand-Père used to wear. This is Beatriz Beaumarchais, entertainment mogul. With small shares in everything we watch, wear, and use for fun, she might own more than the rest of them put together.

"Sit." Monsieur Jean gestures at the table.

None of them bow. Our titles mean nothing here. Louis squeezes my shoulder and takes his seat. I settle beside him.

Jean takes out a vape and starts puffing out rude clouds. "They said you were this passive kid. So I didn't anticipate these . . . problems." Jean has a rough way of speaking that grates on me the moment I hear it.

Louis stares him down. "You knew my father. You should have been able to anticipate me."

Monsieur Jean snorts, which releases a puff of smoke from his nose like he's some mythical beast. "We get it. You've got some balls. Now it's time to play nice."

"I aim to be fair," says Louis. "Nice is a lucky side effect."

"Well, let's review what's not so nice." Jean ticks things off on his fingers. "Disarming important security measures in your quarters, work-arounds for security measures on your tech."

"Love the screen name," adds Madam Rohan, and gives me a slow, mocking wink.

"Don't get me started on you." Jean jabs his vape in my direction. "Refusing sponsorships, whipping up Paréesians over Wastelanders, sabotaging political dissidents, starting a Pixter boycott."

"Down over five hundred thousand users for two days," says Rohan. "We lost over a million in ad revenue."

"And now you want to promise the Third Estate things that can't possibly be delivered," finishes Necker.

"We must allow the Third Estate one hundred more representatives to the Estates General," Louis says. "In the interest of equal representation, we should have had these numbers all along."

"Let's not be cute. One hundred is impossible." A lazy plume of smoke curls from Jean's mouth.

"Maybe Angoulême should have thought of that before he sent androids to shoot at them," Louis says.

"I saved your life, boy," says Angoulême. All trace of the respect he's shown us at events is gone. "You saw that crowd. They would have torn the palace apart, you and your lovely wife with it. Things don't go their way, they burn things, break things, take things. Those are the people you want to bow to? *Non.* They bow to us."

"How dare you." I can't keep my mind from the girl at the gates. Have they ever once looked into the eyes of someone like her? Someone they steal from? "There are starving people all over your kingdom. And you expect them to bow to you? As thanks for their dirty air, food shortages, and impossible taxes?"

"I know you think Wastelanders are your little pet project

and Paréesians are your friends, but this is what comes of poking your nose in. You wouldn't have gotten twisted by their over-blown fears if you'd just left the firewalls in place," says Rohan. "The situation would have been under control."

"Like it was yesterday?" says Louis.

"You should have let us handle it," I add. "We were going to disperse the crowd. Our way."

Beaumarchais throws her head back and cackles, so over-the-top it's clearly just for show. "Darling," she says. "Child . . . you give the masses what they want? They don't stop asking. They just keep taking. Trust me. That's what my business runs on."

"Fair representation in government and protection from leaders who acted like their enemies is more than a fair ask," says Louis.

"But this is what I'm saying," says Beaumarchais. "One hundred today? Two hundred tomorrow."

"One hundred is already underselling when there are three times as many of them as there are of us," says Louis, his voice rising.

"Strength isn't always in numbers," says Madame Rohan, picking at her nails.

"I think the Paréesians proved otherwise yesterday," I say. "And if we were to side with them? Then where would you be?"

"Still in control of the kingdom's infrastructure, and you would likely find yourself dead if you were to pursue such a foolish path," Rohan says.

Louis leaps to his feet. "You would threaten us? I can call the guards right now."

"We control the guards. Sit down. That's what you're not understanding here." Jean puffs out another plume of smoke.

"You're a feisty little fella hiding under all that computer coding bullshit, so let's be really clear. We see everything. We know everything. We control everything. Cross us and . . . well, look how your old père ended up."

I ball my hands into fists so tight I can feel my pulse thumping in my fingertips. Murderers. They're murderers. They admit it. And they don't care.

"My predecessors have put people to death for murdering Bourbons," Louis says with a venom I didn't know he was hiding.

"And we muzzled them," says Monsieur Jean. "Move on us, divide the country into civil war. Sounds like a gold star on your reign. The Third Estate? They're not your friends. They're not your children. They're a pack of wolves. They'll eat you alive when they spot a weakness. Doesn't matter what you give them, they will always resent you. They'll always turn on you. The seven of us here are the best friends you've got. We have given you every comfort and every luxury. In return, you take the heat off us, and you promote us, and you unite the kingdom. So far, you're not doing so great a job at any of that."

"Don't push us to turn to Stanislas instead," says Rohan. "He understands how this works."

"Enough." Louis slams a hand on the table. "I'm not backing down. You turned on them. The Third Estate is getting representation."

"The Third Estate is getting nothing," Choiseul speaks up. "If you don't like it, I can cut the power grid to the city. No electricity. No food. We'll see how well you get along with the Third Estate then."

"You wouldn't," I say, short of breath as I imagine the chaos that would cause.

"We will do whatever it takes. I suggest you start playing along. Do as we say, and this mess will get sorted," says Rohan.

"It's time to unleash the full force of the androids," says Angoulême. "That's what will bring order again. Androids in the streets, setting a firm precedent."

"Or you could listen to them!" Louis shouts. "You could give the people a voice and do something other than use them!"

"Or we could find a way to shut you up," Jean says, voice rising.

My heart is in my throat, but I think of Mama and what she would do. "Wait," I say, too weakly. Too quietly. I take a deep breath so the rest will come out steady. "You run businesses. Let's do business. Let's negotiate. What do we do to get one hundred seats in the Estates General?"

Valois folds long, elegant fingers together on the table and speaks in a throaty voice. "I for one would like to test new vitamin supplements in the Austro market as well as experimental treatments for the wasting disease."

I swallow once. Mama didn't mention Valois, but she will agree. She will agree to whatever gets us out of this. "That could be arranged. Easily."

"One hundred seats aren't bought *easily*," says Angoulême. "Your mother has been completely resistant to a SveroTech branch in the Austro Lands. Beaumarchais has some musical bots she's tested in a live show at her park. It'll help the Austros see the androids more favorably. We'll send those over, with the military models to follow. But the show first."

"The kids love it." Beaumarchais grins.

I feel like I'm saving the Francs only to poison my homeland. My Austros. Louis squeezes my hand under the table. "I can convince her to be more open to SveroTech," I say.

"Brilliant. That will buy you about fifty seats," says Angoulême.

"The deal was one hundred," I say.

"No, it wasn't," says Monsieur Jean. "We haven't made any deals."

"I asked the price of one hundred."

"One hundred isn't for sale. I think we're agreed on that." Jean glances around to a bunch of nods. "One hundred is dangerous when they're this out of control. You're stupid to ask for fifty and lucky we'll give it to you."

"They won't be satisfied with fifty. It has to be a hundred," says Louis.

"They won't be satisfied with anything, which brings me to my next point." Monsieur Jean raises a finger. "There is a condition to you adding fifty seats for the Third Estate. Your choice is to accept those fifty seats, *or* you take our advice, which is no seats, and starting today we double down on the androids at the palace and in the Parée police force. That means if you insist on doing it your way and accept those fifty seats, you're on your own. When it doesn't work, we're not coming to your rescue. We're done with you. Don't want to use our strategies? You'll see where that leaves you."

Louis and I glance at each other. But I know we're in agreement. This has to be better, less risky than no representation and more androids. When Mama said I would have to find my own way, she meant this.

"We'll have to trust the people," I say to Louis.

He nods. "We accept the terms for fifty seats in the Estates General."

"I will contact the Austro empress immediately," I say.

Necker sighs and cracks his neck while Choiseul rubs his eyes. "This should be interesting," he mutters.

Monsieur Jean hops to his feet. "Well, then. Pleasure doing business, Majestés." He puffs out a huge vape plume and bows, dispersing the white vapor. I stare at them, cold as I can. In this moment, I'm not so different from them. I would gladly see them all dead.

They swoop out of the room like a flock of well-dressed crows.

Louis and I sit in silence for a minute. The air conditioner hums in a vent over my head, and I rub my arms. It froze me for the whole meeting. "Do you really think this will work?" I ask.

"I don't know, but we have to try. There's nothing else to do. The alternative was so much worse." Louis has his fists pressed to his eyes. "We dragged you here and married you to a dying land. I'm so sorry."

If it doesn't work, will we have to dance to the tune of the First Estate? At least we'll live. I imagine for a minute that it will be like before, when everything was beautiful parties and positive press, even though that was all an elaborate glitchshow. It's a fluffy thought, as weak and wispy as a cloud. We can never go back.

"I would rather be in a dying land than in the Austro Lands without you," I tell my husband. Then I hold his head on my shoulder while he cries for a kingdom that was dying before he was crowned, probably before he was born. I cry for him too, and for a world I never knew was so rotted at the core.

FIFTY-SEVEN

October 21, 3070, 9:00 p.m.

The fifty new Third Estate representatives are added to the Estates General. The people aren't satisfied. It isn't enough. Especially after the news breaks about the android deal with the Austro Lands. Not when androids put people in the hospital during the protest. Not when they could have killed someone. Not when there are androids here in our palace and the Fersen scandal is far from forgotten. The same old opera photos have been trending again, along with new ones of Fersen dragging me away from the crowd.

So, the riots continue. Sometimes in Parée. Sometimes at the gates of Versailles, where they taunt the android guards. But the guards don't fire. Not without our orders. As Monsieur Jean promised when we expanded the Estates General, we are on our own.

Louis and I work day and night trying to figure out what could calm the people, what could put things on track. We give money, and the Austros are sending some food and provisions for the Paréesians. Actions matter now, not things that I say or post on the Apps. But the problem is clear: the First Estate. We haven't found a glitch in their firewall of power. Mama grows more scared by the day. Louis and I aren't ready to give in, but

Philippe, Stan, and Josephine are leaving. They'll flee to the Austro Lands.

We're gathered in the courtyard in front of their cruiser under a clear sky of stars and a neon glow casting the palace in spooky green and purple. The Parée skyline, glowing red in the distance, seems to make the night warmer with a thick, smoky haze.

Louis hugs Philippe with tears in his eyes. My heart aches because I know that for more than half their lives, these siblings have only had each other. And now they'll be separated. As Philippe moves to Elisabeth, brave Elisabeth who has refused to leave, Josephine takes my hands. She can't meet my eyes as she says, "You were nice. When hardly anyone else was. Take care."

I squeeze her hands. "You too. My mother will look out for you."

Philippe is next, hugging me tight with his lean arms. "See you, sis." His face is pale, highlighting a few freckles on his nose. The confident prince who ran through the halls, flirting with every girl he saw, blasting music at every party, is nowhere to be found. I just see a scared boy. Josef will like Philippe. He'll treat him like a brother.

Now there's only Stan, his eyes dark and brooding. He's far from my favorite, but I'll feel less safe without him. "You've got some guts," he says with just the barest hint of his old smirk. "Be smart. Be safe."

"You too." I hug him around his neck and he gives me a formal kiss on the cheek. When I let go, he moves on to Louis. I have to strain to hear what Stan says.

"You know that . . . I didn't want this. I want you alive more than I want to be in your place."

"I know." They take each other by the arms and touch their foreheads together.

It's too much. I have to look away.

Mercy has arrived. He'll escort them to the Austro Lands. "I'll see you in three days," he says quietly.

I nod. There's nothing to say.

"Is there anything you'd like me to tell your mother?"

"Just ask her to take good care of them."

"Of course, Majesté." When Mercy hugs me, I think that maybe it wouldn't be so bad to go to the Austro Lands. To go home.

I imagine Louis and me exploring the gardens there. He'd be turbo-charged to see the different trees and plants, to hunt pheasants.

Stan puts a hand on Josephine's back and they prepare to board the cruiser. The headlights brighten and its humming grows louder. Louis turns to Elisabeth. "Go," he says. "Please."

"After Maman died, you promised you'd never leave me. At the funeral, remember? Well, that goes for me too. I'm not leaving you."

Elisabeth always said Louis was her favorite. She's never been one for empty words. Louis hugs her tight, holds out a hand to me, and gathers me in too. With our arms in a tangle, we watch Mercy rush our family toward the cruiser. Philippe goes first, glancing over his shoulder to give us a small wave. Josephine and Stan follow. He still has a hand on her back and her chin is held high. Mercy turns and bows to us before he enters the cruiser. The door shuts behind him.

As the cruiser rises, the wind whips my hair, sticking it to my teary cheeks. We watch the lights carry half our family away. I try to fill my mind with images of what it will be like when my Austro family welcomes them to Schönbrunn Palace. The thought almost makes me smile.

FIFTY-EIGHT

October 25, 3070, 8:36 a.m.

Georgette sets my breakfast tray in front of me, the china cups rattling with her shaking hands. They wouldn't let me leave the room this morning. I know why.

Like Louis finding a flaw in a firewall, they found ours. The Third Estate is coming. They've broken through the palace gates.

Georgette's fear makes me braver. I reach for her hand. "Georgette, it's all right. The guards are right outside."

A tear rolls from her eye. "It's you I'm afraid for, Marie. I don't want them to hurt you."

A lump forms in my throat. I let my tea go cold and unfinished, instead clasping my shaking hands in my lap. I'm waiting for something. I'm not sure what. But I feel this might be my last breakfast in Versailles for a while.

Georgette and I jump when we hear a cruiser roar overhead. The windows are sealed shut, so we can't see what's happening, but that sound was far louder and closer than cruisers usually are.

A *boom* rattles the windows, and I suck in what feels like all the air from the room. I've never heard anything like it. Like a cruiser engine, but whining and broken somehow, with more roar.

"What's happening? Open the windows," I say to Georgette.

"I can't, madame. They ordered them shut," Georgette says through a flood of tears.

"*Scheiße*," I whisper, the first Austro word I've used in months. I'm not sure why it slips out of me. I feel so small and helpless, like a mouse in a gilded trap. Maybe I should have left. Should have gotten out while I had the chance, like Thérèse and Mama wanted me to. It's too late for what I should have done. There's only now and survival.

The door to my quarters whooshes open and Georgette squeaks.

Nilsson marches in. "Majesté, come with me. Quickly, please."

But I don't move. Nilsson's eyes are bright blue and give nothing away. This is the first action he's taken in a week. In the absence of orders from the First Estate, apparently all Fersen and Nilsson do is stand at attention, not much different from the statues in the gardens. Seeing him now doubles my fear.

"Where do you expect me to go?" I ask.

"The rioters are in the palace, Majesté. We have to leave."

"Why should I go with you now? You've done nothing but stand in the hallways for days."

His face remains still. "I have orders."

"From Angoulême? He said he's never helping us again."

"Ensign Bisset."

Jeanne? What's Jeanne doing here?

My holofone dings with a message. It's Bisset. Go with Nilsson. I've got his controls.

I don't trust the androids, but I suppose I'll have to trust Jeanne.

"What about Georgette?" I ask Nilsson.

"Just you, madame."

Georgette squeezes my hands, her face red and swollen with tears. "Go, Marie. I'll be safe. It's you they want." She reaches into her collar and yanks out her brother's red bandanna. "Take it. For luck."

"I couldn't. It means the world to you."

"I'll feel better knowing I gave it to you."

Mops dashes up to me, yapping. I reach to scoop him up.

"Just you, madame. I'm sorry," Nilsson says again.

My brave mask breaks and a sob escapes. "I can't leave him!"

Georgette scoops up my little pug, flailing in her arms, trying to reach me. "I'll take care of him. I promise."

With her brother's bandanna in my pocket and Mops in her arms, we have left our two most important treasures with one another. We're equals now.

I let my fingers graze Mops's bristly fur before I turn away, and my heart breaks in new and terrible ways. This goodbye is so much worse than the one I gave my little friend before I left the Austro Lands. He's straining toward me and Georgette holds him tight. "Be safe." I squeeze the words painfully through the tightness in my throat.

"Madame, we must go now," says Nilsson, and he tries to take my arm, but I shake him off as my vision blurs with tears. I follow him downstairs through one of the dusty hidden hallways. Silent tears flow down my cheeks.

I don't understand how it's come to this point. Just looking back at the tangled road here makes my head ache. All I can do is put one foot in front of the other while I try to decide if I should be saying goodbye to every window, every statue, every pillar that I pass. Will I ever come back?

Elisabeth, Louis, Fersen, and a small group of guards startle me as they rush through a hidden doorway in a holo-wall. When I see Louis, it's like there's been a fist around my heart that finally relaxes. He gives me his hand, head held high, but in his eyes he looks absent, like he's disappeared deep into his mind to hide.

"What will they do? What do they want?" I ask.

Elisabeth stares straight ahead at Fersen, her eyes ringed with dark circles from the same lack of sleep we've all been living with. "They want our heads," she says.

"They want to hold us captive in Parée," says Louis.

This doesn't feel real. Or it feels too real. It's like when you stay at a party way too late and realize that the only people left are wasted and awful to be around, while you stand in a mess of spilled drinks and you're so damn sick of the music that you can't imagine how you were having fun just a few hours ago.

Fersen taps a portrait, which swings away to reveal a doorway. As we descend, Elisabeth asks, "Why are we going in the basement?"

"We're going to the garage," says Louis.

"What for?" Elisabeth asks.

No one answers. We turn corners until we enter a low cement room filled with antique vehicles. The sort that don't fly.

Fersen dashes to a giant black vehicle on big, thick rubber tires and wrenches open the back door.

"Jeanne," Elisabeth breathes.

Ensign Bisset jumps out of the vehicle, tapping on a holofone.

"What are you doing here?" Elisabeth asks.

"Sergeant Mercier and I don't like how the First Estate have been using the androids. We're getting you out."

"But you could lose your job, you could—"

Jeanne cuts her off. "I quit. I'm not using the androids the way they did on that crowd. And I wasn't leaving people I care about behind. Not when I could do something."

I turn to Louis. "I thought we weren't going to run from them."

Louis shakes his head. "I don't think we have a choice anymore. We need to regroup. I don't know what would happen if they take us to Parée."

Fersen opens the door to the driver's seat. "We don't have much time."

"Get into the vehicle. We can't take a cruiser. They could shoot us out of the air," says Jeanne.

She steps up to Nilsson, tapping furiously on her holofone. "Nilsson . . . it's been a pleasure. I'm sorry it ended up like this."

Nilsson stiffens, less human and more robot, and closes his eyes. Then he crumples to the floor.

"What did you do?" I ask.

"Basically, factory reset him," says Jeanne. "I can handle Fersen, but both of them at once would be tricky. I had to rewrite some of their programming to cancel out old protocols, and I'm still doing some of it on the fly."

"But we're bringing Fersen?" I want to argue, but I know there's not much time.

Fersen doesn't respond. He's looking at Nilsson. Maybe wondering if the same thing will happen to him. Jeanne tugs at his stiff uniform collar. There's a small glowing object stuck to his neck. "Don't worry. I've got this. He's under control."

"I'm not sure it's a good idea. . . ." Ever since the bracelet bug, when I look in his dark eyes, I wonder if I'm looking at the First Estate.

"Trust me. We might not make it without him. I can't drive this thing, and I don't think any of you can either. Now, we really need to move."

"There's just no time. We're out of options." Louis nudges me. I climb into the weird, bulky machine and settle in the seat behind Jeanne. It's cramped inside. Way smaller than a cruiser, and it smells like mint and vape smoke or something. Louis slides in after me with Elisabeth behind him.

Fersen gets into the driver's side of the old antique. It rumbles to life, shaking us around like empty glasses rattled by a bass hum.

Jeanne clicks something into place in the front seat. "Drive on, Fersen. You'll need your belts on, everyone."

Louis tugs a flimsy fabric thing across me that clicks closed at my hip. I don't know what it would possibly protect me from. The vehicle roars with noise when it reverses. Something about it seems clumsy as we rumble through the garage. It's like I can feel every pebble we drive over. Louis practically presses his nose to the glass as we emerge into the gardens. His eyes are on the many windows of the palace.

"We're coming back, aren't we?" I ask.

I can barely hear his answer. "I don't know."

I thought I was out of tears, but they fill my eyes again. "But I don't have Mops."

Louis sets a hand on my leg. "Noailles will look after him. She might be able to send him to us."

"Are we going to the Austro Lands?"

He gives me the saddest smile I've ever seen. "Don't you think it's time I met your mama?"

"But who will be king?"

"Still me?" He blinks fast, like he really doesn't know the answer.

As we clear the gardens and head for the trees, we pass the field of solar panels. They glow strange and orange, and in the midst of them, there's the flaming shell of a cruiser. I remember what Louis said when I first came here and he warned me that nothing was what it seemed. He said they could shoot down a cruiser if they had to. A huge bump jostles us as we hit a log or a rock. Fersen is driving the vehicle right into the woods, branches scraping the windshield. "I shouldn't have sent androids to the Austro Lands. I should have thought of a better trade," I say.

"This is not because of you," Louis mumbles. "Maybe . . ."

"What?"

"Maybe the end was already starting when I was born. Or maybe it started when my père saw . . . that." He nods toward the front windshield. I was so wrapped up in what Louis was saying that I didn't notice the change. The trees are thinning. I can see light and space in the gaps. Something about the landscape is wrong. All at once, I figure it out.

The wall is gone.

We pass the signs that say not to trespass. The trees become smaller and smaller; they start to lose color, their leaves pale and their bark grayish. Then it's low scrubs and before us . . . emptiness. More emptiness than I've ever seen. We're facing a long, sandy stretch of earth with nothing but scrubby grass and scraggly plants with thorny branches. The horizon is murky, like it's full of smoke.

The vehicle feels very small. I feel small. Like there's nowhere left to hide.

Louis's eyes are wide. "He must have lost his mind when he saw this."

Louis thought our job was to remove the wall.

I guess we did one thing right.

FIFTY-NINE

✳

The Wastelands might be endless. I've been staring at the seat in front of me because looking out the window too long makes me feel panicked, trapped but also exposed in our tiny vehicle in this vast, dusty space. Nothing could be more different from living in Versailles, where every inch is meant to grab your eye, dazzle, distract. There is nothing here. Just us. And this. Just weather and dead things. The air is so thick with dust or smog or something noxious that the sun only just penetrates in a yellowish murky haze.

It's hard to tell if the clouds of dust rolling around on the horizon are windstorms or vehicles. I have a feeling it's the second one, because sometimes Jeanne orders Fersen to change course and he wrenches us to the left or right. I'm not sure how long it takes to reach the border in one of these things.

I sleep out of pure exhaustion. Elisabeth offers me food, but I don't eat. There's nothing to do but watch stretches of emptiness. At one point we pass a mountain of garbage. It breaks up the landscape like a metal giant, all heaps of twisted, gutted cruiser frames and ragged strips of plastic.

Louis watches it get smaller and smaller behind us. "I wonder how far he went." The sinking sun turns the light into a murky blue-green, making Louis pale and washed out. "I wonder what he saw."

Louis's dad must have been a brave guy to go out here willingly. The sun sinks lower. Elisabeth and Jeanne have an overdue conversation that I try not to listen to because it's too private for this claustrophobic space. But they have it now, maybe because even though the border gets closer every minute, it feels like we're running out of time.

I barely notice when Fersen interrupts them to say, "Something is coming."

"Where? Position?" Jeanne asks.

"North at ten o'clock."

For a stupid minute, I wonder how he can see anything. The horizon looks dusty and empty to me. But of course, he has some kind of tech that allows him to see miles ahead.

"Correct the course," says Jeanne.

"It's scattered. They're moving fast." Fersen moves his head in little increments, tracking something that the rest of us can't. "I don't think we can evade."

Jeanne swears. "Maybe we should have flown after all."

"Ten," says Fersen. "Twelve. Sixteen."

Now there are small lights on the horizon. They emerge over bare hills of cracked dirt, zip around like fireflies in the gardens.

"Wrong direction to be the rioters," says Jeanne.

"Wastelanders?" I ask, my breath quick and shallow.

"Probably. I don't think we want to meet them," says Jeanne.

"I don't think we have a choice," says Fersen.

Jeanne curses again.

"We could talk to them," says Fersen. "They're normally

interested in weapons. Supplies. Shall I slow down? They may blow out the tires if we don't."

"What choice do we have?" Jeanne whips her head around, tracking the lights. She's a techie, not a soldier. We have to trust Fersen now. We're at his mercy.

Every muscle seems to tense as I crane my neck to watch the lights on the horizon grow closer along with a puttering, roaring noise. Small vehicles on two wheels zip in and out of the headlight glare, speeding by, flicking in and out of view. Dust kicks up all around. They're circling us. Fersen slows us to a stop. Roaring from the little machines covers any other sound.

I peek out the tinted windows. The people outside look like they're wearing dirty old blankets and animal skins. Rusted helmets and bits of metal strapped all over their bodies, along with big knives with curving blades. And guns everywhere. The people I supported are pointing guns at us. How could someone sweet like Georgette come from people like these?

Fersen cracks his window. "Don't shoot!"

A figure with a rifle covered in little scopes steps closer. His face. What's wrong with his face? It has several big sores, red and runny. Someone flanks him, but their face is hidden by a big, goggled mask full of tubes, probably hiding the same kind of burns and boils.

The scarred man peers into the crack in the window, gun still trained on Fersen. His bloodshot eyes roam each of our faces.

Fersen presses a button and the window slowly moves downward with a whine. "We don't want trouble."

The man with the gun has a rough, hoarse voice, and speaks in an accent and dialect that are unfamiliar to me. "You look like fancy-folk from the château. This is *très bien. Bienvenue.*"

There's a knocking on the outside of the vehicle. A big door in the back swings open and a scrawny boy with bare arms hops in. A gust of warm air stirs my hair and I almost choke. The scent of rot and burning plastic and something like oil fills my nose, seems to coat my throat. It's the garbage smell I used to catch whiffs of in the garden.

The boy who's hopped in can't be much older than Philippe. He looks like a bag of bones, all draped in some ripped plasticky thing. Like the man with the gun, he also has oozing sores, but his are on his torso. They gleam red and wet through the holes in the plastic stuff.

The boy cackles, a wet, sick sound like Grand-Père made before he died. "They got good metal." He yanks off a tire that was mounted to the back hatch and rolls it toward the other scavengers.

"What do you want with us? You can't take apart our vehicle and leave us for dead out here," says Jeanne.

The man with the gun spits in the dirt. "You think you the first château-folk we leave out here? *Non.*"

Louis grabs the seat in front of us and leans forward. Terrified, I grab the back of his shirt. He looks like he's about to say something, but he just stares at the man, who stares back at Louis.

"Ayeee," the gunman says slowly. "You his *fils*, yeah? You got the same face. Should listen when old père tell you. This our turf."

"What happened to him?"

The man with the gun shrugs. I can't take my eyes from the barrel. The bobbing motion makes my blood run cold. These are like strange fragments of a half-remembered nightmare. The gun pointed in our direction. The gasoline stink of the people now pawing through the vehicle with rough, blackened fingers. The fact that this man met Louis's father once, long ago.

"He say he would help us. We let him leave alive. He give no *merci* even. He *bon voyage* and don't come back. Surprised? *Non*. I am not."

Louis shakes his head. "No." He sits back in his seat like there's no life left in him. "He died. Otherwise maybe he would have helped you."

The gunman shrugs again. "You soft like babies. You die easy, *non*?"

"Yeah," Louis mumbles, his eyes out the window on the ghostly, burned, scarred, and masked faces floating around, carrying off our only lifeline in this terrible, dead place. I think he's giving up. No fear in him, no fight. How are we going to make it out of this? We can't trade with them when they have no trouble stealing.

The boy who took the tire is prying a curving piece of metal off the back of the car with a heavy bar. When he puts a foot up, I notice a green scrap of fabric wrapped around his ankle and remember the bandanna in my pocket. I yank it out and wave it at the gunman in the window. "Do you know Georgette? She had a brother who died in the fires. She thought you could . . ."

I don't know what she thought or what this bandanna really means to them. Apparently, neither does the gunman, because he frowns and spits on the ground again. "We ain't the caravan what got burned. Quit waving that rag about. I don't know no Georgette."

"I tried to help you. I told the Paréesians to welcome the Wastelanders."

This means nothing to them. They clearly have no Apps out here. I know they don't care. But it's crushing me how I thought I was doing so much good when I knew nothing about the Wastelands, nothing about how lost and friendless I really was. Or how desperate these ragged people really were.

Before I can think of another idea, there's a cruiser roar from behind us.

"*Merde*," says Jeanne. "Listen, let us out of here. We'll pay you somehow."

The gunman cackles. "*Oui*, now you speak in terms an *homme* o' the Wastes understands. Too bad, *mon petit lapin*. They are going to pay much more. *Certainement*."

I look out the back through the open hatch. People covered with bandannas and masks leap from the cruisers. A woman with a blue scarf wrapped around her head to cover all but her eyes approaches the gunman.

"Cover 'em," he says, and a few other Wastelanders move in while he clasps hands with the woman in the scarf.

A man in a mask aims a gun at Jeanne's window. "Disable the bot," he says.

"He could kill you all in five minutes," Jeanne says.

"No doubt," says the man. "But I would shoot you first."

"Do it," Louis says quietly, and nods at Jeanne's holofone.

Jeanne turns to Fersen. It's strange to look at him and see so much calm when we're surrounded by guns and dead land. This is exactly what makes the androids so dangerous. I can barely think for fear. He could do anything. He doesn't know fear.

"I know your code like the back of my hand and I'm still not sure I really know what you are," says Jeanne while she swipes at her holofone with shaking fingers. "When you wake up, maybe you'll be a revolutionary."

For a moment, Fersen frowns at her. His personality returns, softening his features. His furrowed brow shows confusion. Maybe sorrow? Then his chin dips, and he closes his eyes.

"Check him," says the man with the gun.

The woman in the scarf pops Fersen's door, tips his head back. I can't see what exactly she's doing. She seems to check his eye. "Powered down," she says.

The man in the mask rushes to the passenger side and smashes out the window to pop the door. Elisabeth screams as we're showered in glass. "LEAVE HER ALONE!"

Jeanne struggles, but the man grabs her by the arm and twists until she squeals in pain. "You're under arrest by the Committee of Public Safety and the *citoyens* of the Third Estate. You'll be taken to await trial."

Trial? I look to Louis, and he squeezes my hand. "I'm sorry," he whispers.

The door opposite me opens. They aren't rough when they pull Elisabeth from the vehicle, but halfway out, she screams. The man in the mask carries a crumpled, unconscious Jeanne.

"What did you do to her?" Louis shouts.

Then Elisabeth crumples too.

My breath is coming fast. Way too fast. Like air is getting forced in. The door opens beside me. Louis grabs my hand, shouting, fighting. I flail my arms.

"Get off me!"

"*Arrêtez*! Easy! Easy! Easy . . ."

But they won't get their hands off. I see Louis wrenched backward out of the vehicle.

A wail escapes my throat and I lash out again.

A shout in my ear. "*Arrêtez!*"

Then a pinch in my neck.

It's like I have ice in my veins. Everything is tingling. I think I'm melting. Becoming bits of sand. Once a queen, now I'm just a hundred grains, and I'll blow all through the Wastelands.

SIXTY

October 27, 3070, 1:54 a.m.

Beeping.

    Steady, quiet beeping.

    My eyes are stinging and dry, like they're full of sand.

    The light above me is too bright. Dragging, heavy, hand full of water or fire to block the too-bright glare.

    An IV taped to the back of my hand. I think it's feeding me poison or gasoline, because I don't remember.

    What came before me.
Who
came before
me?

SIXTY-ONE

✳

October 29, 3070, 11:11 a.m.

Am I awake or am I having a nightmare? My head aches like there's a little person inside my skull kicking the back of it over and over. These . . . aren't my clothes. This is like nursing scrubs . . . or a prison uniform. Some soft, tan cotton material. *Was passiert*? Who changed my clothes?

I sit up in a small bed. Really small. Barely fits me. Some creaking, awful thing. The room is mostly bare. There's a plastic container of water, and I down a few swallows. The light is dim and bluish. It's cold in here. I have to stand on the bed to see out the small window above it.

Bad move. I get dizzy the minute I look out. I'm way, way up high and La Tour Ancienne flashes on the horizon.

Parée. I'm somewhere in Parée.

My knees are water, and I fall back on the bed, head swimming and pounding.

Where are my husband and sister? What happened to Jeanne and Fersen?

It's an effort to sit up. Things tilt and objects double. Not that there's much to see. A blank wall. A toilet. I stand and run my fingers along the wall. There's the paper-thin gap around the door. There's the button to open it. Nonresponsive.

I smack my hand against the door. Not that it will do much good. When that inevitably doesn't work, I turn a circle and shout "Hello" to the ceiling. Since I've been watched every other place I've been in this kingdom, why shouldn't I be watched here too?

I sink to the floor and hug my knees. What happens now? Who took us? The First Estate? The Third Estate? What do they want from me? *Jemand, hilf mir.*

Must have been right about the watching thing, because probably fifteen minutes pass and then the door slides open with a quiet *whoosh*.

My heart starts pattering right away. The man who enters the room wears a simple suit. Nothing to dress it up. No LED or holo. Plain navy-blue color. He has graying hair and a plain pair of glasses that look old-fashioned like Adelaide Frasier's were. I don't know if this is a friend or an enemy, but years of training drag me to my feet to bow formally.

The man bows in turn. Though he should have bowed to his queen before I bowed to him.

"My name is Lagarde. For all intents and purposes, I'm your lawyer, Madame Antoinette."

"You can address me as Majesté." My voice sounds hollow.

He has a thick mustache curling up at the ends, and it twitches as if he might contradict me. But he says, "Majesté, then."

"Where is my husband?"

Lagarde scratches at his eyebrow, apparently oblivious to the fact that every second he hesitates to answer is torture. He gestures toward the little bed. "Perhaps we should sit."

I feel sick. I won't sit on a bed with a strange man. My feet move like they're unattached from me, moving me backward away from him.

His mustache droops and his eyes soften. "Oh. Majesté, there are many people who wish you harm. I'm not one of them."

The unexpected gentleness breaks me. "I'm sorry. But I have no idea what's going on." I'm also terrified, but admitting this could be a weakness.

"No, no. I understand. I just thought you'd like to be comfortable."

I fold my arms over my chest. "Where is my husband? Please just tell me that."

"He's down the hall, Majesté."

"I want to see him."

"You will." His voice is rough with sadness in the way of people who have been crying. "Majesté, you've been apprehended by the Committee of Public Safety. The Committee of Public Safety represents the Third Estate and members of the Second who wish to overturn the law of the land."

I let out a rattling sigh. The news does not come as a surprise. "Where does that leave my husband and me?"

"Majesté . . . you are at the mercy of the people and will be subject to their will. The people will decide your fate. You are charged with crimes against the republic. Debauchery, embezzlement, treason, and resisting arrest. Things have moved quickly for the king. I have delayed them for you so we can better prepare a case."

This is too much. I don't understand. Treason? If anything, the people have committed treason against their sovereigns. "What do you mean, 'moved quickly'?"

"His trial was this morning."

"No." I shake my head even though the moment I do, it throbs and aches. "It can't have been. I wasn't there. I slept. He went to trial and I was sleeping?"

"Unconscious, Majesté. They sedated you at the time of arrest. They imagined it would make this process smoother. Easier for them."

"Don't I have a right to be at the king's trial?"

"I fought for it, Majesté. But they didn't want you to testify. I'm sure your words would have softened some hearts. The people in charge here would not have risked that. What we are dealing with isn't justice as I know it. It's a new regime fueled by desperation." Now I see that there really are tears in his eyes. "I'm so sorry, Majesté. Please understand, I'm on the side of the crown. I did not represent him, but I contributed to the case the best I could. The king will be executed tomorrow."

Lagarde's hands on my elbows are the only thing that keep me from collapsing to the floor. If my stomach weren't empty, I'd vomit. This can't be real. It can't. I won't let it be. "How?" I whisper. "How could they do this?"

"When you fled for the Austro border with an android for protection, you resisted arrest and avoided accountability. The public believed the king would turn an army of androids and Austros against them. They took it as treason."

"We just wanted to live." The words gasp from me. "They broke into our home. Violently!"

"I know." Lagarde squeezes my shoulder. "I'm so sorry, Majesté. The violence of the scene . . . the wish for blood . . . it's a dark time for our kingdom. The people believe this execution will bring the light."

"How could they? How could they do this to him?"

"Public opinion is easily molded, Majesté. I hope we can use that to our advantage to spare you."

Spare me. To save my life for . . . what? A kingdom that isn't mine? A world without Louis and the people who I've come to love as family?

"Where are the others?"

"Mademoiselle Elisabeth is also down the hall. She will face trial too. It will give you some comfort to know that Stanislas, Josephine, and Philippe were able to flee the country."

My brothers. Will I ever see them again? I think of them going to the Austro Lands. Could I live for them? For the thought of seeing them again, and Elisabeth, and my mother and Josef? I don't know.

I clutch Lagarde's arms to stay steady. "I need to see him."

Lagarde puts a hand on my shoulder. "Of course. I think I can arrange for that shortly. Is there anything else you need?"

"Just him."

Lagarde nods once and turns to leave. I crawl to the bed and try to cry until I'm out of tears before Louis sees them. But once they start, they feel like an ocean with no end.

They're still flowing when I just barely hear the door *whoosh*. Padding footsteps. I know the hand that's on my back. The bed sinks under me and I roll into Louis's arms.

"Hi," he says softly.

I hold on to him like I'm in raging waves and he's the only rock that can save me. To think that when I first met Louis-Auguste, I wasn't sure if I liked him, and he made me nothing but confused and angry for weeks on end. Now I can't face life without him. "They can't do this."

ALLYSON DAHLIN

"They can," he says in that gentle murmuring voice that is now a precious sound to me. "They will."

"I hate them," I say. It's the first time I've even thought it. But it's the truth. They've ruined us. They gave us everything, then destroyed us like it was a game.

Louis gently pulls me from him and wipes at the tears on my face. "Don't hate them. Please."

"How could I not? They'll take you from me."

He leans his head against mine. "I know. But . . . they're doing what they feel they have to."

"Don't say that. They don't have to do this. Your life is worth more than this. You are worth more than this."

He stares at the floor. He holds my hands, thumbs brushing my wrists in a soothing pattern. "If I was, maybe I would have seen it sooner."

"Seen what?" I ask him.

"That we lived in a fantasy. Our whole world wasn't real. And it was built at the expense of suffering people. My père tried to show me that. But I was too scared to look it in the face. He was right. I'm a coward."

"Look it in the face for what? So the First Estate could kill you like they did your father? Don't you dare blame yourself. They used us. They all did. Every one of them from the First Estate to the Third. They used our power and treated us like cheap entertainment on ViewFi. You were trying to face things, but you barely had time. There has to be something we can do."

How can they not see what he's worth? He's stronger than they know. He's just young. We're barely more than kids. And we were trying. Like Mama said . . . my mother. My mutti can

410 ❋

stop this. Mama has the might of a kingdom behind her.

"They won't have you," I tell him. "My mother won't let them."

"No." He shakes his head. "That would mean horrible war. More terrible than what's coming. I won't do that to this country. I want them to build what they're imagining. That's my job. I belong to them. And if my death ends something that's hurt them for generations . . . then I'll die."

My heart is crumbling. Nothing has ever hurt like this. This is a nightmare. When they sedated me, I never woke up. Maybe it's after we saw the riots and I fell into a stress sleep. Or it's after Louis and I consummated our marriage, when I fell into the deepest, most exhausted sleep full of twisted dreams I never woke up from. I'm going to wake up and Louis will be out hunting already and Mops will be there, and I'll fill my day with whatever Noailles has planned and Louis will go to work and we will fix all of this. We will have the chance they never gave us in this nightmare world. I want to wake up. I want to wake up right now.

"You can't die," I whisper. "You are the kindest, most thoughtful person I know, and you can't die."

"Dying is . . . I don't know. It's not as bad as knowing I'm leaving you and my family here." Louis tears up and I can't look at him. "I promised you a crown and a kingdom. Not this. I'm so sorry."

I press my ear to his heart, still beating for now. "What if I just go with you?"

"No." He draws away from me, gives me a shake by the shoulders that startles me. "No. You'll fight for your life. Do you understand? You can make it out of this. You and Elisabeth can make it out of this. Fight for her. Fight for you. You aren't me. There are people out there who love you. People who want to see you alive. People who need you alive. Live. Try to live with everything you have. Go home to your mama. Just go live. Promise me. Promise me or I can't face tomorrow the way I want to."

"I promise." It's an empty, hollow promise, but the only thing I have left to give him.

"Good." He drops his hands from my shoulders and gives me his sleepy little smile. "Go marry some Austro guy who's twice the husband I ever was."

I wipe at my dribbling nose. "Impossible. Doesn't exist."

"I guarantee he does." He lays a hand on my cheek. Smiling. Somehow he's smiling. "I wasted a lot of time with you. Took time for granted, I guess. If only I knew what I had right away."

"You couldn't have known what would happen."

"I was a big baby, though." He nudges my knee.

"You're just shy," I tease, and poke at his shoulder. As if anything could make this situation light.

"Hey . . . they told me I could stay in your room as long as I want. At some point you're going to get drowsy, then I'm going to leave and go back to my room to . . . get ready. I want you to pretend I'm getting up to hunt. Because there's no easy way to do this, but I think that's best."

I shake my head. "No, I won't sleep. I want every possible minute."

"Please. It would wreck me. Please."

His eyes are large and desperate. I can't refuse him. Fresh tears spring up. "Okay."

He puts his hands on my legs. "Let's pretend I get to try this again. And you just showed up at Versailles, except I'm going to be a thousand times less stupid." He plucks up my hand in his. "Greetings, madame. Somehow you're even more beautiful in person than on the Apps." He kisses my hand more thoroughly than would be considered polite at our first meeting.

It's like a plant pushing from dry ground, but somehow I laugh. "Fake. You would never be that smooth. Even if we had a time machine, you couldn't be that smooth if you tried."

He scrunches up his brow. "I'm not sure what you mean, madame. We've just met. How do you know how smooth I am? I see you've got a weird sense of humor. That's okay, though. I like funny."

"How lucky for you. I'm absolutely hilarious."

So I play along. For hours. Louis tells me all these things he would do. He would give me the Petit Trianon, a beautiful house in the gardens I had admired since arriving at Versailles. We would grow strange, rare plants there. New plants that no one has seen or lost plants that used to grow before the Event. Plants that could feed hundreds and grow in cracked, thirsty dirt. We build a theater. We expand representation of the Third Estate and limit the powers of the First Estate, and cut surveillance, and make the air cleaner. We almost imagine the children we would have, but we don't need words to agree we shouldn't go there.

For a few hours, we're something like happy. I don't want to think about it because I've learned if you think about happiness too much, it starts to break into pieces until there's not much left. We talk and talk in slower, heavier voices deep into the night.

I'm almost asleep now. I might even be dreaming.

I feel Louis's breath on my face. "I want you to know there was no one better for the Franc Kingdom, or for me." His lips press against mine gently. This is the last time they ever will. I start to panic and sleep shakes off me. I grab a handful of his shirt. "Please," he whispers. "I love you, Marie. . . . I love you, Maria."

I have to let him go. There's nothing. Nothing else I can do for him. Slowly, I relax my fingers and his shirt slips from my grasp.

"Sleep," he says, and brushes a hand over my hair. My arms weigh a ton as he slips from them. Everything goes cold as soon as he gets off the bed. I see him for one minute as the door slides open. His broad shoulders and messy hair. I can't see his eyes, but I know he looks back at me once. Then he closes the door.

I don't think I'll ever be warm again.

SIXTY-TWO

✳

I hold on to this hope that something will happen. That the people couldn't possibly kill their king. I hold on to that hope until morning.

I hear a lot of noise on the street, and when I look out the window, there are a lot of people walking to some point in the distance. I can't see where. The fact that I can't be with Louis at the most horrible moment, the fact that he's alone again, is too much to think about. It's crushing the air right out of me.

I lie back down on the bed and tremble.

I don't know how much time is passing.

He's already too far away from me, even though he's still alive right now.

Will they tell me when it happens? Will I know? Do I want to know? I don't. I can't sit here while this happens. These bars on the window separate me from him, and I hate them. These bars in my way, caging me like the Francs have always caged me. Cold against my fingers as I pull at them uselessly until my shoulders ache. I choke as sobs claw up my throat.

The noise outside isn't like anything I've heard before. Some blaring hornlike thing. A warning bell or a monster's roar or a war horn. It rattles the windows.

Is that the last thing he heard?

Monsters. They're all monsters.

Cruiser horns wailing. Now I hear screaming in the streets. I scream too. Scream my throat raw and yank on the bars until my arms burn like they'll fall from my shoulders.

Maybe I should have just died too. Something in me is gone. My heart, maybe. I've never felt so alone.

SIXTY-THREE

October 31, 3070, 9:06 a.m.

Lagarde is here, but I don't care much about anything he's saying. He tells me Louis died bravely. That he denied all the charges against him and forgave his enemies. I'm not sure why that matters now. He's dead. Nothing matters. I can't bear to think how they did it. About what method of murder might have made the masses scream in the inhuman voices I heard.

"Your trial is scheduled in two weeks," says Lagarde. "I tried to delay it more. Many on the Committee of Public Safety feel you've suffered enough. The longer we wait, the more sympathy might turn for you. But that's exactly why Robespierre pushed to hold the trial as quickly as possible. Your mother has tried to negotiate, but they have no interest in her wishes or will. She's very afraid for you."

These words are empty in my ears. Facts attached to some girl who isn't me. Marie isn't here right now. Marie is already dead. "Maybe they should do us all a favor and just kill me tomorrow."

"You can't think like that, Majesté." Lagarde takes my hands in a loose grip. "We must think that we can win. We *can* win."

"Why should I think that? They hate me, Monsieur Lagarde."

"Many love you."

"Not on the Committee of Public Safety."

He pats my hand, a gesture so empty it's almost funny. "They've already taken your crown and your husband. To release you to the Austro Lands would remove you from the country with a little bit of mercy. I believe they could be convinced to release you. These aren't evil people. Just determined ones."

"Can I see Elisabeth?"

"I'll see what I can do." He rises in a creaky way with popping knees.

The hours that pass are numbing. He doesn't come back.

SIXTY-FOUR

November 3, 3070, 1:19 p.m.

I think two days have passed. I just know that I vomited when I woke up yesterday, and then it happened again today. It doesn't make sense, because I don't eat much. Just scraps of bread and chalky nutri-tabs.

I don't really care if I starve.

I don't really care whether I win my trial.

If I go home to the Austro Lands, I'll return in humiliation. The queen who lost the throne. But worse still, I'll return after losing the family and home I loved. I'll return to a world that feels like it's been a lie my whole life. What happened here could happen in the Austro Lands. As long as I'm me, someone out there will wish I were dead. I would spend the rest of my days waiting for them to catch up with me. What kind of life is that? I pass hours lying on my thin mattress, remembering wandering the Schönbrunn Gardens with Mutti's dark dress trailing behind her. Remembering laughing with Thérèse and Yolande at parties, the joy of designing outfits together. No matter how much it hurts, I think of Louis. All the time. Clinging to every detail of every memory. Not believing he's gone while also feeling the pain of it with every beat of my heart.

SIXTY-FIVE

November 5, 3070, 4:51 p.m.

I've been lying in bed for hours at a time with my hands on my stomach. This is the worst *Sehnsucht* I can imagine, because it's not for a place far away, but for a person.

Sometimes I think of escaping. I imagine Jeanne and Axel and the androids bursting through the door to tell me to leave quickly because they are taking me home to Mutti.

Then I remember that I may never feel at home again because home can't exist in a world that doesn't have Louis. It's at those times that I imagine my own death. That I wonder if I will see Louis when this is finally over.

Lagarde interrupts the darkest thoughts. My only visitor in the timeless stream of day and night. He rushes in, brow furrowed, nearly forgets to bow, not that I care anymore about any of the etiquette that formed the false impression of respect.

"How are you feeling, madame?" Lagarde asks.

I shrug because the question is rather ridiculous. I ache and I am likely doomed to die.

"Of course, sorry. I have something important to ask you." Lagarde rubs at his gray mustache. I've never thought much about it, but I'm not sure I've ever seen a mustache on anyone except in history books. It's just not the fashion. I stare at it for lack of anything else to focus on, because I have a hard time looking him in the eye where I know he will see my weakness. "Do you know where Thérèse de Lamballe is?" he asks.

Something else stirs in the ache in my heart. Something nervous and excited. Thérèse . . . I miss her so much. Is it possible she's here too? For her sake, I hope not. "No. Why would I? I'm a prisoner."

"I mean, when did you last see her, and did she tell you where she was going?" Lagarde says.

"No, she disappeared. She was scrubbed from the Apps and the net after . . ." Something holds me back. There is so much about Thérèse I don't know. I don't want to reveal something that might hurt her. "Why do you ask? What has she got to do with anything?"

"Because if you know, I might be able to strike a bargain with Robespierre," he says.

God, they're looking for her too. . . . "I have no idea," I say. "She warned me to be careful and then she left. I would never give her up to save myself. She was one of my only true friends at Versailles."

Lagarde raises an eyebrow. His mustache twitches. "Really?"

"Yes. Why would you think I would give her up?"

"Because she—no, never mind. It's too complicated to explain. She would not have told you in the first place. I don't know why they think we know anything. Foolishness and . . ."

"Monsieur Lagarde, what is going on?" I'm so tired, I don't have the will to keep up or try to guess what he wants with Thérèse or what his twitching mustache implies.

Lagarde shakes his head. "I apologize for bothering you

with this. Robespierre wishes to speak with you. I recommend appealing to his better nature. He has one. I promise he does. Emphasize your innocence. Emphasize your wish to do good and its corruption by the First Estate, but don't reveal too much about your involvement with them. It's a fine line we walk, but this conversation could easily tip in our favor."

Robespierre? I'm meant to confront Robespierre? So he can gloat? "What does he want with me?"

"I imagine he wants to get the measure of you, madame. It will help in his case against you. Or so he imagines. As I said, you know how to charm someone and turn situations to your favor. It's not impossible. You could get through to him."

They want me to perform again. My whole life. A big show. A different face, a different person for every occasion. "I'm not the same Marie I was when I did those things . . . ," I say.

Lagarde nods with sympathy. "I know. I understand. But you must try. You must try because your life depends on it. And being genuine, being frightened, exhausted . . . you don't have to hide this. We can hope he will decide he's punished you enough."

All I can manage is a noncommittal noise in the back of my throat.

"Madame, I must ask you something very important," says Lagarde. "Do you want to live? Will you fight to live?"

"I don't know," I whisper. It's a terrifying answer. But what can I live for?

"I know it seems all is lost." Lagarde's voice is soft. "And you have lost so much. But it is never too late. You are worth saving."

Tears well painfully in my eyes. I can't believe I have the salt and water left to produce them. "Am I?"

"Of course, madame, or I wouldn't be here," says Lagarde. "Now, will you fight for your life? I will fight for your life with all I have."

I think of Louis squeezing my hand. Louis begging me to live.

"Yes," I say.

Lagarde looks at me over the rims of his glasses and nods slowly. "Good. Then we must proceed carefully."

SIXTY-SIX

November 12, 3070, 1:01 p.m.

I'm brought to an assembly room to meet Robespierre. The guy I called a turbo-nerd and hacked. The guy who will decide my fate. It would be almost exciting, if it weren't a matter of life or death.

I don't know why he wants to meet me before my trial. Maybe he's going to gloat. He acted so refined and intellectual online, but he could also be a troll with the best of them. I want to fight. I have more fight in me than I've had since I woke up in my cell.

I'm escorted by a woman unfamiliar to me, but I feel alone in this big room full of long curving benches. The table I sit at is in the middle of the room before a tall podium. Maybe this is where I will be forced to defend myself. As far as I can guess, the place I've been held captive is the headquarters of the Committee of Public Safety.

The woman who brought me to the assembly room has bright red hair and matching lipstick. She sets a coffee in front of me and another next to it, apparently for Robespierre. I'm too nauseous to want it but thank her anyway. She doesn't bow. Doesn't acknowledge me in any way. I'm no longer the queen. This small gesture makes me realize that. How am I going to make it out of this alive?

Coffee steam wafts over my face. My stomach cramps at the smell. The assembly room is large, empty, echoing so that I hear a door open at the far end of the room before I see it.

Robespierre walks down the rows of benches with steady, even strides. He has a square jaw, a tumble of reddish curls on top of his head, and pinched-up eyebrows like he's always frowning. He wears a black sweater over his shirt and tie like some old man, even though he's not much older than I am. But he does have a synthetic pea coat and a round pair of thick glasses tinted dark. He presses the frame and they clear as he approaches, so I see his eyes, glittering in the clever way Stan's do.

He drags a chair around the table so he sits across from me and folds his hands. "Madame. A pleasure to meet you in person."

"A pleasure to meet you at all." I'm proud of the lie. It may be useless. I have no idea what evidence they have of what Louis and I were doing on the net, but I can play innocent.

Robespierre smirks at this. "That won't save you at the trial. I'm not mad about what you did to my account. It helped speed things up, in fact. I think the First Estate punished you enough for your activities on the net, since they've abandoned you and your husband in your hour of need. And now the people have seen to it that you both have paid the price. You're without your protectors. They no longer have puppets and distraction pieces."

He says all this calmly, but he's somehow more obnoxious than I imagined. "Congratulations," I say.

The smirk stretches farther. "I like you," he says. "You have some grit. I hate your institution, but I like you. That's why I wanted to meet with you now."

"What do you want?"

He takes a sip of coffee. Looks me over. It makes me shiver the way his eyes flick over me. Finally, he asks, "Is there any possibility you're pregnant?"

He's already caught me off guard and smashed through my defenses. Why would he think I'm pregnant? Then again, why wouldn't he? Heirs are integral to the Austro-Franc alliance. I clutch at my belly before I can stop myself. Could I be? I try to think of when I had my last period, but my limbs are water and I'm trying so hard not to tremble, I can't think, can't trust my own body. I can't begin to process what it might mean if I was. That I'm not fighting for my life alone. Should I lie? Should I tell him that I am? Would they truly execute both me and the baby?

Lagarde warned me to tell Robespierre absolutely nothing that he could present as evidence against me. So I bite down and keep silent.

"It would be unjust not to inform the jury if you are, though I must be honest in telling you that it will not make much difference to your fate," Robespierre says. "The Committee of Public Safety will vote in favor of your execution. The trial is a formality. We can't let you live. I imagine you didn't take the test because you knew it wouldn't change our minds. You were right. We can't let the Bourbon line continue if that descendant really does exist now as a few scant cells."

How could such a terror have such a normal face? Frown lines and glasses, like the quiet tutor I had in the Austro Lands.

"You're trying to scare me." That's the only reason I can come up with for this little visit. He wants to scare me so I'll flop at the trial and guarantee their win.

But I won't. I won't walk quietly to my death. I won't go

unless I know I've done everything I can for myself.

"No, madame. I'm not trying to scare you. But if you're going to be afraid or angry, or cry and scream, I wanted to give you the chance to do it now. So that during your trial and execution, you can die with dignity like your husband did. That's the most mercy I can offer you. A chance to make peace with your fate."

Can he really be genuine? Is this more intimidation? It's working. I'm shaking like a leaf and press hands to my stomach. "You claim that you stand up for innocent people. How could you do this?"

I see a muscle twitch in his jaw and the line between his eyebrows deepens. "You, madame, are not innocent. That's why you're on trial for crimes that we know you're guilty of. How could I do what? End a regime that's caused the suffering and oppression of thousands of people? How did *you* sit by and let it continue? How dare you claim that you're innocent?"

For a minute, I think about taking the steaming coffee and throwing it in his face. What difference would it make if I'm already as dead as he says I am?

"I've never done anything in my life as cruel and horrible as what you've done to my family. Never." I prod a finger at him, close enough to make him flinch back. "You made me a queen. You did. Your country. Your people. I didn't ask. I was brought here without ever being asked if it was what I wanted. Then you put me on trial for crimes that the First Estate's rules *forced* me to commit. And when I tried to push back against them, you rallied and made everything worse when I was trying to help you. You all made me exactly what I am. Most of my life was a dance that someone else choreographed, and I have no idea how else I was supposed to move. I was never taught anything else."

He crosses his arms. "Well, I'm terribly sorry we forced you to live in luxury while mindless people addicted to Apps showered you with unearned praise and others starved in the streets."

"I gave to the hungry." I'm not embarrassed by my tears. He should see them and feel them. "I didn't starve anyone."

He yanks his glasses off and rubs at his left eye. "I don't think you're a bad person, all right? I think you're a spoiled, vapid girl who never stopped to examine her life. Maybe it's cruel to punish you for that, but this has to end somewhere."

"Send me home, then." I let my lip tremble. If he sees me as a dumb little girl, I will use it to escape. I lay the accent on thick. "Just send me home."

"So you can return with the might of your Austro mother and brother behind you? *Non.* That's impossible. There's only one way out of this. We have to get rid of you to weaken the First Estate. If we're going to get rid of them, we have to show that we can abolish the monarchy first. If you're as innocent and as much of a saint as you claim to be, think of it as a sacrifice for your country and your people."

I shake my head. "Given a chance, I could do so much more for my people. I have more than myself to think of."

Robespierre points at the rainy windows. "Enough with that. You had a country full of children and you've let them starve on your watch and get burned and beaten by security officers." He looks thoughtfully at his coffee cup. "We will never understand each other." For one quick second, I think I see a human in his eyes. But then he settles back in the chair and crosses his arms. He shuts that door to his vulnerable side. "I'm not going to argue anymore. You can cry, shout, curse me, threaten me. It's what I promised."

It's tempting. It's very tempting. But I'll save the rest for my trial. I can defend myself without being undignified. Regardless of what Max Robespierre thinks. If being a queen has prepared me for anything, it's this. "I won't give you the satisfaction."

Robespierre sighs. Everything hard about his face becomes soft. "I get no satisfaction from any of this. I'm doing it so that two people will never have to sit here in our positions again."

I think of the screams I heard after Louis's execution. They were like his hunting dogs when they found prey. "If you do this . . . it all but guarantees that something worse will follow."

The hard mask settles over his face again. "Nice words. No substance. Exactly what I've come to expect from you."

He looks disgusted with me. Me, who's never treated a murder on the streets like a celebration. "Your execution will be public. The instrument is Dr. Guillotine's Laser Blade. You won't suffer. It will be very quick. Seconds." He gets to his feet. "If that's all, we should both prepare."

I try not to feel hopeless as I watch him walk away between the long rows of benches. I can't afford to be hopeless now. But he has been one step ahead of me since this began. I don't think I was ever once in control. Of anything.

SIXTY-SEVEN

November 13, 3070, 7:21 p.m.

I leave my trial numb down to my bones, down to the roots of my soul.

After what I've just been through, I couldn't be happier to see Elisabeth's face. She's lost weight. Her chin is less round. Her hair is limp. Her eyes look big and lost. She holds her hands out to me and I take them. They're too cold.

"They let my brother come to me before he died too," she says.

What she says is not a question. Clever Elisabeth, sensitive Elisabeth knows how to get us through the hardest fact without me saying the words. She pulls me into her arms, but I don't need to cry. I just shake. My body doesn't feel like my own anymore. Elisabeth leads me to her bed and leans my head on her shoulder.

Her bed is softer than mine. Her whole room is nicer. She has a table and chair, a bigger window, a very small holo-screen on the wall that shows lapping waves on a rocky beach.

I've never seen the ocean in person. Not in my whole life. I'll die without ever seeing it. I stare at the churning water and try to explain to Elisabeth everything that happened at my trial. How the room filled with people, and I saw nothing but enemies. How it lasted hours and hours and I felt like I was in a dream, accused of things I never did: Slept with and conspired with androids. Gambled away fortunes at huge parties I threw at the taxpayer's expense. Tried to mobilize all my followers on the Apps against members of the Committee of Public Safety, tried to strengthen the Austro army with androids, then tried to escape from justice into the powerful arms of my mother, the empress.

To be fair, when some of the accusations got too outrageous, Robespierre simmered it down. But he was relentless in his case against me. Some were softer when they spoke to me, like Desmoulins and Lucile Duplessis. When I spoke, some even looked like they might cry.

Like Robespierre warned me, this was a trial I was never going to win. But I gave it everything. I used everything I tried against Robespierre, but I gave it twice the power. I used tears when I needed to. I was stern and afraid and small and large. I did everything I could at all the right moments. In the end, all my training, all my years of performing, still weren't enough to save my life.

I can't tell Elisabeth about the last part.

My test still sits unopened in my cell. But I told the Committee of Public Safety I was pregnant. I don't think it's true. There is no reason it couldn't be. But there is also no evidence it has to be. Regardless, Lagarde latched on to the fact that Robespierre asked me about a possible pregnancy in our last meeting.

So I claimed pregnancy while hoping with every fiber of my being that I was a liar. The claim made some hesitate. Most were suspicious of my lack of evidence. Saw it as yet another reason I'm a shameless liar. Maybe I made a mistake. Maybe I signed my own death sentence by not taking that test. But it was my choice not to know. They took everything else from me. They're not forcing me to face that. Not when it's too late, and it was one of the few things left I could control.

I can't tell Elisabeth about this. The Committee will probably make sure it never leaves the room. And if it gets out, they'll find a way to squash it or spin it. After I pleaded with them, Robespierre looked me in the eyes and for a quick few seconds, I saw the understanding we've been missing. I had a little bit of hope. Then it vanished. He said, "If it were true, she would have presented evidence. Marie Antoinette is a liar. A frightened young woman, yes, but a liar."

That's when I knew I had lost. I sat back down in my seat and was numb for the rest of the trial. I kept my face still, my chin raised. I tried to look like the queen, even though I've lost my title.

Lagarde yelled a lot. I said nothing else.

Now I'm here. And Elisabeth is the angry one. I sit on her bed and watch her pacing the room in quick strides like she's going to go ream Stan and Philippe out over something. She startles me when she grabs the chair and flings it against the wall, where it knocks off some flakes of plaster.

"Sorry," she says. "Sorry. Sorry."

"Don't apologize." I reach for her and she sits beside me again.

"I just . . . How could this happen? How could they find Louis guilty and then you? You're practically children yourselves. You need a different lawyer and another trial."

"Lagarde did everything he could. I was a lost cause." I rub my hand on her·back. Strange that I'm comforting her when I'm the one who's going to die tomorrow. But it makes me feel calmer.

"Just kids . . . ," Elisabeth whispers.

"I'm not sure we ever get to be kids. Royals, I mean."

She's slumped over, staring at the floor. "I'm not sure if we were doomed to be dumb kids our whole lives or if we were born as weird tiny adults. Whatever we are or were, it wasn't normal."

"It was a weird life we had." I squeeze her shoulder. "But up until the last month or so . . . it was a pretty good one."

She gives me a weak smile that reminds me so much of my Louis. "It was all right."

"I'm glad I married your brother. I'm glad we got to be sisters."

"I'm glad you married my brother too. . . . I can't believe he's gone," she whispers.

I lean my head on her shoulder and she leans her head on mine.

I have no trouble believing it now. There's a hole in me that hurts with every breath I take, and that hole is the part of me where Louis is supposed to be. Now maybe I'll see him on some other side. At the very least, the pain will end.

We're quiet for a while. It's raining outside. I hear it tapping on the window, but I keep my eyes on the water in the holo. "Your room is way nicer than mine."

"Yeah. They think I'll be here awhile. But I'm sure I won't make it out either. They won't be happy until every Bourbon is dead," Elisabeth says bitterly.

"What about Stan and Philippe? Did you hear anything? Do you get any news?"

"Yeah, a bit. I just know they made it to the Austro Lands. Your brother met them with a guard. They must have gone to court. I heard they're under your mom's protection."

This warms my heart in a way I didn't think was possible. My brother hanging out with my brothers-in-law. "I was also wondering about Jeanne and Fersen. . . ."

Elisabeth sucks in her breath. "The First Estate took them, I think. Fersen will get repaired. As for Jeanne . . . I have no idea."

"I'm so sorry."

"She risked everything for us."

First, she worried about Jeanne's reputation. Now she's afraid for her life. And now Elisabeth has lost her brother and her first love. It aches that I have to leave her to face that without me.

"That's what I was told, anyway," Elisabeth continues. "I have a lawyer too. Probably as useless as yours. There's a sort of maid who comes in who seems brighter than the lawyer. Her name is Louison. She's nice. She tells me what she can."

"Louison . . ." I laugh a little. "Your brother told me once that everyone in the Franc Kingdom is named Louis or Louise. I guess Louison counts too."

She laughs, but it comes out as a sob. "Of course he did. He's such a dongle."

Elisabeth wraps her arms around me, cradling my head against her collar.

We sit like this for a long time. Until it gets dark. Crying quietly. Elisabeth asks me if I want to stay with her through the night. I do. I'm not like Louis. I can't spend this night alone.

SIXTY-EIGHT

✳

November 14, 3070, 5:00 a.m.

I wake at five a.m. The world out the window is gray and quiet, turning murky as the sun peeks into a cloudy day.

Elisabeth doesn't fuss. She holds my hand quietly. Lagarde arrives at six. I recognize that fiery look Elisabeth gets, but I squeeze her hand so she doesn't yell at him. He lets me record a message to Mutti.

What is there to say? I tell her I love her. I lie to her and tell her I'm not afraid. I ask her not to take revenge on the Franc people because there's no point now, and I have a feeling that there's nothing but dark times ahead for them.

The little maid Elisabeth mentioned, Louison, shows up with a black dress and helps me change in the bathroom. She's a nervous-looking girl with dark eyes. The dress is plain. No frills, nothing shiny. The Francs finally got me to conform to what they like. All the effort I put into fashion feels meaningless now. It doesn't really change how people see a person. No matter what I did or what I looked like, they saw who they wanted to see.

I step out of the bathroom. "Not my first-choice dress to die in, but it will do."

Elisabeth sinks into the lone chair at her tiny table and buries her face in her hands, shaking with sobs. I lean over her and hug her as tight as I can.

"It's okay," I whisper. "Maybe I'll see your brother again."

I wish I believed in god and heaven like our ancestors did. Maybe I can tell myself I do, and for the first time it will work, and the fantasies in my head will become reality.

"Tell him *bonjour* and *je t'aime* from me." Elisabeth rises from her chair and puts a hand on my face and I put one on hers. I try to wish with all my might that she'll live. I wish for her to leave this place, this whole kingdom, and become a doctor. I wish for her to have love and peace, even though she'll never forget what happened and the cold, ugly way the world turned on her family.

Louison silently hands me a black coat.

"Thank you," I say to her. "Please look out for my sister."

"Yes, Majesté." A single tear rolls down Louison's cheek.

I squeeze her skinny shoulder. "It's just Marie now."

"Long live the queen." Elisabeth has her chin raised and jaw jutted, the picture of dignity. She's still the Bourbon princess.

I hug her one last time. She remains tall and firm until I look back over my shoulder as I follow Lagarde out the door and see Elisabeth fall to the floor, face in her hands.

Lagarde takes my arm gently like we're at a formal event at Versailles and he's escorting me. Police with big, threatening laser guns join us at the door and flank us in the elevator. Twenty stories up. Such a long way down.

"Are you ready?" Lagarde asks.

There is no way to be ready for this. As the elevator lurches to a halt, I'm dizzy and things fuzz and go dark. I stumble to a knee. Before my vision darkens, I see the elevator doors open and . . . I see a dark room and a girl who looks just like me. I'm passing out, I think. Vision doubling.

I blink and shake my head. The officers in the elevator with me rush out. As my vision clears, I see them hustling a slumped figure away. The doors close again.

"Who?" My voice feels weak, but my head is clearing.

"No need for alarm, madame. Security breach, but everything is under control. I know you must be frightened." Lagarde has a gentle grip on my elbow.

Frightened. Yes. But I won't show it. I don't want them to see. I have masks and I will wear one.

Outside the elevator, a dark cruiser waits. Lagarde helps me pull my jacket up over my head as hordes and hordes of people scream and take pictures. It's nightmare noise. Violent shouting, wailing cries, chanting somewhere.

There are flashing white police cruisers behind us and in front of us, speeding around to create a flying barrier. The crowds below our cruiser follow us, milling around like a river.

There are people with paper signs, holo signs. Signs of all kinds. Some say BURN THE #AUSTROBITCH. Others say SAVE THE QUEEN. When I see two people with conflicting signs drop to the ground in a tangle of beating limbs, I slide away from the window.

"It won't be long, Marie." Lagarde looks at me like I'm a suffering animal about to be put down.

But I'm not an animal. I'm a queen. And they won't see my fear. They won't see my broken heart. They'll see the icon they made and watch the death of the icon they killed.

The cruiser slowly descends onto a giant platform. You would think it was a stage for a concert. There are huge holo-screens on either side. They're showing pictures of me and my family. Things I wrote on the Apps. Things that are my crimes, I guess.

The stage is lined with police and soldiers. Empty except for a strange white plastic table. There are two curving pieces of sleek white plastic on the end, with a hole through their center. A faint purple glow emanates from the curve, highlighting the seam where the device hinges open—where it will cuff me around the neck. Did Louis make the connection as quickly as I have? Did he see that simple plastic machine, as practical and stylish as a holofone, and know that it would end him?

I can't look at the thousands of faces staring, screaming, jeering, as I step away from the cruiser into the rough hands of two police officers, who march me up to that table.

One last time, I tell myself that it's fine. This is just another event. All I need to do is walk steady. I can do this. Repeat it a few times. Funny how this little method danced me this far through life, only to lead me here and become the last bit of strength I have to rely on.

As I step to the front of the stage, I glance at a camera wheeling around to point at my face, which I know must appear on the screens behind me. But I don't look. Not at the screens or the camera. Everything becomes hushed. A few shouts here and there.

They start reading my charges.

I've heard them all before.

Eyes on the sky. It's cold. The dress isn't warm enough and they took away my jacket. I'm all prickly with goose bumps. The sun is just peeking through the gray clouds in places. It reminds me of Louis and his shy smiles.

As my charge list goes on, the speaker speeds up because people are getting restless, shuffling around. In the distance, I hear more chanting and shouting.

What are they saying? "No blood for blood"? Maybe.

I wonder if I should count myself lucky that I won't see what happens when this is over.

I can't look at the crowd. I don't know what I'm afraid of seeing. It's not like my situation could become any worse. Then I notice someone about three rows in.

I don't know why she catches my eye out of the sea of people. But I'm glad I find her. She has long, dark hair that blows like sheets in the breeze. She might be from Shinkoku. There are tears flowing silently from her dark eyes. She knows I'm looking at her and she doesn't look away. It's like I can feel her trying to give me strength.

I watch her until a police officer takes my arm and pulls me toward that device. Dr. Guillotine's Laser Blade. I stumble and trip over one of the officer's feet. I didn't realize I was dizzy until I started walking.

"Sorry," I tell him. "I didn't mean it."

He doesn't answer. Maybe he doesn't want to be the last voice that speaks to me.

With another officer, he binds my hands behind my back. Something plastic digs into the soft skin over the pulse in my wrist. They lower me to the table, freezing cold against my stomach.

The device before me opens up with a *click*. A hand pushes at the back of my head so I drop my chin over the curving plastic that hugs my throat. Then the top half closes over my neck to collar me. It's as if I'm wearing a terribly bulky necklace. I have to strain to lift my head up to see. The ring around my neck is strangely warm. I smell disinfectant.

An officer steps up beside me, just in front of me as if he wants me to see him. His face is covered by a helmet with a dark riot mask that transmits his voice through a tinny speaker.

He explains in a droning tone that the laser blade will ignite within seconds of activation to cleanly sever my neck. I will feel nothing.

More people are screaming now. Can't tell if it's angry screaming. Doesn't really matter. My eyes search the area near where I was standing until I find her again. The dark-haired girl. She's grabbing the arm of a tall man, slumped against him while she presses a handkerchief over her mouth. She doesn't have any more strength to give me. That's okay. I don't think I need it anymore.

I look at the sky instead. The guard does something to the box and it starts humming. Then those horrible sirens blast. The ones I heard on the morning Louis was executed. Screams become louder, but they can't cover that siren.

The sun comes out. Just a little. Enough to warm my face. Like it's touching my cheek. I have this weird feeling that all this has happened before. Maybe a thousand years ago there was a girl just like me in the same position I'm in. Maybe she never had a clue either. Maybe this will happen again in the future. Maybe history repeats itself.

The laser blade glows red around the edges of my sight, and the humming is so loud.

It covers everything.

It's so loud.

EPILOGUE

I awake to utter quiet. Nothing but a soft hum.

Stillness.

I'm in a cruiser with a single window. Outside that window there is whiteness. Snow?

Maybe I escaped nothing and I'm truly dead.

I remember Lagarde saying to me, *Do you want to live? Will you fight to live?*

I answered yes because . . . I don't know why. If I had died, I might have seen Louis again. It's a gamble but . . . *mein Gott,* there it is. The ache when I think of Louis, the ache that I can't imagine going away. The hole that can't be filled. This pain assures me I must still be alive.

The door to the cruiser control room sits before me. I shrug off several heavy blankets and my vision tilts. Head feels stuffed full of glitch bits, but a panic creeps up on me. Who is on the other side of that door?

Lagarde was the last person I saw. Before I blacked out in the elevator . . .

Where have they taken me now? This is just like when I was taken captive in the Wastelands. Did Lagarde move me from one set of captors to another?

I have never known exhaustion like this that goes bone deep. Heart deep.

Before I can move, the door opens with a soft whir.

Elisabeth stands before me. Her round face, her worried eyes. So much like Louis's eyes. The ghost of him there makes my knees weak. I have to stumble back to sit on the cruiser sofa again.

"Marie," says Elisabeth. "I'm . . . I'm so grateful. But so sorry."

The relief and pain I feel upon seeing her make my head swim. There are many questions I should ask, but I'm not sure I'm ready to process. "Where is Lagarde?"

Elisabeth frowns. "I don't know yet. Safe, we hope. . . ."

"Safe? How . . ."

"It's complicated," says Elisabeth.

I shake my head. "I don't know if this is right. The crowd demanded my blood. The kingdom will be in chaos without it."

"The kingdom was destined for chaos either way," Elisabeth says, and her voice is harsh, cold. "That's not our fault. You don't have to die for the mistakes of my grandfather and the likes of Rohan and Angoulême. My *brother* should have lived—"

"Elisabeth," I interrupt. "I know how badly Louis's loss hurts. I know it was unfair."

"It was murder," she said.

"Yes, but . . . how many more have died since we escaped? Parée must be . . ." I shudder. How many times will that beautiful city burn?

Elisabeth sighs. "I'm sorry. You must be so confused. Marie, as far as the Francs are concerned, you're dead."

I have little reaction to this. I can barely believe that I'm not dead myself. "How is that possible?"

"I don't entirely know," says Elisabeth. "We had to believe

you were doomed. So our goodbye would make anyone who saw it believe it. Like you, I had no idea what happened until I woke up in this cruiser."

I knew my death would be as staged as my life. So how did we get away with this? How is it that the Francs think I'm dead?

"There's someone who can explain better." Elisabeth turns toward the cruiser's control room and presses a button. The door slides open.

First, there's a flash of shock. But I'm used to shock. A twinge of happiness dulls my pain. Thérèse de Lamballe stands before me. There's no longer a trace of pink in her hair. Just a plain brown, drawn back flat and tight from her face in a long ponytail. Her eyes are shadowed. She doesn't smile.

"Thérèse?" I rise, wobbling on weak legs to embrace the friend I thought was lost forever.

"Marie . . . it's good to see you safe."

She is different from the person I knew. Her dark eyes are steady, the joy in them is gone, the skin beneath them a deep brown bruise that speaks of sleepless nights.

"I never thought we'd see each other again."

Thérèse nods. "I wasn't sure we would, but I had to believe it was possible for this to work."

"I'm very confused. Where did you go? How are we free? Elisabeth tells me the Francs think I'm dead. What happened?" She looks away from me, sorrow plain on her face. She is so different from my bubbly friend, like she's aged years in the space of a month. "Who are you?"

"I'm your friend. I haven't always been a good one, but I am still your friend." Thérèse pauses, maybe unsure how to continue. I don't think I can take any more heartache, any more information. But I wait for her to continue. "I was a spy, Marie. I didn't always hold my husband Alex's views. I was a good courtier, I love many of my Bourbon cousins, but . . . after his murder, everything changed. And I turned spy for the Committee of Public Safety because I believed, still believe, that the First Estate and the crown are cruel, unjust, that they prey on our freedom, on our very lives."

I close my eyes. If I had tears left, I might shed them now. First Axel. Now Thérèse. Was Louis my only true friend? "And so you helped them plot to kill us."

"No." Thérèse shakes her head vigorously. "No. I fought with Robespierre constantly. This isn't the way. Killing Louis has only made Francs bloodthirsty. There's going to be chaos. And yet we still need to eliminate the First Estate. So I turned away from Robespierre and his so-called safety committee. Months ago. When I . . . well, when I became your friend. When I saw that you were a good person who deserved better. When you were brave enough to stand up to them. I knew you were a true friend. I had to flee the palace when my allegiance to the revolution and the Committee of Public Safety was called into question. Marie, I wish I could have stopped them in time. I'm so sorry we couldn't save Louis. I'll miss him every day."

My throat is tight, too painful to speak. I want to shout and scream at her. She worked with Robespierre, the same person who turned the Franc people against me. And yet she's still my friend in a world where I have very few of them. Instead I say, "What I want to know is how you whisked me away and how the Francs could believe I'm dead."

"Well, physically, Jeanne is flying the cruiser," says Thérèse. My glance jumps to Elisabeth. She gives me a weak smile. "None of this would have been possible without her. As for how we did it, we used a decoy. After what they believed to be your death, the Committee of Public Safety was content to release Elisabeth."

My vision blurs as my heart races again. "Who?! I never said I would allow another to die in my place."

"An android, Marie. She was an android," Elisabeth says quickly.

I take shallow breaths through my nose, trying to remain calm. "An android? I don't understand how . . . but wouldn't— people believe that?"

"They do. You found out the truth about Axel Fersen. He was a prototype for this project, the replacement of the real royal family with true puppets the First Estate could work through. When you became troublesome . . . the First Estate decided you would be replaced first. I'm sure it's what they've wanted all along." Thérèse spits this last part harshly and slumps into the seat next to the window.

"So there was an . . . android me? A me like Fersen? And you killed her." The thought makes me sick. Axel was never disposable to me. Not a weapon to be wielded and thrown away when they were through with him. And neither was this sister machine of mine. My heart aches for her even as my skin crawls at the thought of my secret double. I try to remember if I saw her before I blacked out. I remember little but darkness. I never met her, never agreed to her death. I will never get to thank this android who died in my place.

"It wasn't easy to get our hands on her. To steal her, have

Jeanne reprogram her, have Lagarde replace you with the android in the elevator on your way to the execution. It's better than a living person dying for you, *non*?" Thérèse still looks bitter. There is a part of me that wonders if, despite what she said, she blames me for all the blood shed at my expense. "I saw her performance. She was perfect."

I shake my head. "You say you're a champion of the people, Thérèse, but you think they're stupid enough to be fooled by this?"

Thérèse shrugs helplessly. "I don't know. But I couldn't let you and Elisabeth be slaughtered."

"Then if they discover the truth, Louis truly might have died for nothing." My statement hangs heavy in the silence.

"Marie. She was . . . she was just like you." Elisabeth swallows, lip trembling. "It was not easy to watch."

"How?" The recognizable creep slips over me, the feeling of eyes on me at all times. Of nothing being private, not my mind, not my body.

"You know how closely the First Estate watches you, records the palace," says Thérèse. "They've been collecting data on you. Captain Fersen obtained much of the material, like your blood sample." My mind flashes to the time his bracelet pricked me. He dabbed my blood with his own handkerchief. Placed it back in his pocket . . .

This shines a light on so many unanswered questions. I know I should be grateful for my life. But I can't find it in me. And I can't ignore the fact that once again, this was all accomplished without my permission, without me knowing.

Then hope rises in me. It's like a shot of sunlight and absinthe all rolled into one. "Then Louis . . . Louis must be recorded too. There must have been an android. . . ."

Elisabeth squeezes her eyes shut. She shakes her head no.

The hole in me sucks out all hope, smothered as soon as it was fanned to life. I ache. I ache in an unhealable way. I think of his wit, his kindness. I think of how they saved me, but not him. "Why?" I manage no more than a croak.

"His model wasn't complete yet," says Thérèse. "We did try, but his trial was so rushed. . . ."

"You could have tried harder," says Elisabeth. There is bitterness in her voice. I agree with her. A part of me wonders if . . . if my android was so good, they must have the same information on Louis. Surely. In some small way, could we have him back? Would I want him back in that way? These questions are impossible to answer, especially now, in the middle of this nightmare glitchstorm.

I try to make sense of a meaningless world. An android to die in my place, but not Louis's. An execution that could appease the Francs as Robespierre hoped it would.

"I'm sorry, Marie. Truly. I can't imagine how difficult this is for you. I wanted your freedom. I want freedom for the people." Thérèse's eyes brighten and I see hints of my friend, the one who loved a scheme and a crowd of excitement. "You don't have to be the First Estate's puppet or their martyr. You're a person, not an idea. The First Estate understands nothing, hoarding wealth and knowledge and everything vital. We have one chance to try something new, to take the power from those who have seized it again and again for thousands of years, and we have the chance to do it right this time. Without burning everything and starting over from scratch. We might fail, we might die, but there's a chance that can't be ignored. We have to find a new way."

Her words should stir excitement in me, and they certainly bring up endless questions. But as Thérèse said, I'm a young woman. I'm not a dead queen from eons ago. I'm alive, I'm battered, I'm scarred. I'm lost.

"Where are we going?" I ask at last.

Thérèse nods to the window. "Right now we're in the Northern Islands. We need to hide somewhere safe and regroup. I have friends who can protect you. However, you and Elisabeth have a choice to make. I have already robbed too much from you. Now the choice is yours. We saved you because it was justice. Because it was right. You aren't beholden to our fight for a free Franc Kingdom that abolishes the First Estate in a way that won't spill blood through the streets. You don't have to continue to be a figurehead. You can bury your Bourbon names and start a new life. You can have the normal life you were never given a chance to have. It's hard. Harder than your upbringing will allow you to imagine. But it is free. I won't make you decide immediately. Think about it. Rest."

Thérèse rises from her seat across from me. She gives a slight bow. The kind that will haunt me forever, no matter what decision I make. "You may not be a queen anymore, but I am still at your service. Take as long as you need to make your decision."

With a quiet *whoosh*, my secretive, complex friend who wore more masks than I ever have disappears behind the cabin doors.

"Do you have any idea what you'll do?" I ask Elisabeth.

"I don't know." Fat tears roll down her cheeks. "I don't know what I want. I want my brother back. I want to go back to thinking the world is better than this."

I want the exact same things, but there is no use wishing for them.

We sit in silence for a while.

Before I can do anything or even begin to contemplate who I am and who I will be, there's something I have to do.

"The android . . . She—was she really like me?"

"You would never know the difference," Elisabeth whispers. "She was programmed to act as you would. To predict your every move and action. Marie . . . she was—you were—so brave. So very brave."

"I want to see."

She shakes her head. "I don't think that's a good idea."

"I have to see. She died for me. This is the least I can do."

Elisabeth, who loved her brother and understood his love of machines, does not comment that this Marie was just a robot. I'm not sure "just robots" exist anymore.

She pulls a holofone from a pocket in her sweater and clicks around. She extends it to me with a shaking hand.

I watch my face, my movements, my expressions like a mirror as I descend onto a platform surrounded by holo-screens displaying the details of my face to the screaming masses. My expression is composed. It is the face I was taught to wear at solemn occasions, where smiles were not appropriate or not possible. The face gives away no fear. I'm not sure I could really do that. This is the android's work, not mine.

I watch as she holds her head high, approaches the executioner and his strange, horrible device. The crowds roars, some with faces full of joy that make shivers rack me, that make me sick. Others cry, eyes spilling over with pity, held at bay by the police with their crackling volt-batons.

Android Marie trips just slightly as she approaches the executioner. I see her apologize. I'm covered in goose bumps because now she is human. Now she truly could be me. This is like a lucid nightmare. Like wanting to wake up but being forced to watch as they list her crimes, settle her head in that strange clinical, plastic cradle.

I did wonder . . . for just a second . . . how the crowd would be fooled when androids don't bleed.

But there is blood.

Mein Gott, there is blood. There is blood everywhere.

I shove the holofone back at Elisabeth and rest my forehead on my knees, willing myself not to vomit. Only an empty stomach saves me.

That's what it was like for Louis. Those were his last seconds.

How could he give himself to them?

How could the Franc people cheer for our blood spattered on a stage? Two people, barely more than children . . . children who wanted to help them.

Adelaide's words come to mind again. Something I remember from one of my early lessons with her. *Greed leads to inequality, inequality leads to desperation, desperation leads to violence, violence leads to more violence. History repeats itself. We must stop this cycle.*

But this has been the cycle for centuries.

How could we ever hope to stop it?

I raise my head from my knees. Then I stand and pull the creases from my plain black gown.

I was once an Austro girl. I was loved. I had a husband. I had a people. I had a following. Now I'm someone different. But I can't erase who I was. I can't give up when Louis gave his life for a cause.

I feel the weight of empresses on my shoulders, the sacrifice of queens, the suffering of mothers and sisters. I feel the pull of time and the sense of repeating circles. I feel my mother's legacy. I feel my false inheritance. I feel the screams of terrified princesses, of forgotten girls, of lost girls, of girls the world builds up to tear apart. I feel the weight of girls like me. Rich, poor, beautiful, witty, kind, cruel, lonely, frightened.

I've made my decision.

I know I am Marie Antoinette. My own Marie Antoinette. I know I can never be anyone else. I know that despite my borrowed name and whatever its history may be, I must do something to change the future.

ALLYSON DAHLIN

On November 14, 3070, #LongLiveTheQueen was
the most widely used hashtag throughout the Franc
Kingdom. For several weeks, it was replaced from
minute to minute with the hashtag #ViveLaRevolution.
The competition continued until December, when
both were replaced with #ReignOfTerror.

ACKNOWLEDGMENTS

I've been writing for years, and it's solitary at times, but the truth is I would have never seen my work in print without the help of some people I appreciate more than I can express in words. I'm so afraid I'll miss someone I meant to mention, and I probably will. I apologize in advance. I think I'll work backward in this list.

First, thank you so much to Kristen Pettit and Clare Vaughn for your fun and amazing editorial insights! Your enthusiasm for this book sparkles and helped me bring Versailles to life in neon decadence.

Next, I need to thank my agent, Merrilee Heifetz, and her assistant, Rebecca Eskildsen, for discovering this book in the query trenches and seeing the potential in Marie, Louis, and me. Your wisdom, passion, and advice have made this book what it is. I can't thank you enough for having faith in me and in this book.

Endless cycles of revisions, self-doubt, rejections, and pitches are a necessary struggle in the writing process. I'm lucky enough to have writer friends that made the journey with me through many Thursday night NaNoWriMo sessions and beyond. Thank you, Alyssa and Steph, for joining in the tears, shipping, headcanons, wild ideas, despair, rereads, sushi ordering, cover dreaming, burrito eating, sprints, laughs, and general writing madness. And thank you, Alyssa, for not only being the wildest Bourbon Brothers fan but for forcing me to make a pact to hang a poster of their spiritual siblings, the Jonas Brothers, in my office. I've gotten some judgment for it, but may it watch over our writing sessions.

Thank you to my sister, Emily, and also Mary Jane, Grace, and Amanda for being some of my earliest beta readers and sources of encouragement. Cynthia and Rachel also get my beta-reader love, as does Elisa Albert for being a huge inspiration and teaching the most insightful, witty, and confidence-boosting writing workshop possible. I left your class determined to read and write relentlessly.

Once upon a time, I worked at a summer camp where some really cool girls passed a battered copy of my since abandoned novel around and argued over who they loved most and what powers they would have in this world. They were so invested that I knew I wanted to keep writing books for kids. I promised Bunk 14 I'd give credit if that book was published. Well, girls, if you're reading this: wrong book, but I try to keep my promises.

Thanks to my sister and cousins for years of fun, imaginary games, and other shenanigans. Thanks to my aunt and uncle for giving me a place to live that one time. Thanks, Mom, for reading me books at bedtime when I was young. I don't think many people have books like *Little Women* and the Dear America series read aloud to them every night, but if they did, maybe more people would love books as much as I do. And, needless to say, without those books, it never would have occurred to me to write one of my own.

Thanks and love to my kitty, Aveline, who keeps me in check, and my Abram, who keeps me sane.

Last, thank you, Dad, who loved France, who would have loved to see me in print, and who was a natural-born storyteller, whether he knew it or not.